Dive into a good book at
www.swimmingkangaroo.com

Need for Magic
Swimming Kangaroo Books, November 2009

Swimming Kangaroo Books
Arlington, Texas
ISBN: Paperback 978-1-934041-85-7

Other Available formats: PDF, HTML, Mobi (No ISBN's are assigned)

LCCN: 2009935146

**British Library Cataloguing in Publication Data.
A catalogue record for this book is available from the British
Library.**

Cover art by Kelly Christiansen

Need for Magic
by
Joseph Swope

Swimming Kangaroo Books
Arlington, Texas

This page is provided for messages from those
who wish to give the book as a present to a friend

Introduction: *Need for Magic* holds two types of magic. The first is that of a high fantasy novel where learned wizards practice ancient forms of power. The second type is the rarest of all magics, true magic. Thus, it is hoped that *Need for Magic* can be enjoyed on two levels. The first is as a classic fantasy novel complete with all the traditional elements of the genre. The second level is as an exploration of social psychology. Social psychology is the branch of psychology that examines how people interact with groups and expectations. Social psychology often concentrates on conformity, obedience, and persuasion. In short, all people have social needs. The index found in the back of *Need for Magic* will provide an academic view of many of the scenes and interactions in the story.

This page is provided for messages from those
who wish to give the book as a present to a friend

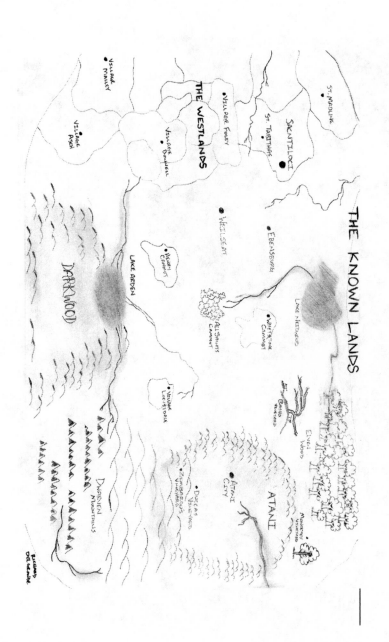

Robert Stenberg

Chapter 1

Even after all these years, watching something suffer and die was still fascinating. The longer and slower the process, the more he could learn from it. The horse he'd bought at the border-town was near death. Its pain mattered no more to him than the grass crushed beneath the wagon wheels.

Despite the many hard miles traveling with nothing but a near-dead horse and a rickety wagon, his black garments showed no wear. His clothes were imbued with the spell *Sospitix*. His scalp was kept shorn with a similarly minor spell. The purification ritual he administered to himself required that he shave his head. The pain of the ritual displaced fear and weakness.

For someone of his power, imbuing the wagon with a similar spell could have been done rather easily. But the wagon would soon prove unnecessary. If he succeeded in his task, he would fly far above the worn, wooden structure that had been his home for far too long. If he failed, he would be dead. Either way, the time of the wagon's usefulness was nearing an end.

The slowly plodding horse, however, was an integral part to his plan. It wanted nothing more than to lie down and die. Only a variation of *Sospitix* mixed with *Adfirmo* kept the desiccated beast alive, albeit barely. The closer to death it marched, the more useful the horse would be.

Lord Sogoth's black clothes made the heat of the sun his constant companion. No discomfort registered in his mind. The squeaking of the axles and the lurching of the brittle wheels were also easily ignored. All that mattered was the task to which he was driven.

The One Oath forced him towards completing the task. It held him like an unbreakable chain and burdened him like a heavy yoke. In becoming a wizard, he, like all other wizards, swore with his mind, body, and soul that he would be relentless in his pursuit of knowledge. He could no more break the Oath than he could will his heart to stop.

With that thought, he propelled himself deeper into his mind. These long weeks on the road had given him the time to practice exercises he'd learned long ago.

The time drew near. The summit of the mountain stood less than a mile away. He did not need to sneak any more than a flea needed to hide from a wolf. Still, he threw *Nascondersi* over himself, the wagon, and the horse. To a casual observer or a weak mind it would allow him to pass unnoticed.

Nascondersi muffled the sound of the iron-shod wheels as they found every stone and every hole on the sun-beaten, rocky landscape. He had long ago passed beyond the boundary of the maps that lay useless in the wagon. Humans could not live here now. He doubted if they ever had or would.

He breathed with a rhythm that helped him hone his mastery of magic and sorcery. Magic was by far the older, and in some cases, the easier method. With enough preparation, spells could be changed to meet almost any purpose. Spells, once unleashed, did not require further attention.

Though he would begin his attack with magic, his defense depended entirely upon sorcery. Sorcery was unlimited, at least in theory. That theory was soon to be tested. Sorcery's only known constraint was the wizard's ability to focus his will. Despite his arrogance, the wizard harbored doubts over his ability to keep his focus through the upcoming battle.

When the terrain narrowed to the point where it could no longer accommodate the wagon, the man in black left it to the elements. He unhitched the horse that was little more than ribs and hair and prodded it onwards.

With each step, his heart seemed to pound louder in his chest. If the horse could sense the tension, it gave no sign. It was too far gone to show fear of death.

To the best of his ability, he moved himself and the horse with stealth. He ducked behind rocks and scurried forward. He, Lord Sogoth, was scurrying. Years ago, the very idea would have been laughable.

A small gravel way led up an increasingly steep slope. He was mere feet from the summit. The countless years of study had prepared him. The mountain stood as he had predicted it would. From his position, he could see the area ahead level off onto a small plateau.

With a dry mouth and a beating heart, he snuck to the rim of the plateau. He crested it with a fear he had not felt in centuries. The legends, the stories, the drawings he had pored over were accurate. Still, he could not believe his eyes.

The dragon lay curled upon a large pile of gravel. Its magnificent scales reflected the sun into colors he'd never imagined were possible. The horse, more dead than alive, did not react at all to the dragon's presence.

With no warning, it stirred. In a graceful arc, it lifted its snakelike head and looked at the intruders as a cat would look at a mouse. The diamond shaped scales played in the sunlight and danced back and forth between red and gold. A rounded feature could not be found on the magnificent form. Every part of it, from teeth to tail, boasted a pointed weapon.

With a sudden shock, Sogoth realized he had not dropped *Nascondersi*. Yet, the dragon stared at him. Surprise was lost. It sensed his magic as he had sensed the dragon's.

Without giving into fear, he leapt into action. He reached for the horse with a spell that he had never before cast. Since the neglected beast was nearly dead, its body was a vacuum devoid of a soul. Mumbling well-practiced words, he opened up the horse's being and pointed *Exolesco* at the dragon.

Sogoth could feel the strength and vitality being sucked from the dragon to the horse. He did not know how many years were ripped from the dragon. The horse's body exploded with the surge of life.

The sound of it hitting the rocky ground could not be heard over the dragon's anguished howl.

Sogoth unleashed his next spell, *Morsus*. Long ago, wizards created it to discipline errant students. He, however, had changed it. What had been created to give the feeling of a blistered finger had been augmented over years of experimentation. Using countless subjects, he had transformed a simple blistered finger into the agony of being slowly boiled alive. To that, he'd added the crippling pain of birthing a child, as well as the shock of multiple fractures.

He threw it at the still howling dragon. The unearthly roar that shook his mind came as the result. With speed the man would not have thought possible, the dragon thrashed its body.

This was the test of sorcery. The muscular tail nearly slammed into him. It stopped mere inches from the man's chest. The tail had met an incarnation of the man's mind. Disciplined thoughts were formed into an invisible shield.

The shield was anchored to the front of Sogoth. It was not, however, anchored to the ground. Even as he flew through the air, Sogoth, purged all thoughts except that of his shield. His back, unprotected by the shield, skidded roughly along the rocky surface. Many years of practice allowed him to ignore what might be broken ribs as he rose to his feet.

To its credit the dragon focused its spastic movements. It leapt upon the man with claws extended. The sight of such an onslaught would cause most men to curl up in terror. Lord Sogoth met the attack with renewed concentration. He focused every part of his considerable mind on the transparent wall two feet from his body.

The dragon landed on the wall. The clear shield did not break, but it and the man were driven back. The dragon worked through its pain and furiously clawed at the man in black.

Lord Sogoth closed his eyes and senses to everything but the shield. The slightest deviation in his concentration would allow the wicked claws to break through and shred his flesh.

With the weight of the dragon's bulk, the man was all but enveloped in a mountain of scales and muscle. The shield around his body was hammered into a transparent coffin.

The dragon inhaled deeply. Lord Sogoth knew what was coming. Flame poured from the dragon's fanged mouth. His sorcerous shield could not stop light or heat. Had he not been prepared with a spell, he would have been reduced to ash and bone.

With the speed of thought, he constructed a well-practiced web of *Diffugio,* which took any concentration of energy and spread it out to the environment. The intense heat of the dragon's flame spread harmlessly into the surrounding rocks.

The dragon staggered backwards. With that, Sogoth stood. He called *Dilucesco.* As it convulsed under blue light that arced from the sky, the smell of burnt dust filled Sogoth's nostrils.

Again, Lord Sogoth uttered the words for his version of *Morsus.* The Dragon collapsed in a moan of despair. The tide of the battle was clear. Sogoth's was the stronger will and the greater magic. Now it was just a matter of time.

The dragon began to stir. Sogoth waited until it lifted its head. By focusing his thoughts, he shaped his shield into a dense block. With his mastery of sorcery, he flung the block at the dragon's head. A force that could shatter large trees knocked the beast senseless.

Sogoth waited and recovered. His exertions had drained him. Never before had he done so much. If the dragon had not fallen when it did, he would have fallen instead. He was lucky. There were countless numbers of things that could have gone wrong, but they hadn't. He was victorious. The underworld could not claim him yet.

The dragon valiantly tried to rise again and again. Each time Sogoth punished it with some manifestation of power. After a dozen instances, he knew it was time.

Sogoth stood mere yards from the barely conscious dragon. He pointed a finger and uttered one simple command. "Rise."

The dragon rolled its huge hourglass shaped irises from behind its lids into the realm of consciousness. Instantly, the dragon winced in pain as if stabbed by some unseen knife.

Again Lord Sogoth commanded, "Rise."

The dragon did not move, either from unwillingness or from inability. Yet again, an invisible lance stabbed through the magnificent beast.

"Rise." This time the flat voice had more force to it.

After so much punishment, the dragon struggled to stand on its mighty legs. With an arrogance that shocked even the now beaten dragon, Sogoth strode towards it. He grabbed a jagged horn that protruded from the dragon's neck and pulled himself onto the dragon's back. He did it with no more thought than a horseman who has known his steed for years.

Sogoth uttered one word, "Fly." To emphasize his command, the man gestured with his arms. Immediately, the dragon grunted and flinched in pain. It was not as severe as the earlier attacks. It was a simple reminder of the earlier lessons. The man in black felt certain he would not have to remind his new servant of the lessons again. Speaking no further, Lord Sogoth rode triumphant as his dragon carried him away.

* * *

"How fitting, to find you working in dung. It is no wonder you stink. That's the best you'll ever be. A smelly bastard." The young woman spat out the last words with contempt.

"I know. You've told me before. I've got work to do." He did his best to sound calm. Keven didn't know why she had the ability to unnerve him. The history of her various attacks on him was long and shameful. After each of her efforts, the proper reply or a better way to defend himself would spring to mind. Too late. Always after the bruise or humiliation was done.

Maybe it was her beauty. Even he who had every reason to wish her ill could not deny her beauty. At sixteen summers she was growing prettier by the day. The entire village adored her. She knew it. The entire village hated him. And she loved it.

"I know you've come here for some reason. I wonder what it could be." He tried to embarrass her into leaving as he struggled with heavy sacks of grain. Fine grain dust filtered out and stuck to the sweat on his neck. He did his best to be calm. If he let her see how her words bothered him, it would only get worse.

"Are you trying to be clever with me?" she challenged.

He thought he might avoid the worst of the situation if he ignored her. She became frustrated by his attempt. She could not accept any hint of his competence in anything. He was the bastard stable hand. Everyone knew it.

"Constance," he said with attempted care. "I have to get these sacks off the wagon and stored in the barn before Goodman MacGregor leaves for his farm. Master Banolf said I have to stack them straighter than a dwarven line. If I don't, I'll hear it from him and Goodman MacGregor."

As soon as he said it, he realized his mistake. He had given her the perfect opportunity to make his already miserable day worse.

"Why? How hard will they box you if they think you are dawdling?" she giggled.

He was continually amazed at how she could change her tone from a hissing viper to that of a charming maid.

"I don't know, and I really don't want to find out. So please, I need to finish this." He hefted the next sack of grain and tried to square it on top of the last. As he set it down, the dust could be seen in the rays of sunlight sneaking through the cracks of the stable.

"Please? My, aren't we being nice today. I'll tell you what. If you say you're sorry and bow to me, I won't tell them how you have been talking with me and forgetting your chores. No, wait, say you're sorry and *curtsey* to me. Then, I won't tell."

"Curtsey?! I'll not do it. I have sixteen summers and so do you. Isn't it time we get over this?" Keven replied.

"Are you sure you won't do it? Are you that eager to anger Banolf and feel his fists? I think you will. All you have to do is say you're very sorry for bothering me, curtsey like a lady, and I'll not tell. It is easy. You put one foot behind the other and bend like so." She demonstrated how easy it was.

Despite his dislike for her, he could not deny she presented a pleasant view.

"Come on, Keven, it is easier than a beating." Her voice was playful.

"If I do, will you really not tell?" He tried not to let his voice betray how hopeful he was. She would just use his hope against him.

"I told you I wouldn't. Now just pretend you have a skirt on and do it."

Keven knew that Master Banolf would not make a beating easy on him. He never did. Keven could suffer this humiliation to save himself. He had suffered worse. Yes, he had suffered worse, he argued with himself. But those were forced upon him. He did not have to choose them.

Mentally he held his nose while he put one foot behind the other, lifted the skirt that was not there and curtsied. "I'm sorry, Constance, for bothering you. Will you forgive me?"

"Of course I will. All you had to do was ask." With that, she turned around and skipped out of the barn. Her girlish bounce showed her womanly features more than if she had walked off like the adult she was becoming.

He wondered if she would tell. He never knew how she would react. Sometimes she would lie, other times, not.

It took some time, but he unloaded the fifty sacks of grain. The last ten of them had to be put in the loft. That was the worst part. Climbing the ladder with a sack weighing three stone. The thin leather on his feet let him know how narrow the rungs of the ladder were.

The loft. He tried to think of it as his sanctuary. Above the stables of the inn was where he and his mother slept. He knew he shouldn't complain. Everyone told him so.

His mother frequently reminded him how they had no other place to go. Keven was sure other towns had inns with pots that needed scrubbing and customers who needed to grope. But, as bad as Village Donnell had been to them, there was no guarantee the next town would be better.

Banolf frequently reminded Keven how lucky he was. He had a dry place to lay his head and good food for his belly, if he worked. Banolf was a large man. Bald on the top of his head with just a few hairs reaching over to meet the thin patch on the other side. He crossed the apron strings in front and tied them so tightly that his belly looked to be swallowing the strings from the outside.

It was hard to decide if Banolf's wife, Mistress Bitte, was better or worse. She simply did not see Keven. She did not ignore him. Ignoring takes conscious effort to overlook that which one does not want to see. Mistress Bitte was far past that. She simply did not know or care about Keven. She allowed the barmaids and his mother to give him plates of food, but she would see right through him. He was not worthy of her notice.

Keven did not have time to rest after the last sack was carried across the large stable floor. He heard the voices of Master Banolf and Goodman MacGregor. After Banolf saw the farmer off, he entered the stable.

"Well boy, looks like you moved the grain without spilling it. Did you put it in the loft like I told you?"

"Yes sir," Keven replied. He did not know why Banolf wanted some of the sacks in the loft. There was plenty of room in the empty stalls, and when they were needed Keven would have to haul them down the awkward ladder. Still, Keven knew better than to protest. The less he said, the less of a reason Banolf had to cuff him on the head for not knowing his place.

"I've got nothing for you until the guests finish supper. Then you'll help your mother clean the pots. Watch for folks coming or leaving this evening. I'll not have any of my guests waiting for their horse." He said the last in a menacing tone.

"No sir, I wouldn't let that happen," he replied. He was hoping there would be no more instructions. Time of his own did not come often.

"Be off, then, but I warn you. You be here to earn your keep after supper." Banolf, like many big men liked to step close to emphasize the importance of their words.

Keven walked out of the dusty stable quickly. In truth, he did not have any idea of how to spend the afternoon. It was a fine day. The heat of summer had given way to a slight breeze that took away the effects of the sun.

Keven did not have friends. The only two he had ever made, Father Sean and Erin, had moved away. The children of the Goodfolk did not interact with him much. Years before, some of them had wanted to and had even disobeyed their parents to play with Keven. Gradually though, they shunned him. As time passed, they too would join in taunting him about his father.

His mother either wouldn't talk about his father or couldn't remember. Being astute, he did not press the issue. She was raped, drunk, or fooled into a roll in the hay. Whichever way, Keven knew his beginning was not a source of joy to her.

As he walked the tidy, well-kept village, Keven thought of his plight. Keven reasoned that the Goodfolk knew he had a decent mind. Still, they wanted nothing from him. Adults whisked the children away from him. Shopkeepers would not let him in. Even the priests barred him from the small church at the edge of town. The Book of the Word had no forgiveness for him.

Fornication was a sin. It was not an accident. He knew, and had been told countless times, that his mother had purposefully turned away from The Creator and spread her legs. For that, she and her sin-child would not be able to receive the ministrations of the priests. Because of his mother, The Creator was not for him.

Frequently, the priests would roam the village talking with the Goodfolk and bestowing their blessings. Whenever the white robed men would see him they would make a sign warding against sin.

As he walked through his Westland town, he remembered fondly the one priest who had looked beyond his curse. From the first time he saw the man with his skinny frame and kindly eyes, Keven instantly knew that Father Sean was different. Keven had six summers when the priest came to his village. He was one of the few adults who had ever shown him compassion.

Father Sean had given Keven the greatest gift he had ever received, a book. At first, Keven was simply happy to have something, anything of his own. In time, remarkably little time according to Father Sean, Keven had learned to read. Father Sean let him see other books. Some even had pictures. On the page and in his mind's eye, he saw elves, dwarves, witches, and even dragons. Keven devoured them all with the eagerness of a starving man breaking his fast.

None though were as good as that first book, The Magic Stick. It was nothing more than a child's tale about magic and impossible monsters. The day Father Sean had gently placed it in Keven's hand was one of the few of Keven's life he could call good.

"Keven, please have this. When I woke this morn, I found it on my table. My door was still latched from inside. I do not know how or who, but I know of no one in this village more deserving than you. I only ask if the rightful owner finds it and wishes it returned, you must give it to him."

Nervously Keven asked how he would know the proper owner. Father Sean tenderly opened the thick leather cover and pointed to four letters. I.P.L.G. Keven was amazed that the little marks were letters. With that, Father Sean taught him the other letters and how to put them together.

Even now, years after Master Banolf had ripped up the book and thrown the pages in the dung heap, Keven remembered every word of every page.

He hated Master Banolf for that. Some wrongs cannot be forgiven. The Universal Church decreed the sin of his mother could never be cleansed. Keven struggled with that everyday. Mixed with that was his hatred of what the Goodfolk wished for him. Even now he pushed himself to forgive because of the second gift Father Sean had given him. To replace his beloved The Magic Stick Father Sean gave Keven his very own copy of The Book of the Word.

Keven took a chance and sat on a hitching post across from the bakery as he fondly remembered the exchange. He ignored the dignified bustle of the Goodfolk as he buried himself in his memories.

At the time, Keven had earnestly tried to refuse Father Sean's gift. He had only nine summers. Children, especially bastard children, were not supposed to have such a book. With gold-rimmed pages and silk ribbons for page markers, it was fine enough for a prince. Father Sean had simply used his warm smile and said, "Son, if I don't give it to you, I haven't learned its lessons well."

That memory never failed to bring a lump to his throat. Perhaps it was that memory or the one connected to it, the memory of Father Sean leaving Village Donnell. The rumor that the Goodfolk gleefully spread was that Father Sean was misled by the confused ideas of the doddering pope.

The ancient pope's belief that peoples' faith in the teachings of the Universal Church grew stronger if they questioned them was seen as nonsense to the increasingly powerful bishops. Father Sean had been recalled to Sanctaloci, the seat of the Universal Church, for preaching that one's ability to read and interpret The Book of the Word was just as important as obedience.

The sound of giggling brought him out of his musings. He looked across the dusty lane to see Constance and two of her friends looking at him. His cheeks immediately flushed red. Whatever they were up to, it could not be good for him.

He marveled at how they seemed to possess all of the grace of elven queens. Did girls practice how to act, he wondered.

They continued to giggle and whisper as they pointed in his direction. He saw one of them curtsey. Then, all three dissolved into hysterics. When they had composed themselves, they marched across the lane to him.

"Hello, bastard boy," a girl named Chrystine cooed. "Can you show us how ladylike you can be?"

"Constance, you said you wouldn't tell." Keven tried to sound like he was an adult shaming a youngster.

"I said I wouldn't tell Master Banolf. And I didn't. Still I wonder who else might be interested. Maybe Gunter?" She had perfected the art of speaking as a sitter would to a child.

Gunter Magson was a large boy whom most considered to be a man. His body had everything Keven's did not. With blonde hair and blue eyes, the girls of marrying age swooned at the thought of him. His shoulders were broad and draped in heavy muscle. Keven knew plenty of farmers and craftsman who worked twice as hard but did not have half his muscles.

Gunter's father was a soldier who rarely came back to the village to see his family. The nobles of the Westlands were locked in seemingly perpetual battles over land, rights, and ideas of honor. Keven sometimes wondered if having a strong king like neighboring Atania did would prevent a lot of suffering.

Keven knew that with the rumors of a coming war, Gunter would not see his father for a long time. But it was Gunter's dream to be a soldier. He usually practiced his soldiering on Keven who had the bruises to prove it. He did it for two reasons, he was bored and he could.

Keven didn't wait to hear what else the girls had to say. He quickly turned and left. Whatever would come out of their mouths would end up causing Gunter to find him and beat him. Of course, the fact that the girls would look on would add shame to the pain.

He came to the old blacksmith's shop. Its doors were barred, and the great forge behind the building was cold. There was no ringing of metal and no pumping of billows. The silence of the foundry echoed in his heart. He'd met his other friend, Erin, here.

Erin Dunn came to Village Donnell with her father six summers past. Her mother had died in childbirth, and as a result, she was brought up by her father in a way that made the Goodwives frown in disapproval. Perhaps because she was not seen as a proper young lady, Erin hadn't hated him as everyone else had.

From his readings, he would describe her as a pixie. Her hair was kept short because her father did not know much about raising girls and because long hair near a hot forge made even the toughest father wince at the possible tragedies. She was smaller than Keven, and he was small for his age, but Master Dunn worked her harder than any apprentice in the village. He was not a cruel man, but to him, learning work was more important for children than playing. When work was finished, he would leave her to her own wishes. The fact that Master Dunn did not prohibit his daughter from playing with Keven put the man into the very small category of good people Keven knew. He did not say much to Keven, but he always had a smile and a hello for him. Both were genuine.

Erin had often worn boy clothes. At first, she was a curiosity to Keven. With short hair and breeches and longshirt, she had looked like a boy. She even liked to wrestle and chase. However, as the years wore on, Keven was glad she was a girl.

They seldom had time for anything but work. When they could sneak away, they did everything together. They explored the woods near to the town. At age twelve, the woods were a good place to seek adventure.

Many things were discussed in those woods. On a few timid occasions, Keven and Erin spoke of the future and of getting older. With characteristic shyness, and no one to guide them, they decided that their futures would be best spent together.

Those plans were shattered when Erin and her father had moved away. One of minor lords of the Westlands had started a war of reputation with his neighbor. King Festinger did nothing to prevent such wasteful use of people by his vassals. At least, that was the rumor that had reached his town.

Master Dunn knew that if there was one thing honor hungry lords needed, it was the skill of a blacksmith. Master Dunn' preference was for making tools, not weapons. Thus a quiet life in a remote village was what he had hoped for himself and his daughter.When the lord's soldiers had come for him, the Goodfolk of Village Donnell watched in silence and did nothing to stop their neighbor and friend being taken away. Though easily bigger than any of the soldiers, Master Dunn had not put up a fight. Keven remembered watching and wishing Master Dunn would take one of his hammers and smash the heads of the soldiers. Keven had silently screamed as he watched Master Dunn pack up Erin and his tools and go with the soldiers. That memory had not faded.

Lilandra

Roberta Vaughan

Chapter 2

He hated waiting. It was humiliating. He was the King of Atani, damn it. Even as an angry curse was about to fly from his mouth, he calmed himself. This was merely a nuisance. Let her pretend to be a queen he thought to himself. She can flit about and trade in gossip. She was but a fleeting thought in the minds of foppish nobles.

He sat in his high backed, ornately carved chair and waited. The chair was heavy oak and had the great lion of Atani carved into it. While his expression remained passive, inside his irritation was growing, expressed only in his unconscious tapping of one finger on the table.

He looked around the room for the hundredth time; it was a reflex. Defeat found the unwary. Thick candles hung from the walls in simple iron holders. Even the chandelier, which had a place of prominence in the room, was utilitarian. Black iron may not be fit for a King, but weighty matters did not find answers in a room decorated to please popinjays.

"Good news, Your Highness. The people are celebrating in the street," she announced as she came in. "The farmers are producing more; the smiths and craftsman are working double. And everyone is cheering because of the end of slavery." She kept her eyes locked on his to gauge his reaction.

"Curse you woman! How dare you? You have no authority to do such a thing." Though he struggled to keep his tone even, the flush of his face showed his anger.

"It was your daughter who actually signed the decree. She is the princess, you know? Does the law allow you to rescind such an order so soon?" She casually teased him with her question.

"If you've read the law enough to have her make such a decree behind my back, you know full well that there is a waiting period. There are precedents that must be observed."

"Perhaps after the lawful time you can rescind the decree. I wonder how the citizens will react. I wonder how your daughter, Helena, will react?"

The smirk she showed angered him almost as much as how she manipulated his daughter of seventeen summers.

"She is a still a child. She knows nothing of such matters." His voice was a taut cord stretched between ire and confusion.

"Have you listened to her recently? I know you have spoken to her. I am sure you know there is a difference. Perhaps if she had a mother? Maybe that is why she clings to me."

Her audacity at being so forward with the royal family's tragedy stymied the usually domineering king. He sat in dumbstruck silence.

She continued, "I hear that the soldiers are even asking for extra practice. They are preparing as though they have wanted this their whole lives. Can you imagine what Atani will be, when we are ready?" The last was not a question, it was simply a confirmation that her plans were working to perfection.

It was hard to judge her age. There was an ancient wisdom in her eyes that contradicted her smooth skin and youthful looks. Although his pride would not allow him to be attracted to her, he still had to admit she was beautiful.

Her dark hair shone across her shoulders, but, of course, her present hair color was only a passing style. She changed her hairstyle and color almost as often as she changed gowns. Donius suspected she did it just so she could measure how quickly the noble ladies would imitate her latest fashion.

Her dress was designed to appear modest, but revealed her striking figure that every man in Atani lusted after. Her blue eyes were big and engaging and gave her the look of someone who was far younger than what she claimed as her twenty-six years.

She flounced into a chair that was usually occupied by the most accomplished of his generals. Her upturned button nose and her full pouty lips made him think of a whimsical noble girl whose greatest threat was causing a scene during a ball. Donius had seen her act this way before. He had also seen her appear and act as regally as any queen twice her age. Her commanding presence was enough to intimidate even the most experienced field commanders. He had even seen her act wantonly with some of his soldiers. It wasn't what she wore or what she said individually. She simply could change herself.

"Yes, freeing the slaves was the best thing," Lilandra said as she examined the back of her hand. "The people now rally to serve the nation. Long subjugated family and friends are returned to their lives. You must not have known how fearful your subjects were of the slavers' yoke."

A resigned sigh snuck past his lips. It was an argument in which he had participated many times. He chose to ignore the more complicated economic argument of nationalizing personal property. Very few citizens truly realized that even unsavory parts of the economy were necessary. He chose instead the more simplistic moral argument.

"Slavery is a part of society. It is a tool to keep order and keep the wretched fed. It is neither good nor evil. Should we let people die? Should we let the great capital of Atani be filled with human refuse?"

14

"Humans do not choose to be refuse, Your Highness." She added the last with a tone he could not identify.

"Do not insult me by thinking I will believe your witchy lies. I am not a commoner to believe I only have to follow you to my dreams. I am the King," he said with an icy calm that so many found unnerving.

When she did not respond, King Donius of Atani continued on in a voice that sounded like a scholarly lecture. "People make choices everyday. If the consequence of those choices is poverty, then they must accept that. That is the law."

"And that leads them to the slavers?"

Her question was a mocking jab at him. That he had let this woman gain so much influence in his kingdom bothered him. Still, he had reasons to keep her around and happy. He exhaled, tired of arguing a longstanding and successful social policy, but determined to maintain his kingly grace.

"You know as well as I do that no one is given to the slavers without good cause. What would you have the good citizens of Atani do? Pay their taxes only to house prisoners who do not work? Should the citizens see their taxes go to those who make poor choices? You know well enough that slavery is good for Atani. It is a good deterrent. Any potential cutpurse who sees the eyes of a slave will keep his knife to himself."

"But what about the slaves?"

"The slaves are no longer citizens. They gave up that right when they could not meet their obligation to their family and to Atani. Sloth cannot be tolerated. The fear of falling into slavery motivates those who would be lazy. Ambition motivates those citizens who work hard for their family. It is a good system; the people understand it. You cruelly fill their heads with dreams that figs and plums will fall from the tree without being harvested."

"My good king," Lilandra purred. "I have no love for slavery."

"No honored, Regent." If words were knives, she would be bleeding. "You have no love for anything that is not you. How dare you presume to preach the ethics of slavery? What do you call my daughter? Does she not follow you blindly like a slave?"

"My most noble king," she cooed in a sensually mocking voice. "I see no chains since I have helped you rule this kingdom. Your daughter follows me because she loves me. It is the same with the citizens. I do not force them to love me. They are free to choose their own fate."

He let the hold on his boiling emotions slip. "You vile witch. You have bespelled my daughter, and you think you have stolen my kingdom." He said the last as if it were more than a personal offense, as if he could think no worse evil.

"Have caution, Your Highness, you would not want your daughter to hear of us bickering. Your daughter is at the difficult stage with which many youths struggle. She does not know what to believe. Many parents

15

have lost their children due to a lack of patience. Fret not, she sees me as a guide. She trusts me. Without me, I fear you may lose her."

* * *

Keven woke up before his mother, before the animals below and before the sun. He always did. He tried to lie for a while longer, but his bladder was a cruel master. His too small shoes were dry enough to wear after letting them air for the night. Running errands in the rain the previous day had made his barely cobbled shoes squish with every step. Being dry, however, made them stiff and rough. The leather would soften with wear, but it would be a merciless process.

Rather than force his feet into the unyielding leather, he wrapped them in rags and headed down the ladder. They didn't offer much protection, but they did guard against the chill of the morning. A dozen horses stood, heads drooping, in various stages of sleep. Some of the horses were master Banolf's, some belonged to visiting guests. All were in stalls that needed to be cleaned.

As he quietly walked out of the stable to the privy in the back yard, he wondered why he just didn't pass his water in the stable. It would be so much easier, and no one would know. Well, he'd know when he unloaded whatever supplies Master Banolf ordered for the inn. That act would partially confirm the town's idea of him.

He wished the supply wagons would arrive soon. He didn't like unloading them, but he hated waiting to unload them more.

Keven, of course, did not know much of his mother's life before he was born. He did wonder what had made her commit such a sin as having him. She should have known by the moon when it was safe to be with a man or of herbs to cleanse her body of the sin that became him. Hardly an instant passed when he did not silently question her, pity her, and curse her for the life she had given him.

When he was young she had tried to spare him some of the torment that went with being the son of a sinner, but each passing year saw her less and less inclined. Maybe it was because he was getting older. Maybe it was because she was simply tired. She used to intercede when Banolf used a belt on his backside, and Banolf would invariably turn the belt on her. After a while, she deliberately shied away if it appeared Keven might be in danger of a beating.

Keven knew that she could not protect him anymore than a tree can protect its seed. As he walked back from the privy, he looked at the inn and its outbuildings. Master Banolf was a rarity for a commoner. Many Goodfolk strutted about as if they had the wealth of a noble, but few, except Banolf, actually did.

He had seen the inn grow in the past few years. Banolf had several storage sheds and buildings behind the inn, all built well and painted white. Keven remembered the days it had taken him to paint them. The work hadn't been difficult. It was the days after it that had caused him the trouble he remembered. Each time he tried to scrub off the white paint that covered most of his body, something prevented him. The tub or buckets to haul water were missing. For a week, the town had their fun mocking the ghost boy or the future priest who couldn't wait to wear white.

Banolf insisted that every part of his inn impress his customers. Even the manure shed was painted white and locked. Keven understood why Banolf would lock tool sheds and storage buildings, but he could not understand why Banolf insisted on locking the door to the manure shed.

The kitchen had not yet begun producing its morning aromas; those smells would soon be waking the guests up. His empty stomach wished the morning meal would speed along.

He had been up in the guest rooms a few times when beds and other furniture had to be moved. Without much conviction he prayed that one day he could sleep in one of those beds. There were even chests of drawers. One of the rooms had an actual mirror. Rarely having money, Keven did not know how much a room cost for a night. But one day he swore he would know the comforts of a true mattress with clean sheets.

As he rounded the corner of the stable, he saw his mother coming down the ladder. He wished he could do her chores for her to let her rest one day.

"Good morn, mama." He tried to sound cheerful.

"Oh, good morn, Kev. Mistress Bitte and I should have food for breakfast soon."

Keven wasn't sure if she was trying to make his morn better or if he was doing it for her. "Mama, I'm going to get started before the stink gets too bad."

She nodded and headed in the direction of the kitchen. Reluctantly he went to pick up the shovel.

When Keven first started working for Master Banolf, he was told that to clean the stalls, the horses must be out of them. Banolf believed the horses didn't like the shovel, and they didn't like people behind them. In only a very short time, Keven had realized he could do the dirty deed with the horses in the stalls. It took two tension filled weeks to convince Banolf that Keven's way was better. He was good with animals.

Keven had had a dog once. Several summers ago a big, mangy thing that looked like a wolf had come around the inn with a hurt paw and ribs that showed through its skin. Keven hid it, stole food for it, and nursed it back to health. At first, it did not trust him. Eventually, he won the feral dog over so that it would eat from his hand.

The horses did not like the dog's presence; neither did Master Banolf. Keven knew the dog to be smart because it would disappear during the day and come back after dark. The dog broke that pattern only once.

Keven remembered it well. It was one of his few triumphs over Gunter. Gunter had come into the stable to cause Keven misery. He liked to build up to the actual beating.

As Gunter was backing Keven against a wall with his chest puffed out, they both heard a noise. It started with a hissing intake of breath before turning into a growl of pure hatred—a growl so fierce, the boys felt it in their bones. The dog was in the stable, teeth clearly visible and coarse fur standing on end.

Both boys froze, terrified. Gunter turned and put his back against the wall so he was next to Keven. The dog's yellow eyes followed him. It took a step forward. Gunter slid further away from Keven, and the dog's eyes followed him, but it did not move.

Gunter slowly slid out of the stable and out of sight. The dog then trotted up to Keven, licked his hand, and trotted off. The dog showed itself a few more times after that, but it eventually stopped looking for meals behind Mistress Bitte's kitchen.

He never told his ma or even Erin about the dog and Gunter. He didn't want to soil the memory with having to convince them it was true. It was one of the few things he alone possessed. To keep the memory special, he did not let himself indulge in it. So, with a resignation to his duty, he put the shovel to use in the filth.

* * *

He guided the dragon with only the slightest pressure of his knee. The great dragon could have easily banked or rolled and have been done with its hated rider. It did not. In the short demonstration of his power, Sogoth had trained it well.

He would take this triumph and use it to achieve even greater heights. Like anything else, with the correct combination of will and mechanism, everything was achievable.

Clouds were both above and below as the wings effortlessly glided on unseen currents of air. Even Sogoth who was accustomed to thinking of himself as superior to all in the known lands had to marvel at the beauty of the dragon.

A smile spread across his stern face as he approached the Atanian capital. Despite her haughtiness, she would have to admit his greatness with this gift. No one had done or could do what he had done. He was now a Dragon Master.

The dragon flew in ever-lower circles around the city. The target was clearly visible because it was the biggest structure in the city. Suddenly, the dragon folded its wings and dove toward it. Sogoth again experienced the fear he thought he had banished.

He was unprepared for a fall from this height. Normally, he could handle any physical danger, but this was different. His battle to subdue the dragon had temporarily depleted his power. *Situtum domus*, the spell that would instantly return him to his sanctuary was something for which he needed a clear mind and a calm moment. It could not be done from the back of a plummeting dragon.

As Lord Sogoth prepared for death and what unpleasantness he knew awaited him after death, the dragon unfolded its great wings and landed. It was as silent and graceful as a simple barn cat jumping from a window.

He looked up and saw the empty Atanian coliseum surrounding him. It was huge and built entirely of white granite and polished marble. The sun's reflection in the specks of the rock made the structure seem even bigger than it was.

The silence and the steady ground were welcome. He needed time to recover and plan for his exit. Though less spectacular to the uneducated, his exit spell took far more skill than riding a dragon.

* * *

"But Papa... you don't understand."

Tonay Denisio was a good person and was generally happy. Her father had cared for her well, even after her mother died. She was a pretty girl with more than a few interested suitors. The suitors were good boys, hoping to be good men. There was nothing wrong with them except that they were content with life in the village of Ducca's Vineyard.

"Tonay, I was young once. I know that farm life is not what makes dreams. I also know that dreams don't make supper."

"But what am I to do? Spend my whole life on one farm only to go to another when I marry?" Her tone mixed disgust, urgency, pleading, and hope.

"Have I done that bad by you, girl? Has this farm been that so bad to you? Have you not had food and clothes?" He tried to hide it, but there was more than a little hurt in his voice.

"No Papa, I just don't want to spend my years with the animals. I don't want to go to my grave smelling like pig droppings." She tried to be gentle with her words.

It was an exaggeration. Her father's farm was as clean as a farm could be. She did not even dislike living on a farm. It was simply that she did not know if she liked living anywhere else. The tidy farm was all she knew.

"You say it like you're noble born, girl. I have listened to your words, but they make no sense. You want to run off because you think war is exciting. Listen to your own words. A girl with a sword." His tone cut gashes in her dreams.

"But Papa, I need to try. All I know is this farm and animals. Maybe there is something better for me out there." Why did he think she would never come back? If she went to Atani City, she would surely return.

"I'm sorry, girl, but that is the end of it. I need you here, and Atani City is no place for you." He said the last firmly. He knew dealing with young ones her age was tricky, girls more so than boys. Damn, he swore to himself, *if I caused my father half as much grief as this girl causes me, I will beg forgiveness a hundred times when The Creator brings me to Him.*

Seeing that she was not getting anywhere, yet again, she stormed off. Why didn't he just let her go? She yanked the front door open hoping it would break. But, no, he had built it too well. Like everything else on this farm, it was boring, functional, and overly sturdy.

She marched through the clucking chickens. She didn't really want to kick them, but felt so powerless that she needed an outlet. For the past few months, she had heard nothing but talk of the coming war.

At first, it had been only curiosity. Messengers on horseback would come to the village, and then word would spread as fast as fire in a hay barn. People could hardly wait to hear the latest news. The people who were the first to hear would then be surrounded by others who wanted it retold after the messenger urged his horse to the next town.

She and the rest of her girlfriends had, at first, little interest in talk of squads, training, and swords. That is until she heard something that changed her life. Regent Lilandra wanted women and girls too.

The rumors, which were added to almost daily, said that women and girls would be needed to support Atani's armies. There were even rumors that women would one day fight on the lines. All of the men and most of the older women dismissed such talk as cow dung. But she saw more than a few women with a far away look in their eyes.

Tonay knew what they were thinking. What if? What if she could get off the farm and out of the village? What would the world show her?

Maybe she would not be married off to a boy who was thought to be a good match. Maybe she could be a war hero or something other than a farmer's daughter and a common wife.

She almost giggled at the thought. Women war heroes. Well, why not, she asked herself. Regent Lilandra said that women were needed for the war. Tonay was almost bursting with wonder. The Regent of Atani needed her, a farm girl.

As she marched across the yard to continue her chores, she looked at the animals. They were in pens, wore bridles, or were tied to a hitching post. Their future was this farm, the same thing day after day until the farm outlasted them. She realized she was no different. She had to break free. With that revelation, she began to plan. It wouldn't be hard to get away. Her father trusted her.

* * *

Princess Helena did not know what to do with her hair. For as long as she could remember, people had had nothing but the highest praise for it. She knew a lot of that praise came because she was the heiress of Atani. She also knew that her hair was the envy of many ladies at court.

Falling naturally in curly, golden tresses, its color had even been compared to the morning sun by the court's minstrels. Servants competed for the privilege of brushing it even while she contemplated cutting it off. She'd had the same style since she was a child. There was nothing childish about it; all of the past queens of Atani wore their hair as she wore hers. For days now, she had battled with herself, counting the reasons for and against such a monumental decision.

The problem was that she was not known for anything else. Of course, she was happy people thought she was pretty. Still, she wanted them to think of her as more than just King Donius' pretty daughter. She wanted them to think of her as someone important, someone who could control her own life.

She had worked hard to change the opinion of the many nobles who frequented the castle for social and political functions. It had first started when Helena tried to subtly impress the various ladies who rode into the castle to hear the latest gossip.

The ladies of the noble society would accompany their husbands on the many political meetings King Donius hosted. The ladies would all make their arrival a show. The gowns were elaborate weapons in a competition that would challenge even the most cunning strategist. Each woman would try to out do the others in appearance with the rules in this social combat changing almost weekly. The rules emphasized skill in making alliances, creating impressions, and above all else, hiding the fact that the competition was important.

At first, when Helena was old enough to join the ladies, they merely tolerated her because she was the King's daughter. Helena, a quick study, rose quickly in the ranks to become a serious contender in the great game of importance. It did not take her long to realize that success in the small pond of the women's competitions still did not earn her respect in the ocean of real power. She wanted out of the pond.

She wanted the men's approval; they held the power. Her father had done an admirable job of educating her for being the eventual Queen of Atani. But, the nobility looked at her eventual ascension as a necessary evil. To them, it would be an inconvenient time that would end when she was relieved of power. Atanians, she was told in a thousand subtle ways, needed a strong King not a pretty Queen.

She still felt the humiliating burn of condescension from the men sitting around her father's war table. They allowed her to stay as they would allow a toddler to attempt to pick up a broad sword. It was far too difficult for a toddler to even move the heavy weapon, so there was no cause for concern. Helena's attendance at the political meetings was an amusing distraction. Her well thought out suggestions fell on deaf ears. She realized that she did not matter to them.

The situation had made her appreciate Lilandra's arrival even more. Helena knew her father loved her, but Lilandra understood her. Lilandra seemed to feel Helena's need and could salve her pain.

Within months of her arrival, Lilandra was silently acknowledged as the undisputed victor of the constant struggle of women of nobility. She overwhelmed them with her beauty, cunning, and utter disdain for their efforts. By emulating her, Helena, too, made their attempts at importance seem childish.

Lilandra also impressed her father and his advisors. Helena wanted so badly to impress them as Lilandra had. They listened to Lilandra. In fact, a few of them feared the woman who was now regent. The reason was simple: Lilandra did not need them.

In a very short time, she climbed higher in the esteem of the King and of the common folk. She made the advisors' positions superfluous. Only by demonstrating their usefulness were they likely to retain their positions. The haughty nobles of Atani now frantically searched for something Regent Lilandra might need.

The best thing about Lilandra's rise in the court of Atani was that she did not forget about Helena. She always found time for her young student.

Helena looked forward to her daily lessons with Lilandra. She worked hard at being the best student she could be. Never before had Princess Helena feared a tutor. She had always been the princess and could simply refuse to cooperate. However, with Lilandra, the slightest look of disappointment was enough to crush the girl's spirit.

For the hundredth time, Helena wondered what Lilandra would think if she cut her hair. Helena feared asking her because she knew Lilandra would gently reproach her for caring about frivolity. If she cut her hair, maybe the Dukes would take her a little more seriously. It was silly, agonizing over such a decision. Helena simply wished she knew what Lilandra would say. The woman always seemed to have the right answer.

Even after two years of tutoring the teenaged girl, Lilandra still understood Helena's needs more than anyone else. Lilandra had done so much, given so much that Helena was desperate for a way to show her appreciation for her tutor.

* * *

It wasn't too long before a small group of soldiers marched into the stadium. They had stopped in formation that looked small on the huge field. Seventy paces separated them from where Sogoth stood and the dragon lay behind a wall of *Nascondersi*.

One of the soldiers shouted in a voice that cracked with uncertainty, "Hold fast for the Most Honored Regent of Atani, Her Ladyship, Lilandra." The words barely carried across the vast field.

Sogoth did not see fit to acknowledge the announcement.

Her power was growing, he noticed with admiration. She took her time in crossing the field. Her dress was impeccable, her face a mix of a girlish pout and queenly disapproval. Surely, there was no man who would not melt at her every request. Except her brother.

"Lord Sogoth, you have disturbed the peace of Atani. I am their Regent, standing in place for their King. This disturbance will not be tolerated." She drew herself up to her full height and pulled her shoulders back. She closed the distance between them so her escorts could not hear what she did not want them to.

"My dear sister, it is good to see you as well." He approached her, but did not embrace her. Whatever emotion was between them did not permit that.

"Brother, why have you come?" Her tone had a mix of curiosity, exasperation, and wariness.

"To give you a gift." It was said simply as if there could be no other reason.

"Fine," she said cautiously, "What is the gift?"

"This!" he said as he swept his arm backward to the sleeping dragon as he allowed *Nascondersi* to dissipate. He took pride in her shocked expression. She was not easily ruffled, but a dragon pierced even her cool mask.

Lilandra was accustomed to being one step ahead of people, thus she hated losing control or being outmanuevered. She needed to seize the advantage back from him.

"Sogoth, I have seen what you are capable of. Too often. This one though," she waved her hand at the dragon, "is simply your best one yet."

He shifted a little, and the slightest softening of his expression flashed for the briefest instant. There it was. Even he was not immune. So

23

easy, she thought. Sprinkle a few compliments, lace it with awe, and male pride was hers to control.

"Whatever am I to do with this creature? Is it even alive?" She let a trace of girlish helplessness intrude.

"I assure you, it is very much alive, though a bit worse for our journey here. As for what you do with it. That, dear sister, is up to you. Make him your royal pet, your official symbol."

"Sogoth, I do not want, nor do I need a dragon." Sibling rivalries did not fade easily. "It is in the middle of our coliseum. We are to have games in two days. My people have come to rely on seeing me at the games. How can we have games with this in the field?"

"If you don't want him, fine. I merely thought that you might enjoy a gift that no one else has ever had. If it is that you fear my gift," his tone turned sinister, "perhaps I can help with that as well."

"My dear brother," her saccharine words dripped from her painted lips, "you chose your path to power, and I chose mine. Let us leave it at that until the final reckoning."

"Dear sister, why did you choose this soft Magic of Need? Why do you not use a true path of power?" He did not ask the last. He said it with authority that made anything he said a fact. "With enough power you could do anything, even control this beast." He didn't even attempt to hide his boasting tone.

He furthered his arrogant criticism. "You are the Regent of this land, and still you could not stop even the most common of soldiers should he decide to have his way with you."

"You have chosen your path, I have chosen mine. The softest silk is still stronger than the hardest steel. Brother, would even your most loyal of men come to your aid if he believed you could not strike him for his inaction? No brother, if they believed they would not be punished, they would stab you in back. Are you so sure of their fear of your power?" It was an argument they had had for countless years. Though neither would admit it, they each wondered if they had chosen the right path. They both also feared the day when their paths would bring them together as combatants.

"Sister, in the end we will see who has more control of their rabble. The dwarves' dark cousins heed my call. With those goblins, I will build an army to cover all the known lands. As my strength grows, so will the dwarves' respect for me. They will not intrude on a struggle of strength. It is their way; they respect strength. The elves surely will hide in their trees. In the end, it will be your army against mine. In the end, though, such pawns will matter not."

He closed his eyes and rudely ignored her for a few minutes. Suddenly and simply, he disappeared from her vision. It was not just that she couldn't see him. He was gone. She was glad her guards across the field could not see the astonished look on her face. She had heard about such a spell. It was *Situtum Domus*. It was a one-way escape spell. She knew the instant Sogoth vanished, he appeared somewhere safe. It took an amount of skill few wizards could claim. Lilandra was immeasurably glad he could only use such a spell to return to his home. It would not do to have him simply appear when and where he wished.

She quickly recovered herself; she too had power. She thought again about her position and plan. It was flawless. She thought to herself, *you see, dear brother, you only control through fear. My power comes from their love of me. I fill their need, and as long as there is pain, there is need.*

* * *

Keven went about his daily routine with an unusual spring in his step. Today began two days of feasting and merriment. Keven cared little for the reason of the celebration, only that his chores would be lightened. There would not be a lot of unloading supplies during the feast. The inn would be bulging with the guests Banolf would pack in. Those guests would bring horses to groom, but that hardly bothered him.

Banolf had hired a storyteller for the evening. Keven hoped he was a good one. With his lightened load and with Banolf distracted by customers and their coins, Keven looked forward to an evening of entertainment.

Once again, Keven was cleaning the stables. As far as labor, it was one of the easiest chores Keven had because it did not require much lifting. Like everything else Master Banolf owned, the stable was of superior quality. The stable had ten stalls. Master Banolf owned three horses. Because the inn was usually full with travelers, Keven often had to put more than one horse in a stall. It made clearing the muck that much more unpleasant.

It always amazed him how horses could turn what seemed to be a little bit of hay and grain into such huge piles of dung. When he had finished cleaning, put the shovel on the cart and prepared to drag it off, the big chestnut, Caelv, whinnied. The horse was Master Banolf's favorite. Keven paused a moment to pat his face. He would not let himself have deep feelings for something that Master Banolf treasured. He knew the horse would never be his, yet he cared for the stallion as he did all of the horses. Keven felt sympathy for the young male because it was built to run, not to be kept in a stable day after day. Master Banolf had bought it from a trader because it was a good steed, but he was an innkeeper who seldom traveled.

Keven grabbed the handles of the two-wheeled cart and began to drag it to the manure shed. He was thankful that it was not far. The cart was big, heavy, and it stunk. Keven was also thankful that the farmer who came to get the cart brought his own. When the farmer came he would take the cart Keven put in the shed and leave his own empty cart inside. Keven did not want to think about having to move the dung from one cart to another. He silently marveled to himself how Banolf could make money selling dung.

The iron lock that secured the shed was the one lock for which Banolf trusted Keven with a key. It opened easily, and Keven swung the heavy door. He pushed the cart in carefully. There was only an inch on either side once the cart was in.

Right as he was about to close the door, he was grabbed from behind. Instantly, he knew it was Gunter. The second shadow had to be Richsen. Keven struggled with everything he had. He knew what they planned. With only two of them Keven thought he just might get away. Then, Gunter tripped him. Richsen quickly grabbed and picked up Keven's feet. With Gunter pinning his arms to his sides, Keven was held helpless in the air.

"Stop!" Keven yelled. "You're gonna' make Banolf mad!" Keven hoped the threat of upsetting Banolf would deter them from going further. He did his best to twist free.

"Make us stop!" Gunter challenged. With that, they heaved Keven into the shed onto the cart filled with horse dung. Keven felt his body sink into the soft offal. Before he could right himself, the door slammed shut, and the iron lock clicked.

"Have fun in there, dung boy," they taunted. "Maybe your ma will come rescue you."

Through small cracks in the shed wall, Keven watched them run off. He got to his knees and experimented with the door. It was locked; he was trapped kneeling inches deep in manure. He swore at his cursed luck. He was a man but still no more able to fend for himself than a helpless child.

He didn't know what to do. He knew no one would hear him in the inn. His mother, the serving girls, and mistress Bitte would be too busy with the pots. Master Banolf would be in the great room convincing early celebrants to buy more ale.

He swore in frustration. *Why? Damn it. Why me? Why can't I stop them?* He swung his fist as hard as he could against the rough-hewn interior planks. It hurt, but the pain felt good. The pain in his hand distracted him from the pain he felt in his soul. *Why, Why, Why?* With each utterance, he slammed his fist against the wall. He knew he must have been bleeding.

Open wounds and manure might lead to sickness, but he didn't care. He was covered with the foulness; he had no choice but to sit in it while he waited for others to let him out.

He let the frustration drive his thoughts. *Why?* He had never done anything to them. They saw him as weak and of no value, but there was more. Things of no value should be ignored. No, he meant something to them. Keven began to think. It was all that he could do. Thoughts connected with other thoughts in dizzying patterns. This would be the last time, he vowed.

Gareloch

Tommi Tissari

Chapter 3

Lilandra was resting on a velvet couch in her wing of the royal palace. Though her well-formed body was splayed in a comfortable position, her sharp mind was working furiously. That was the normal state for Lilandra. Her beauty and grace gave the impression of divine equanimity while her mind was busy with the next moves in the great game that was life.

She savored the truth that her plans, crafted so long ago, were working as well as she had imagined them. Of course, it wasn't easy. There was any number of occurrences that could have proven troublesome. Quite a few might yet cause her problems.

As she sat in her receiving room, which was connected to her sumptuously appointed bedroom, she made a mental list of what decorations and upholstery needed to be changed. It wouldn't do for the Regent of Atani to have to suffer the same furnishings month after month.

The hand painted ivy that crawled up the wall was old. The elegantly detailed painting of a flock of birds that adorned the ceiling would have to be painted over. Even the red velvet on which she reclined would have to be removed and replaced with something. Green, maybe, and satin. That would make a wonderful change.

Her cunningly calculating mind winced at the wastefulness such frivolity encouraged. It had to be done, though. As far as her comfort, the color of the walls and the coverings of the furniture mattered not a whit. It was the need that it created and the need it fulfilled.

In all of the scurrying that her whims produced, there were plenty of smiles to be seen. People enjoyed working, especially for her. Getting paid for working was good. But people seemed to enjoy working towards a big, shared goal if they were recognized. It was simple. People needed to feel important. If she provided that to a few hundred craftsmen with the simple changing of her chambers, her future plans had to be safe.

King Donius was becoming less of a factor everyday. Even the strongest men had weak points. She was lucky he did not know what his own weaknesses were.

Subtlety was the key. By being the royal tutor to Crown Princess Helena, Lilandra had gained access to the places and people of influence in the great castle of Atani. Since then, it was her myriad of skills that had caused her rise in the esteem of so many.

Her beauty was a big part of it. She understood beauty in a way that few others did. Unlike the clucking hens that were the noble women of Atani, Lilandra understood that beauty was a means, not an end.

Additionally, she knew that each person understood beauty differently. For the common soldiers who now would gladly lay down their lives for her, beauty was too much eye makeup, a low-cut gown, and a not so subtle hint of the possibility of a roll in the hay. For the crowds of citizens who increasingly threw roses at her in the street, beauty meant looking as good as they dreamed, but not so good as to be unapproachable. For the nobles, her beauty had to seem intriguing but not threatening. Nobles were quite jealous of their standing with each other. It would not do to scare them. She had to let one group of them think one thing, while she would work on something different for others.

Beauty was not the only tool she had in her kit. Her flowing hair could be pinned up sensibly. Her flirtatious gowns could be left in the wardrobe; she could look intimidating. It wasn't until a few months after her arrival as Helena's tutor that she brought out other tools. Nobles were the easiest. Their constant struggles with each other and their need for approval from the king made them hang their needs out like a merchant hung his shingle.

It was not as clumsy as extortion. Sure, they all had their weaknesses. One lord needed to hide his debts. Another lady needed to conceal the shame of lying with a servant. It had to be much more delicate. The lord who had debts was, at the heart of it, worried about his security. With a few words and a few gestures, she enabled him to feel more comfortable. Whether he then lost his land was irrelevant. His need for security was filled.

The lady who enjoyed a different type of service from her male attendant simply needed to feel desired. In the lady's simple mind, she had worked out the idea that if she was not desirable, she was not anything. A few confidential, woman-to-woman talks had let the woman feel needed. If a woman as beautiful as Lilandra said the lady was desired by many men, how could she argue?

From those two instances and others like them, word of the beautiful and talented royal tutor spread among the nobles. Her popularity spread as the ever-jealous nobles sought her out, lest a rival might gain more of her time. Having the nobles' public approval, if not officially declaring her valuable, increased her standing with the many officials and bureaucrats in the castle's employ. That was where her plans began to bloom.

The unnoticed castle staff made wielding power possible. Of course, the King made the decisions, but his staff supplied the information that permitted him to make decisions. The best ruler is only as good as the information he is given.

Because of her success with the nobles, many of the castle staff began giving her the respect they would only give the highest lord. Nobles to them were a curiosity that was best to be avoided.

Lilandra changed that. In her eyes, they were not unnoticed servants. They were people who needed to talk about their families and their lives. They were people who needed to hear that they mattered. Nobles and kings rarely spared a kind word for a purser who would report accurately on the limitations of the castle's finances. They only wanted to hear that there was enough money for all of their grand schemes.

It cost Lilandra nothing to seek out some of the King's staff and give them the kind word they had not expected, but desperately needed. For the groomsmen, she wore her hair and gowns in a way that would have them happy just to have her near them. For the maids, she would dress down so that they would not feel overshadowed. Every woman, even the hardiest of servants, needed to feel beautiful. Lilandra filled that need.

It took more than a few conversations for them to trust her. It was just not done. Nobles did not make commoners feel better. By asking the opinion of commoners, she changed the role they saw themselves in. Eventually they relaxed their guard and sought out her approval. They needed to have her think well of them. She became privy to a lot of information. The unseen and unheard servants saw and heard more than the king's spies.

With the adulation of many of the nobles and with the eyes and ears of the workers of Atani, Lilandra was well on her way to beating her brother at a game that had begun so very long ago. However, what she thought was a small lead in their private contest had been shortened by her brother's latest coup.

What the hell was she to do with a dragon? Her brother had not violated the vows they had pledged to each other. He had not directly attacked her or interfered with her plans, but he had put her in a position that very well might expose her weaknesses. Again she swore to herself, what the hell was she to do with a forty-foot dragon! She rarely cursed in public, except when such words might get her needed attention. It never ceased to amaze her how some men reacted to a woman who used words they only thought about in the bedroom.

The dragon's scales were truly brilliant in even the dimmest hours of night, she had to grudgingly admit. Its power must be immense. Until she saw it, she was not sure dragons existed. She, unlike so many others, knew there were real wizards, and wizards did not give up their secrets easily.

Lilandra suspected that even they did not have much if any knowledge of dragons. She wistfully wished Sogoth's gift was what he said it was. She knew him well enough, though, to know that he never gave a gift that did not contain at least one hidden barb.

Militarily, the dragon could be used in so many ways. Fighting was not where her skills lay. As a Mistress of Need, her powers were far more subtle, but no less effective. Sogoth was a Wizard of Sorcery and of Magic. Though not the best at either art, the fact that he had met a dragon and conquered it spoke volumes of his power and ambition.

But if the reports were correct, moving the damn thing would be impossible short of calling Sogoth back. How he would love, she swore, being called to help, reveling in her need.

Her animal trainers had tried using food to wake it. Their hesitancy and plain fear was overcome after they had been convinced that she personally needed their expert services. They would have had as much success getting a hill to eat.

The soldiers tried to force it to move. Even the strongest swing of the sword produced nothing but a sore arm and a few sparks. The engineers and machinists confirmed what she knew. It would take weeks to construct the necessary riggings and part of the stadium would have to be destroyed. The sleeping dragon was just too big.

Though she had never been inside the Wizards' Palace, she knew what real magic was and how difficult it was to acquire. Of those few who called themselves wizards in Atani, she knew none had the right to do so. The test to be a wizard and the terrible price that test demanded seemed to scare the life out of the ones who passed.

Some who had true magic might be in Atani, but she had never found them. Those who claimed to have magic could fool themselves and the peasants who believed their words. It seemed anyone with any ability at separating a fool and his coin was calling himself a wizard.

Each charlatan she asked about the dragon gave her a different reason why they could not wake it: the moon was not right, the weather had not allowed the herbs to grow, or the numbers did not favor it. She needed a wizard who was a master of the sorcerous arts or even of technology. Not so called wizards of the stars, weather, or worst of all, herbs. They each did their best to hide their inability by using arcane words and wizard speak.

She wondered what Sogoth would do to a wizard such as the ones who were making excuses for their failure. Sogoth's art was not hers, but his methods were effective. In the short run only, she reminded herself.

She had visited the dragon several times since Sogoth's departure. It was hard to believe the beast was alive because it did not seem to breathe. It was as if Sogoth gave her a dragon-shaped piece of granite. She knew the stories of dragons. She knew it could quite possibly sleep until the citizens of Atani were long dead and the city was naught but ruins.

That thought could not be allowed to reach the public. In the days after Sogoth's flight over Atani City, Lilandra let many nobles and commoner alike know what she thought of people who traffic in rumors. Nothing was more detrimental to her long laid plans for the the Dream than old wives' tales of beasts and dragons.

She asked each one of the soldiers who had seen the dragon to keep quiet as a special favor to her. They could not have agreed faster. Each wanted to please and was sorry they had failed to move the dragon for her.

That the coliseum was closed was an annoyance. The citizens had come to expect and look forward to contests and performances at the arena. It brought the citizens together. The poor had yet to be fully represented, but that would change. After the more affluent had participated in the assemblies, a need would be created in the poor. The need would be filled when the time was right. The events allowed them to hear and see her, and it allowed her to know what they needed.

Lilandra began to draw up rumors and plan for their subtle distribution. Citizens would have to wait to see the inside of the coliseum. A date would not be given, only the whisper that something big was being planned for the people. The rumors would mention her and that she was preparing a grand event that showed how much the people of Atani were needed.

* * *

The sun was a few hours away from the horizon as Gareloch rode into Village Donnell after two nights on the road. He could have arrived sooner, but he simply did not feel like rushing. That was what he told himself. If he had to admit the reason, it was that Thistle, his horse, did not like to rush. He had long ago given up trying to control her or even get respect from her. She was what she was; there was no hope of changing her.

This village was like many others. The white washed buildings did battle with the mud from the streets. Gareloch could tell that the Goodfolk of this town, more than most, were particular about the look of things. He was sure that on feastdays, the church was packed with people in their finest. Ah, he sighed to himself, they have to get their hope from somewhere.

He had made an agreement with the local innkeeper to entertain at this feast. It was not bad work. He even liked the stories. Many of the folk had heard them before, but Gareloch took pride in his ability to make an old story sound new.

He especially liked the children. Indeed, he usually had to fight with the innkeepers to have children present early in the evening. Innkeepers must be a race, he thought. They all looked the same, welcomed people the same, and thought the same. Children did not drink or pay so the innkeepers could not see a good reason to let them take up valuable floor space in the inns' great rooms.

But Gareloch insisted. He had a few methods that usually ensured he got what he wanted. Where else, he mused, would the children hear tales of things beyond their plow, grist wheel, or loom? It was their parents' words that chained the children to a life identical to that of their parents. Gareloch's wish was not that the children would leave the life of their ancestors. He simply wanted them to choose that life or any life. He wanted them to have hope.

Thistle whinnied as she pranced a few steps. In his long life, he had never heard of a mare that objected to mud. Even she, as particular as she was, would bear a freshly rained-on lane for the promise of a good grooming at the next village. Good luck to the stable hand who had to take care of her.

The inn was not hard to find. People were coming and going from it as well as just standing in front of it. If Gareloch were a different sort of man, he would take pride in the fact that many of the people were simply waiting for him.

As he drew closer, a few of the Goodfolk recognized him for what he was. The whispers, the elated faces, and the subtle pointing were enough to make most men blush with pride or unease.

When the fat man in the white apron burst through the doors of the inn to welcome him, Gareloch knew he had to be the innkeeper. The man wanted to be the first one to greet the storyteller. If possible, his rotund form swelled even more as he realized people were watching him. His thin hair was pushed back with some potion that he probably hoped made him look friendlier. Gareloch, who had met many innkeepers, wondered if the man used cooking grease. What they would use and reuse in stews would make even a troll think twice before eating.

"Welcome storyteller. I am Goodman Banolf, your humble innkeeper. The Goodfolk have been waiting for you. Welcome indeed. My stable hand should be around to take your mare. Just tie her here while you come inside. She'll be well cared for."

The innkeeper was dragging Gareloch inside while trying to seem gracious and gentle.

"Goodman Banolf, I'd no like ta leave me horse unattended, I'll wait fer yer lad. This horse, she does no like anyone I've no introduced her ta."

Banolf seemed to hesitate as if wondering if this latest development was making him look foolish in front of onlookers. "I'll get the boy. Elven prince he thinks he is. I'll put him to work and box him good, I will. My apologies to you, Master Gareloch"

"Tis no trouble. Days in a saddle make a man glad ta stand a bit before he has ta sit again"

With that Banolf hurried off, muttering angry things about work, chores, and laziness.

* * *

Keven didn't know how long he'd been trapped in the shed. The shadows shifted through the wooden slats. The smell from the manure was overwhelming.

He heard Master Banolf call for him from some way off. The thought of being in trouble was a fleeting one. He would rather take Banolf's worst than stay in the dung. He yelled as loud as he could.

By peering between the cracks, Keven could see Banolf's scowl deepened as he approached. Keven heard him fish for the right key.

"We have guests, and you're playing dwarf in the hole. Well you better get your arse to the front of the inn and take care of the customers. Then, we'll have a talk about you resting like a lord."

As he swung the door open, he glared at Keven and asked, "Well, what do you have to say, boy?"

After a second of staring at the fat innkeeper, Keven exploded out of the shed and stormed off. The look in Keven's eye gave even Banolf pause.

Keven didn't run nor did he walk; he simply moved with a single-minded purpose. Hours of frustration had cooled and condensed into a ball of iron hard rage. He knew where Gunter and Constance would be.

He rounded the corner of the inn and strode to the crowd in the center of the street. He was correct. Gunter, Constance, and others were standing around the storyteller.

"Gunter!" he shouted, "Do you know why your father, the *great* soldier does not come home? He is either dead or lying with whores making bastards like me."

The crowd turned. Gunter stood among them and turned along with them to take in the dung covered boy. His face gawked, astounded someone would dare say anything of the sort to him, especially the bastard. Slowly, that look hardened into the arrogant ugliness Keven was used to, and he closed the distance in four quick steps. As a testament to Gunter's training, Keven did not see the fist until it hit him in the cheek.

Keven found himself on the dusty street with an aching face. It was nowhere he had not been before. He hauled himself up.

"Gunter, you will be lucky to make it a year in the lord's squads. You're tough with only me to fight and Constance to cheer for you. How will you fare on the battlefield? Will you make it till the end of your first battle or will you be simply another nameless corpse?"

This time, Gunter's fist came to Keven's stomach. Keven doubled over but did not go down. After a moment, he got his breath back. He waited until he could speak loud enough for the village to hear.

"Constance," he shouted, "You are the fairest in this town. Enjoy it now. This is the best you will be. You will soon give birth to a litter of screaming babes just like your mother. You will grow large hips like your mother and be chained to a hearth like your mother. No one will look your way. You will be me."

Gunter's fist came again and knocked Keven to the ground. Keven felt the pain in his cheek, and it felt good. It spurred him on. He was right.

"You know I'm right. You hate me. You fear me because I cannot be worse. I am the lowest of this town. You know that, and you know I didn't earn it by anything I did. And you know it would break you. You need me to break because then I wouldn't be better than you."

Gunter's fist did not come. He looked confused. Keven did not care.

"Hit me again. Do it. It won't make me any less right. It won't make you any less wrong." Keven dared Gunter in front of the town.

"And you, Richsen, Brenden, and all of you who follow Gunter and Constance, ask yourself, why? Why do you hate and fear me? I'll tell you why. There is no difference between me and you. I am what you could be. My life cannot get worse, but yours can."

He said each word as if it were a hammer blow, beating years of pain out of his soul. Everyone on the street froze as if their movement might focus Keven's wrath on them.

"And to all of you Goodfolk," Keven was shouting now, "Am I what your Book of the Word teaches is evil? Am I the troll that pillages your virtue? No, but I am everything you fear. You think I am poor because of who I am. Would you be different if you lived in a barn and shoveled dung for a meal? As long as you are not me you think you deserve the title Goodman or Goodwife. What makes you different than me?" The last was not a question. It was a challenge.

No one in the street accepted his challenge. Keven spat the last words out like poison. He looked each person in their eyes. They could not meet his stare. Even the most respected of the village could not face the bastard stable hand.

With his victory established, he strode to the storyteller. What should have been an exchange that contained deference and respect was cut short by Keven grabbing the reins of the gray mare and leading her to the stable.

* * *

36

Tonay had made good progress. Leaving her papa's olive farm was easy. The hard part became getting far enough away that he could not come after her because she knew he would. She would not stand up to him if he did catch her. He had never been forceful with her. She had never given him a reason. But, she knew if he caught her, it wouldn't come to being dragged back bodily. She would obey, like she always did. The thought sent chills of humiliation down her spine.

Uncertainty dogged her every step. Her soft- soled shoes probably would not make much of a mark on the hard packed road, but she would be seen by any number of people.

Though the area around Ducca's vineyard was considered lush, she had trouble finding vegetation in the rolling hills that would offer much cover. If she were to remain hidden, she would have to travel far from the road. That thought continually unnerved her. She wasn't given to believing tales of trolls and goblins. She did, however, know that she did not want to sleep by herself in the wild. The knife she carried was no deterrent to any true threat.

That thought spurred her feet. The sooner she could find some of the Regent's squads the sooner she would be free. She did not want to hurt her Papa, but he would not let her take a chance. Everyone needed to make his or her own mistakes, she believed. How else was she supposed to learn that a kettle can be hot unless she burned herself?

Tonay forced herself to take a path that would steer her a little farther from the road. If she was going to do it, she wanted to do it all the way. If she stayed on the road because she was afraid, she was not ready to leave her father.

Any good tracker could follow her. The dark, loamy soil allowed the most tender grasses to grow. Indeed, Ducca's Vineyard could hardly survive if the fragile crops were not nurtured by the soil.

She had purposely left behind her dresses and slippers. They would not help her in her journey. She also wanted to impress any soldiers that she was a serious girl – no - a woman who could answer the Regent's call for help. Tonay wondered how many others were heeding the call and leaving their life to be a good Atanian citizen. There had to be others. How could people resist, she wondered. Regent Lilandra had done so much good for the people since King Donius asked for her to be his permanent counsel.

Tonay knew her papa tried to be a good man. He was not violent, though he was no coward either. She knew he had served in King Donius' army when he was younger. It was as if her father had nothing left in his soul to be stirred by noble causes. However, as much as she loved him, she could not accept his refusal to listen to Regent Lilandra's call.

She yanked herself away from her musings. Thinking of her father would not put her in contact with the Regent's squads. Maintaining a clear head was the only way to not get lost. She shivered as an image of having to return home and admitting she got lost entered her head.

The army had sent recruiting parties all over this part of Atani. The rumors all said that they were welcoming anyone who would give their life for the Regent. That thought of camaraderie and self-sacrifice spurred her on.

Lilandra herself was the ultimate example of contributing to a greater cause. She saw no difference between noble born and commoners. The noble Regent spoke as comfortably with common farmers as she did with the most learned advisors. The rumors said she opened the castle's larder for the newcomers to the city. She housed all volunteers and trained them to be the best they could be.

Tonay's feet were ever more swift as she picked a path through the underbrush. With each step, she became ever more convinced of her mission. She knew she would not need the food in her pack if she kept her thoughts on serving Atani and Regent Lilandra.

* * *

Gareloch kept his face free of expresson as the fat innkeeper bowed, scraped, and begged his apologies for the incident in front of the inn. Gareloch had ridden in a wrinkled, stooped old man. Now, he stood straight and tall with an air of authority and importance. He was a storyteller, after all. He could switch his bearing to fit his mood or the situation. The innkeeper was a bully. Bullies did not respect friendly old storytellers. Bullies only respected someone who could take something away from them.

It was strange for the innkeeper to call so much attention to what was essentially a fight between two boys. Gareloch, despite his many years of wandering, had never seen a fight quite like the one he just witnessed. The boy who landed all of the punches was the one who ended up skulking away the loser.

Gareloch surveyed the great room. Though it was a typical inn, it was pleasant and clean. Inns usually made most of their coin from men who did not know when to stop buying ale. This inn was clean enough and bright enough that even most women would feel comfortable at the dark wooden tables.

The great room was big enough to hold seventy-five, if they were packed tight and numbed with drink. They would hardly notice, after a time, the watered down ale and the stringy meat. Get them drunk and keep them spending. That, Gareloch knew, was how the innkeeper planned it.

Gareloch turned his attention back to the innkeeper. "I trust my bags will be stored securely in my room." He changed his voice and accent to sound more educated than his customary brogue. Words often made the difference in one's appearance, he mused.

"Yes sir, I will bring them up myself from the stable. Then I shall go back down to the stable and give that boy a long lesson in manners."

"Yes, I'm quite sure you will. Before all of that, I would like some ale and a meal. I'm not sure I could perform well enough if my throat continues to be dry. I would hate to think what this village would think of you if the storyteller you promised could not perform."

The fat man's expression went blank with nervousness.

Gareloch could smell mouthwatering aromas from the kitchen. Ordinarily, he would have complimented an innkeeper on keeping such a fine establishment. Gareloch, however, did not like the man. So, he changed his role from that of a cheerful storyteller to that of a haughty noble, and the innkeeper changed his role to that of a servant.

Gareloch sat at the table and tried to look aloof and bored. "You have done a fair job with this establishment. It fits this backwards little farming village. Perhaps one day you will travel and see what true inns look like."

It worked. The innkeeper could not talk fast enough. He promised Gareloch a great meal, with great service. He went on to mention that the beds had real mattresses.

Banolf was about to leave the table. In fact, he had backed up several paces for fear of turning his back on what he thought was a temperamental storyteller. Right as he turned to go, Gareloch gave him one more direction.

"My good man, I would see the stable hand at my table after he has bathed." He said it neutrally and watched for a reaction.

"Please sir, do not trouble yourself with the likes of him. I shall deal with him soundly. You can be sure of that"

"Yes, well, that is fine. But, I would have him at my table. You may deal with him for the insult he caused your *fine* inn. I will deal with him for the insult to me. Be sure he is not presented to me before I finish my meal. I would not want to ruin my ability to entertain your paying customers. One more thing, I expect the honor of being the first to lay a mark on him. The greater insult was done to me. It is my right."

The confusion on the innkeeper's face was evident. Gareloch's demand was so unusual that the innkeeper fretted it might be yet another slight on his inn. If a fat man could scurry, the innkeeper did.

* * *

Tapio Denisio was not a tracker. Often, he was off his horse, staring at marks in the mud trying to determine if his daughter had made them. He was getting more worried with each passing mile. He knew she was stubborn. But, he had expected to meet her trudging back home and was amazed that there was still no sign of her.

She could not have packed much food or even traveling supplies. He had no reason to believe she knew how to travel.

He remembered how he had felt as a young man serving in the army and seeking glory. This was different. Adventure always had risk. Tonay didn't seem to realize that. Swearing to himself, he climbed back on his horse and spurred it to a slow canter. It was the best the old plow horse could do.

If Tonay was ahead of him, it could not be by much. She had left, he reasoned, right after sundown. For the thousandth time, he wondered if he should urge his horse to go faster or if he should go slower and look for a sign.

He had searched for the whole day and even through the next night before he stopped. He knew it was almost useless to search in the dark, but he could hardly make camp and sleep by a fire while his daughter was out there alone.

His horse needed rest and deserved sympathy. It had given him years of service and didn't have too many years left to give. But, still, Tonay was his daughter. He'd let the horse die under him if it would help him bring her home.

A few years in the army had taught him his limits. He was tired. Still, the constant stream of horrible images kept him pushing his horse. Wolves, goblins, or even a troll might take her. As bad as those were, they almost comforted him compared to the thought of slavers. He knew that once the slavers had their collar on a person, that person's death lasted a lifetime.

How had it come to her running from the farm, he asked himself again. He knew farm work was hard, and the life surely was not glamorous, but it had been good enough for him, her mother, and countless other souls. Tending the animals and pruning the trees and vines was not a game, but it was honest. If a person did not work, they did not eat. It was a simple law of nature that Tonay did not want to follow.

No, she was a good girl, he corrected himself. She was never afraid of work. She could sometimes lose herself in the chores around the farm. He remembered a time when she was to stack firewood. The cord pile of logs was high and should have taken a few days to stack. Tonay worked straight for twelve hours and nearly finished the task. She seemed surprised at her own hard work when he told her to stop for dinner.

When asked about it, she didn't really have an answer. She merely said she was thinking of other things, not the logs. It was as if she was not doing the work. He had seen it many times. Even during a conversation, she would be elsewhere.

This running off was a fool's notion. A woman in the Army! That was bad enough, but she did not seem to understand what it was that a soldier did. Swords were fine things, until you had to pull yours out of someone.

He had honestly tried to understand her reasons. Neither he nor Tonay was slow of wit, but neither could make themselves understand each other. It was beyond a simple argument between the generations. He had been no angel growing up and probably helped his papa to lose the few gray hairs he had. But, this was different. Many people, and not all of them young, were leaving the villages and the farms to head for The City of Atani. They were dropping their hoes or closing up shop and heading north for the Dream.

The Regent's call defied understanding. There was no war to be fought, nor any castles to be built. King Donius kept the city spotless and orderly. There simply was no reason for this new Regent to need so many people to come to her aid.

Nibbling on the olive bread occupied his mind as he walked his horse. He wished he could let the horse graze a bit. But, time could not be spared. With dawn breaking, he needed spend every minute looking. A keen and careful eye was more important than speed, not that the old workhorse could give him true speed.

Tapio also knew that there were worse things than soldiers. He had never actually seen one, but a few men he trusted swore they had met up with goblins. Their stories were enough to frighten hardened soldiers. What goblins did with the bodies of the ones they killed and even with the ones that were only wounded had kept him from eating and sleeping for days.

The weight of his sword at his hip comforted him. He had not picked it up in years. It had lain in his room wrapped in oilcloth and tied with twine. At one time, he had had more than a little skill with it. He had served in the Atanian army and received some training. That training had lasted about five seconds once he was in his first battle.

The thing he remembered most about his first and his later battles was how hot he felt. Fighting was physically grueling. Every muscle and every sense strained to keep life in the body. Unlike a hard job harvesting olives or tending to live stock, fighting for your life did not allow for even a small break. He had fought battles in the dead of winter, but he always remembered being hot and scared.

Perhaps the main thing his training officers neglected to tell him was what actually happened to your enemy's body when your sword struck it. It was usually a wet sound. Sometimes there was the scraping sound of a badly angled blow bouncing off bone. He had seen animals gutted and butchered countless times. Still it just wasn't the same with a man.

The worst was the finishing stroke. Tapio Denisio was, at heart, a gentle man. Of course, he had been strict with his daughter and demanding of anyone with whom he traded. But, he hated and would be haunted by the memories of administering the final blow to a fallen opponent. To cut deep into a man's chest did not often kill him quickly. The man could live for minutes or hours. If you turned away, the man might even have enough strength to stab you in the back. No. His officers had always told him a wounded enemy had to be killed, even when his eyes showed terror and he begged for mercy.

The rush of blood to his hands, feet, and face assured him that the darkness of those deeds still had their effect on him after so many years. Those vile memories motivated him to climb back on his farm horse and search for his daughter. She thought soldiering, battles, and swords were fun.

He was hungry but resisted the urge to nibble more. He knew he would be hungrier later. He could fight the hunger. It was the gnawing worry that sapped his strength and addled his mind

Luck or The Creator's will made him look down when he did. Barely visible in the hard packed mud of the lane was an imprint of horseshoes. The print made a clear edge in the mud. The clear edge meant that time, wind, or another's passage had not rounded it down. It was fresh. It wasn't Tonay's print, but it might be someone's who had seen her. With renewed worry, he spurred on his tired nag.

* * *

Kielasanthra Tylansthra knew she was being kept waiting as part of her punishment. Patience was her weakness and impatience was not well tolerated among elves. For beings that lived for countless years, the ability to be at peace with oneself was critical. Kielasanthra had heard that lecture a thousand times. But she knew it was not herself with whom she was not at peace. It was the elders and their ancient rules.

The garden in which she was forced to wait was beautiful. It was always beautiful. Everything was always beautiful. That was the elven way.

It was not the beauty of her instructor's garden that bothered her. It was that she had nothing to compare it against. To Kielasanthra, she felt like a fish trying to appreciate being wet.

As she sat on the conveniently bent tree trunk, she again noticed the incredible skill that blended the dwelling with the garden. One flowed into the other with barely a seam. That too was the elven way. Nature was life. It could be changed, convinced to grow a certain way.

The tree that so graciously grew in such a way as to offer a comfortable place to rest was an example of her instructor's skill. No tools had been used because tools along with weapons were looked upon with disdain, as crude and primitive. The tree was simply convinced it might be happier if it grew differently. It was a version of magic that was older than elven memory. Kiel had little patience with it.

Her trouble came from the fact she was not fully elven, but was half human. Haste and straight lines interested her. Both were involved in weapons lore. A bow was tolerable to the elves because the curved wood was coaxed from a tree. The bow had significance in elven history that even the long-lived scholars could not fully explain. The straight arrows were tolerable because they were meant to be cast away from the archer. She had learned that from countless reenactments of ancient rituals.

Those same rituals taught of the sword. Swords were, are, and always would be evil, a necessary evil. Elves had no forges; their swords were created from magic. Metal came from the living earth. It grew, albeit much more slowly than even the elves. To coax such a slow growing thing as metal to change itself demanded much. Many elves had to work with powerful magics to create the hated weapons.

As the histories showed, even the patient elves had need of swords. And those blades have been passed down through generations.

The most important lesson one needed to learn about the complexities of elven society was that errors were not to be made. Perfection was the only acceptable level of achievement, indeed, the only way to live. Elves lived for so long that regret had to be prevented. Living with an easily preventable miscue for decades or even centuries did not make for easy living. Regret was always painful. Even small miscues, like the flap of the meekest butterfly could have consequences that might haunt one for ages.

Though comparatively young and only half-elven, Kielasanthra knew about consequences better than most. She was an accident, a miscue of a human male and her mother. Kiel would live for a very long time and each breath Kiel drew brought shame on her mother, shame that would not end for many years.

Kielasanthra had done nothing to earn her mother's shame. She was the best archer of all of the current students of the LeafTender Clan. Her woods lore and weapons craft gave her cause to be proud.

It wasn't Kielasanthra's actions that made many elves uncomfortable. It was her very existence. Kielasanthra represented one of the the worst mistakes an elf could make. Elven females were fertile for only fleeting moments in their long lifetime. That was beneficial, in a race whose members lived for centuries, having several offspring would cause countless problems.

Elven notions of sex and love were quite different than those of humans. Elves were considered physically mature after three decades of growth. From that point until death centuries later, the pleasures of the flesh were a constant temptation to every elf. To be surrounded by constant beauty tested even the strongest of wills. The cruelty of the elven life was that the fertile times for females were different for each elf. It could be in the third decade or even in the thirtieth. They were rare and unpredictable, at best happening only three times in a life.

To complicate things, males who were interested in mating looked at Kiel more and more. She was finding that her beauty was a thing of consternation for most elves. The males had composed flowery poems noting her lithe grace at the same time resenting her for being beautiful but not fully elven. The females were jealous over such attention and her ability to make any bit of clothing look like nature's finest offering. Years of extra lessons with the bow and woods lore had made her body an example of the best nature had to offer.

Love too, was difficult for the elves. Even the dullest of human observers would notice that nothing lasts forever. There are past moments, current moments, and future moments. Things change; that is nature's way. To pledge to be with one mate for the rest of one's moments is foolish. Love, like the most fragrant flowers, grows and dies. Marriages are encouraged to bloom, and allowed to die and decay so that new loves might be found.

Kielasanthra had not yet given herself to a mate. She did not know if the gift of herself would ever be fully accepted. She was seen as beautiful, but would never be perfect in the eyes of other elves. Worse still, despite all of the elven knowledge of life and growth, times of fertility remained a mystery. An accidental child would be a mistake she would not make.

She had sat on this trunk and others like it waiting for many of her instructors to tell her she was not thinking with proper care. She could almost recite the speeches word for word.

As she fought boredom on the comfortable tree limb, she did not hear her instructor exit his dwelling. Little separated his dwelling from the garden. He stood over her and waited for her to notice his graceful arrival.

"Honored teacher, please share with me the benefits of your moments." It was a common greeting from a lesser to a greater.

"Kielasanthra Tylansthra, please spend some moments in my dwelling." The forms of etiquette had to be observed though Kielasanthra was eager to be done with this. She dutifully followed him to a hedge that was thick with stout branches. He led her through an opening that she would not have seen without his guidance.

The inside of his dwelling was a model of elven harmony. The moss was a soft carpet that seemed to care for one's feet. The flowers bloomed in uniformity, and the trees that wove themselves in and out of the dwelling provided seating for many elves. What unsettled her was that all of those seats were filled. She rarely prayed to *Agris*, who nurtures and prunes all lives. Seeing the elders' expressions, however, shook her usual irreverence.

Her instructor took the last open seat, leaving her standing. She faced seven elders who were seated in a half-circle. They were the leaders of the LeafTender Clan. Their calm faces gave her no indication as to why they were in her instructor's dwelling. Surely, she had done nothing she had not done before many times. Still, she was nervous.

"Kielasanthra Tylansthra, you have been unhappy these last decades. Your past moments have made your present moments awkward. Many have tended to you. Still you are a wild vine. Your future moments seem to have you grow in disharmony with others."

There was pain in his voice, and that alarmed her. The genuine sorrow that welled up surprised her.

"Yes, honored teacher, I do not spend enough thought on my present moments. I do not sow with caution. I cast my seeds without thought. I will endeavor to reap better future moments." It was a rote reply she had given many times before. The contrition in her voice was automatic. She would say whatever she must to get back to her bow.

"Yes, we all need to sow with care. May our future moments always reflect cautious action. But the council fears you are not right for this garden. Perhaps you will flourish with different soil. After much consideration, it is thought best if you leave our garden. Perhaps some time with other humans will allow you to grow as you wish."

To elves, control over one's emotions was essential. Acting with emotion caused regret. Regret caused more emotions. It was a cycle that could cause more unplanned reactions than a hundred butterflies flying at once. Kielasanthra Tylansthra felt no emotion at his announcement. For the first time in her nine decades, she felt nothing. There was not sorrow or fear at being asked to leave. There was neither relief nor joy.

"Kielasanthra Tylansthra, we know this is difficult for you. You are the finest ranger to have ever grown in Elvenwood. We think a time of a decade should be enough. Should you wish to return to this garden anytime after that, know that you are welcome."

Numbly, she turned her back on the circle of elders, etiquette forgotten. She had often been described as a wild vine in the garden. She never thought she would be a seed, cast into the wind.

* * *

As he neared the stables, Banolf bellowed. "Keven! Where are you, you smelly cur?"

Keven emerged from the one empty stall with a candle and a book that had been loaned to him by a widow in exchange for weeding her garden of herbs. The flickering light hid any emotion his face might have shown.

"Boy, blow that out before you burn down my stable. You have upset the storyteller. I swear..." But Banolf's anger was such that he could not finish his threat.

To Keven, it seemed as though the fat man was trying to control himself.

"Listen to me. Tonight is the feast night. There will be people lining up to hear the storyteller and buy my ale. If you do one thing to disturb peoples' drinking and buying, I will have you thrown out of town. You and your mother will have nothing but a pot to beg from. You are to get the wash tub, scrub the manure from your body and present yourself at the storyteller's table."

Keven was prepared for just about anything. He had realized or convinced himself he simply did not care about the town, the people in the town, or whatever they might do. But, having to face the storyteller was a little off-putting.

"Now listen, boy, you are to apologize and beg forgiveness. He says he wants the first right of tanning your hide. You had better take it and thank him. If he leaves or does not tell his stories, you will be sorry your mother ever spread her whore legs." With that, Banolf stormed out.

Keven did not react. He felt no need to. There was only so much Banolf could do and none of it could truly hurt him. His imprisonment in the dung shed had taught him a little about himself and what he truly needed.

Joseph Swope

47

Lucius

Lori Crow

Chapter 4

The dreary, gray stone of the halls tricked the mind into thinking the body should be cold. The Wizards' Palace was old beyond counting. It boasted of being well constructed. Over the centuries, there had been many attempts at rebuilding and incorporating ever-newer skills at wizardry into its foundations and corridors. With all of the vaunted knowledge that went into its design, it was still common to feel a draft in almost any hallway.

As Lucius walked, his robes swished around his corpulent feet. He was honest enough with himself to admit that he was not just large, he was fat. As a child many, many years before, he had been ridiculed unmercifully. Though the sting of the children's taunts had almost faded, the irritation at not finding a way to cure his condition was just as sharp as it had been on the first day he had realized he was different from others.

As part of progressing to the level of wizard, he, like every other student of the various other forms of power, had a choice to take several oaths. They culminated in the Trinity, the Duality, or the One Oath. The One Oath was the most basic: all who passed the wizard test had to swear to increase their knowledge. There was no way around that fact. With power came that indelible collar.

Failure to meet that oath was simply not possible. It was magically bonded to the wizard. An attempt to break the oath resulted in unpleasant consequences that no wizard would be foolish enough to risk feeling twice.

Few wizards swore to only the One Oath, to always strive to increase and improve knowledge. It was dangerous to have a wizard whose only boundary was to seek more power. Most newly promoted wizards swore the Duality. It bound the wizard to increase and improve his knowledge and to do no preventable harm to others.

Of course, the word *preventable* had been and was still debated by some of the most developed minds in the Wizards' Palace. But the oath did its job of keeping the peace between wizards. A wizard who was intent on doing harm, would be a devastating force. The One Oath of always increasing knowledge bound wizards to stay where they knew they could learn the most.

Though there had been schemes aplenty to look for knowledge outside of the palace; few worked. Those few endeavors over the ages that were successful were based upon the belief that the Wizards' Palace was not the best place to seek knowledge. While simple in theory, changing one's belief about the Wizards' Palace was akin to changing one's belief that rain *could* fall up. Lucius was jealous of the few who had the ability to truly believe that.

The feeling of being trapped periodically threatened to overwhelm him. He had been in the palace for over one hundred and seventy years. Because the oaths did not wane with age, he knew he would be in the palace seeking knowledge for an even longer time.

Lucius had taken the more demanding of the three oaths, the Trinity. Not only had he sworn to increase his knowledge and to do no preventable harm, he had vowed to actively seek to aid others.

Few people inside the Wizards' Palace needed aid. Those that did need aid were students who fell into two categories. The younger students who struggled with lessons could be easily motivated with subtle applications of *Morsus*.

Older students who were nearing their wizard's test presented more difficult problems. Wizardy required absolute control of tremendous energies. Thus those undertaking the examinations could not be coddled. Still, having students explode, implode, or dissolve as a result of a simple mistake was certainly harm that could be prevented.

Lucius and many others who were bound to the Trinity believed that the consequences of student failure were too harsh. The palace, in its long history, wasted far too many young men due to the rigidity of tradition. Yet, the Council of Wizards upheld the idea that some harm was necessary and not preventable. In that way they avoided breaking the Duality to which many of them were bound.

As he walked the halls, a plate full of sweetcakes in hand, the torches in the sconces ahead of him burst into flame. It was a simple spell, *Diluscesco*. One of the first he had ever learned. The flint he and so many others needed to first perform the spell had long since been cast aside. By far the greater expression of power was that the torches did not produce any smoke. That, to Lucius was amazing. Fire without the smoke was like water without the wet.

Lucius was a Wizard of Magic. Perhaps it was simply because he was trained in magic and not in the other disciplines, but they seemed wrong. Magic was the oldest art. Alchemy was old but its origins were shrouded in secrecy. Technology and Sorcery were too new, too alien for him. He just couldn't trust that those arts of power were dependable.

Producing fire was easy for a Wizard of Magic. In fact, it was easy for wizards of most of the forms of power. It was the Wizards of Alchemy who created the smokeless torches. They claimed it was easy, but hearing their talk of compounds and elements made his head ache worse than a spell gone wrong.

He knew he shouldn't eat one sweetcake, much less have a whole plateful of them. Yet, he could no more not eat them than not draw air into his lungs. One day, he would find or adapt a spell to reshape his body in a way that was permanent and safe.

The long life granted to him by becoming a wizard haunted him in a different way. It offered him countless days of seeing mirrors. Every time he looked in a mirror he saw something he could not control, and he became disgusted with his huge body. That he could not understand it put him at risk of not fulfilling the first of his oaths.

Changing his appearance was a simple illusion that most students of magic learned fairly early. Simply changing the appearance did nothing to the actual substance and was usually temporary. The more difficult changing of the substance was dangerous. The mind and the body were linked in so many delicate and intricate ways that simply changing one's body usually meant changing the very essence of that person.

It could be and was formerly used as a very nasty weapon. By changing someone's body into that of an animal, their self was changed. They were a different being trapped in a body they were not meant for and often did not know how to use. The histories were full of men who were changed into dogs, only to starve because they could not understand how a dog ate. Such things necessitated the Duality and the Trinity.

As he came within paces of his door, it opened. The heavy oak planks were bound together by straps of iron. It would not open for anyone else. Still, it was only a door. Any wizard of any of the forms of power could easily turn the door into a pile of splinters or ash.

When he crossed the threshold into his big, comfortable apartment, the fire in the fireplace roared to life, and the water in the teakettle began to heat. With so many spells around it that were set to his triggers, his apartment was the envy of many lesser skilled wizards.

To his right was his study. The desk was ancient and all but buried with moldy books, ancient scrolls, and tomes that would make novice students weep at the thought of having to digest the pages within. The stacks of magical artifacts were neat and organized. It would not do to have some magical artifacts touch others. It would be quite embarrassing to have to admit to the librarians or the archivists that he, the Acting Wizard Master, had inadvertently erased a book of magic or caused one spelled bauble to contaminate another.

His personal chamber was large and boasted trappings that would make most kings envious. The bed was huge and covered in layers of silk that perfectly reflected the rich colors of the rugs and drapes. The room looked as if an army of maids tended it. There was not a spot of dust or a thing out of place. *Sospitix* gave him the luxury of a well-kept bedroom.

The small room that was attached to his bedroom contained an artifact that was created by a team of wizards who followed the path of technology, and the artifact was relatively new. It allowed Lucius and many others in the palace to do away with chamber pots altogether. Lucius could simply sit down on the chair-like machine, eliminate his waste and not worry about the waste again. Lucius did not understand the machine or much that the Wizards of Technology created, but he knew some of their machines were every bit as powerful as the oldest spells.

He hated being the Acting Wizard Master. Many of the wizards in the palace were all but slaves to the One Oath. Yet, they could not or would not ask a fundamental question. Why was it so important to continually develop their knowledge? It was this kind of obsessive and sloppy thinking that bothered Lucius Guyini in every cell of his large body. None of those thoughts, however, would make reading the stack of reports he had postponed go away.

He let his considerable bulk fall onto an elegant couch with an audible exhalation of air. Hating a responsibility did not make it go away. He set his mind to making the stack of papers go away. With irony, he noted to himself, that despite his knowledge of several ways to turn them to ash or make them simply disappear, he was trapped by them as surely as he was by his oaths.

Just then, the teapot began to whistle. Half moaning in frustration, half feeling joy at a reason to postpone reading for a few more moments, Lucius took his eyes from the paper in front of him. He debated walking across the room to pour himself tea. He knew he should. Sitting on the couch eating sweet cakes was no way to make himself smaller. Still, he was comfortable, and he had the reports around him just so.

There were a few spells that would bring a cup of tea to him. Changing its location, as with a variation of *Situtum Domus* or *Covinnus*, or even simply floating it across the room with the uncomplex *Restitutum* would be like chopping down a tree instead of simply moving out of the shade.

He resigned himself to pouring a cup by hand. Avoiding work often took more effort than simply doing the task in the first place.

By reading the reports in his position of Acting Wizard Master, he had learned much about the palace. Most of the wizards knew three things; the trials of becoming a wizard, the path of power they had chosen, and their need to increase their knowledge.

The palace was created and maintained by a blend of the major disciplines, magic, sorcery, technology, and alchemy. Unlike every other place humans inhabited, food in the palace did magically appear. Even so, that magic had to be organized. Supplies and waste had to come and go but not without the proper use of some type of wizardry.

The security reports were the most interesting of all of the somewhat dull reading. Security, like most things in the palace, demanded a blending of all the branches of wizardry. The paths of technology, sorcery, and alchemy guaranteed that no army in any of the known lands could breach the palace walls. The discipline of magic, using ancient spells, guaranteed that only deserving students could even find the palace. The combination made Lucius and most of the wizards feel secure.

The greatest defense of the palace was derived from a little known and often misunderstood path of power. Only a few in the palace could even manage a bit of the power of the hidden path. They were grasping at straws, merely perpetuating a defense that was set in place ages ago. There were no current masters of this path of power; there were no Wizards of Need.

The power derived from need ensured the palace's defense in a very subtle, yet effective manner. Aside from the legitimate candidates who sought instruction, the power of need made sure that no other people became interested in finding the palace. The hardest walls and toughest defenses could not be breached if no one could find them. But, more importantly, no one could find the palace if they did not feel the need to look.

It was a troubling thought. For ages, wizards had lived and studied within the awesome walls of the Wizards' Palace. The feeling of security that the palace gave the wizards was treasured. Still, there were many creatures both magical and mundane who could benefit from the knowledge contained in the mysterious walls. For all of their power, the wizards in the auspicious palace were no more than prisoners.

* * *

Kiel had traveled roughly southeast. She saw no reason to change, so she let her steps continue to take her in that direction. She hardly needed rest, and when she did, she always found a tree that was accommodating.

Her long strides and thoughts of her father almost took her past the scorch mark of a cook fire without noticing such an obvious sign of passage. Her father was long since dead, and the only thing she knew about him was that he had been a good man. Whenever Kiel had asked about him, her mother would turn away to hide her tears. Kiel was often left wondering if her mother regretted her daughter's birth as elven custom demanded or if the memories of a man who must have been noble and fair enough to win the heart of an elven maiden were just too painful.

As she moved closer with the shift of the wind a stench that had never existed in fair Elvenwood struck her in the face. Even humans could not smell this foul. She saw no carcass, so the source must have come and gone with whoever had used the fire. She could not imagine meat that was rotten being cooked. Or, of meat that was cooked, smelling so rotten.

Subtle gouges in the dirt revealed themselves as claw marks. They were mixed with boot prints that were short enough for a human child, wide, though, and deep. Kiel could make out two separate sets of prints. Whatever had made the prints were short but heavy creatures.

For Kiel or even any elf who had more than two decades, the combination of tracks were unmistakable and easy to follow.

Where they could, her quarry stepped on rocks and exposed roots. Where they couldn't they stepped in each other's tracks. One of their party had to have been carrying a sack of leaves. It was an old trick. Dropping leaves over tracks.

She moved cautiously. Without pausing, she pulled from her pack a handful of nuts and berries. She ate more from nervousness than from hunger. She had no idea what she would do when she came upon them. She smiled ruefully with the realization that this was to be her first lesson without her instructors.

Suddenly, she heard a squeal that was too high pitched to be anything good. To her credit, she was frozen for only a moment. After that had passed, she burst into a graceful trot. Even at that speed, she glided through the woods with barely a branch being disturbed.

Her elven eyes caught two figures about seventy paces ahead of her. She hid behind a bush. Sparse as it was, it along with her brown and green cloak and hood allowed her to blend in.

They were standing still, hunched over. Her pointed ears strained to hear anything. From her vantage point, she could only see their backs.

As silently as a light breeze, she deftly minced through the brush. She gradually moved towards them in a flanking direction that took her downwind. As she drew closer, she could smell rotten meat on the two figures.

Her tracking skills took over. Patience, she reminded herself, patience. From her instructors, she had learned that each person only gets one chance to live each moment. Each step for her was a moment that had to be perfect, or there might not be a next moment.

When she saw what it was they were hunched over, she nearly gave her position away with a gasp. They held a body in their thick hands. A small body, that of a child. It was limp in the way of those whose life had been pruned by *Agris*.

She felt like drawing her bow, but her instructors' voices cautioned her. The mental voices were warning her to be patient; decisions should not be made in one moment. She had no proof that the two had actually caused the body harm.

What she saw next banished her indecision. One of the two who was on his knees holding the limp body lowered its head and took a bite out of the body's neck. Her keen, pointed elven ears could hear the flesh rip as the figure yanked its head back with a mouthful of gore.

Her stomach felt as if it was squeezed by an unseen hand. Goblins this far north were an evil that could not be tolerated. Even her instructors, who unlike her shied from violence, believed there should be no weighing of moments when confronted with goblins. Goblin hatred of elves was legendary. If they saw her, nothing would stop them from slowly ripping her apart.

If she dropped her pack quietly and drew her bow right, she would not have to draw her sword. A shot at fifty paces would be easy for her. Even if they started to run for her, she could easily put an arrow in each before they reached her.

With a deftness and flexibility that spoke of her years of training, Kiel silently shifted out of her pack. Slowly, ever so slowly, she rested its weight on the forest floor. When she was sure it was down, she released the straps. She strung her bow in a swift and fluid motion. Her right arm reached over her shoulder and pulled an arrow from its quiver. Smoothly, she nocked it in the oiled bowstring, drew, and took aim. The yew wood bent in fluid symmetry.

Patience, she heard her instructor say. Each being only gets one chance to live each moment. Take care with your present moments; it prevents regret in your future moments. Gently herding those thoughts from her head, she refocused her aim, released her breath, and let the arrow fly.

Without looking to see where the arrow hit, she reached for another oak shaft and almost had it nocked when she heard the wet noise of an arrow hitting flesh. Before the second figure had realized the danger, the second arrow was on its way to send the creature to its death.

Kiel stood as still as a tree for several moments. She knew they were dead. Her arrows had hit their mark at the top of each one's neck. Swallowing fear, she forced herself to examine the gruesome scene. It was to be the second lesson she learned without her instructors.

As she looked over the three dead figures, several feelings rushed through her. The chief among them was revulsion. If she had eaten more than nuts and berries, she would have emptied her stomach. The creatures she had killed were stout things. Had they been standing they would have only come to her shoulder. They were wide and heavily muscled. Their grayish-green skin was drawn tight over corded sinew. It was their faces though that scared her the most. Their mal-formed noses were little more than holes in their faces. Their lips did not have enough flesh to cover their crooked and pointy teeth. Even in death, their teeth were bared in a snarl.

Ripping her eyes away from the creatures, she saw the other dead body. When she saw the small frame and the big innocent eyes, a feeling of dread and loss crashed upon her. A pixie, a delightful creature that made even the reserved elves laugh. Kiel fought to show no emotions, but internally her heart ached. For a brief instant, doubt over whether she was ready to be independent of her instructors invaded her thoughts.

Like smoke in the wind, her trepidation about being on her own vanished. Sorrow over the loss of the pixie gave way to the excitement she realized she felt. Killing two goblins had been easy and she confessed to herself, enjoyable. She hoped her future moments would offer opportunities to use her bow and even her sword.

Kiel could not tell how the pixie had died. But, the gaping wound in its neck left no doubt that the goblins were involved.

She would do nothing for the bodies; she did not have to. The Pixies would take care of their own. As for the hideous creatures, they would have to lay as they were. Kiel wondered if even the scavengers of the woods would eat the gray-green flesh.

She walked on, questions spinning in her head. What were goblins doing so far north? How could those two reeking, clumsy beasts catch such a nimble creature? Did they use magic to catch a pixie? Where would goblins get such magic? The questions were disturbing. She was sure the answers would be as well.

* * *

"Father, I'm so pleased with you."

He relied on years of weapons training not to show any emotion, though frustration and anger welled up in him like a volcano. He was the King. His daughter was speaking to him as if he were one of her servants. He accepted her impudent tone because he knew his grip on her was tenuous.

"I'm glad to hear it." He wanted to start slowly and blandly, just to keep her talking to him.

"Really, the peasants are much happier with Lilandra's most recent changes. Even the servants seem to mind their duties with a smile. Fear of punishment takes away so much of a person's spirit."

Helena almost glowed when she spoke of her mentor. It bothered him a little that he did not inspire the people the way Lilandra did.

"Efficiency and pride in one's work are virtues," he said flatly. "Lilandra's efforts are laudable. It is true the castle is running well. Maybe there is a spark of joy in the air." He had been having to admit her success more and more.

"Oh, yes, she has many new ideas that will help all people of Atani. She has taught me so much about politics and ethics. So much of what I have learned in the past is wrong."

Did she mean to rub his face in her distance from him? He wondered with suppressed anger. Everything she had learned in the past? That was everything he had taught her. How could Lilandra do so much to his daughter in so little time? When she came out of nowhere and petitioned to be his daughter's tutor, she was filled with charm and confidence. He felt comfortable that Lilandra could polish his daughter to be every ounce the queen Atani deserved.

People jumped to do things for Lilandra. They needed to please her. It was as if her words were treats made from figs and dates and as if his subjects were children clamoring for those treats.

"What changes do you think are most popular with my subjects?" he said, knowing his daughter yearned for respect. Treating her like a rebellious child would only push her further away.

"Really, Father, you should not call them 'subjects'. Especially not 'your subjects'. It's demeaning. But, to answer your question, lowering the taxes was not only popular, it was good for the citizens. You see, Father, we live in luxury. You and I produce nothing. We do not know what it is like to work hard, to make something, and then to give part of that to the King's government."

He had heard these arguments before. In fact, he had argued her side many years before with his own father. He could not make his father see what he had thought was reason any more than Helena was convincing him. He wondered if wisdom could ever be taught to the young.

"You are correct, Daughter. Taxes can be onerous, yet, the simple fact is the security that allows people to conduct their business costs money. No ruler can produce money. You know that." The last words slipped out as he realized his mistake. He could not afford to sound as if he was lecturing. It had to appear as a conversation among equals. It galled him. Still, if humbling himself a little was what it took to make her see reason, he would do it.

"But this is where Lilandra's new ideas come in. She has ordered that all of the coins collected in taxes this year are to be melted down and recast to three fourths of their original size. From the scraps, more coins can be made. As she pays those in our employ, she will have more coins to dole out."

At hearing this, Donius had to turn away. It would not do to have Princess Helena see his jaws clench.

He had spent enough time with the pursers to know how delicate an economy was. Such broad changes could be remedied, but it would take time. Donius knew that if he tried to explain the complexities of the

Atanian currency to Helena, she would simply accuse him of not being open and leave. He decided to try another approach.

"It seems a good amount of the soldiers really agree with her recent changes." If he was to get anywhere, he had to praise the Regent.

"Yes, they really feel as if they are part of something. She fills them with a purpose. They are willing to fight to protect and spread her ideas. Even, I should say, the new recruits who are pouring in. They are very eager to show that they will fight for the good of Atani."

"And you have spoken to the soldiers?" He asked it casually. A summer earlier, he remembered forbidding her to visit the lower ranks of the army. Though many of the men seemed to like her visits, he knew the potential danger. Military discipline was never absolute, and uneducated soldiers should not be tempted with a pretty young princess.

"Absolutely. Regent Lilandra says it is good to be among the citizenry. We need to rid Atani of the idea that the poor are to be avoided. They are to be embraced."

"I see," he said evenly. He had to be careful. If he pushed too hard, she would see him as attacking her precious Regent's ideas.

"Of the poor," he said, "there are many who make poor decisions. They do not tend their crops well or they produce shoddy goods. Many of the poor can be seen wasting their coin in taverns or on slaver's juice."

"Father, it is because they do not know better. If they were given a chance, maybe even some extra coin, they could rise to be anything in Atani!" She tried to keep calm, but she felt the truth in her bones. She just wished that he could understand the beauty of Regent Lilandra's ideas.

"Perhaps there is some merit to what you say. But, I don't think that cutting the pay of the soldiers is a good way to support that idea." He said it as gently as he could. It was a logical flaw in Lilandra's *Dream*. Helena had to recognize it as foolishness.

"Father, that is different." She groaned with impatience. "The soldiers serve because they love Atani. They understand there is something more important than their own need. They are given training, lodging, and meals. They don't need gold. Regent Lilandra fills their every need."

* * *

Keven had been in the great room many times during his stay with Master Banolf and Mistress Bitte. Usually, he rushed through the room on his way to complete an errand. On extremely rare occasions, he was allowed to sit in the great room with the Goodfolk and hear a storyteller or share a feast.

This time, however, he wanted to be anywhere but the doorway of the great room. Keven's heart sank lower when he saw that the storyteller had several plates in front of him. Only a lord had enough money to eat like that. There were plenty of stories of what nobles considered fair punishment.

Keven walked across the room evenly and with a confidence he did not feel. He stood at his best imitation of attention in front of the old man's table and was promptly ignored.

The storyteller made Keven wait for what seemed like hours before he pushed his plate away and sighed.

Keven did not know what to expect. It surely was not a bouncing voice that sounded as if it was hiding a joke. "Ah, so yer the lad who cursed the village like a common beggar. In front of ladies and a visitor ta yer town."

Gareloch had used so many voices and been so many people in his long life, his natural voice was a mix of many times and many places. What came out most often was a thick brogue that rarely showed how formidable he could be.

"Lad, I'll base my actions and my justice on yer response ta me one question. Did ye mean the things ye said? Honesty tis the only way of it with me."

Gareloch, a master of his voice and quite aware of how many ears were sharing his conversation, said it loud enough for all to hear.

Keven froze. He was trapped better than any rabbit in a snare. He could not begin to guess the thoughts of the old man who was so calmly staring at him.

Keven knew the passion his words had carried only two hours before. He could not expect anyone to believe he had had a sudden change of heart. Yet, as much as he wanted to be honest, he could hardly throw dirt on his own coffin by saying he meant the words.

To Keven, it seemed as if the storyteller did not blink. He was as relaxed as a well-fed lord entertaining a peasant's petition.

A sliver of frustration wormed its way into Keven's mind. He was once again stuck by someone who could control him. Would he never be free? The emotions that had welled up in Keven weren't exhausted. No, he had plenty to spare. He thought of those prying ears in the inn, waiting with glee for the chance to see someone besides themselves get hurt.

Keven looked the old man in his clear blue eyes and said, "Yes, I meant every word."

"Ah, if tis the way of it, sit and eat with me. Tis been a long time since I shared a table with a lad of courage."

Keven wasn't sure he heard correctly. The words were thick with an accent he had never heard. But, the tone and the man's gesture told Keven the danger had passed. Keven tentatively slid into the chair across from the old man. He had never actually sat at a table in the great room, only at one of the benches in the back.

"Tell me lad, what tis yer name?"

Keven responded hesitantly. He felt safe as long as he could hold onto his righteous anger. It was hard to do because the old man was confusing him, and Keven felt vulnerable. "Keven."

"Gareloch, tis me name. Now, tell me the short of it. I want ta know what makes a lad say such things so boldly. Ye knew the beatings that would come of it sure as night follows day."

Keven hesitantly began to tell him about Constance, Gunter, Banolf, and the town. He tried to make it short but the old man kept interrupting him to ask more details. Keven was interrupted again by Master Banolf.

"Excuse me, Master Storyteller, if the boy is bothering you, I'll have him removed. He has caused you quite enough trouble."

"My good innkeeper. Does it appear as if I am bothered? Hmm?" Gone was the friendly tone of an old man who seemed interested in Keven's story.

"Well, I…"

"No, I am not bothered. I shall handle my affairs, and you shall tend to yours. Tell me, when a patron sits at a table in your inn, do you often pester them?"

The voice seemed to Keven like a blade of ice. The old man did not give Banolf time to answer.

"Fetch this young man some roast. And I mean a good cut of it. He is my guest till I begin the stories. I cannot begin to entertain until I am sure my guests are well fed."

Banolf's face was a picture of confusion. His mouth moved, but no sound came out. He turned and headed towards the kitchen.

After some prompting by the old man, Keven continued his story. Gareloch was an attentive listener. He took his eyes away from Keven only once, and that was to fish his pipe from his voluminous robes. The pipe was a faded yellowish thing that looked older than the man who stuck it between his teeth. As soon as his lips closed around the stem, Keven could see and smell the strong scent of the smoke coming from the bowl.

Through clenched teeth he said, "Continue, lad."

As Keven finished telling about the events that led up to the fight in front of the inn, Master Banolf appeared with two steaming plates. They contained sausages, a slice of roast lamb, seasoned turnips, and even two sweet cakes. "I have added these to your account, Master Storyteller."

"Yes, that is fine. Now leave us." He waved his hand as if to shoo off a pest. After Banolf left, the voice changed. "So laddy, why did ye no just whack 'em with a board? It might have saved ye some trouble."

"Well that wouldn't have solved my problem. He is bigger and has friends. He will always hit me harder. I needed them to stay away from me. I think my words hurt them more than ten whacks to their heads. I don't think they will come to bother me again. If they do, I will deal with that then. What I said was the truth."

"Tis a rare thing ta think before ye hit. Rarer still ta know the truth of things. Perhaps smelling dung made ye think. I wonder if it would help others." The old man's words trailed off as if his thoughts drifted away. After a quick moment, the thickly accent voiced continued.

"So, lad, ye are a hero for a day. What of tomorrow on the morn? What of the next year? Did ye think of that?"

"No. I didn't, and I almost don't care. I know I do not want to be Banolf's stable hand forever. But, I don't know how to stop."

"Ye must know there is nothing fer ye in this town. I'll be leaving on the morn. Ye've got a quick wit about ye. I could teach ye the way of things. I could use yer help with others."

Keven stammered something unintelligible.

"Think hard on it, lad. I'll be leaving with the sun. It will no be easy, traveling with me. That yer ma, over there? I'll have words with her tonight. Now, I have stories ta tell, and ye have thinking ta do." With that, he buried his smoking pipe somewhere in the folds of his cloak and stood up. "Off with ye now. I hope ta see ye with the sun.

* * *

As Lilandra sat in front of the large, empty fireplace, she put down the stack of papers and let her mind relax. A fire in the large hearth was not really necessary. Atani never really got cold, even this time of year. Still, the castle was drafty. She could have combated her chill with a sable stole one of her many admirers had given her. Instead, she rang the bell and almost instantly a matronly servant hurried in.

"Nessy, I feel a little chill. Do you think a fire would warm me?" Asking for someone's advice, even a lowly servant's was the surest way to make them feel like a king's champion. If she knew any less about people, she would have been amazed to know that the servants bickered over whose turn it was to answer her call. Even so, people were people, and they all needed to feel important. As a result, they would fight to serve others.

"Oh, of course, child. I'll have a fire in here before you can blink. You really should eat, you know. You're too thin. That's why you feel the cold."

"Thank you, that would be nice." Lilandra held her head and said the words in a way she had not in so long. It was a trick many children knew well. If they were sick, a mother could resist them nothing. To Nessy, having a sick Regent gave her a problem to solve. She moved her round frame out of the room at a run.

Quicker than she would have thought possible, Nessy led two thin male servants into her room. Each carried an armload of split logs. Their armloads were too big. In fact, they could hardly see over the wood they carried. It was a trick all men seemed to think worked on all women. Carry a lot, subtly let the watching women know it was heavy, then pretend it was not.

"Oh, please don't hurt yourselves. That wood looks awfully heavy. You must be strong. Be careful." Lilandra knew her role in the ruse well.

"Please, Honored Regent. It is our pleasure to help you. This little bit of wood is nothing."

They were cut off from their attempt to talk with her. Nessy began to tell them how to lay a proper fire. The two men, like anyone, had learned to lay and light a fire at a young age. Still, Nessy felt she needed to instruct them on how to do it.

After the flames had spread from the tinder to the logs, Nessy and the men left the room and closed the large doors behind her.

Lilandra picked up the papers again. She wanted to throw them into the fire. The papers said nothing she could not overcome. She could overcome anything with time. It was just that the news they contained was inconvenient. The reports cautioned against spending money faster than taxes could be collected.

That did not worry Lilandra overly much. She knew that money was but one way, the cheapest way to pay people. People thought they needed coins. That was the magic of it. People did not know what they needed. Lilandra, however, did.

She could spare no expense hiding the dragon. She thought it best to hide it in plain sight. An obvious lie was most easily believed.

She had not used the carpenters' guild since such a job would have soon become widely known. Instead, she had discreetly sought out workers who could construct a building that would hide and hopefully even contain the dragon should it wake. The building was huge, and the wood was the finest the mills could cut. After it was done, she explained to the men that she needed their silence, that she was most grateful for their help. She also rewarded them all with rich assignments in places far from the city.

It was her latest expenditure of the king's money that brought the clerk from the purser's office eagerly to her wing of the castle. He certainly should have turned over his findings to his superior, the chief purser. It was the chief purser's responsibility to let the ruler know of the financial state of the kingdom. But, what was a duty to some became a pleasure for others.

Lilandra knew the young clerk hid his findings from his superior simply because he did not want to give up an opportunity to meet his beloved Regent. His need for approval was glaring. A young man who was slim, bookish, and had several layers of authority above him rarely had a chance to feel proud. With a mix of ruling Regent and beautiful woman, her attention on him was like food to a starving man.

The young man sincerely worried about the state of the royal finances. The large amount and cost of green cloth that had been purchased confused him. He desperately wanted her to notice how intelligent he was when he questioned if it was for the army. Lilandra did notice, and she complimented him for it. She even said Atani needed more citizens like him. Why not? Compliments were more valuable than gold and could be given again and again. No amount of gold could have bought the smile her approval put on his face.

To further cement his commitment to her and the Dream, Lilandra shared a secret with him. The green cloth was not for the army. It was the same color as a gown she planned to wear at an upcoming ball. It had been bought in such large quantities so that the dedicated citizens could show their support by wearing the fabric.

She'd asked him to leave his report with her, telling him she wanted to better understand such an important part of the kingdom. With a smile that almost split his face, he left her with the stack of rough papers.

The changes she had implemented had begun to have an effect. Her reduction of taxes had certainly reduced the money in the royal coffers. Conversly, it had also bought much. When she lowered the taxes, the crowds cheered. It wasn't a big reduction; it was simply that they knew she cared for them. After a certain time, she'd lowered them again. Each reduction was small, but they added up, both in effect on the citizens and effect on the treasury.

Still, the extra coin in purses around the kingdom would buy much happiness. She planned an event in the coliseum. It would be a speech to rally the masses. She was going to wear green. The dress was going to be the envy of all the citizens, noble-born and commoners alike. After her appearance, they would rush out to find green material. Lilandra made sure it was available to them.

With such extravagant expenditures, it was only a matter of time before the royal coffers were empty. She would hide that for awhile. The resulting economic disruptions would cause privation, but she could counter that. Even hungry people could be happy if they believed it was their choice to be hungry.

Money would flow again. There were plenty wealthy kingdoms. Economies abhorred a void. When the peoples of the Westlands learned of the Dream, their money would flow to Atani's coffers.

Kiel

Kevin M. Buchman

Chapter 5

Kiel heard the horses for what seemed like an eternity before she saw the riders. To her pointed ears, the sound of far off horses on wet turf sounded like an army of drummers. The words of her instructors were true, humans were a noisy race.

No, she had to stop herself. If there was one thing she should take from her instructors' teaching, it was that each moment was precious. *Agris* blessed each being with only one chance to live each moment, that included one's thoughts. She was not going to sow rotten seeds of contempt for humans in the ground of her fertile mind. Each thought was a moment, once it bloomed, its existence could never be denied.

She studied them from behind the cover of a few bushes. They were galloping hard enough to push the horses.

They were in uniform and well armed. Each rider had a short sword at his hip and a bow across his back. She could not believe the bow was strung! She could think of no better way to ruin a good bow than by keeping it strung longer than absolutely necessary. She could almost see the hack marks on the bows where human tools had butchered the wood for their purposes.

Conveniently, they stopped about seventy paces from her hiding spot. She could see the smiles on their faces as they pulled up on the reins. Their conversation was light, fraternal, and revealed that they had been racing.

Her curiosity was piqued more than she thought possible. Should she approach them? If she did, she would give up every advantage.

From her hiding place, she could see them, but they could not see her. If she went closer, they would have the advantage of numbers, strength, and speed. But, if she did not approach, when would she ever begin her new life?

"Hail, riders," she called loudly to them as she stepped from her cover.

Instantly, they swung their horses about as they spread out. With the increased distance between them, they made a much more difficult group of targets. As they did that, all save one whipped their bows off their shoulders. To Kiel, their actions seemed fumbling. It took them far too long to notch their arrows. Still, she was at least sixty paces from them with three arrows pointed at her. Even fumbling, they had her well covered.

"I mean no harm. I approach with peace," she called out as she took measured, confident steps to them.

"State your business here," the one without a bow in his hands commanded.

She could tell he was used to issuing commands. He was a big man, tall and broad in a way that elves were not. The hair on his face reminded her of some of the beasts of the forest.

"I have no business. I am a simple traveler, a pilgrim if you will. I have come from Elvenwood to travel and learn." It was neutral and gave away no important information. She was glad she had learned her lessons in the human language.

"It is rare for one of your people to leave Elvenwood."

His eyes were alert. They were trained on her, looking for something. She was surprised when they did not dip below her neck. Most males could not help themselves from looking at what they hoped to see more of.

"It is especially rare for no apparent reason. Either you are lying or you are, as you say, wandering around. But, I think that would lead to wasted *moments*." He emphasized the last in a knowing way.

"It seems you know something of my people." She lowered her hood to show him her ears. "If you know that much, then you know I do not wish you, your party, or your nation ill. I simply wish to travel." Kiel took her eyes from the commander.

The other three members had all but forgotten their bows. They were almost drooling as they leered at her taut curves.

"I ask your name, elven traveler."

"I am Kielasanthra Tylansthra. For ease, please call me Kiel."

"Kiel, I am Lieutenant Rondelli. I am head of this recruiting party. We have come north from the nation of Atani. We ride offering our protection and safe passage to those who wish to live a life worth living under the benevolence of the rulers of Atani, King Donius and Regent Lilandra. It might be that what you are searching for can be found in Atani City. We would be honored to assist you in reaching it. I am sure once you understand what our Regent is offering, you will be very pleased to be there."

To Kiel, the moments seemed to be passing too fast. But, if she was going to learn about them and live among them, she thought she might have to adopt human ways. With too little thought about the present moment, Kielasanthra Tylansthra made her decision.

"Lieutenant Rondelli, I accept your offer. It would be most kind of you to assist me in learning about your ways."

Only a few moments later, Kiel was holding tight to a human male she had just met as they galloped for a strange human city.

* * *

In Keven's relatively short and bland life, he'd had few reasons to be excited. As a result, when he was sitting astride a horse he had tended for years ready to leave the village of his birth, he did not know if he felt like a fool or a king.

He still wondered if this might be a dream, sitting on a horse, his horse, like a lord in front of half the town with more than the usual number of Goodfolk in the village for such an early morn. Many of them were nursing sore heads from a night of drinking and had not been up to a walk home the night before.

He wished the old man would hurry. He was afraid Banolf would convince him that he needed the boy for work or maybe that Banolf wouldn't sell the horse after all. Keven marveled at what the old man's purse must contain. He must have bought half the larder from Banolf. He had mixed emotions as he had watched Banolf's wife stuff hard bread, dried meat, and packs of cheese into the recently purchased traveling equipment. Though he knew the old man briefly, Keven was sure his mother received a few of the old man's coins as well.

Keven drew in a deep breath and looked around his town. The day was perfect, if a bit still. Even the birds seemed to be watching his departure. The white-washed shop fronts seemed to be a little more faded and spattered with mud. The smoke from the hearths seemed a bit more acrid, not like the sweet aroma of baking he always thought it was.

The door to the inn opened and out stepped Banolf and the old man. The storyteller seemed as happy as a man who had just heard a joke. Banolf looked as though he had eaten one of his pickles that had been in the brine too long.

"Are ye ready, lad?" The old man's voice had that same bounce it had had the evening before. "I can tell yer new ta the saddle. I fear fer yer hind quarters after a day of riding. Ha."

Keven had dreamed of saying a hundred things to Master Banolf if he ever got the chance. His chance was upon him, yet his head was as empty as it had ever been.

The old man limped to his horse with a staff, yet swung himself into the saddle with an ease that caused everyone to take notice. Once again, Keven was not sure how old the man really was.

"We best be going. We have a long way." With that, his horse turned slowly away from Banolf and Keven's mother.

Keven's mother's hands went to her mouth, as if to stifle any possible words of regret. With that last vision and a head full of feelings, Keven left the village of his birth. The excitement he had felt moments ago began to fade. He had learned by many painful lessons that excitement was often dashed. In a practiced habit, Keven forced out hopeful thoughts of what might be. It was better to focus on a thought from the past that always brought him comfort, Erin.

He missed her so much. The years since she had left had weighed heavily on him. The ache he felt for her kept him from feeling much else. Thoughts of her overshadowed embarking on a journey with a storyteller.

* * *

That he heard her approach was not unusual. A Blademaster had to be aware of his surroundings. That it distracted him was troubling. His current partner was a young man of no more than twenty-five years. He was in his physical prime. His well formed torso boasted long muscles that were quick and flexible. There were not too many men who could match the power and speed of the young man's sword strokes. The young man trusted that knowledge.

King Donius knew that also. The king, being a Blademaster with many more years on his body than the young virtuoso, did not try to match the youth's speed and power. He had planned to lull the young man into a false sense of confidence that he could beat the older master. Donius was almost ready to show the youth the error of his style when the thought of his approaching daughter prevented him from moving when he should have.

The meaty thud of the wooden blade hitting Donius' shoulder made many of the onlookers wince. It was a testament to his training that King Donius did not show any discomfort at absorbing such a blow. The bruise that would develop would be a lesson that every swordsmen should know; keep your mind free of everything but your opponent.

The younger man's face was a mix of pride and worry. Pride in that he had marked the all but unbeatable King of Atani. Worry that he had struck the King of Atani. Inside a training ring, there was no rank or role except that which the combatants worked out themselves. The king nodded to the young man to end the match and glanced at his angry daughter. As he watched her stand in the courtyard, he could see she was masking her fury. He did not know what had made her angry this time, but he could see that she was carrying herself less like a young princess and more like a woman of power.

She was not so full of herself that she would interrupt his practice. She stood on the edge of onlookers and did her best to be patient. He said his farewells to the young soldiers who worked with him. A little camaraderie was good. They needed to see that the man they served was a good man. He quickly washed and dried his upper body with a towel and donned his shirt. Working without his shirt gave his young training partners a chance to see real scars of real battles. It sobered and fortified them.

As the circle of onlookers disbanded and his sparring partners headed back to their barracks, she approached him. Her gown, her hair, her whole countenance demanded respect from those she confronted. Lilandra's lessons were well learned.

"Father, Lilandra thought it would be good for me to work with some of the former slaves." She said it as an indictment.

"I don't see the harm in that. I don't see the point in it either." He tried not to sound patronizing.

"Well, they won't listen. Well... actually they do listen and obey everything. They will not choose a profession. They will not choose anything. How can they go back to their lives if they wait for others to tell them what tool to use or what food to eat?"

"Yes, the slavers do their job well."

"You seem as if you care little for their plight, as if you do not wish to see them recover."

"Imagine a fly trapped in amber. Even as it becomes completely embedded, it can live for quite some time with bubbles of air trapped with it. Despite how it may wish and struggle it is forever trapped. It can look through its prison and perhaps think, but it can never act of its own free will again. The slavers use slaver's juice to trap the mind and seal it away. A slave may remember his former life, may rail against what training has been done to him. Yet, in the end his will is held fast, forever stuck in amber. However bad it may seem, it is fair. Everyone knows slaver's juice is permenant poisoning, once the damage is done a person can never come back. The withdrawal lasts forever. You know this, and you know you are wasting your time."

Her face reddened as his word reached her ears. The ripple in her jaw muscle let him know he needed to calm her.

They were walking through a rather large corridor where any number of servants could hear. That the people celebrated Helena's decree to free the slaves meant he could not rescind it. More and more of his advisors went to Lilandra first and then to him. He could not afford to be seen arguing with his daughter over decisions the Regent made. People were already whispering things that were disturbing.

"Helena, I and my father before me have always made slavery public and honest. Once a citizen chooses not to be a productive part of our

69

society, that choice and all others are taken from him. The slavers change that citizen, forever. There is no returning them."

They continued walking through the castle. It was a true castle, not a fancy palace such as those in which the rulers of other lands lived. He managed to slow their pace a little. Helena seemed to be in a mood to storm down the corridor. As always, he knew he could not abruptly halt their pace or their conversation. To do so would only serve to send her to Lilandra for more lessons in how he did not understand.

"Father, if the slavers and their cursed slaver's juice are as permanent as you say, why do you still permit the citizens to use it in the taverns and in their homes?"

"Helena, I am king. I am a strong king, but no ruler can control every action of his people. If the people wish to drink watered down slaver's juice, that is their choice. If they drink it too much or too often, they will end up a slave to it. If they let that happen, they will end up begging on the streets. Every citizen knows this. Only fools test it."

"So that's it. We have hundreds of citizens who are slaves and cannot think for themselves, and we have thousands of others who are drinking slaver's juice, and you talk about it as if it was the weather."

"Helena, we have had this discussion a hundred times. Scholars have debated it a thousand times. It is or was a good system until Lilandra put her hand in." He shouldn't have said it, but he could not resist the urge to point out the truth.

"Father, Lilandra is trying to build something for all the people of Atani, not just the nobles or the merchants. All people have the right to feel good about themselves. They need to feel good about themselves. She is trying to make that happen. It can only be good for Atani. Why do you fight her?"

Him fighting her? Was that what his daughter and others thought? Had she come so far as to be the one whom people saw as their ruler? Was he the one fighting her as if he was trying to steal power from her? His mind whirled. Truly things had gone further than he had thought.

"Helena," he said sharply. "In the first place, no one has a right to feel good. They sometimes have the opportunity to feel good. What they do with that is their choice. A position in the nobility can be earned or bought by anyone. In the second place, I am the King! I do not fight anyone for the good of Atani. *I* decide what is good for Atani!" With that, he stormed off. He had to think.

Helena was left staring at her father's back. Just then it hit her; Lilandra was right. Her father was almost irrationally protective of his power. He had a need to feel in control. It was well hidden, but his need was there for anyone who looked hard enough. She turned on her slippered heel and made her way down the corridor. She wondered what other lessons Lilandra would share with her.

* * *

They rode in silence for several hours. Keven constantly looked around at the trees, the sky, and the ground. He was not shoveling dung or listening to Banolf's orders. Keven was on a horse, miles from the village of his birth, and free to do as he pleased. He took a deep breath and tried to remember every detail.

The old man remained a mystery to Keven. From the back of him Keven could not tell if the old man was sleeping. His cloak was wrinkled and tattered, and his saddle was obviously well worn. Keven would never mention this out loud, but it seemed like the old man was also well worn. As if he could feel Keven's questions, he stirred and started patting himself as if looking for something. Keven urged Caelv to quicken his pace. He wanted to see what the old man had hidden.

Gareloch fished a pipe out of his cloak. To Keven's eye, the wrinkles of the cloak seemed contagious, one growing out of the other. The skin on his gnarled hands blended into the tattered fabric. The old man stuck the pipe in his mouth with an audible click as it hit his teeth. The pipe seemed to be a part of him like an extension of his wizened face. A moment later gray smoke rose in the air and drifted back to Keven's nose.

Keven didn't want to spoil the quiet of the ride with chatter, but there was so much he had to ask. He gathered all of his courage and rode up next to the old man's horse.

"Excuse me, sir, but I have a few questions, and well, you said you'd look after my education." He hoped it sounded natural.

"Aye, I did at that lad. What questions have ye?"

He had countless questions. Who was the old man? Why had he paid for Keven to come with him? Where were they going? What came out of his mouth surprised and embarrassed him.

"Your pipe, does it burn when it is in your cloak? I didn't see you light it last night or again this morning."

As if he were preparing an answer, Gareloch sucked in through his pipe and held it a while. He blew out the too sweet smoke and looked at Keven. Keven, however, looked at the smoke. It did not drift aimlessly like smoke from a cookfire. It drifted up in shapes and lines. He felt like a child following the cloud till his eyes could not longer see it.

"Lad, most all things are no what they seem. But, a few are." With that, he stuck the pipe back in his mouth.

Keven kept waiting for him to take it out again and say something else. When it was clear the old man wasn't going to, Keven rushed to think of another question.

"Well, I barely know you or the plans for this journey. So, I don't even know if this is what it seems to be."

"Look close, lad, what do ye see when ye see me or me pipe?" Gareloch offered himself for inspection. His clear blue eyes did not match the old man's wrinkled face.

"Well, I've thought about it since last night's supper. It isn't possible. The pipe should go out if it is not being used. If you have a way to keep it lit, it would burn you or your cloak."

"Ye say tis no possible, yet yer eyes see it. Which is it, lad? No one can be happy with two thoughts fighting in his head."

"I don't know. I don't know what to think."

"Tis good ye admit it. Many will no say those words, even ta themselves. There are some things that exist that the eyes or mind can no see. There are some things that do no exist, but the eye and especially the mind sees anyway. That tis what ye need ta learn."

As the old man went back to chewing on his pipe, Keven tried to puzzle out what the man said. It was not anything new. Certainly Keven had read enough to know the eyes did not know all. Air and wind could not be seen, but they did exist.

"Yer a bastard," the old man calmly said.

Keven was violently jerked out of his thoughts with those words. He was surprised and hurt the old man had said it.

"Tis true though me eyes can no see it? Or tis it false, though the Goodfolk of yer village know it ta be true?"

The shock of hearing it from someone he had begun to trust began to wear off as Keven thought about the questions. Waves of understanding crashed on him only to recede back to the hidden source. It was as if he almost had the answer but could not grab it.

The old man could not see he was a bastard. Was there actually anything to see? Keven was no different than Gunter, Constance, or any of the Goodfolk, yet he was a bastard. It was a fact, a fact known by all. Was it still a fact if it is not known by all? The old man had not known Keven was a bastard until he rode into town. If no one knew Keven was a bastard, was he still a bastard?

When he looked up from his thoughts, the old man was at least twenty paces ahead. Keven did not know how long he had been thinking. He did not think it had been long, nor did he notice the old man spurring his horse to gain the distance.

Keven wanted to ask more, but he did not want to lose his current path of thought. He was close to something important.

* * *

It had been five days. She was cold, out of food, and more than a little afraid. Tonay knew that if her father found her, she would gladly go home with him. As much as she wanted to succeed, desire and pride could only a carry person so far, and she was hopelessly lost. She knew she was somewhere north of Ducca's Vineyard, but beyond that, she had no idea where to go for food and shelter. She was reduced to huddling under bushes at night.

She was frustrated by not being able to ignore the fears that crept into her mind. When she was a young girl, she had learned that if she kept her mind occupied with pleasant thoughts, childish fears could not intrude. Over the years, she had honed that ability. When she let her mind roam, she could ignore the drudgery and sore muscles that came with farm work.

Tonay guessed it was the fact she was tired and hungry. She could not keep her focus on the things that made her happy when her mind was sluggish. It bothered her that she could not control her mind. She was a cold, tired victim of her surroundings.

That was how they found her. It was hardly the impression she had been hoping to make. She was anything but the serious, competent citizen she had hoped to portray. Her breeches were stained, her hair hung about her face, and worst of all, she looked desperate.

The squad, however, did not look a whole bunch better. Her idea of Regent Lilandra's squads was the picture of gallantry. She had dreamed of crisply uniformed squads of soldiers who were eagerly looking for people who were willing to give themselves to the Regent. Their uniforms were to be the brightest red of Atani's colors. Their steeds were to be all white and finely groomed. With perfect silhouettes and prancing steeds, those who were to escort her were to represent all that she hoped her new life would be. These did not meet her fantasy. In fact, they were quite bedraggled.

There were ten of them. The first soldier that found her looked like a footpad. To her shame, she even squealed when the man happened upon her. She followed him to his commander. There she saw that some were mounted on horses while others walked, leading their mounts. They all wore rough-hewn shirts of differing colors. Some of the breeches were so tight, the men wearing them should have been embarrassed.

She was quickly given a few bites of rations and made to feel a bit at ease. The squad did not seem to be in a hurry. In fact, they all dismounted for a time. Many of the soldiers ignored her.

The questions about her did not come from the squad. Rather they came from the leader. With at least a week's growth on his face, he looked like a cutpurse. He, unlike the others, wore a uniform coat. From his insignia, she guessed he was a lieutenant.

Her guess was proven right through their conversation. With each series of questions and answers, she was more at ease. Lieutenant Deccia had a sincere smile that came easy through his scraggly beard. He was a young man, but had a worn look about him and carried himself as one who was in charge.

At first, the questions were simple ones, more polite than anything else. Once she explained who she was and what she was looking for, the conversation became friendly. Lieutenant Deccia was surprisingly forthcoming.

He took a real interest in her. When she spoke, she knew she had his full attention. When she told of her adventure over the past days, he was impressed. He, in a few short moments, let her feel something seventeen years of farm work had not: respect.

"Thank you," she replied as gravely as she could. "What do I do now? What are my responsibilities?"

"For now, you, with all the others will see to our daily routine. You will help with filling the water skins, collecting firewood, and other tasks. If you wish to stay with us and accept your rank, you will submit to my authority unquestioningly."

"Yes sir!" It seemed like the appropriate thing to say. She had answered her father with those words many times. She had never said them with so much hope and pride.

"Sir, if I may, are we going to Atani City? Will I be with this squad for a long time?"

Lieutenant Deccia chuckled slightly. "We will head to Atani City. For now we are your squad. You will learn what you can from the other members of this group. Everyone has something to give. When we reach Atani City, you will probably be assigned to a position that will allow you to contribute what you can to the Regent's call."

Tonay almost shivered with excitement; it was coming true. Lieutenant Deccia seemed to understand how important it was for people to give themselves to a higher service.

"For now, First Recruit Tonay Denisio, while we rest the mounts, you need to find a stout branch that will become your practice sword. You will begin your training at our next stop. You will be the last of the recruits this trip that we will escort to Atani City."

* * *

"'Tis as good as any spot. We'll stay here. Lad, ye go fetch some firewood and water. Don't forget to tend ta the horses. I'm sure you know the way of it. Remember ta have care with the Lady Thistle, she bites when yer no looking. I'll see about turning these dried rations in ta something fit ta eat."

Keven tried not to groan from the soreness from being unaccustomed to the saddle as he walked to the stream and back. He should be thankful he wasn't serving Banolf, but he was still serving someone else. He would rub Thistle down first. Though Gareloch frequently reminded him of her temper, Keven never seemed to have a problem with her.

As he began to free the horses of their burden, he noticed the crackling sounds of a fire. He turned to look and noticed the old man several steps away from the small cook fire. He was squatting on his haunches and rifling through one of his packs. Then, he hobbled back to the fire and began putting pinches of some dried herb into a pot. Around him lay bits of the food Mistress Bitte had packed for them.

"Excuse me, Master Gareloch, how did you light the fire so fast? I did not hear the sound of flint and steel."

"Lad, I've been on the road enough ta know the easy way of things. I could ask ye how ye manage ta turn yer back on The Lady Thistle and no get bit for it. Mind the horses now, and I'll have us something that many innkeepers would be proud ta call their own."

Keven continued to unstrap the tack from each horse. Gareloch traveled with a prodigious amount of gear. Most of it, Keven thought, could easily be left behind. The tooth and body powder would be the first to go. Thistle had the worst of it. She looked like a wagon that was largely composed of bags of books.

Keven went back to brushing and rubbing the horses. They certainly had not been worked hard on the lazy walk that had taken them so far from the village of his birth. Still, Keven knew enough about horses to know that a good rub down was important to them and their willingness to walk the next day.

He dutifully checked the shoes. He was no ferrier, but he knew enough to see trouble. He could see no stones or seeds in any of the hooves.

His mind, as it often did when it was turned loose, found pictures and memories of Erin. He relived the same memories over and over, but he never tired of them.

With the horses tended to and his stomach empty, Keven turned back towards Gareloch's cook fire. The victuals Mistress Bitte had sold Gareloch were ordinary travel rations. But, whatever was in the black pot smelled delicious. Keven plopped himself down on a nice spot of moss and waited.

The crackling fire and the peace that came from being weary chased away any painful thoughts, even those of Erin. It occurred to him that, in time, his memories of her might fade into blandness. He wondered if frequent indulgences in their past would wear away the comfort and pain of his love for her or would the exercise of reliving his time with her keep her essence preserved in his mind.

Those thoughts were banished by Gareloch putting a dented metal cup in his hands. The taste lived up to the aroma, and Keven was quite content to eat his dinner slowly and think of nothing.

As he lay down, his thoughts meandered in an unfamiliar direction. He had not prayed since he was a small boy. Keven's relationship with The Creator and The Book of the Word was practically non-existent. His life, compared with that of others in Village Donnell, had been hard. He had always believed he had little reason to give thanks. He had less reason to believe prayers of supplication would be answered.

Erin, however, gave him a reason to go through the hollow motions of praying to a Creator that had ignored him for so long. Keven silently begged whoever answered prayers to be able to ride to wherever Erin was and seal the promise they had made in the woods.

* * *

The caravan was impressive. Twenty heavy wagons each pulled by six stout horses. The axles were not rough-hewn trees slathered with animal fat, nor did the wheels creak and groan as if they were going to buckle at any moment. The wagons were all made from metal.

The metal did not shine like a gleaming prince's sword. It was dull gray and intimidating for its look of strength. The lines on each wagon were remarkably straight with square and true angles. With most wagons, any child could pick out the differences between each one. Each of these metal wagons was an identical copy of the one before it. The craftsmanship required to create such sights was beyond the comprehension of the many peasants who looked on in wonder.

As amazing as the vehicles were, their drivers and escorts were what truly drew the eyes of every human. Dwarves. It had been a long time since many of the poor farmers who worked the land along the road had seen dwarves. Some of the younger ones had simply believed them to be merely parts of fables to delight children. Like the moon blocking the sun, sightings of dwarves outside of their mountains occurred rarely in one's lifetime.

With some of the escorts on shaggy ponies and others on foot, it was hard to count the number of dwarves. Rumors would of course spread and with each telling the numbers would grow. The escorts and drivers were alert. Those running alongside would often dart into the back of a wagon. Just as often, another dwarf would spring from a different trap door to once again trot alongside.

Even from a distance, their short stature could be seen. Short, no more than eleven hands high, but their broad shoulders spanned almost that width. On any other creature, such proportions would look ridiculous. On dwarves, it simply fit. Their beards were of varying colors, some were red, some were blond, and a few were so dark they almost looked blue.

They were well armed with hammers, axes, and even a short sword or two. The weapons reflected their wielders; they were stout, heavy, and not to be underestimated.

The dwarf atop the lead wagon was named Haft Oreshael. He was the leader for two main reasons. He was one of the few dwarves in the caravan who spoke the human tongue. More importantly, he was the one who put up the money and promised to pay the others.

If it came to fighting, they would duck into the wagons and use the heavy crossbows to teach the first waves of attackers a painful lesson. The metal skin of each wagon would give every dwarf a protected firing platform. Once the bolts were exhausted, each dwarf would grab a weapon and pound the soft humans as if they were freshly smelted alloy. It would be a long fight. The dwarves would eventually lose a pitched battle in human lands, but Haft almost wished it would happen. The posthumous glory of being immortalized in ballads and tales of battle would almost make up for the lost gold.

As much as he craved a reputation for daring, Haft Oreshale had not organized, recruited, and financed this expedition for glory. There was money to be made, a lot of it. The letter that had come from Atani was unlike any that had ever come to the dwarves. Humans were always requesting trading rights and special treaties. They were all routinely ignored, until Atani's request. Dwarves loved to trade. More than that, they loved getting the better end of a bargain. Humans, however, had little that dwarves needed.

Therein lay the problem. The humans wanted dwarven goods, but they had little to trade in return. Humans offered gold, but the Dwarven Nations could mine their own. It was a pathetic situation for the humans. The less they had to trade, the more they needed dwarven goods. Because they had so little, they were in the weaker bargaining position. The humans did not realize this. Begging one to trade with you was no way to begin to haggle.

That was until Regent Lilandra, representing the people of Atani, sent her missive. Her words and meaning were debated for months in the ale rooms of many dwarven clans. Her tone was different than that of other humans. It was not flowery or full of promises of profits, but blunt and to the point. She said the Atanians had things the dwarves needed, and Atani needed the dwarves. No other human had ever before been so blunt. Other humans were so worried about diplomacy and offending, almost as bad as elves.

Even with the unusual tone of the request, most dwarves dismissed it. What could a nation of humans have that dwarves could need? Haft saw the situation like few others did. To him, it was the question akin to whether to start a new mineshaft. Of course, existing shafts would continue to yield a known amount. However, the chance of a new, rich vein was too much to ignore. This expedition to far off Atani was just a simple test dig to see if there was value in the rocks.

He emptied his accounts, borrowed even more, bought what he could, and hired all who were willing. Unlike humans, dwarves would never willingly go into debt. Debt was weakness, and weakness was abhorrent. It was that dogma that caused many of his fellows, some as close as brothers, to scoff at his idea.

By traveling countless miles into foreign lands, he would be put in an indefensible position. Worse still was the bargaining position he would find himself in when he finally reached Atani City. He and his caravan would have traveled a long way. They would be tired, hungry, and at the end of their supplies. They would have invested much time and effort just to get to the bargaining table. Getting a decent price would take a stroke of luck.

Whoever sat across from them at that table would know these facts. By taking this risk, Haft was in a position of weakness. The humans would be in a position of strength. They could offer any price and lose nothing by being rejected. Haft would have no choice but to accept their prices and then would have to hope for a good price on supplies with which he could travel home. Even the youngest dwarf knew not to show weakness in a bargaining situation. The one who could hold out longest made the best profit.

The weapons they'd brought to sell were dwarven forged, but crafted for a human. The war hammers were the finest steel but were hollowed out for weak-armed human use. The swords were much longer than the dwarven short sword.

It was the crossbows that were the biggest risk. Haft had two wagons full of the powerful, long-ranged weapons. It was the mix of metals that gave the bow its particular spring. Though there were many exaggerations, Haft knew the crossbows he planned to sell could completely bury a three-ounce bolt in an oak tree at forty paces.

The risk was that though other races admired the weapon, they believed they could not use it. The first consideration was the weight of the weapon.

The other considerations were a reflection of the weaknesses of the other races. Most thought that only the phenomenally strong dwarves could use such a weapon.

Many times, over many kegs of ale, Haft had sat with others and discussed the lands and the races. Of course dwarves were stronger, but that was simply because each dwarf decided to be so. That was the key. That thought, like so many other truths, only appeared after so many flagons of ale.

Strength was made up of many things. Elves could pull the cable back if their minds were not weakened by history. The elves lived too long. They would rather use their long bows than the more powerful crossbow. Pulling the cable back to its pin was work, hard work. The effort made even some dwarves sweat. Goblins could never produce that kind of effort. They would quit work as soon as they thought they could get away with it.

Humans could pull back the cable. They were perhaps the most capable of the races, but they feared pain. Of course, pulling fifty stone with a simple cable might cut the flesh of the fingers, and the humans seemed to value their soft pink flesh more than they did the strength the weapon brought. Fear of pain was the ultimate weakness.

Donius

Jennifer "Cia" Ellison

Chapter 6

They broke camp as they had done for the past several days. The big adventure Keven had thought he was starting had not yet materialized. Each morning, he seemed to care for both horses a little more. The old man simply smoked his pipe and waited for Keven to finish his chores.

Often, when they had finished traveling for the day, the old man promptly lay down and took a nap. It bothered Keven, although he knew it shouldn't since Gareloch was old. Still, having to set up camp, unpack the horses, gather firewood, and fetch water had not been what he had expected.

He reined in his frustration at Gareloch. The old man's leg must hurt greatly; it was all he could do to hobble around the cookfire with his twisted walking stick and cook the stew. The routine was only marginally better than his routine at Banolf's inn. He did not want to seem ungrateful to the old man, but he was not pleased. He did his best to keep up his end of the conversation, but Gareloch's responses were increasingly short.

As they rode on, it became apparent to Gareloch that Keven was sulking. "Lad, yer acting as a wee one who does no get his sweet. Tis no way fer a man such as ye ta act. What thoughts are in yer young mind?"

"Well, I mean no disrespect, sir. I truly am grateful for you taking me with you to learn and become educated. I don't think I have learned much. I have been with you for a while, and I still tend horses and fetch water."

"Well, lad, now that ye've spoken up, what do ye want?"

The old man's face held a small smile. Keven was not amused. He felt the old man was having sport with him.

"Well, I don't know. You said you were going to take me away and teach me. You said you might even take me to some real schools." Keven tried not to sound accusatory.

"Lad, if ye do no know what ye wish ta learn, how can I teach ye?" He said it as if he were explaining that fire was hot to a child of four summers.

81

"Well, can you teach me to fight or even to tell stories?" Keven hated to sound foolish, but Gareloch kept looking at Keven as if he were measuring the young man.

"Tis more than a wee bit of difference between the two. If ye could only choose one, what would it be?"

Another test, Keven knew. Only, he did not know how to answer.

" I don't know. I guess it would depend. I couldn't get a meal at an inn by fighting, but I couldn't stop brigands or goblins with a story." Keven hoped his noncommittal answer sounded intelligent.

"So, yer saying tis more a question of knowing what ye need. Needing one and having the other can put a man between two millstones."

"Well yeah, I guess that is true." Keven understood only part of what Gareloch said, but he did not want the old man to know that. "What do you know, Master Gareloch? Can you not teach me that?"

"Lad, if ye knew everything I knew, ye would be me. Do ye want ta be an old man?" He gave Keven a look of amusement that gave Keven the idea that he was a king's idiot for not knowing such a thing. "Ye have youth and hope. I have naught but memories of better days."

"Well, what should I learn? What do you think is important?" Keven was resigned to admitting he did not know.

"The best place ta start is learning what ye don't have. Learn what ye need first."

"But how? Will the school you told me about teach me what I need?"

"Lad, do ye have a stump instead of a head? If I had me walking stick with me, I'd see just how hard that head of yers is. No one can tell ye what ye need. No, tis no true. There are plenty who will tell ye what ye need. But, ye need ta know the truth of yer need."

Keven felt like he was trying to make a wall out of hay. His thoughts would not take shape, and Gareloch just kept throwing more hay on top of his pile of thoughts. He needed to ask a question to which he could understand the answer.

"What if a pack of wolves or goblins comes after us? Neither of us has a sword or even a bow. I know what my need would be. But, I wouldn't know what to do." Keven wanted to make the conversation light. He used goblins to add humor to his point. Everyone knew that goblins only existed in stories.

"Aye, ye have the right of it there; ye don't know what ta do." The old man ended the sentence with a tone that suggested he'd given Keven the answer. He continued to ride in his shabby cloak with a content look on his face.

"But that is what I have been trying to say. I don't know what to do."

After a few minutes that were agonizingly long to Keven, Gareloch started to pat himself all over. He eventually felt his pipe in one of his many pockets and brought it out. With a childlike grin, he stuck the pipe in his mouth and immediately began to exhale the sweet white smoke.

"Lad, if ye could learn the sword from an old man like myself, would ye do it? Or would ye rather learn the trick of lighting a pipe with no flint?"

"I'd like to learn the sword. Your trick with the pipe or our cook fires is good for convincing children that you are some kind of magician. But, I'd like to learn something that is real."

"Aye, I see, lad." Gareloch took his pipe out and blew smoke rings that seemed to dance in the air. "A real sword fer a real need."

Keven was learning that Gareloch had a certain pace to his conversations. He seemed to enjoy them and liked to stretch them out.

As they rode on, the silence was broken by an ominous buzzing. An arrowfly landed on Keven's arm. He reacted wildly and scared the pest off with a clumsy wave of his arm.

"I'll teach ye what ye want; I'll teach a bit of the sword if ye can answer me a question. If ye cannot, then ye will have ta learn the wee magic trick. Pay me heed now, lad, what would ye have done if ye did feel the bite of the arrowfly?"

"Well, I would have…"

"Lad, before another word leaves yer mouth," Gareloch called over his shoulder, "do ye think ye might want ta think a bit on yer answer?"

Keven took the advice of the old man. They rode on in silence for the rest of the day.

* * *

The humans she rode with were different from the grace and culture she was used to. Everything with them seemed too abrupt, so brutish. She understood their explanation for speed.

They were not cruel with their horses, but they did not listen to them, either. The campfires they built were sometimes fed with wood that was hacked from a living tree. They meant the tree no harm. In fact, they did not even seem to be aware of the tree at all. To them, it was a thing to be used. Still, they tried to be polite to her in their own clumsy way.

Each night, they had offered her some of their food. She politely refused as she hid her revulsion. Dried animal flesh that was carried for days hardly seemed a meal for anyone other than goblins and their ilk. She often wondered about the goblins while she was riding with the humans. Why were they so far north?

e did not tell the humans of her encounter with the goblins. She
_everal reasons why: all were reduced to the fact that once she told
them the knowledge was theirs, and she could not take it back.

Would they react as she had? Shoot first, examine later? Probably;
they did not seem to fear regret. A powerful attraction pulled at her. For
decades, she had trained and honed her skills as a ranger. If she followed
the lead of her elven instructors she would never use her skills.

The journey to Atani City was uneventful. As they neared the city,
she saw more and more human farms and settlements. With effort she
avoided gaping. She did not want to have to live with the regret of causing
shame to herself or the humans who toiled so bleakly. The rickety shacks
were square things made from almost straight lines. They were wholly
unnatural and looked ready to collapse.

Despite all she learned about humans on her short journey to their
city, she was amazed at the sight of the city itself. It was huge with stone
buildings that reached for the sky. From her vantage point she could see
no trees. The city seemed to be a chaos that humans were trying to tame
with straight lined streets.

"There now, Kiel, that is the castle itself. It is where the ruler of
Atani stays. We shall take you there. You will be given the most cordial of
welcomes."

If her instructors wanted her to learn of human customs, they could
hardly have plotted a better curriculum. Barely a few weeks out of
Elvenwood and she was already being offered an audience with their
ruler. Of course, by riding into the city with them, she was relinquishing
every ability to protect herself. Alone in a city of countless humans was
hardly a comfortable way to spend her future moments. It was definitely
not how she wanted to spend her last moments. Still, if she was to learn,
she would have to take the tough lessons with the easy ones.

The men in her party seemed to speed up as they approached the
city wall. The road was crowded with all manner of carts, wagons, beasts,
and humans. The riders sped past them, shouting that they were doing the
Regent's bidding. Again, they repeated the cry that they were on official
Atani business.

Both she and Lieutenant Rondelli thought it would be best if they
hid her elven identity with her hood until she was properly situated in
Atani.

Kiel's sharp senses could not keep up with the myriad of sights,
sounds, and smells that assaulted her. She was accustomed to the
tranquility of the forest. The forest, though never quiet, had a rhythm to
its activity. Watching humans dart and move in all directions on the
cobblestone streets filled her blood with excitement. It was so different
from the staid and boring forest. Humans, it seemed, lived for action.

She became a little unsettled as Lieutenant Rondelli steered his horse at full gallop right through the gates to the castle itself. She did not trust his skills as a horseman. He relied too much on the bit, the reins, and the saddle to control the horse. Kiel winced as he pulled the reins hard. The horse skidded to a halt, and she was very nearly thrown over Lieutenant Rondelli's shoulder. That would have caused her great shame. It seemed that was the human custom, to rush through everything. Without even thanking the horse, he had her dismount and then follow him through a large doorway that entered the castle. She barely had time to grab her bow from the horse's back. Her other things she could leave for a while, but she would not be without her yew bow.

Lieutenant Rondelli stormed through the castle. Had she not heard the pride in his voice, she would have assumed he was angry. But, then, who knew anything about humans? Perhaps walking fast and stomping through a castle was the custom.

"Kiel, I'm so glad I could bring you to Atani. Atani is a special place. People have begun to work together, to help each other for the good of our nation."

He said those words over his shoulder, his riding cloak billowing behind him. She had no trouble keeping up with him. Though his pace was fast, he moved clumsily, while Kiel glided along in her own graceful stride.

As they went deeper into the castle, she realized she was hopelessly lost. She, once again, had let her past moments put her future ones in jeopardy. She trusted Lieutenant Rondelli, but still, she did not know why he was hurrying. From what little she knew of human haste, this was more than a little rude. He had not offered her accommodations or refreshment.

"I'm taking you to Regent Lilandra. She'll be most pleased to see you."

"Is she your ruler?"

"She is... Well, it's best if you meet her. I can't wait to tell her how I found you. She is always eager to hear from any citizen. Of course, no one would want to bother her with small talk. She is too busy for that, but she would never let you know it. She always seems to have time for a word with everyone."

Even his speech had sped up. Lieutenant Rondelli reminded Kiel of a youth who had seen his first pixie and could not wait to tell his elders. She could not help but feel the excitement that seemed to float about the castle.

"She'll have time for you. That is for sure. She will be pleased with me when I tell her how I found you."

Kiel wished she knew more humans to compare Lieutenant Rondelli against. What she thought was a disciplined and cagey man-at-arms was acting like a youth about to receive a sweetberry dessert. Maybe this was how they all lived, moment to moment without a thought about how their moments connected. He seemed so free; she wondered if she would ever be that free.

They swept into a large chamber that had hundreds of humans milling about in differing sized groups. They were talking to their own group while simultaneously listening to the groups around them. Her hood made observing them with discretion difficult.

Lieutenant Rondelli pushed through them with no more grace than a bull in an orchard. Kiel felt a rush as she noticed his seeming indifference to the subtle violence of pushing through a crowd. A small smile showed itself on her mouth as she thought of how her instructors would recoil in fear at the thought of such casual violence.

Kiel tried to look around to learn as much as she could. Their clothing and hairstyles seemed frivolous and were even worse than the garments that some of the elven maidens favored. At least the fancy elven gowns were flowing and graceful. These humans seemed to favor clothing that restricted movement, especially the females. Kiel could practically feel them sweating and suffering in such gowns.

Lieutenant Rondelli abruptly stopped. Were it not for her long years of practice in watching a person's movement, she might have run into him.

"A thousand pardons, most Honored Regent." He waited to be recognized. The person he was addressing was a female who was sitting on a throne. The throne sat on a raised platform, so despite her seated position, she could look Lieutenant Rondelli and Kiel in the eye.

Kiel had no way of gauging her age. She was beautiful, even for a human. She looked to be innocent and vulnerable, though her eyes held strength.

"Ah, Lieutenant, it is always good to hear from a dedicated soldier. Without your bravery, we all would not enjoy the security we do."

The grisled officer blushed with the idea that someone as important as the Regent herself would praise him. "Most Honored Regent, I have brought a friend to Atani. She is someone who might witness and add to our Dream of every person working for a common good." With that he guided Kiel to meet the human on the throne.

Kiel did not know if she should bow or what gestures were appropriate. She did the only thing she thought would help, she lowered her hood.

A gasp rippled through the crowd, and Kiel found herself the center of attention. She could see the countless pairs of eyes sweep up and down her body. She was hardly presentable for a formal introduction. Her long hair hung unadorned about her shoulders. Her riding cloak did nothing to hide her form-fitting leather breeches. Dirt and the smell of the lieutenant were on her clothes.

Kiel felt no embarrassment. The small discomfort she had came from knowing that she did not have a hint as to what her future moments might entail. The discomfort was barely noticed next to the feeling of power that grew in her as she realized the humans wanted her. She was at the mercy of a horde of humans who had lust in their eyes.

The woman on the throne stood. Kiel had lived among the fair elves for over nine decades, and few among them could match this human woman's radiance. Her eyes were the bluest of blues. Their dark pupils seemed to be arrows that pierced Kiel's very soul. Kiel did not feel threatened; still, the woman's gaze was unsettling.

What at first seemed to be the beauty of a frozen mountain-scape, immediately melted into the warm loveliness of a woman welcoming a long awaited friend.

"Welcome, Mistress Elf. I am Lilandra, Regent of Atani. We are honored to have you visit. We extend an invitation for you to stay with us. We would be honored if you did."

It was a warm and honest greeting despite the necessary formality. Kiel immediately realized she liked this woman's sincerity.

"I am Kielasanthra Tylansthra of the LeafTender Clan. Please call me Kiel. I would be honored to accept your invitation to stay and learn from you." Kiel hadn't realized the silence of the crowd of observers until that silence ended with several exclamations of approval. Regent Lilandra smiled in a way that made the awkward attention of the crowd seem warm.

"We, of course, would be happy to help you learn whatever it is we can teach you. There is a condition, however." Although Lilandra's tone was serious there was a hint of amusement in her eyes. "You must teach us. There is too little known between elves and humans. I would like to change that. I think and hope you would be invaluable in that effort. Please help us in our effort to improve our nation."

Kiel wished her former instructors were here to see this. In her most recent moments, with very little consideration of her future moments, she made a rash decision based on trust. Now, in her present moments, she was valued and recognized as important. The farther she got from her instructors, the more she was aware of their limitations.

"Kiel, we in Atani are attempting to build something. We are attempting to reach beyond our petty individual needs and give to our neighbors and our nation."

Many of the courtiers who were observing nodded and voiced their agreement. Humans, it seemed, were more harmonious than her instructors had taught.

"Oh my, The Creator forgive me and all of you rude people. We have not offered our guest refreshment." There was a good natured spark in Lilandra's eyes. She certainly had not meant anyone to feel rude. Her courtiers obviously felt comfortable enough to laugh at a shared faux pas.

With well-practiced and subtle movements, the servants appeared with silver trays and matching goblets. Kiel took one with a good feeling. Sometimes present moments simply worked out for the best.

"You too, Lieutenant. You have served Atani well by introducing us to our new friend. Please have a cup and join in celebrating. Though many of our citizens give their best, few have been able to match your contributions to Atani. Please feel pride knowing that Atani is better today for your efforts."

At first, Kiel had been so occupied with the warmth and grace of Regent Lilandra that she had forgotten about the man who brought her here. When she noticed Lieutenant Rondelli, she saw his eyes were filled with pride as he held the silver cup of wine. The silver cup was cradled by one hand while his other rested on the hilt of his sword. Kiel tingled with excitement as she saw that even in their most elegant situations, humans were never far away from violence.

* * *

Keven hurried to set up camp and unpack the horses. Gareloch had a knack for picking good sites: there was a nearby stream that made fetching water easy. Thistle and Caelv were unpacked and hobbled as fast as Keven could manage, and the small shelter of trees yielded a surprising amount of dry wood for the fire.

As Keven walked back into their camp with an armload of firewood, Gareloch stirred from his customary nap.

"Ah, lad, when yer bones are old, nothing suits the body better than a quick rest." As he rolled to his knees, he picked up his twisted walking stick and used it to lever himself to his feet.

"Stack the wood properly, lad. Then stand a pace back." With that, the dried sticks astonishingly grew several small tongues of flame. Keven had second thoughts about his choice of the sword as he saw the cook fire burst into life.

Those flames reminded him of the fact that, try as he might, he could not explain Gareloch's pipe. He wished he could study it. He knew he could never sneak it out of the old man's cloak. And doing so or even asking to see it would be cheating on the tests that Gareloch was giving him. He did not know the exact rules, but he knew what was cheating and what was fair play.

Keven knew Gareloch would not take out his pipe while he was tending to supper. Hobbling around the fire required his walking stick, and the old man needed at least one free hand to prepare the stew.

Keven waited for the perfect time to bring up their earlier conversation. Waiting was tough for him. For every answer Gareloch gave, three more questions sprouted in Keven's head.

When Gareloch pronounced supper was ready, Keven was relieved. Only after the old man was settled could he renew the conversation.

"Well, lad, what about that arrowfly, what would ye have done?"

"I would have killed it." It was a simple, truthful answer. Just like the one he gave at the table in Banolf's inn.

"Why, lad?"

"Because it stung me." With that, Keven felt the trap closing.

"So?" That one word demonstrated to Keven that he had failed this test.

"So, well, I didn't want it to sting me."

"No, lad, I'll have no lazy thought from ye. Remember we were talking about *if* it stung ye what would ye do *after* the fact?"

Keven didn't respond right away. He tried to cut through to where the old man wanted him to be. Gareloch continued.

"All actions stem from needs. After the stinger tis in ye, what tis yer need?"

"To get it out." Keven was confident of that reply.

"Is it? The poison is already in ye."

What seemed to be simple common answers suddenly seemed to be like a child's understanding of the world. Keven did not know what to think.

"Lad, would ye care about the wee stinger if it did no hurt?"

"Well no, I guess it wouldn't matter then."

"So, lad, if ye could stop yer pain, would ye still kill the pest?" It was said with the finality of someone slamming the door shut. Keven knew he had not answered the question. "Tomorrow, lad, we'll talk more."

As if to end the conversation, Gareloch took out his pipe and started puffing. Since he was seated for the night, Keven assumed he had stowed his walking stick away with his pack near the horses.

Gareloch had a far off look on his wrinkled face. The look said that Keven's answer would come when the old man was ready.

* * *

Tonay had dreamed of meeting Regent Lilandra countless times. In all of her fantasies, Tonay had never visualized that to do so she would have to fetch water and wood for a bunch of ragged recruits.

She was the only female and as a result, finding her own bushes each morning, each night, and at every rest was awkward. There were a few comments on her shape and what they thought she really wanted by joining the army. The comments meant nothing to her. She concentrated on being the best First Recruit she could be.

Traveling was hard, but Lieutenant Deccia kept her dream alive. He seemed to be the embodiment of the Regent's call. He was professional and hard but only because his position required it. His every word, thought, and action seemed to be focused on getting as many rough recruits to Atani City as soon as he could.

After a few days, she had learned the rhythm of her new squad. As a result of the recruiting party's success in gathering new recruits, they had more citizens than mounts. Lieutenant Deccia said it was common for a recruiting party to be so successful. Many citizens understood that there were things more important than petty desires.

The horses had to be rested often. In addition to the mounts, the low rations caused the party to take as direct a route as possible to Atani City.

Even though they were moving directly toward Atani City because they could accommodate no more recruits, they stopped several times each day. After the horses were watered, each recruit lined up for sword practice. At first, she felt foolish waving a stick in the air pretending it was a sword, but that feeling of foolishness was quickly washed away with sweat.

The practice seemed as if it lasted hours, though she knew Lieutenant Deccia would never let the squad stay still for long. She wondered if her shoulders would ever be the same. Practice consisted of swinging her stick with both arms as hard as she could at the shoulders of her fellow recruit lined up directly in front of her. She was to stop her swing no farther than one thumb's width from her partner. At the drill leader's call, she would then become the target as the recruit across from her swung his stick.

She lost count of how many times she did not stop her swing early enough. Her apologies seemed feeble and weak. Her partner also missed his mark. With the first of his accidental impacts, she sucked her teeth in pain.

Despite the pain, she was determined to do her best. Lieutenant Deccia bellowed to the recruits that holding back was giving in to fear. That was equal to death on the battlefield. He also said hitting your partner showed a lack of control. That, too, would also mean death on the battlefield.

For Tonay, the regimen was tough. In fact, just traveling was difficult. She had never really ridden a horse for any length of time. The rest breaks were anything but that. The sword practice took what little strength she had. Her one escape was in her mind; she would review the drills in her head. It was just like on the farm when she would keep her mind occupied. She figured that if she could imagine herself doing it right, she soon would.

It was slow going. In her mind's eye, she could see what her body was supposed to do. Sometimes she managed to do it. It surprised the regular soldiers and recruits when she would occasionally anticipate their moves and respond with feline quickness. That was rare. She still had much to learn, and any errors resulted in painful welts.

The treatment was doled out equally to almost all of the recruits. Tonay, though, sometimes received a slightly different version of the drill. When she made a mistake the corporal who sometimes eagerly volunteered to become a sparring partner would not hit her as he hit the others. They received blows on the head, shoulders, or anywhere the corporals could reach. Tonay, however, received the blows in only one place, a smart smack on her bottom.

The smack certainly did not hurt much. It did, however, burn. With every smack the soldiers, and even the recruits, would snicker and make a comment. It was humiliating and frustrating. The harder she tried, the lighter the pat was. The comments became almost worse than the welts. She tried to imagine the correct counter moves. The embarrassment would not let her concentrate. Thus, she could not imagine the fight as she needed to.

"I wouldn't want to hit a lady anywhere she doesn't need it," was a favorite comment from the soldiers. The version of the drill she received allowed the soldiers an easy excuse to ask about her bottom.

Tonay did not know what to do. She knew that complaining would make the situation worse. The difference in treatment ended rather abruptly. During one rest, Lieutenant Deccia observed the drills.

"Corporal Cini, is there a reason you are using a different training method with First Recruit Denisio?" His tone left no doubt what he thought of the practice.

"Well, sir," he began nervously. "She is a woman, and we did not want to injure her."

"Corporal Cini, who do you serve?"

"Regent Lilandra and King Donius."

"Corporal Cini, have you not heard the Regent's decree? Do you disagree with her thoughts on the equality of all people?"

"No sir!" Corporal Cini replied in an effort to regain some of his rapidly ebbing pride.

"Corporal Cini, if this recruit was all that stood between you and a soldier from the Westlands or even a goblin wouldn't you want her as well trained as possible?"

"Yes Sir!"

"Good. I'm sure you'll make the necessary adjustments. Carry on."

At first Tonay was thankful until the sticks began to fall on her unprotected body. Then she almost wished she could go back to a simple smack on her backside.

Slowly, over the next few days, she and the other recruits were learning to avoid the most obvious mistakes. The sharp blows from the recruits were becoming less frequent. When contact was made by the soldiers, she and the other recruits were often able to turn away from the worst of it.

The progress to Atani City was slow, but Tonay was learning. She was making something of herself. She was following her own choice.

* * *

He was beyond tired. Tapio Denisio had lost track of the days that had been filled by heart-wrenching searching. He had no idea if Tonay was just over the next knoll or if she was leagues away. His tired mind strained to hold onto the hope that she could simply be around the next bend. Certainly she could've become too exhausted to continue or maybe she realized she had made a huge mistake.

The road to Atani City had become more crowded the farther he traveled from the farm. Any prints or wagon tracks he discovered always seemed to lead to a party that had not seen a young woman. Of course, a few travelers offered to help him look if they could share her with him. He was too tired to be offended or angry. He just wanted his daughter back.

In his exhausted haze, he noticed that all of the traffic seemed to be headed in one direction, towards Atani City. Most of the wagons and carts were so overloaded, he could hear the axles creak despite the thick coats of black grease that covered them. It seemed farmers, smiths, and craftsmen were headed to Atani City. Their reasons sounded hauntingly familiar: they were answering the Regent's call, like any good patriot should do.

The travelers were quite cheerful and routinely offered some of their food with their greetings. Their refusal to accept payment for their kindness sounded much like Tonay's reasons for leaving.

"We're all Atanians right? It's only natural for citizens to help citizens," one father said as his family walked beside his team of horses.

"It isn't right for us to have much while you have so little. That's what Regent Lilandra says. She wants to redistribute the wealth so everyone is equal."

Tapio noticed that their tone became decidedly chilly once they realized he was not going to Atani City to serve.

When he realized a traveling party no longer wanted him accompanying them, he rode on without a discouraging word. He had initially dismissed Tonay's excitement about Regent Lilandra and her new ideas, but in meeting so many travelers who shared Tonay's fervor, he became more than a little unsettled. Like moths to a flame, they were drawn to Atani City.

"Ho, citizen, from where do you come?"

His hunger, exhaustion, and the thoughts of Regent Lilandra allowed him to be distracted. As soon as he noticed one rider approach him from the side of the road, three men stepped from the bushes with crossbows drawn and aimed at him. From the way the man on the horse carried himself, he was obviously the leader. His expression was friendly, but Tapio could feel the crossbow bolts aimed at his back.

"I am Tapio Denisio, I'm a farmer from Ducca's Vineyard."

"Well met, Citizen Denisio. I am Lieutenant Spudolli. I am the leader of this recruiting party. It is good to see so many good citizens answering our Regent's call."

"Yes, of course, we all must give to receive." Tapio remembered Tonay saying something like that. He hoped it would be enough to satisfy these soldiers.

"That's quite a blade you have there, Citizen Denisio."

That was exactly what Tapio did not want, attention. He needed them to leave him alone. "It's not much of a blade, and I'm not much of a swordsman." Tapio hoped his casual tone would bore the soldiers.

"Ah, humbleness. Regent Lilandra says that is a good quality in all citizens. Come, we will travel together. Perhaps we'll encounter more citizens who wish to give to their nation."

The tone was light, but Tapio noticed the crossbowmen did not lower their weapons. Tapio felt the trap closing around him. By resisting even politely, he would cause these men to take even more notice of him. He needed to stay calm and give them a reason to let their guard down.

"Yes, it would be good to share the road with others who understand their duty to give to their nation." He had to play the part; there was no chance of outfighting them. It had been a long time since he had swung his sword. Even if he could pull it from its scabbard without cutting himself, he knew he would have three bolts in him before he took a step.

"Recruit Denisio, that is a fine sword. I think it would be best for you to hand it over to me. These roads can be dangerous. Bandits might see such a treasure and attack you."

Tapio thought for only the briefest of moments. The ruse was obvious and so were the odds of him keeping his sword and his life. With a forced smile plastered on his face, he handed over his sword.

"Come then, ride with me." Lieutenant Spudolli offered with false cheer and turned his horse to head towards Atani City. The three crossbowmen never unloaded their weapons.

Maybe this was a blessing. The Creator did work in mysterious ways. These men might take him right to Tonay. She was headed towards Atani City to join the army. He was now headed towards Atani city, and it looked like he had just joined that same army.

They were well-equipped, though they showed no armor. Their horses were of fine stock, and their uniforms looked relatively fresh. That they had three crossbows was impressive. Each of the crossbowmen he was now traveling with had a short sword. Their saddlebags bulged and their quivers held at least a dozen bolts each. They were well rested and disciplined, while he was very tired. Dejectedly, he realized it would be sometime before he could get away from Lieutenant Spudolli and his men. With a silent prayer, he rode on with his new squad.

* * *

Kielasanthra Tylansthra wished that her instructors could see her. She was given a large room in the Castle of Atani. Granted, it was confining and dreary, but it was the best the humans had to offer. Even the brutish humans, as they were called by her kin, could recognize her talents. If the Regent of Atani valued and needed her, why could not her own clan?

The walls of her large room were made of gray stone. How the humans managed to find so much stone to build something so large was amazing. They had not even the skill of coaxing the earth to give up the stone; they surely did not have dwarven skill of measuring and cutting. Even Kiel, who had only read about dwarves and their skill, could see how poorly the rough edges of each block fit together. It seemed the humans had used more mortar than stone in the creation of the castle.

That they had made it was a testament to human adaptability and their desire to do something with their short lives. Why they had made it was a testament to their foolish ways. Kiel could not imagine how many short human lives had been dedicated to building something so crude and unnatural as a castle of stone.

The stone floor of her room was so rough, Keil shook her head with the shame of it. The floor, like other parts of the castle, had stood for many years. Whoever had attempted to carve the flooring pieces of stone was long dead. Yet, the monument of his will, the floor, stood for ages. He must not have understood that there is only one chance to live each moment. For him, there was one chance to make even a cold stone floor a thing of beauty. He did not seize his moment.

The uneven floor was covered by a thick rug, and it stretched nearly to each of the walls. There was a fire laid in the fireplace, but she did not light it. She had spent her life in nature. Cold was a part of nature, she would not hide from it now that she was among humans.

Humans, she'd read, felt secure behind walls. Her instructors pointed out the folly in such thinking. Hiding behind walls only trapped the person who was hiding. Building a castle for defense was equally foolish. Certainly the walls were high and the moat wide, but every enemy in all the known lands knew where to find the person hiding in the castle. Maybe, she wondered, they secretly hoped for a siege. With a mental thrill, she imagined herself standing on the ramparts firing arrows into attacking bodies. At such a range, she'd never miss. Being with the humans was right she realized. In all of her time in Elvenwood, she had never felt free to explore her desire to put her skills to use.

She could not wait to start her new role for her adopted nation, Atani, leading a squad of humans on a scouting expedition. That she was to lead thrilled her to no end. The Regent Lilandra was quick to notice that Kiel was a born leader who only needed an opportunity.

In addition, Kiel was to educate the members of her squad in elven tracking and woods lore. She had not met the members of her new squad, but she had to admit she was eager to impress them. More importantly, she did not want to disappoint Regent Lilandra.

With that thought, Kiel realized there was nothing to do in her room. Exploring would pass her present moments. Despite the bright day outside, the small windows of the corridors made shadows her companions as she walked.

The servants she passed were courteous. They did their best not to stare as Kiel found herself walking to the throne room. She did not realize it at first, but she hoped Regent Lilandra would be there. The woman was always happy to talk with her. Unlike her instructors, the Regent listened. She had time for everyone, but especially for Kiel.

Bronwyn McIvor

Chapter 7

Keven woke with a start. Something was wrong. He was about to stir and get to his feet quickly when he felt an old, weathered hand across his mouth. As Gareloch slithered across Keven's body, Keven could see a wild-eyed look in the old man's eyes. He understood in an instant that silence was critical.

He lay there for uncounted minutes while a dozen questions assaulted his mind. When his patience was about exhausted, he heard the rustle of leaves. From the sound of the disturbance it was more than one pair of feet. He strained his ears till he felt like they were growing larger on his head. He heard sharp whispers that were in reality little more than grunts.

He did not know what was in the woods surrounding their camp, but from the desperation the old man had showed, it could not be good. As his imagination began to wake, fearful images that came from children's stories flooded his head. He was ashamed to realize he wished for the comfort of Banolf's hayloft.

The corner of his eye captured some movement, but he dared not turn his head for a better view. He did not know why the intruder, or intruders, did not immediately grab him. They were stomping around no more than a few feet from where he lay.

That Gareloch still silently laid half across Keven gave Keven plenty of reason to remain still. The weight of Gareloch made Keven very aware of how much his chest was moving with each breath. The rising fear in him made him inhale ever deeper.

Keven knew it was only a matter of moments before they were discovered. The shadowy images at the edge of his vision had come closer. From his position, he could not count the number of pairs of either clawed feet or boots. The boots were a sickly gray that had unusually square toes. To Keven's wild imagination, the boots even looked to be made of iron.

The clumsy footsteps pounded nearly every inch of the campsite, but amazingly, they did not step on either Keven or Gareloch. The harsh voices were uttering sounds that could only be described as ugly. For an instant, one of the intruders came close enough to allow Keven a proper view. As soon as it happened, he wished it hadn't.

The intruders were like no people Keven had ever seen. They were short, but powerfully built. One of them had a nose that was flattened so that its huge nostrils looked to be holes in its face. From the dim moonlight, Keven could not clearly see colors, but to him, the face appeared to be a dark shade of green. Its hideous head was covered with a riveted helmet that looked a lot like a stout pot.

To Keven's horror, the thing stared at his face. At that moment, Keven knew the thing was evil. His heart froze, and his eyes would not blink. He wanted them to blink, to shut out the nightmare.

It bent down to look at the prone men; its face was a mere foot from where Keven's head lay on his rolled travel blanket. Keven did not know why the thing did not simply kick him with one of its heavy boots. Keven mentally braced himself for what he knew would be a brutal impact.

Amazingly, the thing lost interest in Keven's face. It simply blinked its misshapen eyes and moved on to study a different patch of ground. Keven would have exhaled a huge breath had he inhaled any air. His fear had prevented him from breathing, and he was thankful.

With agonizing slowness, the creatures began to move away from the center of their camp. Their heavy boots made impacts that sounded like kegs dropping from a cart. The thought of those boots stepping on his face almost caused Keven to weep. As the rustles in the leaves became fainter, he exhaled a sigh of relief.

Gareloch slowly rolled off him but motioned for Keven to keep silent and still. Keven tried to sink himself into the forest floor. He had never envied a mouse its burrow before, but at that moment, Keven wished he had a hole in which to hide.

As Gareloch sat upright and peered around, Keven tried to make sense of what had just happened.

Keven had faced beatings and endured shame before. Nothing, however, in his young life had prepared him for the feeling of stark terror that now enshrouded him. He did have pride enough to attempt to control it. Still, he knew his clenched jaw and cold perspiration were beacons telling the old man of his fear.

"We should no see them again this night," Gareloch pronounced. For a storyteller, his tone was that of a king giving an edict.

Keven's mind was simply not up to questioning. He had stared a nightmare in the eye and was spared for no reason he could recognize. It was all he could do to raise himself to one elbow and look at Gareloch.

As if sensing the boy's confusion, Gareloch simply said, "Goblins, nasty little buggers. Tis a good thing they did no see us." His light brogue was small comfort to Keven's near shattered emotions. The old man sensed this and continued with his cheerful banter. "Some are near human in how they look but still uglier than a dwarven maid. Others, lad, look worse than what the bards sing of. Some have scales and a tail, some wear iron boots for kicking, a few have claws on their feet to hold down their still squirming meal. No one knows the way of their differences.

"Lad, ye did well for waking up ta that. I have seen men tough as nails that did no hold themselves as ye did. Sit here and rest a bit as I see ta the horses. They seemed ta have left the horses, tis strange. I do no like the idea of goblins in a hurry. Tis good they did no bother with the Lady Thistle; she would have given them a time." He laughed at his own joke. Keven could not believe the old man thought the ordeal was funny.

Gareloch produced his walking stick and pushed himself up with it. When he was to his feet, he walked to the horses with surprising grace. The gnarled piece of wood that was supposed to help him walk appeared to be no more than an afterthought.

Keven tried to get to his feet, but he simply could not convince his legs to work. He realized that the fire had gone out and their few possessions were scattered about. He wished the fire was still warm. Though the night was not cold, his spine held a deep chill.

"Ah well, we can count our blessings, the horses are fine. But, I am a wee bit restless. Sleep will no come easy this night. A pot of tea might be the way of it." Gareloch used his stick to ease himself down in front of what had been the cook fire. The black earth had clear boot prints in it.

Gareloch reached for some of the unburned sticks Keven had collected. He piled them in the center of the fire ring and then reached for a pot that miraculously was still half-full with water.

"Come, lad, shake yer head a bit ta get yerself thinking again. Twas not so bad as ye first thought naught but a bit of goblins. Come sit by the fire and some tea will set ye right."

Keven rubbed his face and crawled over to the ring of stones that held the cook fire. He winced as his knees shuffled some of the leaves that had been his bed not long before. The crackling of leaves sounded obscenely loud. A shiver of fear ran through him at the thought of the goblins hearing the sound.

"Ah, lad, tis the way of it. Just when ye need a fire, all ye have is ash and rock." With that he looked at Keven. The old man's eyes softened a bit as he peered in earnest at the boy's eyes.

"Speak ta me, lad. The buggers are a ways away now. They'll no hear ye. Don't let 'em in yer mind. Push 'em out with yer own thoughts."

"Were they really goblins?" It was all Keven could say, but it seemed to satisfy the old man that the boy had some of his wits about him.

"A small gang of goblins. Tis rare ta find them in such a wee number. We had the luck of it with only five. If there are five here, there must be more somewhere no too far."

Keven had too many questions fighting to be the first one asked. The strongest of the questions was an attempt to reconcile what he saw with what he thought could not be. Rather than ask a useless question, Keven forced his mind to accept that he had been nearly stomped by creatures he had been told did not exist.

"What were they looking for?" Keven heard his own voice, and it sounded hollow. He was still digesting the nightmare.

"Tis hard ta say with goblins. Surely, they were looking fer a meal. Goblins are no choosy when they get hungry. Most things that live or once lived are fair game fer 'em."

"Would they have eaten us?" Keven tried to put a little life into his voice. He did not like how close he had come to giving into his fear.

"Well, lad, tis hard ta say and no pretty ta think, but tis possible. Tis a good thing they did no see us."

"I don't understand that. Why did they leave? One of them stared right at my face!" Keven tried not to shiver at the thought of that hard face looming over him.

"Ah well, goblins do no have good eyes. They use their knothole-sized nostrils ta smell their next dinner. They knew something was here, but they could no see us."

"But, he was right on top of me. Nothing is that blind." Keven's curious mind was starting to shake off the grip of the nightmare.

"Aye, lad, ye are sure of that fact. Yet, yer eyes know different. What ta believe? Tell me, lad, what tis in me hands?" Gareloch showed Keven two open palms that had more wrinkles than dried fruit. In several quick gestures, Keven lost track of where Gareloch's hands had been. With a flourish, Gareloch produced his beat up pipe seemingly out of nowhere.

"What did ye see, lad?" he challenged.

"But that is a simple storyteller's trick." Keven protested as he took up the challenge.

"Is it now? Did it no fool yer eyes? What if I said the simple trick came from a palace of wizards?"

Before Keven could answer Gareloch's question, the old man waved his arms around in quick motions. Keven lost track of the number of times the old man's hands went behind his back and in his cloak. Astonishingly, the old man seemed to pull his walking stick out of his sleeve.

"What about now? Are ye so blind ye did no see me put the stick in me robe? A simple trick. What can ye trust if tis no yer own eyes?"

Keven was too proud to ask the old man to do it again. He knew that by asking he would prove the old man's point.

The woods had returned to normal nighttime sounds. Crickets were chirping their calls, and the woods felt right again. Keven relaxed a little as he knew the goblins were farther and farther away.

"Lad, what ye want ta learn is no what ye think. Even the goblins themselves will teach ye something if ye ask the right questions. Ye have the right of it. Why did no they see us? Tis only a magic trick as ye say."

Keven kept silent for a few moments. Conversation with Gareloch could be agonizingly slow until the old man began to hand Keven ideas, and the pace increased as dizzying as a king's juggler.

"Now, lad, about yer lessons: tell me with the goblins what did we need? Two swords or a storyteller's trick?"

Keven was starting to recognize Gareloch's traps. He did not want to give up on the idea of wanting to be a swordsman, but he knew having a sword would not have helped him against five goblins.

"Tis as good a time as any ta learn yer trick. Ye owe me that, and I want some tea. No sword of yers will heat the water fer me. Lad, fetch me some flint and tinder from yer pack."

Keven struggled to get to his feet. Though he knew the goblins were not near, it was still an effort to expose himself by standing up. He got the tinder box from his pack and resumed his position at the fire pit.

Gareloch was puffing on his pipe as he rummaged through a pack of his own. He found the items he needed and turned back to Keven.

"Put the flint in yer left hand as ye normally do. Now put the tinder on the ground where ye want the fire ta be. Listen ta me close now. Ye owe me the effort of it, so do as I say." Gareloch opened a large book to a weathered page. Keven had camped with Gareloch several nights and did not recall seeing the book before.

"Lad, breathe as ye would when coaxing a wee spark. Breathe in just a puff and breathe out an angel's breath. Do that now, just as I say. Do no stop til I say when."

Keven felt foolish holding flint and breathing at a spark that was not there. As Keven began his seventh breath Gareloch told him to repeat the words he heard.

"Lad, do no change yer breathing. But, within the breaths, say the words I say ta ye."

The words that came from Gareloch were clear enough, yet they did not want to stay in Keven's head. He repeated them with the same rhythm Gareloch offered them. As he spoke the words, he noticed the feel of them. It certainly was not the sound of his voice. He could not remember the sounds as they left his mouth. Yet, the feel of the words was definite. They flowed from him with each of his breaths.

The flow of the words changed and became more real. Keven could not see them, but he felt them mix with his gentle breaths. They intertwined and swirled at the base of the small pile of dry tinder.

Keven relaxed even further and closed his eyes. He kept breathing as Gareloch instructed because it felt good. Each breath felt like a stretch after a long slumber. The words were becoming more solid. And just when he felt them reach their pinnacle, they drifted away. Keven was sorry to feel them go, but holding on to them was like keeping the wind in a net.

He knew in an instant what had replaced them. With a quiet confidence, he opened his eyes and saw the smoking tinder. Gareloch blew on it and added some twigs.

"Aye, lad, tis the way of it. Tis always a mix of things yer first time. But, I tell ye true, no one I know did it finer their first time. No one."

Keven knew he should be excited, but he was not. It was not the goblins that took his astonishment away. It was the feeling of peace he felt. Saying the words and breathing had felt right. It was part of him.

He didn't want to spoil the feeling with words. He just sat and enjoyed the flames in a way that he never had before. They were his.

The peacefulness quickly gave way to exhaustion. He felt like heavy blankets of sleep were pressing him down.

"Aye, lad. That tis the way of it with *Sublevato*. Tis tiring ta work yer first spell. Ye've had a night ta remember. Ye've earned yer rest. I'll set watch fer the night." Keven barely heard the last few words. He simply fell backwards and was soon fast asleep.

* * *

His workshop was his sanctum. Most wizards seemed to prefer cramped alcoves overflowing with artifacts and books. Lord Sogoth's standards were considerably higher; his workshop was a cavernous chamber that occupied much of his small castle. It was finished with black marble and polished to reflect the light that had no apparent source and was cold in every way that a place could be cold.

He stormed through the halls imperiously, his black boots making great echoes with each step. Though his power in both sorcery and magic was nearly unmatched, even he could not escape the heavy yoke of the One Oath he had taken so long ago. Always, he felt unanswered questions and unfinished work in the back of his mind.

From his earliest days, he had been cursed with an inborn love for knowledge and power. He had always been driven. Anyone who knew him, including his dear sister, knew he was destined for greatness. Such ambition was a blessing in his early life; few could stand in the way of his wants. Those who tried learned quickly to avoid him in the future.

His success in the Wizards' Palace had not come cheap. Though he owned the right to call himself Wizard of both Sorcery and of Magic, he'd had to pay dearly for that right. It took a while before he realized the true cost of such power.

The price was insidious. His conscience was crippled. As a result, he had become quite adept at looking away from the light of goodness.

Though his workshop was not cramped with artifacts as those of the wizards who had not found a way out of the palace, he did in fact have quite a few items that were imbued with power. The most powerful, and therefore the one he most cherished, was a round, clear globe that sat upon an ornately sculpted, three-legged stand. In fact, it was more than clear. It was so utterly transparent that it could not be seen unless the light was right. That light could only come from a Wizard of Magic.

As Sogoth approached the two-foot wide sphere, the lighting in his workshop changed to accommodate his wish. That it changed without any outward sign of his making it so was a testament to his facility with advanced magics.

For long minutes, Sogoth stared intently at the globe that was barely visible, a motionless observer intently handling forces few could comprehend. After an indefinite amount of time, the sphere became more visible. Colors of every hue swirled and coalesced. Scenes of the world beyond his sight became visible. As they did, he relaxed.

The magic globe provided information, and information, he had learned long ago, was power. As long as he was looking into the globe, he was free from the threat of the One Oath. Knowledge and power. Few would believe they were more of a curse than a blessing.

With concentration, he could direct the orb to show him scenes from any of the known lands. The Westlands sat unaware of the plans against them. Their petty, feudal skirmishes were distractions from their internal failures and their external vulnerabilities.

From his time as a novice in the Wizards' Palace, Sogoth knew there were probably other orbs and at least a few other wizards who escaped. Because no other wizard had come knocking on his portcullis, he had to assume *Nascondersi Cacumen* was successfully hiding the emissions of his magic use.

Sogoth's Wizard's Price left him able to know which deeds caused harm to others but not until after such deeds were done. If there was, in fact, a Creator, Sogoth knew he was damned many times over. In pursuing knowledge, he had committed acts most would consider unspeakable.

Before he paid the Wizard's Price, Sogoth had given little thought to his conscience. Only after it was rendered irrelevant did he wonder about its importance. A Wizard's Price always demanded things of value. By denying him his conscience, it affirmed the importance of it.

He ripped his thoughts from that torturous path. If he was damned, there was nothing he could do about it. His Wizard's Price prevented him from atoning for past deeds. Therefore, his only hope lay in amassing as much power as he could. Wizards lived a long time, and the more power they had, the longer they lived.

He directed the focus of the orb much further south. The denizens of Darkwood were stirring; creatures of all types were infiltrating the lands of man. Though some were quite powerful and magical in nature, it was the most mundane of the Darkwood residents on whom Sogoth based his plans. Goblins.

No one knew how many of them existed. They resisted organizing. Sogoth almost smiled as he thought of gangs of them pouring into human lands and overwhelming Lilandra's army.

Goblins were interested in only one thing, weakness. They sought weakness in others as much as dwarves sought strength in themselves.

The racial laziness of Goblins would keep them content to engage in the same cyclical flow of violence they had always delivered to their own kind. Sogoth had introduced certain magical artifacts to lift them out of their self-defeating ways. The artifacts had little power except the ability to make it easier for the wielder to cause others pain. A few wands and a bunch of rings were distributed among the ever-changing goblin tribes. Of the artifacts he left behind, a few had enough power to make even goblins stealthy enough to catch a pixie to create confusion and fear in the north.

Each chief was given an artifact. He immediately took joy from using it to cause those around him to squirm in pain. Sogoth had designed them to turn on the wielder after a certain amount of energy was discharged. Thus the one causing the agony would soon find himself on the ground in his own bath of pain. The others would then set upon the suddenly writhing goblin and pummel him slowly. Goblins could not resist tormenting any thing that displayed weakness.

Sogoth gave each tribe the knowledge that there were countless defenseless humans in the north. Human children were weak; their old were infirm and feeble. There were plenty of such humans on the path to his castle in the north. If any goblin could make it to his castle, they would be given weapons to make others scream in a way no one had heard before.

Their excitement at the prospect of causing so much harm to so many whipped them into a frenzy that overcame their natural instinct to remain lazy.

The magical orb revealed that gangs of goblins had come as far north as the villages surrounding his castle. It was time to greet them, reward them, and send them back with enough booty that their kin would pour forth. An army of goblins was hardly an elegant weapon. Certainly the well-trained Atanian army would cut down scores of the brutes in an open conflict.

But no matter how precisely a trained soldier could swing his sword, he would tire. Goblins did not. By some legends there were more goblins in Darkwood than there were swords in the known lands.

* * *

Tonay knew they were making good progress despite the challenges of moving too many people with too few horses. She was the newest member and as a result, she had to ride in the rear position on the horse. At first, it bothered her. All recruits were supposed to be equal. The one time she did manage to ride in the forward position, her partner had been creative with how he held her.

When she had first felt his hands roam from her waist to her chest, she was mortified. She wasn't in a position where she could effectively strike him. She stiffened with shock and indignation.

She could not decide if she should shout out or if she should deal with it quietly. Either course of action had its problems.

If she made a disturbance, the others might find the reason for her indignation humorous. Additionally, it might further show her to be different from the other members of the squad. No, she thought. It was her problem. She would solve it.

His hands moved slowly across her wool shirt. He wasn't rough, in fact, he was tentative. Still, she almost retched with revulsion. She was no stranger to letting boys explore. This was different, though. She almost shook with impotent rage. Tonay forced herself to be still, lest she twist back to elbow him in the face and fall off.

Once again, she realized any girlish reaction or asking for help would demonstrate to him and maybe even to herself that she was different from the other members of the squad.

With her right hand she smoothly grabbed the index finger of the man's right hand. She made sure her thumb was on the back of his middle knuckle. Slowly, she began to bend. With ease, she pulled his hand off her shirt, but she did not stop straining his joint.

From the way his body stiffened, she knew it hurt. She could have easily broken the finger. Instead of going that far, she silently held it at the point of nearly breaking. Tonay knew he desperately wanted his finger back intact. He could do nothing about it. She kept up a steady painful pressure. Neither she nor her partner spoke any words for the rest of the ride.

As angry as she first was, a warm feeling of assurance enveloped her. She could take care of herself. It was satisfying to know that she was living the Dream.

As she held his finger in silence, she tried not to let any thoughts enter her mind. It was difficult. Thoughts seemed to pop into her head anyway. She remembered her papa saying that nature does not like empty spaces.

Her mind came upon the sword drills. For that last week, several times a day, she had suffered hardly any bruises. But, while their frequency decreased, she noticed them more. It was not because her instructors or fellow recruits were hitting harder. The awareness stemmed from the frustration of seeing how her mistakes had led to the strike.

Her fellow recruits became easy to beat. They were too reliant on their bodies. The soldiers, however, knew better.

She focused her thoughts on what she knew of them. She tried to remember every detail of her opponent as he moved. Envisioning it took all of her concentration. That allowed her to not think of the lout riding behind her. She could see her opponent's shoulders, hips, and footwork. She tried to see the weakness.

There was an opening. When an opponent swung his sword in a wide arc, the proper counter was to quickly stab forward. Straight attacks were always faster than circular ones. That was why the corporals always seemed to jab her and the other recruits painfully in the gut.

The imaginary fighters in Tonay's mind danced. The figure that was her opponent stabbed in a quick straight motion to her middle. She stepped to his weak side in a circular motion. With a half-slash, she could put her stick smartly on his left kidney.

She came out of her trance with a slight smile on her face. The peace and confidence in her allowed her to drop the pervert's finger. Soon after, Lieutenant Deccia called for a halt.

It was a small clearing with a trickling creek that would allow the recruits plenty of room to practice. Her legs were stiff and her rear end was sore, and she desperately wanted to wash herself.

After the cretin behind her dismounted, she swung down to take care of the horse. She liked animals, and her father had taught her the importance of getting a chore done quickly and completely.

After the horses were tended, the recruits were called to line up. It was to be a live sparring drill. One of the corporals yelled for them to begin. Instantly, her opponent sidestepped to his right. He was right handed and was doing exactly what he was instructed to do.

Tonay moved in and out of his range. Each time she did so, she made herself appear slow. When she felt she had gauged his speed, she stepped just inside his range. As he swung, she moved straight in with speed she had been hiding and jammed the end of her stout stick in his gut. He went down with a groan. His groan was loud enough to cause the others to stop their sparring and look in her direction.

"First Recruit Denisio!" Lieutenant Deccia bellowed.

She immediately froze in her best imitation of an attention stance.

"Yes Sir?" she shouted.

"Why did you hit your fellow recruit so hard?"

She was puzzled. She knew that the wrong answer might leave him disappointed in her.

"I practice hard like you taught me because the Regent has given us all the opportunity to be the best we can."

With a mix of military pageantry and hard, military discipline, Lieutenant Deccia spoke words of approval to Tonay. "First Recruit Denisio, you show great promise with the sword and even more with your understanding of how to serve Atani."

"Thank you, sir." She tried to appear calm, even gruff. It wouldn't do to have everyone see her beam with pride.

"Recruits," one of the soldiers hollered. "Change partners."

This time Tonay was faced with a man who had a young face. She wondered if she looked as young to him as he did to her. He was the nicest of her fellow recruits. Though they seldom spoke, they had exchanged smiles.

"Begin!"

They circled for a few moments. Then, he attacked with a great overhand swing. She saw it coming as soon as he began, giving her plenty of time to prepare her counter. The end of his stick whistled past her face as it continued downward to the soft ground and impacted with a wet thud. Tonay immediately stomped on his practice sword. It was yanked out of his grasp and lay trapped beneath her foot. With a smile, she tapped him on the shoulder. The whole exchange took mere seconds.

"Stop! Switch partners"

Tonay faced a recruit who was much larger than she. He leered at her. It was not malice, but simply the expectation that she would not be able to stand up to him. She kept her face calm and remembered the peace of concentrating on one thing, the dance of her mental fighters.

He began the fight by running straight at her. It so surprised her that she had to dive out of his way. She rolled out of it and came up on her feet, seeing him smirk at her with confidence. They danced back and forth, with their practice swords making loud smacks. She was gulping mouthfuls of air, but it did not dispel her sense of calm. While she was fighting, she did not think of her father, running away, Regent Lilandra, or of failing. While she fought, she was safe.

He charged again. He led with his stick leveled right at her chest. She waited until the last instant. Without thinking, she dropped into a crouch, thrust her practice sword between his running feet and watched him fall.

"Stop! Change partners."

With a light sheen of sweat, Tonay shuffled over to her next partner. Finally, she thought to herself. It was the recruit who had been so free with his hands.

His lesson was about to continue. As soon as that thought was done, she stopped herself. That was not how she wanted to begin this fight. If she thought of his hands or her pride, she would not think about moving. She tried to remember the calm of the fighters in her head.

"Begin!"

They circled each other. Both recruits were trying to best apply what they had learned in the last week. He began his charge swinging back and forth. He was left-handed, so Tonay moved to his right. He was fairly well balanced, and his constant swinging acted like a shield. With a light flick of her stick, she smacked his sword hand. It hurt, and she could hear his exhalation of pain.

With his hand hurting, he was tentative in his attacks. Tonay kept her mind free of all thoughts but one. She looked at him not as the man who had taken liberties with her breasts, but as someone on whom to practice. She moved with grace. Quick as a cat, she double tapped him on his right shoulder.

For the next few moments, she danced in and out of his range. Each of her movements seemed to end with her stick hitting him at least twice. To Tonay, it seemed as if she were outside her body watching herself fight. She did not know how many times she touched him with her sword. She was only aware of the elegant chess match with the other fighter. Each move he made gave her an opening.

"Stop! Recruits, rest for five," Lieutenant Deccia bellowed. "First Recruit Denisio face Coporal Cini."

Corporal Cini walked towards Tonay. He swung his arms in a stretch and smiled at her. Since Lieutenant Deccia's command for the men to treat her equally, she had been.

"Begin!"

Tonay began swinging back and forth with all of her strength. She kept just out of his striking distance. She let him think she had no plan. In her mind, she kept the image of the two fighters.

She let herself step inside his range. He took the opening and thrust forward in that efficient move that had given her so much trouble. She saw it coming before he began. To his straight attack, she countered in a circle. Her deft side-step took her to his left elbow. She was inside any possible back-swing he could manage. With a flick of her wrist, she laid her stick on his kidney and then the back of his knees to bring him down.

"Stop!"

Tonay looked down at Corporal Merini. With a surprised look, he rolled himself onto his back. He extended his hand for her to help him up. She was surprised by the gesture of camaraderie in defeat. It was hard to imagine he was the one who most enjoyed putting the flat of his sword on her rear end. She helped him up as the others watched. Truly, the Dream reached everyone.

Lieutenant Deccia strode to her. "First Recruit Denisio, you have demonstrated skill with your weapon. You have shown an understanding of the cause we serve. You have shown a willingness to put the squad ahead of your needs."

To Tonay, his words were bits of pleasure washing over her soul. She knew she was smiling though she tried to fight it.

"For these reasons, I deem you worthy of a promotion. From this moment on, you will be Second Recruit Tonay Denisio. I have no insignia to give you. Your role in our journey will not change much. When we get to Atani City, this new rank will mean nothing, but those of this squad will know of your commitment to the Dream."

Tonay's only regret was that her papa was not here to see it. It wasn't because of spite. She wanted him to see her so he could be proud.

* * *

She tried to practice the breathing techniques and mental exercises that her instructors said led to peace. She couldn't. She supposed that if she could she would still be in Elvenwood calmly evaluating every thought and feeling with the others of the LeafTender Clan.

She had given up her customary traveling clothes. This occasion demanded it, and she was happy to comply. In her short time in Atani, she had heard about assemblies in the coliseum. All citizens spoke of the citizen ceremonies with reverence and excitement. To be asked to speak at one was an honor she knew she would never have received among her race.

For her appearance, she had donned a beautiful gown. At least, her human hosts believed it to be so. Elven delicacy required wispier clothing that seemed to be a part of the wearer. Humans, it seemed, like to make statements with their garments.

Her gown was a collage of blues. The long skirt was made of satin. There were patches of velvet and velour on the shoulders and bust. To complement this, the Regent herself had lent her a necklace of diamonds. Kiel was thrilled.

The cut of each stone reflected the sunlight magnificently. She knew the square cuts would be offensive to some elves, but she did not care. The best aspect of the necklace was that Lilandra had loaned it to her. It was the Regent's personal property, not a piece from the Atanian collection.

Kiel surveyed herself in the mirror and saw a reflection that was confident in its beauty. More than that, she knew she looked happy. Each interaction with a human caused her to feel more at ease. The peculiarities of the humans were less and less important. This was the right place for her. She was accepted.

With the humans she was free: free to think, free to act, and most importantly free to express. For elves, true expressions of emotions were rare. Emotion was spontaneous. It often led to regret. That could not be permitted.

After thinking on the Regent's request for her to speak, Kielasanthra Tylansthra realized she wanted to do it. The Regent and the people of Atani had welcomed her warmly. Regent Lilandra suggested Kiel simply speak from her heart. To Kiel that was easy. Her heart was full with contentment and fulfillment at being a part of the Dream.

So, here she was, in a room inside the coliseum of Atani waiting to be announced. These demonstrations let the citizens of Atani share what it meant to be Atanian. They were able to see the Regent, the princess, and sometimes even the king. The good feeling that came from and descended upon the crowd was an excellent reminder of why they sacrificed so much for the Regent's Dream.

When she heard her name and the trumpets, her stomach did flip-flops. She noticed that the herald pronounced her name correctly. He must have practiced for some time. It was moments like this that would make her present and future moments seem rich.

She glided along a narrow walkway high above the floor of the stadium. She could hear the crowd hush as she became visible. The silence only added to her nerves. She approached the balcony that was next to the royal balcony. She could see that only the Regent and the princess were present.

Feeling like a vision of pure elegance, she made it onto the balcony from which she was to speak. It was hard for her to believe that a building so large, that contained so many humans, could be so quiet. Her elven upbringing recoiled at the thought of so much stone and cut timbers. Despite that, she also felt pride at her new nation's accomplishment. At the railing, she paused. She hoped her voice would not fail her.

"Citizens of Atani, I came to you as a guest. I am from a different land, indeed, even a different race. Since I have come, I have been welcomed. This welcome was unconditional. It was only after I asked that I was told how I could be a part of the Dream. That is what I truly want. Like you, I know that the Dream of equality and happiness is greater than any one being."

Kiel paused. She was pouring out her heart. She felt more human than elven. At the pause, the crowd erupted in cheers. It took some time for the din to die down.

"It is an example of the love and feeling for all beings that the Regent Lilandra offered me a position in the great army of Atani. She knew I was not born here, she knew I was different, yet she offered it to me, an elf." She paused again. Her emotions were raging through her.

"So, I am pleased to say I accept. I will serve you and the Dream as one of you. I came as a guest. Now, I hope you consider me a sister of your nation." If she thought the last eruption of the crowd had been loud, she was almost deafened by this one. It went on for several minutes. Thankfully, a steward came to her side and gently guided her to a seat on the balcony.

Kielasanthra Tylansthra felt like she was floating. Her feelings were so high, she wished she could cheer alongside the citizens in the seats below. An elf cheering!

There were a few speeches after hers. It was hard to pay them attention. Though she knew it was impossible, she felt as though all of Elvenwood could fit inside the coliseum. To assuage her nerves, she kept trying to count the number of humans present. It must be several tens of thousands. She read that human females could give birth to as many as ten offspring. Seeing the mass of cheering humans convinced her it was true.

In the center of the coliseum where games were supposed to be played, there was a large wooden building. The sight dampened her elation a little. Square wooden structures were unnatural. She did not need her elven education to see that it was recently constructed. It was also huge, so large that it took up at least a third of the playing space.

"What is the purpose of the wooden building?" Kiel asked the older noblewomen sitting next to her. The gaudy earrings the spinster wore pulled down on her already wrinkled earlobe. She wondered if human males found that attractive.

"Nobody knows, dear," the old women responded.

Dear? It amused Kiel that the old human thought she was older than Kiel.

"The Regent is not telling anyone. She will only say it is a surprise for the citizens of Atani."

That made Kiel smile like a youngling elf. As she sat on the embroidered cushion on a seat in the stadium, she thought about her new role as an officer in the Atanian Army. Though she had never had to enforce rules, she had seen it done many times while the elders asserted their role over her. She hoped she could imitate them well enough to earn the respect of her new unit. After nine decades of having to listen to others, she had finally found something that spoke to her.

* * *

King Donius was well schooled in tactics and strategy. He knew the importance of out-thinking an opponent. It was always preferable to out-maneuver or let the enemy plan with wrong information.

Lust for battle rarely won the day. A Blademaster had to master pride and realize his weaknesses. Donius had been fighting a losing strategy, expecting to win because he wore a crown. That was foolish, and it would not happen again.

He marched purposefully through his castle. With his royal cape billowing behind him, he marched on. Servants scurried out of his way; they must have sensed his mood. He paid them no notice. Though he had no sword strapped to his waist, he was ready for a fight. His hard-soled boots were tapping out a cadence that should have given anyone warning that he was coming.

At this time of the day, he knew she would not be in her bedroom. He strode to her office. That she had acquired an office in his castle was an insult. She was a tutor. At most she needed a desk in her room. He had no idea how she had convinced his staff to acquiesce to her requests. Why was he not informed of her moves?

Without knocking, he stormed in to find her sitting behind a desk looking at papers. That enraged him. What reports was she looking at? Did his advisors bring him the same information?

"Lilandra, you have gone too far. Your self-proclaimed regency ends now. You will at once return to your original room and wait to receive updated instructions as to your responsibilities and restrictions in *my* castle." His tone was as cold as frozen steel. Any normal person would have simply collapsed under his royal authority.

Lilandra dropped her eyes to the paper that was in her hand. She continued reading for some moments. When she was done, she looked up and spoke.

"You know, these reports show that just about everything in the kingdom is doing well." Her casual tone and the lack of reference to his title was like a slap in the face. "The army swells in numbers due to recruiting. Farms, smithies, and mills are all working harder and producing more. Crime, even in the most remote towns, is down. And most importantly, the people are happy. What exactly must stop, Your Highness?"

This time, the inclusion of his title was as insulting as the previous exclusion.

"There is a reason the crown is not easily worn or won. You have no possible idea of how short these increases will be. Can the farms continue their record production past this year if no field is left fallow? Can the mills and the smithies continue to make their goods if all of the young men and *even women* are in the army? You have set a grand party. But, the people will soon feel the morning after."

"My dear king, I gave no orders to make these changes happen. I simply let it be known that it would be good for all Atanians to join together for a common cause, to make Atani even greater."

"You gave no orders? Of course you gave no orders. You are a simply the princess's tutor."

"Let me explain a few things to you. It is true I gave no orders. The title of Regent you allowed your daughter to give me is all but meaningless. Yet, the people rally around my every whim."

He countered. "Subjects are easily swayed. They have no head for the true issues."

"Perhaps you are right. But, let me ask you, if these easily swayed peasants have worked as hard as they have just because I've asked them to, what do you think they would be capable of if I ordered them?"

For the first time in his kingship, Donius was unsure.

"Are you threatening me?"

"No, I would never do such a thing, Your Highness. I am simply suggesting that the people of Atani love me. They know I love them. I let them see me, I let them know me. They *need* me. You are simply a king they have always obeyed. Ask yourself if you were in their shoes, how would you feel about a king like yourself?"

He dismissed that question as he would swat an arrowfly.

"That love is fleeting. They will turn on you when unexpected, bad rumors spread, or times change. Then they will come back begging forgiveness and asking for assistance. It is how people are. No true ruler builds his house on a foundation of shifting sand."

"Thank you for the wise advice," she said dryly. "Where you have tolerated and even dismissed rumors, I embrace them. Rumors are how people talk and think. Of course, they are not true, but people hear and say what they need."

Her eyes bored into him. "I shall make this easy for you, Your Highness. Your servants and advisors all vie for my attention. The soldiers look forward to my visits. The subjects eagerly await any word of me. Their whole lives revolve around what I will wear at my next appearance in the coliseum."

"That means nothing!" he barked. "I am the king!"

"Are you sure it means nothing? Tell me, Your Highness. Let's compare the people to your daughter. To whom does she look to for advice and guidance? Of whom is she increasingly scornful? I wonder if your daughter or the people had to choose one of us, who do you think it would be?"

The words hit him like a thunderclap, but he rallied. "They have no choice. I am their king as my father was before me. I am a good king, fair and just. People do not get to choose their ruler for the very reason we are discussing. They do not know what is best for them. They will always choose lower taxes and easy solutions. That is why they need a strong ruler."

"That may be true. The ignorant wretches that love me do not know what is good for Atani, but they have need. I fill their need, and they love me. The same with your daughter. She has need of my approval like a slave has need of slaver's juice. And you know what? I give it to her as often as she needs. She keeps coming back for more. What would happen if you cut her off from that? Would she thank you?"

He had nothing to say. Fighting over a kingdom and political discussions came easily to him. Words, when it came to possibly losing his daughter, did not.

"No, Your Highness, she would not thank you. Just as a slave would protect his master rather than be free, your daughter follows me. Your subjects need me. You cannot dismiss me. In fact, it is fortunate for you that I do not have the people express how little they need you. When was the last time Atani had an open rebellion? Do you doubt for one moment that they would storm the gates if they thought I was harmed?"

King Donius, the Blademaster, the accomplished battlefield commander, and the rightful King of Atani was humbled. He had nothing to say. This was the first time he had ever been so thoroughly beaten at anything in his life.

"You may go now, Your Highness. But, in the future, do come quickly when I call. I might have some need of you."

As he closed the doors behind him, he could not determine if her smile was more wicked than beautiful. It did not matter. There were ways to make sure she did not smile again.

* * *

The summer day grew warm, and Keven had long since abandoned his cloak and shirt. He rode only in his breeches and undershirt. He observed the old man who rode several lengths ahead. Gareloch did not seem to be affected by the heat. He still wore his cloak, and his shoulders were hunched, as if he was sleeping. Keven wondered how he didn't fall off the horse.

He nudged Caelv into a canter and closed the distance between them. Keven wondered if horses got bored. When he came upon the old man's left side, Keven noticed that he was indeed asleep in the saddle.

Keven steeled himself. The more he spoke with the old storyteller, the more he was intimidated by him. Whatever bad would come as a result of waking his enigmatic traveling companion was far better than dying of curiosity.

"Sir?" Keven spoke softly, but in the quiet afternoon, it sounded as if he had shouted. The old man did not stir except for opening his left eye enough to glare at Keven.

114

"Lad, yer too young ta know the way of it. But sleep tis the thing. Waking a man from a good sleep is worse than robbing his purse. Aye, but not so bad as waking in the Wizards' Palace. Hah."

Whatever the old man thought was funny, Keven did not know. He did notice, though, the old man had mentioned a palace for wizards again. "Um, I'm sorry, it's just that I was hoping you would teach me more things."

To this response, Gareloch opened his other eye and turned to face Keven. "Ye do no know what ye want ta learn. Ye do no even know why ye want ta learn it. How can I teach someone like that?"

"I do know what I want to learn. At least some of it. I do not want to be weak. I do not want to be put in a pile of dung or told what to do by anyone." His words came out more forcefully than he intended them to. He wanted to impress the old man with how rational and intelligent he was.

"Some would say there are different kinds of weak just as there are different kinds of strong. Which one do ye want?"

Keven did not know. He was afraid that one wrong answer would have Gareloch sleeping in the saddle again. He forged ahead and hoped the old man liked his answers.

"I hate not being able to do things or control things. If the goblins saw us, or if slavers come for us, I would want to stop them." Keven was sure that was a solid answer.

"So, lad, tis physical strength ye want. Would ye like to be able to lift a wagon or best any man in yer town?"

"Not just those. If you can teach me to light a fire with … well with whatever it was, could you teach me to be strong? Is it possible?"

Keven tried to say the last with calm detachment. From his hard lessons at being denied the things he wanted, he had learned he had to hide his desire. To let others know what you want is to give them a chance to take it away.

"Tis a fair enough question fer now. But, ye still have no answered the why of it." Keven relaxed a little. It seemed as if Gareloch was not going back to sleep soon. In fact, his pipe appeared in his mouth. Almost instantly, he began blowing sweet-smelling smoke rings near Thistle's mane.

"Well, what if that tree over there, or something like it, fell on my mother?"

"Aye, ye have the right of it, what if?" That Gareloch could ask a question that sounded like an answer but was not, amazed Keven.

"Well," Keven said slowly, "I'd want to get it off of her."

"Why?"

"Well," Keven stuttered in frustration, "she'd be hurt."

"Exactly." The old man puffed on his pipe with a slight gleam in his eye. To Keven, it seemed as if he was gloating over a victory.

They rode on in silence for awhile. Keven was desperately trying to find the lesson he was supposed to be learning.

"Lad, let's play that yer ma is lying under something heavy. She is hurt and can no move. Ye have a choice between moving the heavy load or stopping her pain. What would ye choose?"

Gareloch puffed on his pipe as too many thoughts swirled in Keven's head.

"Lad, not too long ago ye were wishing fer a sword. It seems all lads do. No one seems to want ta be a healer. Healing is fer old women. Every lad knows it. But tell me, lad, how oft in yer life do ye need a sword and how oft do ye need a healer?"

Not wanting to be so easily beaten, Keven countered. "Would a healer have helped us with the gang of goblins? It seems a person's needs change a lot." Keven was proud of his answer. The old man couldn't possibly argue with it

"Aye, now ye have the way of it." To Gareloch, his answer was satisfying and complete.

"But…"

"A good talk," Gareloch cut him off, "like a good meal can no be rushed. It spoils it. Each thought is a mouthful that must be chewed with time. Do no choke on yer thoughts."

Keven knew the old man was right. He paused for a few moments he hoped were enough.

"So can you teach me more than one thing? I'd like to know how to do a lot of things. If the stories are true, there is a lot of magic." It was a good question, Keven thought. Gareloch certainly knew more than a few tricks.

"Aye, lad. But, which one first? If ye had ta choose, what would it be? That tis the question. What is yer biggest need?"

As if sensing the young man's impending reply, Gareloch cut him off.

"Have care, lad, do no answer me now. Chew yer thought awhile, enjoy yer thoughts. They are the only thing ye truly own. Now, let's break fer the day. These trees are the way of it. Ye tend ta the horses, the water, and the firewood."

The small copse of trees bordered a surprisingly steep hill. It did not take him long to unsaddle the horses and give them a long enough tether to graze. He then had an easy time finding firewood. What he first thought was only a small group of trees revealed itself to be a decently sized woods that filled a small valley with a stream in the bottom of it.

Each of his tasks brought him back to the camp site. Each time he saw Gareloch hobbling around with his stick unpacking different packs.

With a dark thought he quickly squashed, Keven noted how the old man seemed to be crippled only when it was time to set up camp. Keven couldn't even remember seeing the walking stick strapped to Thistle's side.

"Hurry now, lad, fetch the water. I have no mind ta die of hunger. The rations Goodwife Bitte packed are getting harder by the day. We'll need ta boil them ta get them down the gullet."

When Keven came back to camp with the last of the pots filled with water, he saw the old man in a familiar position. He had his pipe in his mouth and was sitting near a ring of stones that surrounded a small stack of the firewood Keven had found. The bedrolls were laid out.

"Come now, lad. Ye can no expect me ta do all the work. Ye need ta light the fire. Tis the way of it."

Keven caught the old man's meaning instantly. Part of him cautioned himself that he should look for sleight of hand. Those thoughts were quickly buried under a flood of excitement. He sat down on his bed roll and prepared himself.

"Ye know the way of it. Take the flint in yer hand. Put yer thoughts on the tinder. Now, listen ta my words and say them as ye hear them. Mind yer breathing."

What had happened the night before came back to him as easily as moving his arms. He slowed his breathing and was careful to inhale through his nose and exhale through his mouth. Gareloch's words were simpler this time. There was a connection between the words he repeated and the feel of the air as it left his body.

After an unspecified amount of time, the words, his breathing, and his thoughts came together as one. The focal point of the triad was the dry tinder underneath the larger pieces of wood. Even with his eyes closed, he knew the spark was there before he could smell the faint aroma of burning tinder.

He continued with the breathing and the mantra. The fire had a life of its own, but he continued for the sheer pleasure of it. The merging of his thoughts was a mix of the feel of a warm sunray, the taste of an apple sweet, and safety of a quiet place to sleep.

"Tis quite enough, lad. Tis good ta do the task and be done with it."

Keven handed him the piece of flint.

"No, lad. Ye keep it. Save it fer next time."

With the distraction and the fact the old man was not providing the words for Keven to repeat, his thoughts unraveled. Feeling the disappointment at seeing it dissolve reminded him of saying goodbye to Erin.

That thought crept upon him like sweet melancholy. He still missed her even after all the time that had passed. He could almost feel her embrace. Her smile, her laugh were right there for him.

"Let yerself take some sleep. I'll wake ye when the stew is ready. 'Twill be awhile."

As sleep came upon him, he searched for Erin among his dreams.

Joseph Swope

Mateusz Poblocki

Chapter 8

The steel caravan ground to a halt. The long journey had had its effect on even dwarven crafted wagons. Some of the axles squeaked and a few of the armor plates were loose. Still, it made an impressive sight. The young guard on duty at the southern gate of Atani City did not know how to approach the many dwarven armored wagons in front of him, so he remained at his post and waited for them to approach. He did know this was an opportunity to make himself known. Unusual circumstances were what made reputations, even heroes.

With surprising agility, one of the bandy-legged riders swung down from the driver's seat. His stocky legs did not give on impact with the ground. He hit the ground like a stone.

With efficient gestures and a few guttural words that sounded more like grunts, the dwarf who jumped down had set his escorts to action. It became clear to the ever increasing crowd that some of the dwarves were forming a group that planned to enter the city. Many of the other dwarves climbed on top of the wagons with crossbows. All of the spectators, even those who had no real knowledge of weapons, knew what a dwarven crossbow could do.

The small band of five dwarves began their walk to the gate. Few people in Atani had seen a dwarf. Rarely did they come out of their craggy homeland. To the people who looked on, it was a grand sight to see five stout dwarves purposely striding toward the city. For the young guard who was in charge of watching for unusual activity, this spectacle certainly qualified.

"Halt." He sounded official. At least, he thought he did.

Though at least a few of the dwarves spoke the human tongue, they ignored the guard and kept walking toward the gate.

The young guard knew he had a duty. He had been recently promoted and hoped to meet the Regent one day. That was, after all, the reason he had left his father's shop. With determination and a twinge of nervousness, he put himself in front of the dwarf who was obviously in charge.

"What business do you have in our city?"

For an answer, the lead dwarf grabbed the guard's throat more quickly than anyone would have thought possible for such a stocky form. The soldier at first was embarrassed by how easily he was taken off guard. After only a second, he realized the dwarf had an iron grip on his throat. The soldier could not speak for the dwarf's thumb pressing painfully on his Adam's apple.

The soldier grabbed at the arm of his attacker. It was granite. Though no one actually believed dwarves were carved from stone, the soldier certainly understood how such tales got started. He flailed wildly as panic set in.

"Boy, if I let you go will you stop bothering us?" the dwarf said gruffly from somewhere deep in his beard.

The soldier nodded furiously. It was all he could do. The dwarf's grip released, and the young soldier fell backwards onto his rear.

"See lads, it's like I told you. Humans are so scared of pain they'll give like a weak tunnel. This one was given a duty. At the first little pinch, he begs for me to treat him like a babe. Ha!" With that, the burly dwarves mocked the man on the ground and stepped over him.

* * *

Acting Wizard Master Lucius toured the palace. Though he disliked having to do it, he made himself find positives in it. Without the burdensome responsibilities, he would never voluntarily walk the halls. Long ago, he would have thought the exercise would do him some good. He had since learned that not even the strictest of regimes would overcome his need to eat. Such was the price of being a Wizard of Magic.

For Lucius, touring the castle often was a reason to have another meal. Walking and devouring a leg of lamb was nothing new to him. The gray stone walls that surrounded him as he walked were made from huge blocks set in place ages ago. Attached to the walls were several sconces that held smokeless torches. His tour of the seemingly endless wings of the palace brought him to a classroom with an open door.

For someone of his bulk, being unobtrusive was difficult. Still, the students of sorcery did not notice him due to the intensity of their concentration.

The room was a large square, fifteen paces to a side. It was filled with wooden benches upon which were perched some thirty students. The benches were more suitable for a tavern than for students practicing the complicated, yet powerful, art of sorcery.

The students' gazes were firmly planted on the wads of paper that were set on each of the ancient and scarred tabletops. The wizard in charge of the lesson was a man Lucius did not know by name.

After a nod of acknowledgment, the instructor returned his attention to the class. To any uneducated observer, the lesson seemed like an exercise in being still. Nothing moved in the classroom, not even the students.

Lucius knew what the exercise was, though since sorcery was such a mystery to him, he probably knew less than the students of how to complete it. Each student was to move the wad of paper in front of him. Though he had seen it hundreds of times, Lucius still could not fathom how a person could simply move something without a formulated spell.

Magic was easy to understand. It was natural. It, like gravity or heat, was a part of the natural flow of energy. He remembered the idea of magic words being taught to him as similar to an echo. Some words, when said at a certain time, in a certain way accelerated natural energy.

Sorcery was different. He had heard the premise of it many times. As many Wizards of Sorcery had tried to explain to him; thoughts come from the mind and are of the mind. Yet, they are not trapped in the mind. Just as a person can direct his thoughts to lift his finger, they can direct their thoughts to act outside of the body.

With a perfect coincidence in regards to his last thought, one of the crumpled balls of paper suddenly moved. It was only a few inches, but it drew every eye in the room, especially those of the young man who moved it. The young man was hardly more than a boy, nineteen at most. His surprised expression betrayed his youth.

"What have we been practicing?" the instructor said in a tone that all teachers used. Though it was phrased as a question, it was delivered as a rebuke. "Will and mechanism. You cannot let yourself be distracted, even by success." With the last words, he glared at the young man who moved the paper. "It is hard to work without nerves or muscles. Until now, you have learned that your body is you. You are so much more than your body. Heat, light, your thoughts, all energy must travel somewhere. The questions you must answer yourself are from where do thoughts come and to where do they go?"

The instructor paused, giving his students time to think. "We do not have spells or even machines. With either of those mechanisms, affecting the paper would be easy. Wizard Master Lucius would you be so kind?"

His request caught Lucius a little off guard. Suddenly, many sets of eyes were on his considerable bulk. He took his hands from their folded position inside his sleeves. With a wave of his hand and a few whispered words, every ball of paper in the room suddenly burst into flame. The paper burned for only a moment. After a required dramatic pause, Lucius waved his hand again. The piles of ash instantly returned to the balls of paper they had been only moments before. While the class spontaneously broke out in applause, Lucius absently wondered whether the magic of his spell returned the smoke to the paper or used particles of paper elsewhere to recreate the balls.

"We have no spells." The instructor continued. "There is only mechanism and will. The greater the one, the less is required of the other. You cannot form solid thoughts outside of yourself - yet. Right now, your mechanism is weak. As your ability gets stronger, you will not need so much willpower to do such a simple task. Now then, back to your exercises."

With that, all of the students refocused themselves on their balls of paper. With a nod to the instructor, Lucius slipped out of the arched doorway and back into the musty halls. Like so many who had come before them, the youths in the classroom were simply not equipped to make decisions that involved wizardry. They were working as hard as they could, running down a road to an imagined goal of power. It was a shame they would never really be able to use their hard won power in the way they imagined. They would not return to their village to show off their new abilities.

Those who never made wizard status yet possessed considerable power were occasionally a topic of discussion and debate. These 'failures' could not return to their previous life where they would surely become lords; they were in the custody of the palace. A half-trained wizard loose in the countryside could never be permitted.

Ancient spells woven into the palace itself kept those who failed the test occupied with mundane endless tasks. Lucius as well as countless other wizards had, over the years, investigated those who worked tirelessly at tasks that would never be completed. Rarely though, was there an instance where Lucius could gain complete information.

Lucius recalled a particularly troubling conversation with a failed wizard on one of the palace's parapets. The eternally young man stood there day after day recording the number of clouds on a slate that was wiped clean with each rising sun. The determined man either could not or would not spare more than a moment for conversation lest he miss a cloud and throw off his tally.

The dreariness of the hallways weighed upon Lucius almost as much as thoughts of those bound to such a fate. With arching doorways and few windows, the Wizards' Palace seemed to dampen all but the cheeriest of spirits.

As big as the palace was, it was clean. The adepts of sorcery were tasked to use their thoughts to move air. The minor hallway gusts pushed dust and other things into any one of a number of chutes the Wizards of Technology had installed.

The more he walked, the more the corridors felt like a prison. He desperately wanted out. What made him angrier than being imprisoned was that those few who had found a way around the oaths did not share their knowledge. In fact, only one such wizard had ever returned to the palace. That wizard was the true Wizard Master. He dropped in and left as he pleased.

Other wizards resented his power or more specifically his arrogant disregard for his power. He was both a Wizard of Sorcery and a Wizard of Magic. How he honestly believed that there was knowledge to be gained outside of the palace Lucius did not know. Lucius did know every time the Wizard Master left on some whim, Lucius was stuck with the responsibility of keeping the Wizards' Palace from being harmed by its own residents.

* * *

Keven awoke to the prodding of Gareloch's walking stick.

"Is the stew ready? How long have I slept?"

With a chuckle Gareloch answered, "Look at the sun, lad. Tis well inta the morn."

"I thought you were going to wake me for supper?" Keven put his arm over his eyes as a shield from the intrusion of the morning sun.

"Aye, lad, I woke ye. Ye did eat almost a pot full. Ye were asleep while ye ate. That was the way of it. Hah, ye had yerself quite a conversation while ye slept. Twas good there were no goblins about. They would have heard and had a laugh at ye."

Keven had heard of guests who, while staying in the inn, would walk the floors as they slept. He was not sure if the stories were true, but he believed Gareloch. He was learning there was much he did not know, even about himself.

"Roust yerself now. We can no move too far with ye on the ground like ye are. I've reheated what ye left of the stew. I expect yer hungry. The Lady Thistle and yer steed are saddled and ready ta go. We're all waiting on ye."

To Keven, it felt like getting out of his bedroll was more effort than unloading ten wagons for Master Banolf. He would not have thought doing the little magic he did would have been so tiring. That thought made him giddy. He was doing magic! His mother, the Goodfolk, and every adult he had ever encounterd as a child had gone out of their way to ensure that he did not believe any of the tales of visiting storytellers. A flash of memory of Banolf destroying his beloved Magic Stick showed itself in Keven's mind. Keven immediately released any resentment towards those who had taught him to disbelieve. He seemed so far away from them now; their petty need to take from him did not matter.

The thought that he was doing magic more than any other gave him reason to get out of his bedroll. Tonight, he thought, he would do it again.

The day's ride was like all of the others they had had. There was little to distract Keven from the many questions that were about to burst from his head.

"Master Gareloch, am I really doing the magic well? Really better than anyone else? And why do I get so tired?"

"Questions, lad, slow tis the way of them. As fer the magic, what do ye want ta hear? If I told ye that ye had the way of it, would ye want ta learn any less? If I told ye that ye do no have it, would ye want it any less? No, lad, tis no a question worth asking."

Keven realized Gareloch was right. He asked a question without trying to think of the answer himself. He was a little embarrassed to realize he was seeking praise.

"Why do I get so tired after I do magic? It feels like we only do it for a few minutes. I've worked much harder than that and not been as tired."

"I know a little of yer life with the innkeeper. Ye did more than a wee bit of work. Aye, working with good thoughts is tougher by ten than plowing the biggest field."

In a flash of inspiration, Keven had a thought. "Is that how you get what you need, by using different thoughts? A thought for each need." He was beginning to understand that thoughts were not simply something that happened to him. They were mechanisms to get what he needed.

"Aye, lad, yer finding the way of it. Ye still have a long journey, but tis a good step."

"Please then, teach me what you know. Please teach me how to have power. If you know a little of my life, you know I have nothing and probably will have nothing. You took me away from that. You and your teaching are all that I have."

Keven was surprised at the emotion in his voice. He realized he spoke the truth. A deeper truth than he had realized before. He needed the old man.

Just as Keven finished his surprisingly passionate plea, a large buzzing pest flew straight into his left ear. Keven immediately flinched and slapped his hands to his ear, swatting the thing. The brief feeling of its legs and wings in his ear continued to give him gooseflesh. His ear still stung from the effects of his clumsy slap.

"Nasty buggers, arrowflies. One tis bad enough, tis luck it did no bite ye. A whole swarm can kill a man. Luck indeed. Ye'd be itching fer days." Gareloch puffed on his pipe and rode for awhile in silence. Keven knew the old man had heard his questions. He also knew that rushing the old man would do no good.

"Lad, ye ask a lot. I've told ye slow tis the way of questions. Ye do no even know which one ye want answered first. Two different things ye did ask of me. Be careful of wanting what tis in another man's head. Mine, like others, is no filled with flowers and sweet scents. Aye, there is more.

Once ye learn something, can no be unlearned. If I gave ye a reason to doubt yerself, could ye ever forget it?"

Keven squeezed the reigns in frustration. He felt like he had opened his heart to Gareloch and the old man was ignoring him, making him wait.

"But fer me teaching ye how ta do things, tis a good question. There are several ways ta filling yer need in the lands.

"The way of the will that most folks know is physical force. If they wanted ta clear a field of stones, they would simply use their muscles ta move them. Tis the way of yer town. Tis the way of the big lad in yer town. He had his way with ye because he had the way of physical force. His mechanism was better than yers. His will prevailed.

"With that, is getting others ta fill yer needs. A feeble, old lord can rule a mighty army. He uses others' muscle to fill his need ta rule. He uses different sets of muscles ta keep his army obeying him. Threats, lad, have the way of force even though they do no always come ta blows.

"A better way, some think is ta barter. There are some who have others fill their need by filling the needs of others."

Keven forced his face to remain neutral, lest the old man think he did not understand something.

"Think on the fat innkeeper. He needed the stables clean. Ye needed food and a place ta sleep. Ye needed food and a bed more than he needed clean stables. He had the way of it with you. Tis the same with a woman and a man. One has more need than the other."

To Keven, Gareloch's words were dancing around his question. He was impatient to get to what he wanted.

"Yes, but what about magic?"

"Lad, if ye only knew the question you asked," he said shaking his head as he puffed on his pipe.

Gareloch, it seemed to Keven, had the ability to say a sentence that sounded very wise, but did not give answers.

"Magic, lad, as ye think of it, is actually many things. Tell me, what is a wizard, a witch, or even sorcery?"

"Well everyone's heard or read all the stories. A witch is someone who could not get a man so she turns to the Dark One and bespells her man. And a wizard, I guess no one really knows what a wizard is."

"Lad, ye've said something that tis false, but has the way of truth. I do no say there are witches. But, if ye ever do meet one, lad, I'd guard yer tongue. As fer wizards, ye have the right of it. Few know the truth."

Keven did not want to let on how eager he was to hear of wizards. He had heard many stories and spent many nights dreaming of his favorite book, The Magic Stick.

Caelv dutifully followed Thistle, who seemed to be the one deciding the path. A long ignored question came to the surface of Keven's mind.

Where were they going? He had been with Gareloch a while. He was indebted to the old man and was eager to learn more of magic. Still, he found it a little unsettling that he had no idea where they were going. Keven, however, knew better than to ask a new question.

"Ye have danced around the same question enough ta tire the most stubborn mule. Keven, ye still have no answered me. Why do ye want more power when ye already have so much? What do ye hope fer?"

The use of his name startled Keven. He had not heard Gareloch call him by his name--he was always just 'lad'. Keven noticed the old man staring directly at him. It was Gareloch's blue eyes and piercing stare that let Keven know this question was a test.

"What do you mean, so much? I have nothing, I'm a bastard who couldn't swing a sword if someone gave one to me. I don't even have a last name. I have to use my ma's."

Suddenly, Keven felt a sharp pain in the back of his neck. He slapped his hand on it quickly. He was unnerved by the still buzzing arrowfly that was crushed beneath his hand. Where did the damn things come from and why had he not heard its tell-tale buzzing? Keven swore to himself.

"'Tis no blessing to be so ignorant. Lad, ye have power, and ye have magic. When ye want ta walk, do ye know the how or the why of yer legs working?"

"But that's not magic."

"Tell me, lad, ta an old women who can no move her legs, is walking no magic? She has the will ta move, but no the mechanism. Magic is just another mechanism. Ta ye, the lad in yer village had power ta best ye everyday. To some, a master archer has magic in his bow. No, lad, think harder. What power do ye have and what do ye need?"

Keven thought as quickly as he could. He kept his eyes on Gareloch to keep the old man engaged in the conversation.

"Power is being able to not have things hurt you." Keven guessed. "I don't want to be hurt." Keven hoped Gareloch would find the answer acceptable.

"By what things, lad?"

"Well," Keven stammered, "if this horse started to buck and throw me, I wouldn't want to fall."

"If the horse was running ta a cliff, would ye want ta get thrown?"

"Well sure..." Keven was determined not to get confused. "Sometimes I would want to get thrown, sometimes I wouldn't. I'd just like to be able to control what happens to me."

That was it, Keven realized. He wanted control. That was what he'd been waiting to say to Gareloch and to himself.

"Aye, lad, ye have the way of it now. But, yer saying ye want ta have control over what happens ta ye by controlling things around ye. Does it no sound a wee bit daft ta think like that?"

"No, it's just like everything else. If something could harm me, I want to have control over that thing." The more Keven spoke his ideas aloud, the more he liked them.

"Lad, yer standing on the river bank fearing cold water. Yer thinking of ways to warm the water. Why no just walk away? Do ye change the river or change yer need ta swim?"

Something clicked. Of all the conversations Gareloch and he had shared, this one felt right to him. It was as if a hidden window suddenly appeared to him.

Keven was so lost in his thoughts that he did not realize they were entering a town until the horses were walking into the village square. He looked around and saw that it was more neglected than Village Donnell. The day had followed the sun behind the horizon, and the town was quiet for a summer evening.

Gareloch or Thistle, Keven was not sure which, led them to the town's inn. It was the same size as Banolf's inn, but it was certainly not as well kept. Keven realized it would be the first time he had ever been in an inn that was not Banolf's. The thought of possibly sleeping inside an inn was exciting. He dared not hope that Gareloch had enough coin for a room or even a bed.

There was no stable hand so they took care of their own mounts. Keven did the actual tasks with the horses. Gareloch simply slid out of his saddle and limped with his walking stick. Keven made short work of unsaddling the horses and filling the stall's bin with enough hay. There was a barrel with a bucket from which Keven could fill the trough for Caelv and Thistle.

After the horses were put up for the night, Gareloch led Keven to the front of the inn. The dull sound of conversations filled the room.

Despite the summer evening, the fireplace had a healthy fire in it. There was an iron spit that hung over the fire and was embedded in the stone. Both Keven and Gareloch were delighted to see a roast and a pot hung on the spit.

Immediately the innkeeper approached them.

"Welcome, travelers. It is an off night. We have roast lamb and spiced potatoes. I just opened a keg of ale this morn. Do you have the coin to pay?"

"Aye. We have the coin ta pay fer a meal and a room. A copper now and two in the morn. I'll be buying rations fer the road from ye, if ye have 'em ta sell." With that, Gareloch took out a purse from his many pocketed cloak. The purse jingled suggestively as Gareloch fished out a coin. The innkeeper took it and was gone in a flash.

While they were eating, Keven could not help but hear parts of the conversations that surrounded him.

"Atanian raiders are taking more people than slavers..."

"We need more rain. If only the king..."

"You won't see me volunteer. Our Westland king and nobles can't seem to stop fighting each other. How are they going to stand against Donius?"

"Talk like that will get your head on a block..."

Keven tried to follow the words. However, the rich food and the cool ale reminded him of how tired he was. He wished they would need a fire in their room. He wanted the feeling of magic again.

"Master Gareloch, can we practice tonight in the room?" Keven hoped it did not sound too eager.

"Lad," he lowered his voice. "No one here wants ta hear ye recite old stories. Ye speak too much already."

Keven was at first confused by the old man's answer. He was about to ask further, but the stare that came across the table was enough to drive the point home. Keven said no more.

After dinner, Gareloch put away his pipe. It was the first time Keven saw the old man empty it and tamp it out. He made sure it was cool before putting it in his cloak. He struggled to get out of his chair and limp across the warm, smoke filled great room. Going up the steps to the room was tough for Gareloch. Keven wondered why he did not use his walking stick.

When he followed Gareloch into the room, he saw with astonishment that there were beds in the room. Real, off the floor, wooden framed beds. With mattresses! That pushed the disapointment of not being able to practice lighting a fire out of his head.

* * *

"But M'lady! Surely you do not think to visit those savages." The shock and indignation on the steward's face were plain.

"Dear Vini, you are the most attentive of all of my advisors. I trust your instincts. But, in this, I think it is wise to meet our *guests* on their terms." She rolled her eyes as she uttered the word guests. She knew her steward would appreciate sharing a joke with his beloved Regent.

She looked every bit the queen. Though she still only had the title of Regent, an ever-growing number of citizens regarded her as the true ruler of Atani. Her plan was coming along nicely.

"You must see that the dwarves need to feel their journey was important. Most shopkeepers and horse traders would disagree with me, but I think if we make them feel wanted and needed, they will lower their prices."

"But they are dwarves and are taught to haggle from the time they pull their first wagon. They respect only strength. If you go to them now, they will see you as too eager."

Lilandra knew that he truly did care for her safety and for the good of Atani. By being a Mistress of Need, she knew what he most hoped his words would ensure was her recognition of him as an important advisor.

"It is true they are not citizens, but they too can benefit from the Dream we all share. They have traveled far. Their supplies must be low. Making them wait does not show our commitment to our higher ideals. They deserve our respect."

"Regent Lilandra, truly you have a gift. You see the good in all things." He said the last with nothing less than awe in his voice.

Every noble's eye tracked her graceful exit from the great room. She headed toward Helena's rooms. She knew that the only thing that traveled a castle's halls faster than rats was gossip. The nobles would be quick to ask the servants if they had seen her and where they thought she was going. They needed to know where she was at all times.

Lilandra saw Helena approaching her from the opposite side of one of the great corridors. The princess was followed by a few retainers and lesser nobles. The girl was building her own following of people who needed her.

They greeted each other with dignified warmth. Helena, of course, adored her tutor, and Lilandra was careful to show the proper type of affection for her student. Indeed, were it not for the young woman's deep adoration, Lilandra's plans would not have progressed so nicely.

"My dear Princess, I wonder if we could have a moment to ourselves. I'd like to show you something, if it pleases you." Lilandra made sure to make her statement sound as much like a request for permission as she could. If others saw the much sought after Regent begging for the princess' time, the princess' image and worth would grow. That in turn would only serve to further Lilandra's plans.

"That would please me. I do have some time now," the princess responded regally.

The two women meandered through the castle, remarking lightly that it was a dreadful place. Helena would occasionally comment on how the walls and design of the castle separated its inhabitants from the rest of the citizens. Lilandra encouraged her student to wax poetic.

It didn't take them long to exit the castle and begin to stroll some of the streets of Atani. Everywhere they went, merchants, laborers, and other citizens stopped what they were doing and gazed in admiration, but they did not disturb the regal duo. It would not do for anyone in Atani to openly treat another as better than himself; all were equal in Atani. That was why the Regent and the princess walked so freely.

There were other, more subtle ways the citizens of Atani expressed their love and appreciation for the Regent. Many of the shirts, blouses, and even banners that hung from the second story windows were bright orange. It was the same color as the gown the Regent had last worn in public.

"The citizens do seem to be enjoying your latest color selection," Princess Helena said with approval.

"Yes, it does seem to brighten things. The streets are cheerful. The people's faces are full of contentment." Lilandra spoke with only a hint of patronage. "Maybe you have learned enough to understand some things. These walks I take, wearing different colors are important. If they run out and buy colors they last saw me in, it is an indication of how much they are with us. From that, I can gauge how much the citizens are paying attention to the Dream."

She paused to let the message sink into the younger woman's mind. This was a critical juncture. Lilandra was not totally sure how the young, idealistic woman would react to such a tactic. Her youthful purity might recoil at the necessity of such manipulations.

Lilandra continued. "The most important thing is that they can buy the right colors. There is no point in showing them fine clothes and lofty ideas if they cannot reach them. We must teach them success one small step at a time."

Helena's face was blank as she pondered Lilandra's words.

"You are someone to be aware of. The people see it, too. Soon, it will be the colors of *your* gown they strive to display."

It was but a subtle flicker across the princess' face, enough to tell Lilandra what she needed to know.

"Now, about your father: how are things between you two?" Of course the older woman knew the answer. Getting people to say things aloud, however, was important to getting them to change their thoughts.

"Things are difficult. He is stuck in the past."

"Yes, parents often are. But your screaming matches have become the talk of the castle. And that is no way to earn the respect of those who hear such behavior. Tell me, does the screaming ever work?"

"No, he simply refuses to see what Atani can become. It's like he is fighting it."

"Let me offer you some advice. Men, even fathers, like compliments. They crave them. Compliments, especially on an adversary, work better than insults. Insults threaten people. When insulted, people close themselves off. Compliments open people up. Try it with your father."

"There is nothing to compliment him on!"

"Think Helena, when he yells, do you listen?"

"Why should I? He's wrong. He doesn't see the Dream."

"Isn't it the same when the situation is reversed? Do you think he listens to you when you shriek like a young girl?"

"Well... he is just so stubborn. He denies that his own citizens deserve to be happy."

"Yes, I know that. But if he does not listen, you continue to holler and scream. Why?"

"You mean I should just give up?"

"No, never give up the Dream. It is more important than any one person. But you can break a good switch over a mule's head, and it still won't move. The smallest carrot, however, will have him following you for days."

After a pause, Lilandra suggested, "You need to find the carrot that he will follow."

* * *

Waking in a bed was something Keven had never experienced, but he instantly knew it was something he wanted to repeat.

"Up, lad, an early morn is the way of it. We'll make no miles with you lounging like a lord in bed." With that, the old man left the room to find the innkeeper.

Keven swung his feet over the frame and then began washing the slept-in, road dust and his own sweat off him as best he could. Keven was once again thankful that Gareloch had bought some extra clothes for him from Mistress Bitte.

It didn't take him long to find Gareloch and the innkeeper as they finished haggling over the cost of the lodgings.

Gareloch gestured to Keven to pick up two sacks that were bulging with supplies and rations. With Keven in tow, the old man hobbled to the stables. Caelv was his usual well-behaved self. He greeted Keven with a cheerful flick of his tail. Thistle, on the other hand, was quite surly and attempted to bite Gareloch.

The old man moved surprisingly quick as he chuckled in response to the foul-tempered attack.

"Ah me, Lady Thistle, I wish I knew the answer ta yer riddle, but I do no have hope for it."

After putting the saddle and recently purchased sacks on Caelv, Keven went to assist Gareloch with his grumpy steed. It didn't take long before his soft words and gentle scratching had the mare ready to be saddled and mounted.

"Tis quite a skill ye have with animals, lad. A good future ye could have working in a stable. I have seen but a wee few animals trust like they trust ye."

Keven was bothered by Gareloch's comment. Was the implied suggestion a seed of future rejection? Was Gareloch tiring of his company? The comment so unsettled Keven, he swung himself up on Caelv and cantered off.

For the first hour, Keven led the way down the road. He did not know the way, but Gareloch did not try to pull ahead. Keven was still piqued at the comment Gareloch had made in the stable. His feeling of frustration intensified when he realized he did not know where he was leading his little party.

He looked back at the old man and found him quite contentedly munching on a sausage. The old man's eyes held the promised answers, and they tempted Keven more than the breakfast the old man was enjoying. Keven swung his eyes to the road in front of him. He knew this was a test, but once again, he did not know the rules. His frustration won out, and he called back to Gareloch.

"Are we going the right way?" For pride's sake he kept the frustration out of his voice.

"I'll trade ye answers. Ride with me and I answer ye and ask one of ye."

Keven had only ridden Caelv for a short time, but he had been using the reins less and less. Caelv responded well to Keven's knees. With barely a signal between them, Keven and Caelv waited for Gareloch and Thistle to catch up to them.

As Gareloch caught up, he reached into his voluminous robes and pulled out a small package wrapped in a clean kerchief and handed it to his younger companion. When Keven opened it, he was pleased to see two plump sausages.

He had tasted better, but he was hungry, and the two sausages disappeared in a matter of minutes. The spices were just strong enough to require Keven to reach for his water skin. He wiped what was left of the sausage off his lips and tucked the kerchief in one of Caelv's saddle bags.

"Sir," Keven began. "Where are we going?"

"'Twas no yer question, lad. I said I'd trade answers with the question ye asked. Tis no right ta change the question after the bargain has been struck."

Keven knew the old man was having sport with him. "Are we going the right way?" Keven exhaled in exasperation.

"Yes. Now fer the answer ye owe me. Why did ye wait nearly an hour before ye turned back ta start yer questions?"

Keven had not been expecting that question. As soon as it registered in his mind, embarrassment crept into his cheeks. He had ridden off from the stable and sulked for an hour. He had acted like a child hoping Gareloch would ride up and apologize.

"I want more than to work as a stable hand. I know there is no shame in it. But, I want more."

"Tis as honest an answer as ye could give. Why then did ye ride off like a child? What was yer need? Was it ta stop the sting of me words? Was it ta find the end of this road?"

Keven rode in silence for a moment. He knew the old man did not want an answer.

"Sir, the town we left, the people seemed less happy than the folks of Village Donnell. You had me guard my tongue. What were we guarding?"

"Lad, ye are no the only one whose life had the way of pain. Aye, there are different pains. There are different needs. Need and pain are often the same. Ye can no have one without its brother.

"Yer life had its share of manure at the table. Tis truly the way of it. But ye had hope. Ye had hope that ye would no always be a stable hand. Ye had hope that the fat innkeeper would keep ye fed. The folks of the town we just left, they are good folks. They were born with needs like the rest of us. But, their lord, and his lord, and King Festinger of the Westlands add ta the need, tis ever the way of it."

"Why did you tell me to guard my tongue? We don't have anything to do with their needs or their lord."

"Tis simple, really. The coins I have in me pouch are no in their pouch. The nobles take coins from the towns. We show up with coins. Did our coins come from their work? That is their question though they do no know it."

"Didn't you tell stories for your coins? You did not steal them from the folks in that town. You earned them."

"Lad, I'll no debate the right of it. Some bend the truth ta fit their needs. The truth is the taxes the lord collects. He says tis ta help the people. Ta me mind, the people would no need his help if it weren't fer his taxes. Lad, work can fill need. Work can even fill hope, but no if the work is stolen by taxes."

Keven thought on Gareloch's words. He had never had to think of taxes, though he had heard Banolf curse them enough. Keven rarely saw a coin that was not someone else's. The few times he earned a coin from the fat innkeeper, he realized how hard it was to gain and how easy it was to lose.

"But sir, that is not the only reason you bid me quiet. It was when I asked if we could practice magic." Keven was happy he was bringing the conversation to magic.

"For most, magic tis a thing ta be feared. Mind ye, I did no say tis the right of it. I only say what tis. Imagine a dwarven crossbow. If yer lord or his knights found one in yer village, there would be trouble. By keeping others weak, the few hold onto their power. Aye, the Westlands are only free fer the nobles. Tis the truth of it. Perhaps one day the people will see the injustice of it. But, there is precious little hope of that. Tis the same with magic. If ye learned enough, would ye still fear a man with a sword? Could ye no melt his armor or break his sword?"

Keven did not respond. He hoped his silence would be taken by the old man as a cue to continue.

"People want what can meet their need. Magic can fill some. Coins can fill some. Hope fills most. If ye have enough of one, ye do no need the others. If ye can cast a spell ta guard yer home, ye have no need of the lord's knights. If ye have enough faith in the Universal Church and The Book of The Word, ye do no need coin or magic.

"Coin and faith are the way of people's belief now. Magic is no trusted. The lords and priests know the way of rumors. The people are eager ta believe the words of those who can fill their need. If people can no fill their own need, they must turn ta those who can, the priests and lords."

"I can understand why people use coin to fill their need. Why The Book of the Word or The Creator?" Though it was phrased as a question, Keven wanted no answer. His mind was set. "I have prayed many times when I was young. Not one prayer has been answered."

"Sixteen summers have ye. Tis far too young ta give up on The Creator. The Church is made of men. Are all of the priests in Sanctiloci bad? Keep praying, lad. He hears ye. Who else knows yer need better?"

"But, I didn't even know magic is real. I think most people would want to know."

"Aye, some would want ta know if they heard the truth of it. But, lad, rumor tis the way of it now. Tell me, is a witch still a hag who tricks a man ta her bed? What did ye believe before yer mind saw the truth of magic?"

Keven was embarrassed at his own ignorance. That thought brought his mind back to something Gareloch said before.

"Can you tell me about the Palace of Wizards?"

"Tis possible ta tell ye some. Mind ye, until yer taken as a student in the palace, yer no ta admit ye know what I tell ye. Tis no guarantee that they'll take ye on. I can only bring ye ta the gates. I know a few tricks, but no like the wizards in the palace. Indeed, the Wizard Master is funny about those who have no been invited inta learning their secrets. He is no ta be trifled with, that one."

"The Wizard Master? Does he know a lot of magic?" The questions slipped out. Keven hated to interrupt Gareloch for fear the old man might suddenly stop such an interesting topic.

"Now, lad, ye can no ask questions faster than I can answer them. Always find the first answer then move ta the next question. Always, lad.

Ta do different, tis sloppy thinking." Gareloch paused to make sure Keven absorbed the admonishment.

"The Wizard Master tis the most powerful of all the wizards at the Palace. Mind ye, they do no all like him, but they admit he is the one ta rule. He has skill enough tis true, but he is no a leader. They do no follow him. The wizards are content ta stay in the palace and increase their power."

"If he is so powerful, can't he force the others to do what is right?"

"If he did, lad, he would break with his oath of the Trinity."

"What oath?"

The old man held up a hand as if to ask Keven for patience. He began to pat himself all over. Once he had his pipe in his mouth, he continued.

"Now, the oaths. When a student is ready ta be a wizard, he must choose his path and the level of oath. The most binding oath is the Trinity. Those who swear the Trinity bind themselves, ta seek ta fill others' needs, ta do no harm, and ta increase their knowledge. There are two other oaths. The Duality binds wizards ta do no harm and ta increase their knowledge. The One Oath merely binds wizards ta increase their knowledge. Every wizard must take at least that oath, ta always look fer more knowledge. They can no escape it."

Keven was doing his best to commit to memory every word Gareloch uttered, while trying not to seem too eager.

"There is more ta choose than the path. Few ever get ta make the choice. The Palace is a hard master ta please. Most who begin as students do no have the power or the need ta suffer ta the wizard level. I can no say more on that."

Gareloch continued to puff. The smoke plume was grabbed by a slight breeze fanning their faces, blown into his white hair and beyond, giving an overall impression that the old man's head was on fire.

"Are you a wizard?"

"Careful with yer questions," Gareloch said in warning.

"I'd like to learn everything about magic, wizardry, and sorcery."

"Ye wish ta learn everything, do ye? Hah. Ye best live ta be older than an elf. Ye do no know what ye are wishing fer. Before a student can take the oaths, he must first know his path. There are many types of power. Magic, sorcery, and technology are the most common. There are some who follow the path of Alchemy. Each path is as different as a dog, a wolf, and a cat."

Keven could not help but feel a wave of disappointment tinged with shame wash over him. Still, he wished he had a tablet, ink, and quill.

"Aye, the greatest achievement is ta be a Master of Need. Some say it can never be mastered, few have hope. We've talked enough from horseback, let's rest the horses and ourselves."

Gareloch steered them off the road to a lone oak tree in a field. It was a beautiful specimen. The two riders stiffly slid off their mounts. They let the horses graze while they found shade against the broad tree trunk.

"You said that need was a type of power, like magic or sorcery. I don't understand."

"What ye have been learning is magic. With the words and the ritual, ye have been lighting a cookfire. Tis a good trick. Sorcery is easier ta get in yer head, but tis harder ta do. Tis like trying ta move water without a bucket. Need, lad, tis the hardest."

Keven felt the piece of flint that was in his pocket. "I still don't understand. What is hard about learning that you have need?"

"Lad, all things that live have need. Oft ta find them ye just have ta look at what they do. This tree, what does it do?"

"Well, not much of anything really. It just sits here." As soon as the words were out of Keven's mouth, he felt a hard flick on the top of his head. He realized he had intercepted a large acorn that was falling towards the ground. He looked at the large seed pod and could not quite believe what just happened.

"Lad, if I'm ta teach ye anything, ye have ta use yer head for more than catching seeds. Does the tree no reach fer the sun above us and the water beneath us? Ye think on that while I close me eyes."

Keven leaned against the trunk as Gareloch promptly began to snore. Despite how much he had learned from the old man, he had more questions now then he had had at the beginning of his journey. Where was the Palace of Wizards? Keven had a rudimentary knowledge of the map of the lands from pictures in the few books he had seen. Were they headed toward it now? How could magic be a secret if there was a huge palace dedicated to it? Would he ever meet the Wizard Master? The thoughts fell on Keven faster than he could record them in his mind.

The day was peaceful with summer heat kept at bay by the shade. The horses were grazing. Envy gripped Keven as he noticed a lone hawk in the sky flying in lazy circles. To fly like that, so free. He wondered if the hawk had needs.

A short time later, he was awakened by Gareloch's snores. With one particularly loud snort, Gareloch woke himself.

"Up, lad, the road does no come ta ye."

As Keven stirred, he noticed the hawk was flying much lower. Gareloch hobbled off to collect the horses grazing a few paces away as Keven lazily made it to his feet. When Keven reached his arms above his head to stretch the last of the nap away, he saw a quick shadow and heard a rustling.

With a suddenness that froze him in place, the hawk landed on Keven's outstretched arm. Keven remained frozen and moved only his eyes. The hawk was magnificent.

Keven saw Gareloch, too. He was standing with the horses, silent and still with an unreadable expression on his face that appeared to be part shock and part caution. Keven was not reassured by that look.

After a few moments, the hawk flapped and moved itself higher to one of the branches in the tree. Keven let his hands down. It was only then that he realized the bloody scratches on his arm. They did not hurt much, but they solidified the shock he felt over the hawk landing on him.

Gareloch rode up to him, leading Caelv by his reins. "Maybe the Wizards' Palace will take ye after all."

Yvo Waldmeier

Chapter 9

Many of the regulars who came to the Vine's Gift were unsettled by the party of new comers that occupied a table in the far corner of the main room. The Vine's Gift was a reputable establishment, though just barely. It was located close to the south gate of the city, and as a rule, the farther one got from the castle, the farther one got from the castle's laws. It appealed to the poorer sort who often drank too much because they had too little. Cheap wine and watered slaver's juice were the drinks of choice. There was dinner to be bought but most would rather spend their money on hiding from their thoughts in a stupor.

The tavern was styled more like something from the west. It did not have the customary Atanian open design. Buildings in Atani were built to take advantage of the normally mild weather; the Vine's Gift was built with stone and mortar. It looked sturdy and felt like it could withstand the coldest of winters. Perhaps it was the architecture that drew the unwelcome party in the corner.

They made an odd sight, five dwarves in a tavern that drew its business from regular neighborhood wine drinkers. Though Atani was known for its vineyards and wines, the dwarves made it clear to Denio, the tavern keeper, that they wanted ale. Lots of it. Before they had walked in, Denio felt confident that his basement full of kegs would last him weeks. With his five newest customers, he was getting nervous that his store of kegs would not last the night.

When they had burst through the old doors of the tavern, Denio started sweating. It was not simply from the intimidating and rowdy air dwarves naturally possessed, nor was it from the saying that drunken dwarves soon changed to brawling dwarves. Rather, it was from their reputation as ferocious hagglers. He assumed when they walked in that the price of ale in his tavern was beyond his control. He was wrong.

He was unimaginably relieved when the leader of the party threw a sack of coins at his chest. The sack was heavy, and the dwarf threw it with quite a bit of force. Still, Denio hardly minded the bruise that would develop later, relieved he'd been paid in advance.

Despite the best effort of the regular patrons to keep their eyes on their glasses, the volume of the dwarves' rowdy conversation made them difficult to ignore. Too often, there was an especially loud outburst from one of the dwarves. The humans could not tell if the outburst was a hardy laugh, a venomous curse, or some dire threat. Whatever it was, it made the humans nervous.

It had been hours since they had come in, and the regulars, the innkeeper, and even the nervous barmaids had had enough time to study them covertly. As many of the stories said, dwarves were shorter than almost all adult humans. They certainly were not smaller. Each one seemed to be a mountain unto himself; their frames were wide enough to make packing into a booth difficult. The rickety wooden benches were barely able to hold their bulk.

Their feet did not reach the tavern's dirty floor, but that did not diminish the respect they commanded. The serving girls saw up close, each of the dwarves' hands was large enough to wrap around even the biggest of ale mugs. They were thick hands, with fingers that looked like fat sausages. The sight of them reminded each human in the Vine's Gift of the fabled strength of dwarves.

Between the five of them, they ate a large roast in a matter of minutes. Tenia and Evia, the two serving girls he employed, could barely keep up with the pace of the dwarves' consumption. The only time they stopped putting meat in their mouths was when they had to wash down half chewed chunks. The forks the girls had brought went unused until the dwarves realized they could have sport with them. The humans in the tavern were made more than a little nervous as each of the five dwarves imbedded the forks, to the base of the tines, into the hard wood table top.

They ate a lot, but in time, their hunger was sated. Their thirst however, knew no limits. Tenia and Evia's trips back and forth were so frequent and numerous, they made a clear trail through the accumulated dirt on the floor between the kitchen and the dwarves' table. Round after round disappeared quickly down their bearded throats. Their thunderous pounding on the table top produced ripples in the wineglasses of the other patrons.

It was good they paid in advance. Neither of the serving girls nor Denio could have kept count of how many mugs were drained. It was said that ale was the only thing that kept the dwarves from ruling all of the lands. From the display before him, the tavern keeper began to understand the words full meaning.

Denio was brought from his thoughts by a squeal from one of his serving girls, Tenia. She was being handled roughly by a table of regulars. They apparently were not happy that she was ignoring them in favor of the dwarves. One of the men was holding both of her wrists. His partner had his hand on her behind. He was grabbing large handfuls of flesh and leering maliciously.

Denio had seen Tenia endure the pinches and playful pats of many drunken customers. She could usually handle herself with a table full of drunks. This was different. He could see the men were hurting her, but before he had to do anything, she kicked the man behind her and twisted out of the other man's grasp. The two men laughed riotously. They were joined in laughter by all of the other drunken humans.

Strangely though, the dwarven table was quiet. They had watched the proceedings with dark expressions on their faces. Since Denio was the only human male in the place who was not drunk, he was the only one to notice. Tenia retreated to the kitchen, and the din of the tavern returned to its normal level. The dwarves turned their attention back to their stories and their mugs.

Denio had not been over to the dwarven table. He admitted to himself, he had not looked for a reason. He was scared of the dwarves and was glad Tenia and Evia were the ones who had to serve them. At first, the girls were frightened of the stocky drinkers whose voices sounded like they came from the deepest caverns.

Denio was surprised to see that, after a while, Tenia and Evia would come away from the dwarves table blushing. Both serving girls had worked for Denio for a while, and they had heard all manner of drunken banter. Denio could not imagine what would make two experienced barmaids blush like little girls. Despite their blushing, the girls seemed to relax around the dwarves.

Once again, he heard one of the girls cry out. This time it was Evia who was draped over the lap of one of the men who had earlier accosted Tenia. The man had help. One drunk at his table held her wrists so that her hands touched the floor. Another man kept her from kicking by positioning his chair over her feet. A string of curses flew from her mouth as the man whose lap over which she was bent began raising her skirt.

"Maybe some quick discipline will teach you how to treat the customers." he slurred from drunken lips.

The man who was preparing to slap her hindquarters often drank watered down slaver's juice, and Denio knew it was only a matter of time before the man's decline would pick up speed. The pull and effects of slaver's juice, even watered down, could not be resisted.

Evia thrashed about. She was a tough girl who was certainly not shy about telling a man what he could and should do with himself. Even she could not free herself from the humiliating position these three men forced her into. Denio wasn't sure if her ordeal would end with a simple thrashing of her bottom.

With her bent over and her skirt pulled up to her back, her underclothes were on display. Her raspy voice did not let up its curses and oaths of revenge. Those, of course, only made the men laugh harder.

Denio was not a big man, nor was he a courageous one. He had stopped plenty of fights as a tavern keeper, but he had learned that sometimes, it was best to let a bad situation go on. There were three of them and one of him. The three drunks also had an audience that would not be happy if they could not see the shameful show that was about to begin. No honest worker deserved to be punished like a child. The men were bullies. If he let it go on, Evia would have a very sore behind and an even more bruised ego. If he attempted to stop it, he could get seriously hurt.

His indecision was rendered irrelevant. The man never laid even one slap on Evia's behind. From across the room, a pewter mug was thrown at Evia's would-be-spanker. The flying mug caught the man completely by surprise, the impact snapping his head backwards. Denio was surprised it did not produce a bloody gash.

Then, Denio saw one of the dwarves slide from the bench and wobble across the bar. "If you're so eager to hit," Denio heard him say, "you're welcome to hit me."

How he had thrown that mug so accurately Denio would never know any more than he would ever know how not a drop spilled from the mug the dwarf carried with him.

Evia was still being held in position.

"Now this seems to be a fight for the weak, three males against one female. Our stories must be true if it takes three human males to best one human female."

The challenge was casual. It was also surprising in that it was issued by one drunk to three drunks.

"Go back to your table, little man," the leader of the humans sneered. "In fact, go back to your land. Take your ugly friends with you."

Denio knew the man had to be thinking with slaver's juice on the brain. The man was no fighter, and the dwarf looked to be carved from stone.

"I'll make a bet, human. I'll give you the time it takes me to finish my mug for you to make me sit down. I will not strike you or attempt to stop you from striking me. To take the bet, you must let the female up."

The dwarf calmly took a sip as the man thought about his words. Denio did not know what it meant when a dwarf did not gulp ale, but he was glad he was not the one on the other side of the challenge.

"What do I win?"

"First, you can continue to beat this female. No other in this place has the strength to stop it."

The dwarf turned to stare at Denio. Denio looked down in shame.

"Second, you'll have the pleasure of making me sit down. Third, my companions will be happy to pay for your drinks."

Denio expected the other dwarves to protest. They did not. They simply stared from beneath bushy eyebrows and watched the developing contest.

"What about them?" The man gestured to the four dwarves who were still sitting at the table.

"They will remain where they are. This is a fair fight, one on one, not three on one. You must let the female up, then stand up, and start fighting. I will simply stand here until I'm done with my mug."

Without any warning, the man unceremoniously pushed Evia off his lap. As soon as her saved bottom hit the floor, she was on her feet again. Her eyes threw daggers as she retreated behind the bar.

The man stood up to face the dwarf. His drunken eyes studied his shorter opponent. He feigned and gestured as if he was going to strike the dwarf. The dwarf did not flinch. He simply brought his mug to his lips and took a small sip.

After the sip the dwarf slowly and almost reverently lowered his mug. Right as he did, the man swung with all of his might. His fist connected with the dwarf's cheek with a meaty thud. As a testament to the force of the blow, the dwarf's head turned violently.

The man swung again, then followed with several more blows. Each was aimed at the dwarf's head and face. After the vicious flurry, the dwarf's lip and nose were bleeding. Still, he simply took another sip.

With a worried glance at his fellows, the man gathered his courage for another volley. Someone handed him a bottle. He swung hard, and the bottle shattered against the dwarf's rock-like head. In only a few moments, blood began to trickle down the side of the dwarf's neck. The only movement of the dwarf was the mechanical action of him bringing the mug to his lips. This time however, he drained the remains in a single gulp.

The man swung again and connected. The dwarf, however, ignored it, took a step, and grabbed the man by his coat. In a smooth motion, the dwarf forced the man downward onto his knees. From that position, the man could not swing his fist effectively, although he tried. In a quick wrestling match of hands and arms, the dwarf managed to grab one of his hands.

The huge dwarf hand enveloped the scrawny human hand. The dwarf began to squeeze. The man thrashed and squirmed. He pounded on the dwarf's chest, but to no avail, pain evident on his face.

"Please, I'm sorry. I was only taking your bet. I don't want to fight you." The man's face was a pleading mask of pain.

"What about the female? Did you mean to cause her harm?" From his tone, the dwarf clearly did not really care what the answer was.

"Ow! I beg of you. Please stop."

"Give me your other hand," the dwarf rumbled.

A quick squeeze by the dwarf made the man wince and quickly bring up his other hand. The dwarf took that one in his other meaty grasp.

"Why did you give me your hand?" the dwarf asked.

"Because you told me to," came the strained reply. The man was clearly in pain.

"So?"

"So, I didn't want you to break my hand."

"But now I have both of yours, and you can do nothing. All because you fear pain. You, taverner, why did you not aid the female in your employ?"

Denio was uncomfortable with the dwarf's attention. As a result, he said nothing.

"Your silence betrays your weakness, your fear of pain. You made a bargain with the female. She serves the customers and obeys you. You pay her and protect her. You broke a bargain."

From his expression and his tone, Denio knew to the dwarf, that was a high crime.

"You! Female human. You have served us well. You upheld your bargain. You have demonstrated strength in serving us when you were scared. Do you want this human to feel pain?"

The man on his knees looked up with fear in his eyes.

Evia was startled by the dwarf addressing her. She was a simple woman with only nineteen summers and hardly any education. She was not particularly gentle, but she did not take joy in others' suffering. The dwarf's question was simply too much for her.

After a period of silence, the dwarf disgustedly cast away the man's hands. "Humans," he spat. "Worse than a twice beaten dog. Letting pain and fear rule their lives."

He staggered back to his table. As he did, Denio saw a few of the humans who had watched the confrontation draw their knives.

There were about twenty drunken men in the tavern, twenty against the five dwarves. After what he had just seen involving dwarven toughness, he knew the outcome of this upcoming fight. As he steered Evia into the kitchen and locked the stout door behind him, he hoped there would be no bodies when it was done. Regent Lilandra really wanted people to stop fighting each other, and he did not want his name attached to any sort of disturbance.

* * *

Keven would do his best to steer each conversation towards magic and the reason Gareloch should teach him more, but Gareloch would subtly steer the conversation back towards the questions of need. Each time the young man thought he had his traveling companion cornered, the old man would counter with an unexpected question that left Keven speechless.

They were in no particular hurry. The warm summer months were bearable. Even Thistle seemed to become more agreeable- at least she was with Keven. They ate surprisingly well; Gareloch had a box with enough spices to make Mistress Bitte jealous.

"Lad, when ye've visited as many places as me, ye learn the way of traveling," he would say frequently.

The midday breaks and the nightly camps were pleasant. Gareloch all but stopped teaching Keven fire lighting, saying Keven had the way of it. The only thing to salve Keven's disappointment was his increasing interest and ability to debate the old man.

It was almost as much fun to try to beat the old man with questions as it was to make the tinder burn with ancient words and breathing, almost. When riding Caelv or just before he fell asleep, Keven often recalled the feeling of freedom and power that accompanied casting the spell. It was as if magic allowed him to touch his own soul.

During this time, Keven knew he was learning. Exchanging thoughts and questions with the old man allowed his thoughts to flow more quickly. He was less and less caught with his tongue hanging out by the old man's verbal sparring.

Keven became flexible, he could adapt to the changing tide of the old man's conversation. Earlier Gareloch had challenged Keven to think of nothing for more than a few moments. Initially, Keven could not do it. After a fair amount of practice atop Caelv, he could hold off intrusive thoughts for longer and longer stretches. It was a feat of which he was very proud.

Keven had become so accustomed to the life of easy traveling and questions that it was more than a shock when he realized he and Gareloch were not alone in the world. One morning, after they had broken their fast and saddled the horses, Gareloch's whole bearing changed.

"Make no noise, lad, and silence those beasts!"

The sharpness of Gareloch's voice made Keven shiver and stopped him in his tracks.

The old man was ten paces ahead of Keven and peering through some brush. He absently held his pipe in his right hand. His left hand was holding aside a branch. After several tense moments, he gestured for Keven to come see through the brush.

Keven crept up to him as silently as he could. The old man winced as each of Keven's foot falls made a noise in the woods floor. Still, Gareloch encouraged Keven to see what was beyond the brush.

When Keven first saw the target of the old man's stare he was unimpressed. Beyond their wooded campsite, beyond the brush that hid them there was a group of riders at least two hundred paces off.

"Damn! Tis bad!"

Gareloch's whisper carried no more noise than a leaf falling to the ground. Keven did not even try to speak. He did not trust himself to be as quiet as the old storyteller. He squeezed the piece of flint in his pocket to keep himself still.

"An Atanian scout party. They are getting bold ta come this far into the Westlands. Tis no right."

Keven and Gareloch stared at the party for a while. Each of their horses was easily a match for Caelv in size. All of the riders had swords, and three out of the four had short bows strapped to their saddles. The fourth one who rode in the middle of the formation had a huge bow strapped across his back. He could not imagine how the hooded figure could use such a bow. Keven had only a little experience with a short hunting bow; even those bows had enough tension to make holding the string steady a chore. He began to think that the two hundred paces separating him from the riders was not enough.

Keven was distracted by the clicking sound of the old man sticking his pipe in his mouth. The old man had never shown such a look of contemplation. Keven desperately wanted to know what Gareloch's thoughts were, but he knew better than to disturb the old storyteller.

What he saw next caused him to gawk. Gareloch took the pipe out of his mouth with his right hand and held it in the air. The gnarled wooden pipe seemed to grow and continued towards the ground like a drop of sticky liquid reaching for the floor. In no more than a few eye blinks, the pipe had become the old man's walking stick. That was why he had never seen the two together!

Keven heard the old man whisper words that he knew he would not remember. Gareloch's voice changed and became hollow. There was no trace of mirth. From the length of them and the intensity with which they exited Gareloch's whispering lips, Keven knew the old man was not simply lighting a fire to boil water.

Although he did not see it, he did begin to hear a distinct whining buzz in the air, but it was louder and lower than he was used to. He knew the sound to be that of an arrowfly. But from the sound, he could tell there was more than one, a lot more.

Keven saw a brown cloud descend on the riders. It was so thick, he could barely see through the swarm. From the buzzing that approached a roar, he knew there were too many to count. The arrowflies were not choosy. Horses and rider were attacked equally.

The spooked horses were not reassured by their flailing riders. As the horses reared, Keven could hear the echoes of curses. It didn't take long for the formation to break.

The riders and bucking horses sped off in different directions. The riders were waving their arms and slapping themselves. Their efforts were worthless. As they rode further away, Keven could see smaller clouds follow each rider.

An eerie silence descended as the thud of the horses hooves faded into a silence that was broken by a chuckle from Gareloch.

"That is the way of that, lad. Arrowflies are usually harmless. A bite does have some sting ta it. A swarm is something even a troll must run from." The smile on his face was one of self-satisfaction. "With luck, they'll ride fer miles. Mayhap they will no come again ta the Westlands so soon. Tis bad business having Atanian raiding parties this far from their land. It only speeds the war."

At seeing the multitude of questions on the young man's face, Gareloch bid him to mount his horse.

"Come, lad, we'll talk as we ride. The questions look ta pop from yer eyes."

* * *

It was hard for many of the common folk not to gape. Of course, they had heard that all citizens were now equal. Treating fellow commoners equally was easy when everyone was poor. But, seeing the Regent and the princess walk the streets was too exciting to resist.

The dirty faces that peered from open windows and crooked doorways were straining to hear anything they could from the two angels. Though they had heard of the Regent's Dream and they desperately wanted it to be true, in their hearts they knew there was a wide gulf between the women walking the street and their sad lives.

The princess and the Regent had been walking for miles, strolling really. The farther they got from the castle, the less the people cheered. Diminished too was the amount of bright orange that was a testament to the love the people felt for their Regent.

"The citizens here are much more subdued," the princess said. She knew her teacher could also see that there was less orange about, but she wanted to hear what her Lilandra had to say about it.

"It is these for whom we must work the hardest. It is tempting to think that these citizens do not care about the changes in Atani. In truth, they are afraid to care. They have been hurt so often by so many things that they dare not hang their hope on a few words from some noble."

It amazed her how Lilandra could quickly see and sum up people's needs. She had a gift for helping people.

149

"Princess, these people who live closest to the city gates have been forgotten for so long. Now, I know that they have indeed made some poor choices, but they are our brothers and sisters. Atani will not reach its full greatness if people like these are left behind."

"How do we help such people? Often they do not seem to want help. Maybe my father was right. Maybe that is how poor people are."

"Helena, all people can and want to reach upwards. All parents have dreams for their children." The Regent let her words sink in as they continued their walk. She knew the destination, but the young princess did not. Helena would be quite surprised when she met her first dwarf.

"Regent Lilandra, what about the coliseum? Too often it is only the nobles and merchants who are able to hear your words. Can we not invite even the lowliest?" The princess' face lit up with hope that her teacher would approve of her idea.

"Truly, you will make a fine ruler someday. You have a way with understanding people." The compliment was given with such skill that Helena almost shivered with pleasure.

"We can invite people on the edges of the city as well as new recruits. They have to feel the goodness that is building in our land." The young princess was almost giddy with excitement.

Few people could resist the lure of a crowd when that crowd decided to feel a certain emotion. Helena prattled on for a bit; spouting ideals had become second nature to her.

"What is being hidden in the coliseum? The whole city is guessing and gossiping. Is it a statue?"

The thought of what lay within was a bucket of cold water on Lilandra's warm feeling of contentment. What the hell was she to do with that damn dragon?

"That, dear child, is my surprise for the people of Atani. Though we can not have games in the stadium, we can have an event for the meanest of our citizens. But, for now, you had better prepare for a test of what I've taught you in negotiations."

With Lilandra's last statement, the princess was distracted from her questioning. The less people thought of the newly constructed warehouse in the middle of the stadium, the better.

"We are headed out of the city gates," the princess declared. "It must be to meet with the dwarven contingent."

Helena was quick and many were threatened by that intelligence. Lilandra was not, because she knew the secret of intelligence. Lilandra knew people rarely acted with their minds. They acted almost exclusively from their emotions. Smarter people were easier to convince because if they wanted to believe, they would make their own reasons.

The elf was a perfect example. After pointing her in the right direction, Lilandra was pleased to see the elf's dedication was growing of its own accord. The speed with which she shed her elven principles and became willing to strike at anyone who threatened the Dream brought a smile to her full lips.

"Yes, we are. They came to our city only days ago. They have come a long way with the first of what could be a lot of needed supplies and weapons."

"Why don't we have them come to the castle and negotiate properly?" The teachings of her father were deeply engrained.

"Why do you think that is, dear?" It was Lilandra's favorite method of teaching, answering a question with a question.

"Security. The dwarves don't know us, so they don't trust us. If they came into the city far enough, they would feel powerless," the princess answered proudly.

"And what of their goods?" Her teacher challenged further.

"They would not want to leave them unguarded. Of course, they want us to come to them."

"So why should we? Why should we give in to what they want?" The teacher continued the lesson.

"Because it is one battle they will think they have already won." Princess Helena beamed with pride. She was constantly searching for ways to impress the Regent. She was sure she just did.

"Excellent! You really have learned. It is no wonder many of the nobles seek your regard. Tell me one last thing, what do dwarves pride themselves on and how do we use that?"

"Strength." The princess said confidently. "We need to have them feel strong. If they feel threatened, they'll fight for their price twice as hard."

"Exactly. That is why it is only you and I, two women, going to meet a caravan full of battle hardened dwarves. Advisors and guards would only complicate the matter. We had to do it today because from the tales of their drunken exploits over these last few days, our taverns and inns can not take them much longer."

Princess Helena had been outside of Atani City many times, but she had never simply walked out of the south gate with only one other woman for protection. She had to stifle a gasp when she saw the small metal village that the dwarves had apparently brought with them.

Upon closer inspection, Helena saw that the buildings were actually large wagons made of metal. There were five wagons whose sides were facing her. From her vantage point she could tell that the wagons made a precise square around a fairly large area. Where the back of one came close to the front of another, metal plates were fastened. The whole thing looked like a small, metal castle keep.

Helena was amazed to see the Regent keep walking towards the strange armored village. There was no hesitation in her tutor's manner. A dwarf who was sitting on the roof of the wagon nearest the opening called to her.

"Ho! State your name and why I should let you pass." The voice was rough. It held no trace of politeness or deference.

"I am the Regent of Atani City. It was I who invited you to sell your wares to our nation. I bring with me the princess of our land. We, of course, cannot force our way into your camp. Would you allow us to enter?"

"Is it just you two? Do you have no guards?" There was surprise in the gruff voice.

"It is just us. If we came for business, we knew you would not harm us. We seek a bargain."

"Perhaps we can trade with you after all. You show strength by coming to our camp without even a knife. That is good. I'll let you pass. Once inside ask for Haft Oreshale."

Helena tried not to gape like a child. Inside the perfect square outlined by wagons, she could see neat piles and rows of equipment and supplies. There was truth to the old saying 'straight as a dwarven line'. There was not a thing out of order.

One of the dwarves was writing on papers tacked to a board as he overlooked some of the piles. Lilandra, upon noticing him, walked directly to him.

"Are you Haft Oreshale?"

"I am. Who are you?" It was a blunt response. It was what the books said Princess Helena should expect from dwarves.

"I am the Regent of this land, Lilandra. I would like to buy some of your wares." Lilandra's last statement went against everything Helena's father had taught her about negotiations. Never, never, tell your adversary what you want. Always take as much time as possible, let them make the mistake.

"Regent Lilandra, welcome!" A broad grin split his mustache and beard. He stuck out his hand. Helena was surprised when she saw her usually elegant teacher jam her hand into the dwarf's. Helena could tell she was gripping it as hard as she could.

"Welcome to you also, Master Oreshale." She filled her voice with a gusto that matched the stocky dwarf. Lilandra looked around the camp and said, "I would not want to lead a group against you and your dwarves. Your wagons look formidable. Bringing such a large caravan so far must have been difficult."

"It was not easy, but it was not difficult." The burly dwarf made a concession to formality. "Would you like to examine our goods?"

"No, I don't think so. I trust dwarven workmanship, and I trust you. We will purchase it all."

The bushy eyebrows rose. "Trust takes strength," he offered.

"And only those who are weak need to cheat," Lilandra responded.

Helena had seen Lilandra talk to countless people in the time she first came as a tutor. She had learned to recognize different gestures, expressions, and intonations. From that, Helena knew that Regent Lilandra had begun to negotiate as soon as she had seen the dwarf in charge. Her body, her speech, even her whole manner worked together to give the dwarf what he needed.

Helena knew from her lessons with Lilandra that people did not want gold. They wanted the feeling that came with having gold. She wondered if dwarves were so different than humans. Watching Lilandra give the dwarf everything but the gold reminded her how lucky Atani was to have someone like Regent Lilandra.

* * *

Kielasanthra Tylansthra was angry and enjoying it. That was rare for Kiel; elves seldom gave in to feeling emotion. Rarer still, was actually showing emotion. She wished she could show it beyond impotent gestures and words. She needed a target for her sword and bow.

She cursed and sputtered oaths that no human had ever heard. Despite the difference in language, her soldiers gave her a wide berth. When someone so beautiful and deadly as Kiel was angry, it was best to stay out of the way. Even her horse pranced in nervous response to her anger.

Her expedition had started well. They covered much ground heading west from Atani. The pace was not important to Kiel. She was just happy to be outside, away from the castle. Her squad's good spirits began to fade as they realized there were not many towns to the west of Atani. Though scouting, not recruiting, was their primary mission, her soldiers, Corporal Tapeni, Corporal Marsali, and Corporal Ginelli were eager to bring people to Atani. It was hard to recruit when they did not come across any people. The area between the Westland and Atani had few settlers.

Kiel's sharp eyes were the first to see them; goblin tracks. After examination, Kiel and her men determined there were ten sets.

Excitement coursed through her, a chance to kill again. The realization that she was impatient to kill was like shedding confining clothes. Her time with the humans had allowed her to find her true self. Fear did not enter into her mind. She and her men were on horseback and each of her squad carried a bow. There was little chance of a gang of goblins surprising and overtaking them. Still, goblin tracks did bring with them a host of nasty possibilities.

Potential problems from goblins and real problems from a swarm of arrowflies pushed her past her limit of elven restraint. There was something aside from anger. She had to admit; there was a little bit of fear in her. Was there magic involved in the attack from the arrowflies? Was it a threat to the Dream? Anger boiled anew as she thought of someone threatening what had given her so much, the Dream.

She could feel the welts growing under her clothes. Most of the time, arrowflies were clumsy pests that would simply bump into a person and then fly off. When they attacked, they were anything but harmless.

The close fitting clothing she usually wore was easier to move and work in. If it gave her troops something to look at, so be it. But despite the closeness of her clothes, the damn arrowflies had wriggled into them. Her sword and bow had been useless.

Each of her troops was stoically ignoring the fire that came with each arrowfly bite.

"Captain Kiel, those bites will fade in a few days," one of her troopers tried to soothe. "Try not to think of them."

"Corporal Marsali," she responded in a clipped, frosty tone. "It is not the discomfort of a few arrowfly bites that bothers me. Arrowflies are a part of nature. They swarm. It is a fact. But not this time of year. It is unnatural. That is what is disturbing."

"Captain, with all respect, they are gone. There is nothing we can do about them or our bites."

"Corporal, once again: Arrowflies swarming this time of year do not have a natural cause. Therefore, there must be an unnatural cause. It is possible that they attacked us by accident, but are you comfortable with that assumption?"

She arched her perfectly formed eyebrows. Corporal Marsali was a good soldier, young and bright, but his seemingly incessant questions he was adding to the burn of her numerous bites.

"But what could cause arrowflies to swarm and attack?" he asked. "Even throwing rocks at a hive will not cause them to attack like they did."

"Exactly, corporal. That is what we should find out. There are many in my homeland with skill enough to do such a thing, but it is doubtful any are here. An arrowfly swarm is a useful weapon for dissuading those who would intrude too deeply into Elvenwood. Someone or something set them on us. I think magic is involved. Magic combined with an unprovoked attack has made our future moments clear; we will shoot at the first sign of those who attacked us. Whoever did this is a threat to the Dream and no better than goblins." Kiel scanned the horizon as she spoke. Her beautiful elven eyes discovered nothing.

"Just as the arrowflies' attack began suddenly, it stopped suddenly. We rode blindly for several hundred paces, then they simply flew away. That, too, is not natural. We are lucky. Just as something caused them to attack, something also stopped them."

Once understanding began to set on the soldiers, they too began scanning the horizon. Kiel did not point out to them that if she couldn't see anything, they would not either. Each moment she spent with them would affect their future moments. If she casually pointed out their shortcomings, they would stop trying. That would cause her regret for the rest of her moments. These three humans of her squad were good. They believed with their heart in the Dream. She had to protect that. Atani had adopted her. Regent Lilandra had given her far more than her clan ever had. Kiel would willingly die to repay that.

* * *

"Who were those riders? They looked armed and tough." Keven knew better than to downplay his fear. Gareloch seemed to know what the young man was thinking before it came out of his mouth.

"Aye, armed they were and tough as dwarven leather. Lad, I do no expect ye ta know much of the world being raised in a barn. I'm just a storyteller, I know little of politics. But, I'll tell ye what I can. The Westlands have enjoyed relative peace for the last few generations except for minor skirmishes between bored nobles. Some say tis one of the few things the priests in Sanctiloci have done well, subtly convincing the various nobles that the glory of coin is nobler than the glory of the sword. Aye, and that peace was shared by Atani. It seemed as if folks knew that losing a few coins was better than losing yer life."

Gareloch paused as he puffed on his pipe. Keven had a thousand questions about the pipe and how much magic Gareloch knew. He also knew better than to ask them now. "One question at a time lad," he could hear the old man say.

"Things have changed a wee bit now. Atani has become restless. They have raided some of the border lands. It does no make sense. Tis folly, ta be sure. King Donius is a fair king. Hard as iron ta be sure, but sensible as he is tough. He does no rule by his emotions, and he knows the value of a coin."

"Is that why they are sending riders across the border?"

"Tis unknown ta all, except King Donius himself. Atani tis a wee bit different than the Westlands. King Donius was raised from birth ta be the perfect king. Until this mess, he nearly was. He is a Blademaster true. He knows the folly of war as sure as anyone. Since before he could read, he was schooled by the best tutors."

They rode in silence for some time. Keven's only indication about Gareloch's thoughts came from the dark look the old man wore. Keven, as usual, fought the familiar battle with himself. Should he try to reason answers from what he knew or should he ask the old man?

"What were the riders after? As fierce as they were, they surely were not enough to start a battle here in the Westlands."

"Lad, clear the sap from yer ears. I said no one knows. They could be looking fer plunder or scouting roads for future attempts. There are rumors that Atani is taking people from the Westlands."

"Like slavery?" Keven chimed in, trying to be helpful.

"Just like the young. Never letting a man finish his thoughts."

He paused longer than he had to, for effect, Keven thought.

"Tis the way of rumor, lad. Some say the Atanians are taking folks as slaves. Others say they are taking any who want ta share in their glory."

Keven did his best to think on what Gareloch said, but he did not have the patience. "What kind of glory?"

"Lad, I'll wager with ye a bit. If ye can go fer a meal with no asking a question, I'll answer anything ye want as fast as ye want."

Keven didn't see that he had a choice, so he agreed and let Caelv trot to the small gathering of trees. Thistle, of course, resisted hurrying. Keven took his time tending to the horses and his other chores.

"A wee bit of practice will no do ye harm. Gather some wood and I'll get the book." Keven was about to ask him if he was sure, but thought about the wager. Without a word of acknowledgement, he set off to gather sticks.

It wasn't long before he had the sticks piled up, and he was seated with Gareloch. To impress the old man, he began his breathing. He imagined his mind as an empty book waiting to be filled with the words Gareloch would say to him.

Distantly, he heard the old man say the words with a subtle rhythm. The silky words appeared on his mind's page as soon as Gareloch said them. They vanished as soon as Keven repeated them. In a surprisingly short time, Keven could feel the small tongues of flame.

He did not feel the heat nor smell the smoke. He simply knew that the flames had been created and were happily gnawing on their meal of dried twigs.

"Let it go, lad, ye have done yerself proud. But, tis enough of that fer now."

The tone was soft yet firm. Keven had heard that tone before when Master Dunn had talked to Erin in the forge.

Reluctantly, Keven opened his eyes. Unlike the previous times, he was not tired. In fact, he felt like a starving man who only ate half his fill. As if seeing his thoughts, Gareloch thrust some dried bread and hard cheese in Keven's hand.

"Ye do have the way of magic, lad. Tis true enough for anyone ta see. Mind my words now. Ye still have a wager with me, so do no interrupt with questions that can be answered with yer own mind. Let yer ears be the way of it."

Keven nodded. He felt that if he said anything, a question would inadvertently slip out.

"What do ye want, lad?" It was a simple question, but Keven was a bit put off by the intense gaze that came from the ancient blue eyes that were staring at him.

"I don't know. I want to know more of magic. I want to find my friend Erin. She was my girl in the village before the threat of the coming war took her away. I hope to marry her."

A look came across the wrinkled face that was tinged with sadness. "Have care, lad, hope is a sharp sword with a slippery handle. The tighter ye hold it and the more ye swing, the sooner it'll cut ye.

"Mind well this question. If ye get what ye want, what ye most want in the world, what then? Marrying a lass tis a fine thing. Being married ta a woman is no what most lads bargain for when they take a knee. Learning magic is a fine thing. Once ye have power, what then? Give me no answer. The answer tis fer yerself alone."

Thoughts of Erin inflamed his feelings for her. The old man's wisdom could not compare to the memory of his lost love.

"Lad, get the clouds out of yer eyes. I can see ye do no have time fer the words of this old man. I have more ta teach ye. Ye have the way of magic, tis true. Ye even have some idea of yer need. But there is more. The words of magic are from a different time. Most can do no more than repeat the words. Tis a dying art. Few have the way of writing new words of magic."

Sitting in the small copse of trees, Keven listened intently. He did not want to miss a thing when Gareloch spoke of magic. The urge to ask a hundred questions was almost too much for him.

"Put yer hand up. Just so. That's the way of it." The old man grabbed Keven's hand and instructed Keven to leave it in the air when he released it.

Almost instantly, Keven felt something touch his palm. It was as light as a gnat and as sticky as a spider's nest. The feeling changed. It became more substantial, firmer. It became an invisible bar pushing his hand down. It did not hurt, but the force was irresistible. Keven's hand went down, pushed by the unseen force.

"Before ye ask a question and lose yer wager, tis sorcery. There are no words, no potions. Tis my thoughts ye felt. Nothing more. Each man should own his thoughts. Few do."

Keven did not know what to say. He simply stared at his hand and hoped the old man would continue to teach.

"Ye must know the way of it before ye bruise that potato ye call a mind. All people, aye, and probably elves, dwarves, goblins, and who knows what else, are made of three things: Need, will, and hope. They're the way of everything.

"Need and will battle everyday. Every man has needs. Every man has will enough to meet some of his need. No man has enough will to fill all of his need. T'would be a dark day indeed if such a man came ta be. Need and will, lad. Ye need food, and if ye want it bad enough, yer will find the way of eating."

Keven stared at the old man whose pipe seemed to simply appear in his hand.

"Need and will, tis the way of all animals. But hope, hope tis the way of men. If ye have no hope that ye can control yer need, ye have nothing. Men use their will ta fight their need. Only if they have hope can they one day conquer their need. Without hope of being free from need, we are just animals.

"Will is the way of sorcery. Work takes two things: the will ta get it done and the mechanism that puts the will in the world. Without the proper mechanism, the work is harder, and the will must be stronger. Tell me, lad, can ye dig a hole with no shovel?"

"If I really needed to. I would have the will. I would do it with my hands," Keven said proudly. He was beginning to understand.

"Lad, ye do have a potato, but perhaps tis no as soft as I thought. Now, if ye want ta pick up that stick by yer foot and ye could no move a muscle, how strong would yer will have ta be?"

"How is..." Keven caught himself. "If what you say is true, the will would have to be impossibly strong to do work with no mechanism, not even a body."

"Aye, tis no easy. If there is a mechanism, only a fool does no use it. Tis possible ta no use yer body. The mind is a mechanism, lad. More of a mechanism than a hammer, shovel, or even sword. The question is: why do ye want that mechanism? What work do ye need done?"

Keven felt like he was grabbing at sand. His hand could only hold so much as the sand slipped though his fingers. The more he tightened his grasp, the more sand fell away.

"Enough words, ye'll no know the way of it till ye feel it fer yerself. Now, reach fer the stick with yer arm. Do ye feel a space between wanting yer arm ta move and it moving? There is. Ye must separate yer mind from yer body. Think now, feel yer mind. What does it tell yer arm ta do? Take those thoughts, lad. Those thoughts are yer will. Take those thoughts and put them outside of yer mind. That is the way of sorcery. Put yer thoughts on the end of the stick."

Keven felt like he was trying to push a wagon with ropes. Pushing did no good; the ropes simply tangled. The more he pushed, the less control he had.

"Stop. Have care, lad. Yer potato is no much, but ye can no mash it on yer first try. Mind yer breathing. Take yer thoughts and will them ta be outside of yerself. Shape yer thoughts, lad. Even a feather will no move from yer breath if ye do no shape yer mouth."

Keven tried it again. He thought about moving his arm and the thoughts that allowed him to do that. He took those thoughts and tried to wrestle them around the stick. He felt nothing. He couldn't even be sure his thoughts were even outside of his mind.

"Tis enough, lad, ye can no do it on yer first try. No one can."

"Well, why didn't you tell me?" he said, frustrated that his attempt had been in vain.

"If I had, ye would no have hope and would no have applied yer will. Besides," he added glibly, "ye cannot succeed on yer second try if ye do no end yer first. And that squares our wager.

"We'll camp here, lad. We've wasted the day among these trees. Tis folly ta move again to find camp a few miles down the road. See ta the horses. I'll boil the water for a stew."

Keven was a bit surprised to see the sun had set. When he came back to the cookfire, he found Gareloch with his nose in a book Keven had not seen before.

After shoveling a few mouthfuls of Gareloch's tasty creation into his mouth, Keven lay down on his bedroll. He tried to stay awake to reexamine his swirling thoughts. Sleep came before he made any progress.

Sogoth

Marc   Herman

Chapter 10

Sogoth sat on his carved throne. To lesser wizards, the gargoyle topped masterpiece would be a magical treasure. To Sogoth, it was merely a place from which he could plan his next endeavor. His strangely callused fingertips absently stroked reptilian scales that were imbedded in the pale granite. Each of the intricately carved scales contained a spell that he had long mastered.

How long he sat mattered no more to him than the exact origin of the lone piece of grey dust that lay on his left sleeve. He found it bothersome that the distracting thoughts of dust and his body's needs intruded increasingly often. By his reckoning, it had been nearly a week since he had attended to them. He would take his supper when the pangs of hunger would interfere more than the interruption of eating.

For his supper, there was no delicacy out of his reach. With *Arcessito,* fruits from any of the known lands and the seas beyond could appear steaming or chilled. Such trivialities brought him no pleasure, for only fools seek pleasure of the body. Pleasure comes from that which cannot be touched. Knowledge and mastering the struggle to attain knowledge were always the highest good.

For Sogoth and all wizards, time was counted differently. One of the first lessons an adept learns at the Wizards' Palace is that the years a wizard might live are barely worth counting. Diligent pursuit of the One Oath extends a wizard's life. Exactly how long he would live Sogoth did not know; the only way to attain that knowledge was to extend his life until the knowledge was his.

His lessons in the power of knowledge began well before he felt the call of the Wizards' Palace. A cold chill he had not felt in ages crept through him as he thought about his first teacher, his mother.

Despite being a talented healer, those who knew her painted her as the wife of the Dark One himself. Still, peasant women from towns near and yon would make a difficult trek to see her to birth their whelps. Accepting whatever crudity with which they had to pay, Sogoth's mother helped them all.

A healer has the knowledge of desperate people's secrets. Oaths of secrecy become porous when pain rules the body. So his mother flitted from one needy body to another, collecting secrets and knowledge as a bee collects pollen. Unlike the clumsy bee, however, she could deftly use what she collected.

Memories he was not sure were his own showed scenes of women with distended bellies screaming in pain. By his tenth birthday his mother was bringing him to all of her calls. There was nothing, no injury, no sickness nor birth from which she would permit him to shield his eyes. He was not brought so that he could fetch water; indeed, that was the lesson. Any peasant boy could fetch water, tend a fire, and stay out of the way. Even the strong-armed husbands who put the babies in their wives' bellies were as much use. Knowledge, his mother repeated, was the only power.

In all of his travels, Sogoth had never once encountered a woman like his mother. Nor had he ever encountered a soul who had the smallest resemblance to his father or sister. His mother collected secrets like a dwarven banker collected coins. And, as any dwarven banker could attest, one coin or one secret has the power of ten when it is spent right. His mother ruled half of the town by the knowledge of others that she used like a puppeteer.

The fact that his father was so opposite was something Sogoth could never quite grasp. Every person of the village, even the ones in his mother's thrall, loved his father. There was not a man of the town who would not eagerly buy him a drink at the tavern. More interestingly, there was not a farmwife within miles who would not raise her skirts for him.

Sogoth's father had a knack for making every person like him. It wasn't an act; he simply seemed to enjoy spending time with every person with whom he crossed paths. The one person he seemed not to care for was his son, Sogoth. Despite every scheme for approval Sogoth's prodigious young mind created, his father steered clear of the boy.

Hunger clawed its way into Sogoth's mind, blunting the delicate thought he was fondling. The boorish need to eat allowed common, albeit fragmented, memories to drift in. Despite the vast differences between Sogoth and every other person he had known, Sogoth, could not remember much of his childhood beyond what he had learned at his mother's side.

As a result, Sogoth had used his magical abilities to augment his memory of his past. Often the added memories did not come from within his mind. Sogoth had memories that he could not possibly have acquired as a child and the exact mechanisms of the acquisition of such memories were unknown to him. Perhaps the One Oath would drive to him to learn how one day.

Sogoth had memories of his parents from before they were married, and so, he suspected, did his sister. By earlier inventories of his mind,

Sogoth discovered that he had more memories than a man of his age should have. So, in a paradox he had yet to untangle, he was older than he was.

The cause of such a paradox stemmed from his parents' union. A memory that he should not have of their courtship flowed into his mind.

Sogoth saw the unmarried couple under their favorite tree near the creek. He could not deny the youth and beauty of either of them. Sogoth had long since given up quaint notions of propriety and had no qualms about remembering his parent's love making. Right as they were to begin to commit the most pleasurable of sins, the terrible scream of a horse ripped apart their ardor.

Sogoth's father didn't bother to button his grey shirt as he ran to the sound. Whenever a horse broke a leg, an injured person was usually nearby. His mother ran too, knowing that injured people often made their wounds worse by moving too much. The sloping hill to the creekside gave Sogoth's parents the view of an overturned carriage foundered in the water. Without breaking stride, both of his parents waded and then dove into the deceptively powerful creek.

The old women huddled on the upturned side of the carriage had faces that were as white as the habits that framed their wrinkled faces. There were no men about so one of the wizened ladies must have acted as the driver. Perhaps that is why their wagon was half submerged.

"Erneth. Help Erneth!" one of the wizened nuns screamed as she pointed to the horse.

As Sogoth's father pulled himself onto the splintered axle of the finely crafted carriage, he could see the pitiful state of the horse. The clear water magnified the horrific angle of its foreleg and did nothing to conceal the blood that seeped out around the exposed bone. The horse, bound by the harness and the weight of the carriage, lay on its side. With courage borne of desperation it held its head above the water. In an instant, Sogoth's father knew the horse would drown. It might take hours, but it would tire, and there was no way to get the beast out of the water.

"They can't make it by themselves," Sogoth's mother announced over the rushing water. She was right; she usually was. The frail nuns would find no footing on the slippery creek bed.

"Come with us," his father said pleasantly, as if it was a casual invitation to dinner.

"Our carriage? Our horse?" The protest was tight with fear.

"We can worry about that later," came Sogoth's mother's cool reply. It was a tone she had used often when an injured person worried about the blood on his clothing.

"But our belongings, they are very important!"

"I'll come back to get them after we get you to shore," Sogoth's father offered cheerfully.

The closest of the old women clutched at his outstretched hand. Hers was thin and cold, his was meaty and warm. In an awkward procession, Sogoth's parents escorted the three old women across the waist high creek to the muddy bank.

Despite the fact that they were safe, fear pulled their lips even tighter across their yellow teeth.

"I'll get your things," Sogoth's father said over his shoulder as he waded back into the water. Sogoth's mother was busy looking over the older women. Despite the warmth of the day, cold wetness could sneak up on old bodies.

In each of the five trips to and from the carriage, Sogoth's father avoided looking at the huge dark eyes of Erneth, the horse. The animal knew it would drown and every attempt to fight that fact brought excruciating pain from its shattered limb.

After his fifth trip back to the bank, the nuns had regained some of their composure after warming up and seeing the contents of their carriage piled in the mud.

"My son, thank you for your service. Truly you serve The Creator. Our belongings are most important to His work."

Feeling awkward at the attention, Sogoth's father turned and waded one more time into the powerful water.

"My son, please do not risk yourself again. We have what we need to pay you."

The plea fell on deaf, determined ears. Though he had salvaged the fine boxes that had been strewn about the inside of the carriage, he had left some common items half-submerged in the water.

By bending at the waist he reached into the window of the carriage one last time to retrieve a dagger as long as his forearm. Befitting the rest of their possessions, it was a fine blade with a keen edge on it. With it in his hand, he stood over the horse. Sogoth's father had hunted deer often and seen plenty of stock animals slaughtered, but a horse whose eyes reveal sheer terror was a different matter.

The blade did its job as dark warm blood mixed with the speeding creek water. Drowning was a hell Sogoth's father would not permit of any of The Creator's creatures.

The memory evaporated as Sogoth's hunger roared into his awareness. He stood up and fought dizziness as he made his way toward his table. He would not feed as some commoners did. He would dine at the head of his ancient table on a meal the like of which he had enjoyed long before he was born.

* * *

King Donius was a proud man. His position and background made him so, but he was not blind to his flaws. In dealing with Lilandra, he had been outwitted at every turn. Until he clashed with her, he had considered himself a brilliant strategist.

To be beaten so by a woman was humbling. He tried to deny that conclusion by continuing to match wits with her. With each new attempt he thought he would emerge the winner. To his credit, Donius stopped his attempts earlier than some men would have. Only a fool continues losing tactics and expects a different outcome.

That thought that allowed him to make alternate plans. He would have preferred to beat her on her terms. He knew, however, it was the victory that counted, not the method.

With that, he strode to her chambers. Without acknowledging the guard at her door, he entered. He did not burst in full of rage. Rather, it was with the self-assured pace of a man who was no longer playing by another's rules.

King Donius made sure to confront her in private. By doing so, he could use some methods of persuasion that would not go over well if they were known publicly. A king was much freer to do as he wished without the eyes of a nation watching.

He stood in her chamber like a lion confidently surveying its next meal. Too often he had tried to bully her with strong words and his royal bearing. A bully was only as good as his willingness to carry out the threat. He had held back for the sake of Helena. But now, Donius was quite willing to sacrifice his daughter's feelings.

For her part, Lilandra matched his state of calm. That he was the one who was angry proved a lesson she had learned long ago. Those who were upset had the problem, not the person or thing that caused them to be upset.

"My dear King, I assume that you are upset. I act only with the best interest of Atani at heart." She maintained the sweet façade.

Unlike many men, he did not respond to her more sultry charms. He glared down at her with a cold stare he knew intimidated opponents on the battlefield as well as those at the negotiating table.

"It is true that my daughter and my subjects love you. Somehow you have spelled them. But, in the end, it is not important what they think. I am the king. I shall give you one last chance to say your goodbyes and remove yourself from Atani."

The calm manner in which he gave her the ultimatum surprised her. He had given thought to this.

"What of your daughter, do you deny that she gives more credence to my words than yours?"

"To do otherwise is to deny what is. Facts are facts; some are more important than others. I do accept certain realities that you have brought to this city and this land. But, by accepting, I do not yield my right and duty to rule my kingdom."

"How very noble of you. Is this worth losing your daughter?"

"You have been warned. Leave my land or lose your life." With that, he turned and strode out of her office.

His thoughts almost returned to their normal state of confidence as he thought that witches could die the same as other people. He had seen enough and dealt enough death for any man. He certainly did not fear it, not for himself and not even for his daughter. Life was rarely fair and even less so for a princess.

Donius was born and bred to be a ruler. Duty came first, always. Helena was only one piece of Atani. If dying was her duty and watching her die was his, then so be it. But could he truly think as anything other than a father? His heart almost seized with imagined grief as duty clashed with memories of his Helena in his arms. He would do anything to keep his daughter free of Lilandra's slavery.

It would not come to that. Lilandra was remarkably popular, and he had, in fact, been negligent with certain things. There might be some turbulence as many of the citizens realized their beloved Regent was dead. It would be painful, but it would be good for them. The best things in life are often the most painful.

Yes, he thought to himself, a few weeks after Lilandra was gone, the people would forget she had even existed. As he strode the castle halls, he almost let a smile cross his face.

He did not know the specifics of it. He simply knew that in a week, if she were still in the castle, she would meet her death. Every king had secrets; strong, effective kings had lots of them. One of Donius' was his knowledge of the assassins' guild.

There were rumors of its existence in every town and hamlet in every land. Most of the rumors were told over cups of wine and mugs of ale. The stories got better as the cups became emptier. Of course, the guild was not capable of all of the things attributed to it. It was, however, capable of creating clean solutions to messy problems.

His requirements were simple; he in no way could be connected to the event; it had to appear as a natural accident, preferably in public. If his name were attached to it, the messy problem of Lilandra would become a stinking bog of headaches he did not need.

He knew a few of their methods. If Lilandra's death was to be public, he would not be surprised if it came from a riding accident. He had even heard of one victim whose clothes were secretly soaked in odorless oil. When the victim went to poke a fire, his clothes went up like a giant wick. It happened in front of a dozen witnesses.

However it would happen, he knew that the sack of gold he had one of his loyal men leave in a forgotten sewer was a cheap solution to a festering problem. He almost whistled as he headed to his throne room to pass judgment on criminals who needed to be punished.

* * *

Kiel was a demanding taskmistress. She ruefully admitted to herself that she did not want her instructors to see her now. She constantly had to remind her squad that they could never take back a step they made. Each step was a moment that could not be relived. Silent tracking demanded all of their concentration.

They were good students. She did not know if they would ever be as good as she was, and it pained her to think that as it reeked of the arrogant thoughts of her homeland. It was assumed in Elvenwood that humans were brutes who could not learn the finer arts. Kiel did not know if it was true, and the possibility that it was truly scared her. If humans were so inferior to elves, would not she be half as inferior as well?

She simply could not allow it to be truthful that humans were less than elves.

Regent Lilandra saw it as well. All things, elves, humans, males, and females were needed. They all had worth. It was what kept her troopers so dedicated to her. They saw Kiel as a link to the Atani they knew could exist, an Atani where everyone was equal. As a testament to the power of the Dream, Kiel had become free of the irrational elven fear of violence. Through the Dream, she saw more clearly. There were those who opposed Regent Lilandra and those who might be of use to her.

She had instructed her men to tie their mounts to trees that were well inside a copse and to set out on foot. They protested at first, but she explained that a horse's heavy hooves could hardly be stealthy.

She knew students often fought learning; she had. Learning meant change, and changing oneself was the most difficult task of all. Still, her three soldiers seldom made the same mistake twice. It was a testament to their belief in Regent Lilandra's Dream that they would change themselves.

She had them keep their swords sheathed, but arrows nocked. Her troopers initially did not like creeping around without their swords in hand.

Kiel explained that if they planned their moments well, no one would get close enough for a sword to be effective. It was much better to see the enemy from afar before he saw you. If they used each moment as it should be used, no enemy should get within striking distance. Once they saw her logic, they were eager to learn as much as she could teach.

She had never thought of herself as wise. Indeed, nowhere in any of her past moments was there the possibility of being a teacher. Yet, here she was leading three human males through woods and fields, teaching them woods lore. There was a good feeling in imparting her hard earned knowledge to those who were eager to learn. She did her best to limit her words; examples were more useful than explanations. So, they learned as they stalked.

What pleased her most of all was that if they gained enough skill, they could then instruct others. If the process continued, the distance between elves and humans would close and that would please the Regent.

Kiel quickly pulled herself from her thoughts. She almost stepped on a dry twig. That would hardly do for an instructor. She had one chance to show her troopers to the best of her ability. If she made a mistake, that chance would be wasted, and her troopers would have a less than perfect image of how to stalk.

Kiel continued to lead; each man was in a different position behind her. She had stopped pointing out obvious hazards. It did not take long for them to learn the worst places to step. Green leaves could make a sound. Even hard mud would reveal their passage. It was as important they did not leave signs as it was they found signs of others.

The magic she sensed with the arrowfly attack convinced her something or someone evil was out there. She continued to move with grace and had to remind her troops that they did not only have to mask their sounds from other potential enemies, they had to mask them from all of nature's creatures. If birds reacted to their passage, someone might notice the birds' reaction. Nothing was so loud as the silence of birds.

The training exercises were built into the very serious reconnaissance. Each day they went further from their horses. They covered less ground, of course, than they would have by staying on their horses, but it gave Kiel a chance to explore the area around the arrowfly attack.

A chirping bird call made its way through the trees. To most, it would be unnoticed, but to those who knew, it was the wrong time of day for such a call. After following it to its source, Kiel found Corporal Marsali squatting over a patch of dirt.

"I think I've found something." The eagerness of his voice was unmistakable.

To their credit, neither of the other two troopers rushed over to Corporal Marsali. They maintained discipline and minced through the branches to where he stood.

"Well, Corporal Marsali?" She was amazed at how her tone sounded just like that of her instructors whenever they were challenging her.

"It looks like only one man. He was not worried about being followed. He passed here twice, the first time going this way, and the second returning. He was carrying water."

"Very good, Corporal. You have done well. Why don't you take us to where this trail leads?" He beamed like a youngster at the honor she had given him.

Following the trail took a long time. It was not that the trail was difficult; whoever had walked it had no knowledge of woods lore and left plenty of tracks.

They were fanned out through the woods with Corporal Marsali at the point, Corporal Ginelli twenty paces to his left, and Corporal Tapeni was twenty paces to his right. Kiel, being the best shot of them all, hung behind and left at thirty paces.

Despite their discipline and her supposed elven patience, it seemed like ages before Corporal Marsali came upon an empty campsite. They were all eager, yet anxious for a little action. After making sure the area was clear, Kiel and the others joined Corporal Marsali.

"Well, Corporal Marsali? Again, what do you see?" The campsite was littered with signs, and Kiel was curious to see what he and the others would notice.

"There were two of them, both men, and they did not stay long. Nor did they take any effort to hide their presence. Whoever they were, there doesn't seem to be anything special here."

He sounded confident, and Kiel hated to criticize him.

"Corporal Tapeni, Corporal Ginelli, do you notice anything out of the ordinary?" After a few moments of scanning the campsite, they both shook their heads.

"Look at the remains of the fire. The ash pattern is peculiar. There is only the residue of thick logs. There is no evidence of kindling or fatwood."

It took each man some time to digest that information. Kiel could almost hear their thoughts as they silently asked how a fire could be lit with only thick logs. It could not be.

"There is much we don't know about this campsite and those who stayed here. But I'll wager my bow they are connected to our little incident with the arrowflies." She let that sink in before she issued the next order.

"Fan out, arrows nocked. Let's return to the horses and find these people. If it is a wizard, I expect you to follow my commands exactly. Hesitation with a wizard will be your last moment. A wizard is like a poisonweed. He must be killed on sight." Though their blank faces did not show understanding, they did show trust. As silently as they had come, Captain Kiel's troops disappeared into the woods.

Helena

Crow

Lori Crow

Chapter 11

He was called Pedro now and apprenticed to a blacksmith in the smithy section of Atani City. The craftsmen were all working as many hours as their bodies would let them. The government was buying any and all weapons, though the blacksmith's guild still controlled how much could be produced. That was important to keep prices high. But each smith secretly made more than the guild permitted, and the Regent's pursers did not seem to care. The smiths were told to make as many swords as they could and that the Atanian army would buy them all. Short swords and spears were needed in great quantity.

Pedro did not know much of making weapons, so appearing to be a bumbling assistant came easily to him. There wasn't an hour that went by that he did not manage to knock something over or even burn himself. Good work, he knew, took some self-sacrifice.

Just because Pedro did not know much about making weapons did not mean he did not know about using them. He was surprisingly well trained for one so young. Pedro had passed no more than twenty summers- at least that is what he thought his age was; nobody knew for sure. Neither his mother nor his father had raised him.

In fact, he had no idea who they were or why he had not been raised by them. They could have died, they could have given him up, or they could have been sentenced to the slavers. Pedro only cared in the strictest academic sense. He had been well cared for. He was educated beyond what most nobles considered erudite.

His education, however, was unlike any other in any of the lands. He was raised by an extended family that taught him and others like him skills that would later help the family maintain their income. From the earliest age, he and his foster brothers were schooled in the ways of knives, poisons, deception, and escape.

Despite the subject matter, their education was quite professional and efficient. For years, he had been trained to be able to throw a knife without looking like he threw it. Many storytellers would be jealous at his ability at sleight-of-hand. Getting someone to drink from a poisoned cup was easy. Putting the poison into the cup unseen was difficult. That skill and others were why he and his extended family had been contacted.

Pedro was not contacted directly. In fact, he had received very little information. Though he knew the locations and faces of his foster family members, Pedro knew that communicating with them was all but forbidden. Too many years and too much money were at stake for anything but the briefest transmission of information. In this instance, his message came from a drunk who was besotted with slaver's juice. The message simply instructed him to get a job at a smithy, any one would do. Once that was done, he was to make plans and ready possible methods. More information would follow.

As far as the drunk who slurred the message to Pedro, his fate was unknown. Using such people was fairly common. One of his family would befriend such a person, buy them drinks, and make sure that the watered down slaver's juice was not so watered down. Once the person was drunk enough, they would be instructed to perform a task and promised riches if they did. Once the task was done, the drunken sot was left to his own devices, sometimes with payment. The next day, the drunk would need the slaver's juice. In time, the patsy's will would be destroyed, and he would be a pariah. At that point, he would cease to be a liability.

Pedro and his family were not without morals; they did not relish violence or senseless death. Being educated, they realized that life and civilization were complicated and precious. They also realized that death and violence occurred everyday. It was often better to direct some of those events rather than let them occur randomly. People had to die. If some of those people became his family's targets, then only two things changed. The target died earlier, and the family got paid.

So Pedro's last few days had been spent studying the shop in which he was now employed. He did his observing covertly. He was perfect for it. He was of average build, he was not too unkempt, but he would certainly not be mistaken for a young lord. Though he bumbled about, he did perform enough tasks adequately to keep himself employed. His boss kept him busy, but not busy enough to prevent Pedro from seeing how the forge's door was often left open. He noticed too that many of his boss's finest swords were hung from a large chandelier-like display rack. Any one of those heavy swords could fall at any moment. There were broken crossbows, tools that could be tripped over, and scores of blades that might have an infectious substance. It was true that his new job was fraught with danger.

It did not take too long for the next bit of instruction to come to him. This time the messenger did not know he was the messenger. A lord had come to the shop seeking a sword. Part of Pedro's duties was to tend to the customer's horses. As his training demanded, he routinely studied everything. The lord's horse had a fine saddle that was well worn. The saddle had an innumerable amount of scratches in it. Some of the scratches had been placed there by a member of his family; it was a language that few people knew, none outside the family. The scratches were not deep. In a short time, with constant riding, the message-bearing scratches would be worn completely away by the lord's buttocks.

The message was clear and simple. Regent Lilandra. When Pedro realized who his target was, he shuddered with excitement. Not in his wildest dreams had he thought he would ever be assigned so powerful a target. At least not for years. That she was a target of his family did not overly surprise him. People died everyday. But, no one paid the family to speed the death of poor people. His family's targets were almost always rich and noble.

The noble rode off, his bottom quietly buffing away the covertly scrawled message. Pedro wondered if any other messages were being delivered today. Certainly, his family had other clients.

Rumors quickly spread through the smithy section of Atani City that Lilandra was to visit the smithies today. It was a fine day with plenty of sunshine, and the city seemed to be bubbling with excitement. There was talk of a new statue being constructed in a wooden warehouse inside the great stadium.

The citizens meandered about in the streets seeking each other's company to discuss how their gowns were similar to the Regent's latest display. They gossiped about the success of the recruiting effort and how no one could possibly be successful against the growing Atanian Army. Of course, the main reason they were out in the streets was they hoped to catch a glimpse of their beloved Regent. Even Pedro's usually gruff and serious boss was in the street talking to other craftsmen.

Pedro, however, was not in the street. His boss had given him plenty of work to do: the overhead sword rack had to be checked and possible tripping hazards had to be examined. Indeed, even the metal filings that lay strewn about could have sharp edges that might permit something to enter a person's bloodstream through the smallest puncture.

From his position in the back of the shop, he could see that his boss and those around him became slightly more active in their gestures. The Regent was coming. His education had shielded him from the hysteria that many people felt for the Regent.

He could only imagine the crowds doing their best to not mob her. She would not appreciate that; she would not want them fawning over her as if she were better than they. Pedro, of course, knew that all people were not equal. No one paid the family to make a target of a farmer.

As she walked down the crowded lane, there were occasional cheers, but mostly people simply waited and desperately hoped for her to notice them. To some, it would be the highest honor to have the Regent choose them to converse with.

Pedro automatically began his tranquil breathing techniques when he realized she was indeed heading to his boss' shop. The exercises came easily to him. The family had trained him, his brothers, cousins, and uncles how to appear casual while delivering death. Excitement led to mistakes. Mistakes led to discovery. Protecting the family was the single most important lesson he had learned.

Maintaining his composure was difficult. When she entered the shop, he saw she was more beautiful than the rumors had foretold. She was not, however, arrayed in a fancy gown and draped in jewels. She was wearing a simple skirt, blouse, and boots. Boots! What type of noble felt comfortable enough to wear the clothes of the working people?

His boss followed her in, chatting all of the way. She patiently listened to his thoughts and even told him that they were good. His flush was deeper than forge-heated iron. She asked probing questions about how much he produced, what he needed, and what hindered him from producing more for the growing army.

She, like anyone who was unfamiliar with a blacksmith"s shop, was careful not to touch anything. People who had not trained with weapons were afraid of them, as if they could jump up and hurt them of their own accord. Pedro watched for his moment. He was ignored by his boss simply because his boss wanted all of the Regent's attention. That was how Pedro preferred things. It was always better if the target did not notice you.

The Regent crossed the shop and passed directly underneath the sword rack. That was not the moment. He remained calm. He had to stay true to his training.

After a brief conversation in which his boss affirmed that her changes had given him a chance he would not have otherwise had, she thanked him for his input. As she turned to leave him, Pedro continued his chores. He had to move a heavy anvil that was at his feet to a corner of the shop. It was very heavy, and he had to be careful with it.

Pedro was careful with his steps; he had to put his feet in just the right place. He did not want anything to go wrong. A misplaced scabbard made him stumble. He pitched forward into the back wall. The heavy anvil came down on his hand crushing the bones easily. Good work, he knew, took some self-sacrifice. The impact on the timber that held the roof was severe. It immediately shook the heavy sword rack loose. To Pedro and the others who watched the events, they seemed to progress in slow motion.

Pedro swore, his boss swore, the crowd outside the shop swore, even Lilandra swore. They all did so for very different reasons. The sword rack fell to the floor while all who watched held their breath. It missed impaling the Regent by a hair's width. If she had not moved quickly, Atani would have been mourning their beloved. Pedro could not understand what had gone wrong. He had done everything according to his training. He could not believe that the operation was compromised.

Pedro was quick to get up and rush to his Regent. He was, of course, sure to display his mangled hand. That was his protection. The sympathy he would garner at having such a grievous injury would shield him from any suspicion. Everything was simply the result of a bumbling apprentice. It wasn't until the shaken Regent left the shop that two thoughts entered his head. The first was confidence that the family had other plans. The second was the extreme pain that came from having fingers pointing in too many directions at once.

* * *

The days passed uneventfully. There were no visits by goblins or sighting of Atanian scouts. But to Keven, each word from the old storyteller was as exciting as an epic battle. Gareloch parceled out information at his own pace. Sometimes he flooded Keven, sometimes he left him parched.

"Sir, you mention people's will, yet you have also told me that wanting things is bad."

"Tis no wanting that tis bad. Tis wanting what ye do no need." After some time and a few rings of smoke, he continued. "Both are important. Without will and the hope that ye can no improve yer own future, ye are no human, yer less then an animal, yer a slave." Keven was struck by the intensity of the old man's words. Compared with his customarily joking manner, the tone drove the message home.

"So it is good to be able to control everything in your life."

Keven barely finished the sentence when a large beetle flew directly into his mouth. Shocked and stunned, Keven spent the next few moments ungracefully hacking, coughing, and spitting. Just when he thought he had removed all of the bug from his mouth, he would feel a thin wing or a prickly leg.

"Have I been talking ta the trees, lad? Ye must have hope ye can change yer future, if ye have *need* ta change it. Have caution when thinking what ye need, but never give up hope."

"But hope for what? What is so important that I should believe in it?" The desperation in Keven's tone betrayed his need for an answer. Any answer that would give him reassurance he was not adrift in the sea of life.

"I have no the way of it. Will no be so easy fer ye. Tis what every man must find fer himself."

The old man used words as a child played with a favorite toy. Keven was not surprised to see the old man several paces ahead. Gareloch had obviously determined Keven needed to digest their last conversation.

Keven, however, was not put off. His time with Gareloch had given him confidence and validated his need to learn. He heeled Caelv to close the distance.

"Sir, what is it you hope for? What are your needs?"

"Have care, lad. If ye truly understand the question, tis more personal than any other. No, lad, I'll no answer ye. Anymore than I'd want ye ta tell me if ye knew yer own answer.

"I will tell ye this. Ye must have care. Too oft a person chases a want only ta find tis naught but a shadow of what he needs. Most folk's needs are but simple feelings. They do no know the way of it. Money, the regard of others, love. Most folk think these are what they need. They are no. Ask why a man needs these and ye *begin* ta have the way of it.

"No man can escape it. Tis a harsh fact, but tis a good thing. Think, lad, what if ye met all of yer needs? What would ye hope fer then? Ye would no be yerself. Ye'd be The Creator. Ye'd have no reason ta wake with the morn.

"I've told ye much. Most of it has the way of wisdom. Heed it well, think on it much. The most powerful of magic, sorcery, and the other paths is need. If a wizard can truly understand his need, he is ta be feared more than any gang of goblins or a host of trolls.

"Such a man would have little ta fear. Such a man would have no weaknesses. Tis doubtful even the wizard with the best mind can reach such a level. Aye, there are rumors of one who has reached such a level. But, tis only that, a tale men tell in taverns about a female who can turn minds."

Keven listened intently. He was sure he was only understanding a tenth of what the old man said.

"The mind alone rarely conquers need. It seems that is the way of life, ta have need. There is an escape. If a man feels the need of others more than he feels his own need, he will be free."

Keven felt like his mind was a net with holes in it. He was desperately trying to catch all of the thoughts Gareloch was throwing at him. Many of the thoughts were on the tip of his consciousness. He let them slip when he became distracted by a new idea. Evidently, Gareloch felt he had divulged enough. Keven was almost relieved to see the old man suddenly riding apart and smoking his pipe.

* * *

For a peaceful farmer who used to be a soldier, it was unsettling to discover how quickly knowledge of killing and hurting came back. It did so in a flash. Old muscles that had grown accustomed to the hard but predictable work of farming were alive with fire. The impromptu training sessions were little more than an organized beating. But violence, once learned, was not easily forgotten.

The training sessions started the same day he was invited to accompany the recruiting squad. From that moment, they had kept their hostility barely under control. They were bullies in uniform. That they believed they were serving the Regent gave them a certain legitimacy that they confused with authority to hurt in her name. From the subtle shoves he received as one of them walked by to the outright laughter as he received a particularly vicious blow, Tapio Denisio knew he was not among friends.

He was able to ignore it though. They were simply bullies. Any man who had as much life experience as he had had learned to deal with bullies. Additionally, he had seen enough violence in his time in the King's army to steel him against minor attempts at intimidation.

Though he knew such a thing as the Dream could never be achieved, in principle it was a noble idea. These thugs knew nothing about the Dream for which his daughter left him. What if she was found by brutes like these?

His feelings about Tonay made the best attempts by his new squad seem like little more than the buzzing of an arrowfly. Nothing mattered besides finding her. She was his daughter, and she was alone in a world that she was unprepared for. Just the thought of her being found by men like the ones who had found him made him shiver with both rage and dread.

He used his rage to build an inner fire that became so hot, it burned away impurities such as fear and dread. His anger became a forge in which the sword of a single-minded determination to find his daughter was created.

Day by day, the one-sided training sessions became longer and more onerous. Lieutenant Spudolli would order Tapio to face one of the two corporals. They would take great pride in slipping past his defenses and smacking him hard on the shoulder. When he did attack, they easily avoided him. His frustration was intense; he knew what his body should do, it was just not doing it as it had years ago. He was wasting time while his daughter could be moving farther away.

He also felt a deep humiliation which grew by the day. It was not simply that he was getting hit at will during the early training sessions, it was that he could not leave to make water without their permission. He knew it; and they knew it. They loved having power over him.

The frustration and humiliation he almost constantly felt seemed to twist his very soul. Both of those feelings were simply proof that he was no closer to finding Tonay.

Their continued harassment, the frustration, and the degradation did not bury Tapio. Their efforts provided him with a constant source of fuel for his pyre of rage.

Tapio's feelings burst free one afternoon. The third stop of the day was determined to be a good time for a training session for Tapio by Lieutenant Spudolli. Before he had even lined up to begin the farce of training, one of the corporals poked him hard in the back with the wooden practice sword. Something in Tapio snapped. Never before had Tapio reached his breaking point, not during battle, not even when he found that Tonay had run off. But the last act of senseless aggression from a man who was preventing him from finding his daughter was enough to make Tapio break from himself.

Without any outward sign, Tapio spun his body and swung his outstretched arm. It connected with a force that knocked the corporal to the ground. Before the man had finished falling, Tapio was on him. With a savagery that would have scared him only days before, his fist connected repeatedly with the man's face.

Before the melee had gone too far, Tapio was kicked off the man, but through his rage, he could barely feel the dull pain of the impact. Tapio rolled with the blow and came quickly to his feet. He held the wooden sword in front of him.

The other corporal, sensing an easy win, rushed in. Tapio was waiting for him with the awakened skills of a man who had been in battle many times before. His moves were efficient and brutal.

The corporal sped in with his sword arm ready to swing. Young men, Tapio knew, too often relied on their strength. While the man was preparing for what would surely be a very powerful swing at Tapio's head, Tapio quickly jammed the point of his sword in the corporal's face. The blunt wooden tip entered his mouth and broke his teeth. It was fortunate the younger man stopped his momentum, or he would have been killed.

As the corporal writhed and moaned, Tapio's awakened instincts drove him. He immediately searched for the other men. He found them fifteen paces away holding crossbows that prevented Tapio from advancing on them.

"Hold! I will fire if you take a step," Lieutenant Spudolli said with no emotion.

Tapio forced his mind to assert control of his rage. At fifteen paces, Lieutenant Spudolli could not miss. If he died, Tonay would be left alone to face a world that would delight in beating the naiveté from her.

"So what now?" Tapio asked. Lieutenant Spudolli had not fired. Yet, Tapio had injured two of his corporals. He suppressed a glimmer of hope that he would be free to go.

"You have shown some skill. The Regent will be that much happier to have you with us. It is time to mount the horses. One trained swordsman will fill our quota just as fast as a band of untested youth."

Kiel

Alexandra Feehery

Chapter 12

It took Keven quite some time to digest what Gareloch had told him. That did not mean he was content to sit on questions of a different sort. The two were lounging under a tree, taking one of their mid day breaks.

"Where is the Wizards' Palace?" It was as good an opener as any, Keven thought.

"I'm but a storyteller, lad. Do ye think the wizards in the palace would tell just anyone where the palace is? Do ye think they want peasants and other rabble just walking ta their door? Secrets, lad, secrets are the way of the paths of power."

To himself, he agreed with the old man. It was a foolish question; he should have thought before he spoke. He should have rephrased the question.

"Well, if you do not know where it is, how do you know we are traveling in the right direction?"

"I have seen the palace once."

Keven persisted, "If you have seen the palace, you know where it is."

"Lad, pick the wax from yer ears. I said I do no know where tis. But, I do know where it was. I hope it will be there again."

As if to stop further questions, Gareloch continued: "Aye, lad, the palace does move. A palace as big as any castle. It has sat next ta a village for generations with no one in the village knowing it was there. Yet, in one day it can be found in another land. Secrets, lad, I do no know the way of them."

Keven knew he would not get anywhere once Gareloch admitted he did not know something. So, Keven tried a different approach to bringing knowledge out of the old storyteller.

"How many wizards are there?"

"'Tis a fair question. I have no the number of them. Hundreds may come ta the palace ta learn. Fewer and fewer progress ta the next level."

Despite the questions that were almost bursting from him, Keven kept them to himself. The old man had the certain tone that meant he would continue if he were uninterrupted.

"Many have trouble with taking one of the oaths. Tis true oaths are broken everyday by common folk and nobles alike. But when a wizard swears an oath, tis something different. A wizard takes one of the three oaths, with his blood, bones, and soul. Those who understand the way of it should have trouble swearing ta something that holds them fer the rest of their years.

"Very few walk the whole road ta the final test. Few who do begin the wizard's test survive. And none of those who finish survive whole."

Gareloch's usual pause in his speech extended too long for Keven. The younger noticed that Gareloch was certainly not thinking of the present conversation. His wizened face showed wrinkles of pain and regret.

"What do you mean by not surviving whole?"

"Each one who passes the test and is raised ta wizard's status must pay a price. The price is oft very dear. Wizard's status means long life. The magic demands something fer that gift. No wizard knows what he must pay until he undergoes the test. Tis different fer each wizard. Refusal ta pay the price means death. The coin asked fer their lessons tis heavier than gold. Do ye still want ta learn the ways of wizards?"

To a casual observer, it would have appeared as a rhetorical question, but Keven knew the old man wanted Keven to answer it. Gareloch did not want to hear the answer; he simply wanted Keven to have the answer.

"Is that what happened to those wizards who studied the magic of need? Did the final test kill them?"

"Tis another fair question. Lad, sometimes ye seem ta have more in yer head than straw and dreams."

Keven took that to be a high compliment.

"Need is no something can be taught by wizards or anyone else. Though it can no be taught, it can be learned."

"Has anyone learned enough about need to control theirs?"

"No, til now no one has."

"You mean it is impossible?"

"No, lad. Nothing tis impossible. But controlling all of yer needs tis as likely as having a friendly talk with a dragon."

"Dragons? Are they real? I have no reason to doubt after what I have seen with you, but dragons?" Keven knew he sounded like a young boy, but he could not help it. Ever since he read The Magic Stick Keven had tried to imagine what a dragon would be like. "I'd like to see a dragon."

Gareloch snorted, "Fine, lad. Just be sure yer an old man cause twil be the last ye see of anything."

"Are they evil?" Keven replied.

"No, lad. They're dragon. They're not evil or good they're just... dragon. They do no wish anyone harm, they just do no wish anyone ta be."

"Are they all like that?"

"Lad," he patiently explained, "they're no like anything. They've lived before there was evil and good. This is their world, or so they believe. We're just ants in their picnic. I fear the day they wake and ride the winds again. I hope I'm long dead when they do come. I do no want ta see what they'll do."

"Have you ever seen one?"

"Are ye daft in the head? Did ye no just hear me? If I saw one, would I be here talking ta ye?" Gareloch was staring at Keven with indignation written on his face.

"Well, how do you know about dragons?"

"I've been a storyteller fer a long time. I've heard a lot of the stories and read a few books of the wizards. They all say the same thing. That's the way of it."

"I've read books about magic and goblins, but I didn't actually know any of that was real until I saw a goblin and tried magic." Keven's tone reflect mirthful triumph. He knew he had caught the old man in an obvious case of sloppy thinking. By saying his words just so, he knew the old man would soon realize the inconsistency.

Gareloch took a breath so that he could continue to lecture Keven, but just as he opened his mouth, an arrowfly flew directly in. The old man's face became even more wrinkled than usual as he desperately tried to spit the still buzzing, thumb-sized insect from his mouth.

Surpsied laughter burst from Keven as the old man furiously spat. The dark look Gareloch shot Keven only served to increase Keven's laughter. Seeing the old man jamming his fingers in his mouth almost caused Keven's sides to split open.

Gareloch cleared his mouth of the intrusion long before Keven regained his composure. There were a few moments of silence as Gareloch drank from his water skin.

"Twas a fine piece of thinking, lad. Ye have the way of it. Ye'll do fine at the Wizards' Palace." It was a truthful and full compliment from Gareloch. "Aye, but do no let yer head get swelled. Anyone can have one in a row. Let's be on our way. We are close ta the spot, but wizards do no wait for any man."

The rest of the day was like the many others they had spent riding. Periodically, Keven would break the silence as a small chuckle would escape. He did not look back at Gareloch for fear of truly laughing aloud.

Keven heard the buzz of what sounded like an arrowfly and instinctively ducked. It would not do to have one find his mouth so soon after his victory. He saw no sign of the noisy pest.

Expecting to see Gareloch puffing on his pipe, Keven looked over his shoulder and was shocked to see the fletching of a long arrow sticking out of the old man's chest.

Keven looked at the old man, but did not meet his gaze. The old man's eyes were trained on something far ahead of them. Keven turned to see what it was that held the Gareloch's stare.

He heard the thunder of the hooves as soon as he saw the riders streaking towards him.

"Run, lad," he heard the old man croak.

As he turned to look at his teacher, Keven saw a riderless horse. Thistle was standing as she had a moment before, but Gareloch was gone.

* * *

She was tough enough to admit to herself that it scared her. Lilandra realized how close she had come to death. Dying did not bother her overly; she was well past such worries. But the thought of leaving so many uncompleted plans was maddening. In all of the plans, she had rarely thought about someone resisting her so much they would have the ability to kill her.

The nature of the attack, the seeming randomness of it, bothered her. At first she believed it to be an accident of a clumsy, smitten boy. After the adrenaline had worn off, she thought on it. It was no accident.

If such a subtle attack could have happened in a blacksmith's shop, where else could it happen? She would have to keep an extra watch on people and how they acted around her.

Most of the time, women, and especially men, acted awkwardly around her. They tried to ignore her beauty, but in doing so, they over reacted. Not looking at her was as much of a clue as one who could not take his eyes off her.

That was why she had noticed the boy in the back of the blacksmith's shop. He had done what few others could: ignored her until the incident. It was a shame that she could not question him.

Despite her best attempts, she could not get anyone to find the boy. The smith eagerly gave every tidbit of information he knew, but it did not help. The last anyone saw of the boy, he was fleeing down the lane with a mangled hand.

That there was still such resistance to her made simply disposing of King Donius even more difficult. He represented what was secure and stable in their world. If there was still sentiment for him, it was too soon to have Helena officially take the throne. More work would have to be done.

Simply because she could not strike directly at the king did not mean she could not force him to accept the new order. The body of the king might be sacrosanct, but the body of a princess was simply a chess piece to be used wisely. It was a dark thought that hardly fit her mood as she looked upon the city from one of the castle's highest towers. It was a breathtaking view. That engineers could build such a thing as a high tower and not figure out how to move a dragon baffled her. She did not let that thought intrude too deeply. The dragon was safely covered and might even stay asleep long after she and every other citizen were dead.

The breeze was delightful. She was far enough above the city to be free from the mix of aromas from kitchens and sewers. She walked from one edge of the tower to the other. The battlements at this height were merely decoration. This tower was more of a sentry position than a battle station.

A few of the great stones were loose, held in place simply by friction. She could not imagine what a human body would look like after a fall from such a height. Whoever came up to this tower would have to be told of the loose stone. She wondered if the princess knew about it. This tower was an accident waiting to happen.

As if the fates had planned the timing of her arrival, Lilandra heard a tap on the trap door that was inlaid into the floor of the tower. A guard pushed it open and gently releasing the iron ring lest the door slam down hard on the floor and disturb the delicate ears of the princess and the Regent. Once the guard was out of the way, Princess Helena daintily made her way up the last steps of the spiral staircase.

"Greetings, Princess. I am so glad you could join me up here."

"It is good to get away from the nobles. They often lose sight of what is important in our fair land." The young woman believed in the Dream with every fiber of her being.

"It is true, and you are wise to see it." Lilandra watched the young princess shine as she received the compliment. "Princess, come look here. What do you see?"

Lilandra knew exactly where the loose stone was. As the princess came to the battlements that made a railing about waist high, Lilandra actually became nervous. The time was not yet right. First, there had to be a lesson.

"I see the city and the poorer sections"

"Why do you have to squint to see the poorer sections?"

"They are far away."

"Exactly. Your father and the nobles push the poor far away as if they are things to be ashamed of. The poor should be embraced by those who have plenty."

The princess' face softened with compassionate understanding. "My father is wrong. All people are equal. Their station in life and education should not matter."

"You are correct, Princess. Now, come look over here. Look straight down, Princess, what do you see there?"

As the princess leaned over the block of stone, it shifted. She was too far extended to immediately regain her balance. She screamed in terror as the stone shifted. To Lilandra, it seemed to happen slowly. She reached for the princess and grabbed part of her satin dress. But she did not have the strength to hold the full-grown woman. She did, however, slow her fall enough for the alert guard to spring into action. He unceremoniously grabbed the princess in the nick of time as the heavy block fell to the ground far below. The princess was pulled back to the safety of the tower floor.

"Princess, are you hurt?" Lilandra said frantically.

To her credit, the young woman rallied quickly. Helena knew well that a ruler must display courage at all times. "I am fine. Pray the stone did not cause harm. Guard, did the stone hit anything?"

"No, Princess Helena. It merely struck soft ground."

"That is fortunate."

"Princess," Lilandra said, "let us go from here. It is unsafe. We should tell your father of your near tragedy. He would be interested to know how unsafe things are for you."

* * *

Keven was frozen with astonishment. Gareloch was shot, then he was gone, and Keven was facing four armed riders speeding towards him. He wished he had the sword of which he spoke so often.

Though his mind was as still as a statue, Caelv's was not. The well-built horse began to prance uncertainly. It sensed the impending threat if Keven did not. Caelv's snorting jarred Keven from his immobility. He reached for the reins and turned Caelv in the opposite direction of the riders.

As he did so, he heard the sound like a buzz pass his ear. Keven knew that the sound was no arrowfly. It was the sound of fletching as it vibrated through the air. It flew no farther than inches from his head.

"Human! Choose well your next moment. Choose poorly and it will be your last."

The voice was shouted from a distance, but even so, Keven could tell it was feminine and cold. Whoever had shot at him had missed on purpose. So, he dropped the reins and waited for them to approach.

As they drew nearer, Keven could see that three of the riders were men who were, themselves, intimidating. Each had a sword at his hip and a bow drawn on him. Yet even from thirty paces away, the woman's spectacular beauty took his attention away from the bow she had pointed at him.

"Dismount this moment!" the female ordered as she drew closer. "I do not have to put an arrow in your neck. I can put one or several in your leg if necessary."

Seeing her fury and capacity for violence, Keven slowly swung his right leg over the back of Caelv. By the time both of his feet were on the ground, the quartet was upon him. Was Gareloch dead?

She had dismounted with a speed and grace he had never seen before and stormed to him with rage on her face. "Where is the old man? My shot was true. He had not more than a moment to live. I looked away for a moment; he was gone. What type of wizard is he?"

Her strangely shaped eyes brimmed with malevolence as she examined Keven. He had seen Constance's face when she was intent on causing him harm. Constance always had a playful smirk despite her intentions. In this woman, Keven could see nothing but anger.

As she tore her gaze from Keven, she inhaled and exhaled deeply. When she turned to face him, gone was the open rage. Instead, there was a serene calmness.

"Stranger, we mean you no harm. We will not waste time here in the open. You will share what you know. Corporal Tapeni, secure the mare. We will take her. This man is unarmed and of little threat to us. He will ride his own mount."

The woman had an accent Keven had never heard that was exotic and beautiful, but he was shocked to hear her orders. She was intent on taking him, and he knew he could do nothing about it. He watched one of the soldiers, obviously Corporal Tapeni, approach Thistle. When he grabbed her reins, she pulled back from him. When he tried to guide her to his mount, she balked and dug her hooves in.

Without any hesitation, he took out a whip made from knotted ropes and began hitting the mare in the face. Keven winced as the full swing impacted on her nose and head. Thistle whinnied in pain. Without thinking, Keven rushed over to knock the man aside though Keven's slight build barely moved him.

In a flash, the soldier swung the whip at Keven. It landed across his cheek and immediately that cheek felt like a thousand arrowflies had stung him there. Again, the man swung. It landed on Keven's left shoulder, and his thin shirt offered little protection. The pain was intense, but Keven hardly flinched. He felt no need to protect himself.

"Enough!" barked the woman in charge. Then in a more even tone, she said, "Neither the animal nor this man deserves to be beaten. They both act according to their natures."

Upon hearing her command, the soldier instantly stopped. He paused and met Keven's eyes. His expression held the barest hint of apology.

The soldier then went to his horse and grabbed a lariat and from a safe distance from the angry mare, he threw a loop around her neck. He dragged Thistle to his mount and began tying her reins to a lead that was attached to his saddle.

"Corporal Marsali, bind his hands and use this." She threw a piece of leather at him. Then to Keven she said, "We will do our best to prevent harm befalling you. You do not understand your future moments, so it is natural for you to resist us. Please do not."

One of the soldiers caught what Kiel threw and walked towards Keven. "Put your hands out front. Lace your fingers together." There was no malice in his voice.

When Keven had done so, the man covered Keven's interlocking hands with the leather cloth. He then wrapped Keven's wrists with a thin leather thong. The cloth was included in the bindings and pulled so tight that Keven could not even move a finger. The effect was such that Keven's hands were locked away in a sturdy leather bag.

She then directed her speech towards Keven. "You, what is your name?"

"I'm Keven." He thought of saying more, but Gareloch's lessons had had some impact on him. There was nothing he could say to influence their decision to take him. He might have had the will to resist them, but he did not have a mechanism to do so.

"You will ride with us to Atani. I said before, we have no wish to harm you. You and your companion, however, wished us harm. He was an enemy to the Dream. There can be no weakness with those such as he. I know enough of magic to know it was your companion who set the arrowflies upon us.

"We are from Atani, and we follow the Dream. You are definitely misguided to follow someone who would attack others for no reason. We cannot leave you here, you being a student of magic. And we have no wish to kill you. With what you may know, you may serve the Dream admirably. In time, you will understand. But, for now, we must ride."

With his hands bound, it took him some effort to get on Caelv. Once they were on their way, he was paid little attention. They rode for hours with no break.

Keven eventually questioned the leader. "Why are you working so hard to bring me? You are wrong in thinking I can help your Dream. I'm a stable hand. Why do you need me so badly?" It seemed reasonable. Gareloch would be proud at the directness of the question.

"Be quiet, human," the leader replied over her shoulder in a hushed whisper. "Do you wish to tell everyone in a hundred paces where we are?"

She was directly ahead of him. The other soldiers were behind him, in a triangle. Their arrows were fitted to the string but not drawn.

"I don't know," Keven responded simply. "You have taken me prisoner for no reason. Those you might be hiding from might aid me."

With that same astonishing gracefulness that accompanied all of her movements, she swung off her horse and loped to the side of Caelv. She grabbed Keven by the arm and yanked him off his horse. Bound as he was, he could not find his balance and fell to his knees.

"Do you see these tracks? Do you recognize the boot prints mixed with claw marks?" She had her face inches from his ear. Keven looked closely at the tracks. He had seen something like them once. Once was enough for the sight of those tracks to put a chill down his spine. Goblins.

"Would you care to shout out now?" she hissed in his ear. "In a gang as large as they are traveling in, they will not hesitate to attack us. They are fearless in such numbers. You would be their dessert." Her exotic features were made more threatening by the hood that covered much of her face.

She then helped Keven up from the dirt, guided Keven back to his horse, and made a basket of her hands. She offered no expression or explanation as she offered him assistance. As they rode, Keven's thoughts swirled around in his head. Fear and confusion conspired to make the hours of riding with his captors worse than combined torments of his village. Tears were never far from his eyes as he rode on, surrounded by those who had shot Gareloch.

After they dismounted, Kiel pulled the Kevin aside. Her corporals could set up the camp and tend to the horses.

In a much more pleasant tone, she made her introduction again. "I am Kielasanthra Tylansthra. I am a captain in the Atanian Army. You are our guest. We are taking you to Atani city so you may benefit from the Dream."

The sudden switch from violence to pleasantness was more than unsettling. Was she crazy? He did his best to use what he learned from Gareloch. He remained calm and he kept his thoughts to one question at a time. "Will you release me?" It was a blunt question, but he said it as neutrally as he could.

"No. I think it would be best to keep you with us. You do not look like you could survive long on your own. Additionally, I think you'll be happy with what you find in Atani city. There is opportunity there for you. There is opportunity there for everyone." Her hood showed only glimpses of her as she spoke to him from horseback.

"So, I am to be a slave," he challenged. Keven kept his thoughts focused. He had to think of his greatest need.

"I have read about human slavers. They are unnatural, and we are not slavers. Have we forced slaver's juice upon you?"

For the first time he realized what she was. The clues were right in front of him. Her beauty, her grace, and the eyes he had noticed upon first seeing her all told him she was an elf.

Her words were true, but that did not make her his friend; she had shot Gareloch. That he had not seen the old man die was the only thing that was giving him hope.

"Why, then, don't you release me? Yes, there are goblins in these woods, but you can hardly care what happens to me."

"We who follow the Dream do care. At this moment, you do not understand. You will when you learn of Lilandra. I apologize for any discomfort your present moments may cause you. Your future moments will be so much better spent once you see there are things that are much greater than your individual wants. We'll do what we must to show you how true that is."

"So once you bring me to Atani, I'll be done with you?" It was a challenge which Keven knew meant nothing. Whatever she said would not affect the outcome.

"Yes. In Atani there is so much for you and others. You will look at these moments and laugh."

"Well, I have no choice. I will stay with you. Now will you cut my bonds?"

"No. I will not feel unnecessary regret in my future moments simply because you say you will stay. I sincerely apologize for the rudeness, but regret over such decisions is to be avoided."

Although Keven fumed with humiliation, he tried to be rational and to ignore his fear and identify his need. He felt he did everything right; still he was powerless.

* * *

"Damn, Damn, Damn." Gareloch swore.

"Easy old friend, you'll undo all of my *Curatitus*."

The two old men looked at each other. The skinny one lay on a simple bed with a rough blanket pulled up to his white beard. The fat one sat on a rickety wooden chair across from his patient.

"And you're lucky I did heal you, what with the years of debt. You already owe me for countless other favors. I don't know why I am your friend. The Creator knows I'm your only one."

"Because without me ta worry 'bout, ye would just get fatter. Tis a wonder ye can cast anything with those sausage-like fingers."

The non-descript gray stone room held little more than a bed, chair, and table. If asked, the cantankerous patient would say that his room contained quite enough things, though he would probably list the stone walls, ceiling, and floor as furnishings.

"Ye don't need ta say I should have been more careful. I know the way of my blunder. I should have cast *Accipio*, but that damn lad and his questions kept me too busy ta guard against threats."

"You should have been more careful," the rotund wizard said dryly. A shift of his weight caused the the wooden chair to creak its indignation. Lucius turned to the equally ancient wooden table and to the plate of sweet cakes that had not been there a moment before. He knew he should not eat them, but making them appear from nowhere was such fun.

"Aye, tis good I knew *Situtum Domus* so well. I do no think I could have concentrated much." Gareloch had lived many years, but that did not mean he was ready to stop. He was honest enough to admit he had been scared when he saw the arrow sticking out of his chest.

As if to ignore his happily chewing friend, Gareloch said, "That lad, ye should meet him. The questions he asks are as good as any apprentice who has years with us."

"Gareloch, you are the master of the Palace of Wizards; you can easily do things the rest of us only read about. Why do you insist on riding about as a common traveler? The known lands are on the brink of war, you know. You should be in here. Can you really do more good out there?" Lucius said the rebuke in such a way that sounded as if it had been said a hundred times.

"Lucius, I said it ta ye enough that even yer fat head should know by now. The real learning, the real magic is out there with the people. Not in yer books or these *sacred* halls." By the way he said sacred, there was no doubt as to Gareloch's true feeling on the arrogance of the wizards who hid in the palace.

"Yer right, ye know," he continued. "There's a war coming. That's the way of it. And what do the respected and powerful wizards do? Tis the same every time. Even those bound by the Trinity. They sit here and hide in their books."

The wiry wizard master continued. "Do ye know what I saw? Goblins. They walked right through my *Accipio*. Twas only moments before they stepped on us that I threw *Nascondersi* over the lad and me."

"Goblins, so far north? It is a good thing they did not believe you were elves. They would not have been so easily distracted. I'd like to know why goblins hate elves so much. Perhaps the One Oath will drive me out of this place to study it. Anyway, we'll set some wizards to *Aspecties*."

"Aye, it'll do as much good as drinking with yer nose. What'll they do if they do see goblins coming out of Darkwood? Hold a council?"

"Gareloch, you are as stubborn as a dwarf and as crafty as an elf, but your skills avail you naught if the rest of the wizards do not follow you. Why don't you lead them from here? Threaten them, bribe them, hell, even beg them, but don't insult the lot of them by leaving on one of your expeditions." Lucius said though he was tempted to gripe about being left with all the responsibilities of Wizard Master as well.

Both men sat in silence for a while. How long, neither was sure; with wizards, time had a different meaning. They'd had this and similar arguments countless times.

It was uncertain how many sweet cakes Lucius ate. But the plate looked no emptier for all of the big man's efforts.

"The lad, Lucius, he's special. I let him go."

Gareloch and Lucius had known each other for years, since they had both been students in the palace. Though they knew each other well, it was rare that either showed emotion. So, the tone in Gareloch's voice made the big man pay attention.

Lucius was awkward in consoling him. "What are we always telling the students? Don't form your thought before you have all of the information. Besides, perhaps this turn of events will serve him well. This might not end up as hard as the first year in the palace. 'Desperation is a crucible in which what is weak is burned away.'"

"Thanks fer the lesson," Gareloch said hollowly. His normal, witty tone was overshadowed with concern. "What ye say has the way of truth, but he is too young. Every man has his limit. He will break in time. We can no let such talent go ta waste."

Lucius had rarely seen his friend in such a state. He had seen his friend do some things that seemingly violated all known limits of sorcery.

"As powerful as you are, you cannot ride around searching the Known Lands by yourself just for one promising student."

"Lucius, I do no need ta search the Known Lands. If they no killed him, he's in Atani. With what we've talked about these last few days, he is in Atani. I've been to Atani before, I know the way of their colors and the look of their weapons. What I saw were Atanian riders. Ye know it, and I know it."

"Easy old friend. You're probably right. Strange things are afoot in Atani. But why him?"

"Lucius, fer sport I used *Ambedoluær* a bit of arrowflies with him. Aye, he ate his share of arrowflies for sloppy thinking. Once the spell is cast, tis no escaping it. He did no know of the spell, of course, but he trapped me with my own words. I ended eating one, me, the Wizard Master eating a bug. That is what we're giving up."

"Gareloch, you're violating some of the first tenets. Thought must rule emotion. Always."

"I admit, I have emotion fer the lad, but reason points me ta the direction of Atani. That is where he is. Do ye doubt it?"

"No Gareloch, it makes sense that he is there, part of the madness that surrounds Atani taking prisoners for their army."

"What then?" Gareloch spat. "Should I bring it before the Council of Wizards and hope they agree ta act? Should I politely ask King Donius ta release him? I hate no knowing the way of things. Was Keven shot? Did the archer know I was a wizard? Was that why I was shot first? Ignorance tempts men into madness."

"Gareloch, we have other things to worry about."

"Lucius, it's all here. The prophecies."

"Bah. You and your theories. The ancient texts are little better than rotting paper. Even the strengthened Sospitix can barely hold them."

"Ta ignore them is the way of fools. How can any wizard ignore possible knowledge?"

"The One Oath only requires the wizard to believe the acquisition of true knowledge is possible. No one but you really believes the prophecies."

"Keven tis the one. He will face a *wizard of unimagined power. The greater will win and the weaker will lose.*"

"Yeah, I know them, Gareloch, and the greatest *power can only be defeated through forgiveness.* The problem is, you are the one of unimagined power, so that means if this boy, Keven is the one, either you or he will defeat the other one. And forgiveness, try that against *Morsus* or *Dilucesco.*" The large man paused to gain his breath. "And...*what about taming a dragon with no sword?* The prophesies are ravings, Gareloch."

"Tis no the way of it. Do no be so limited."

Lucius knew he could not prove his friend wrong, so he went on to quickly steer to conversation away from the deadlock.

"Perhaps all is not hopeless." As soon has he said the word, Lucius mentally winced. Any word but that one. He tried to cover quickly. "But you have instructed him in some of the arts of power, sorcery, or maybe some magic?"

"I've given him naught but a hammer and a nail. Now, ye think he is ta build a house. No, he does no have the way of power yet. I fear he is a twig swept away in a flood."

"I'll leave you to heal and sleep, even you need to sleep. With any luck that arrow pierced your cursed pride. Will you just please try to not berate everyone now that you're back?"

"Bah, I'm no king ta play politics. These wizards swore oaths, and I am the Wizard Master. That is the way of it, in case they have forgotten. I'll hold their feet ta the fire, and I will make them honor their vows."

* * *

Lilandra knew exactly how the king had resisted for so long. He had had the most important role in the whole kingdom. With such a role he was far better armed to resist her efforts. She had given up on his voluntary support, but with enough pressure, he would soon comply. After he complied, he would then voluntarily conform to the role.

That thought propelled her to his wing of the castle. He had been more active lately. Perhaps it was his belief that she would soon be dead. Though she could not watch every corner and every servant all of the time, she could control the source of her possible assassination.

She came upon the king's quarters and the two large guards who held halberds posted outside his doors. She doubted she could even lift one of the heavy weapons. Though they remained still with perfect military discipline, their eyes showed that they were very much aware of her half covered bosom. The dress was cut too low for what most nobles would consider decent. With a smile, she thought to herself that the ladies who complained loudest would soon be wearing gowns that had equally low necklines.

As she approached the guards, she put on a smile that most men would kill for. "I would like an audience with the king. Do you think he has time?" Her tone was sweet.

The men were given authority to hold the door. Challenging that authority would only strengthen their resolve. Asking them, however, what they thought was something that few did, including the king they swore to protect.

"No one may pass, Honored Regent," one of the guards said automatically.

"Oh," she said dejectedly. "I had hoped to talk to him about the princess' near accident." She pouted just a little bit to let them know they had control of the situation.

"I'm sorry. He gave us strict orders."

"Well, what if I just popped in for a minute? That certainly could not cause harm, could it?" She paused, forcing the man to think.

"No, that would not cause harm. It's just..." The stoic guard was having trouble with explaining his orders.

She pressed her attack. "Well, I can't possibly cause the king harm. He is a Blademaster. I'm just a woman. I only need a minute of his time to talk to him about the safety of his daughter. Please?"

As he was thinking about it, she gave the screws of persuasion one last turn. "Do I look like I'm hiding a weapon in this gown?" She said it with humor. She did a slow turn so the guards could get a good look at her curves. Though they stared hard, she knew they were not checking for weapons.

"I suppose it would be alright for you. You are the Regent." With that, he stepped aside and pushed the door open for her.

As she stepped through, she saw Donius seated at a large desk that was covered with high piles of documents. He looked up with murder in his eyes.

"You are foolish to flaunt your insubordination. Have you learned nothing? You must leave, or you will die."

"Yes about that, we have a problem. I don't agree." She used her casual tone as a weapon.

"You have no choice. I am king!" He said it in a harsh whisper that she knew would have meant death if she were facing him with a sword.

"Donius." She used his first name to drive home the importance of her words. "Do you think that the incident on the tower was an accident? I understand that accidents can happen to me at anytime. But you need to know that accidents can happen to your pretty daughter, as well. If something were to happen to me, your daughter's life would be short. Her death, however, will be long. Do you doubt I have people so loyal to me that they will do whatever I deem necessary?"

"You're mad! You threaten the life of a child, of my daughter? I would rather see her die than be a slave to you."

"Please, let us not bore each other with boastful lies. Your daughter is the one thing you love more than your kingdom. Call off the assassins."

"They do not operate like servants. Once they have agreed, they will not stop. Contacting them is not like ordering a drink in a common tavern."

"We have a problem then. If I die, your daughter does as well. You know full well that you cannot protect her from all who are loyal to me."

He was playing a game of chess with a master. He saw the trap closing, but he did not know how to prevent it.

"Donius, if you can not call off your assassins, then it is simple. You must protect me from them. You are a Blademaster. Protecting me should not be too difficult for you. Remember, if I die, Helena dies."

As the full implications of what she was saying hit him, he almost grunted in pain. The image of Helena's body in a burial dress stabbed his mind. Echoes of the vow he had made to his dying wife to always protect their daughter chased away the terrifiying image of Helena's body. He would never permit any of Lilandra's henchmen to harm Helena. Never.

Donius knew that the assassins he set upon Lilandra could be anywhere. If he were to protect her, he would have to escort her everywhere like a common bodyguard. He would be in a prison more humiliating than one with locks and shackles.

Lilandra smiled both inwardly and outwardly, she knew she had him. He would continue to resist, in his mind at least, but he would soon be bound to her will.

Roxane Babin

Chapter 13

Keven awoke from his first night with his captors surprisingly rested. His dreams had been of Erin; the elf and her soldiers could not take that from him. As long as he had memories of Erin, what they did with him did not seem so bad. In some ways, however, thoughts of her made him more despondent. How was he ever going to find her if he was guarded constantly and spirited off to Atani?

Frustration began to well up in him, but he forced it down, as that would do him no good. He had to focus on getting away. As soon as that thought came to him, Gareloch's teaching challenged it. Did he need to get away? Where did he have to go?

At least he had temporary use of his hands which made taking care of his morning business much easier. Even unbound and unguarded behind a tree, he knew he could not outrun them.

The breakfast was light. Captain Kiel had given permission for a small fire to be built with boiled oats as the meal. Keven knew at least one of his needs, he had to eat. He sat down next to Corporal Ginelli who seemed to be the most friendly of the soldiers.

Keven watched Captain Kiel. She was hard not to look at. Before meeting her, he had considered Constance the most beautiful female he had ever seen. Next to this elf, Constance was a saggy Goodwife who walked with a limp.

She did not partake in the morning meal. Therefore it came as a surprise to him when she approached and sat with him. She handed him a dented metal cup full of unflavored oats.

"Did you sleep well, Keven?" Her voice was polite, even sincere.

"I slept well enough."

"We are not bad. In fact, we are bringing people to Atani for their own good. In Atani, everyone benefits. You will see. In life, all creatures act for themselves. In Atani, people act for each other. No one goes without."

Keven did his best to appear interested. It was not hard. He wondered if she knew how men looked at her.

"Regent Lilandra is not like other rulers. She will be interested in meeting you personally. I promise you, when you meet her, when you hear her speak in the great coliseum, you will know the truth of my words."

"Is there anything I can say to convince you to let me follow my own path?" he asked.

Captain Kiel took a minute to reply. With a regretful tone, she called to one of her soldiers.

"Corporal Marsali, when you are finished eating, bind our guest as we did yesterday. We will be riding soon. I do apologize for these moments of discomfort. They will become past moments, replaced by pleasant moments once you realize why we are working so hard to bring people like you to Atani."

While speaking, the elf suddenly stared off into the surrounding trees. Though she made no overt move, Keven knew she was alert.

She shot to her feet in an eye blink. "Something is amiss. I will return shortly. Have the horses and our guest ready to travel." With that, she slipped into the woods.

After watching her go, the three corporals began executing her orders. Corporal Marsali approached Keven with leather thongs and the cloth.

Keven dutifully held out his hands and quickly lost the use of them. His hands were now one less mechanism he had. He wondered what Gareloch would say. It was a question of need. He knew his greatest need was not simply to have his hands unbound, but he didn't know what his real need was.

In a strange replay of events, Keven saw Thistle resist Corporal Tapeni's effort to untie her from the tree to which she was hobbled, biting him hard on the arm.

Corporal Tapeni hesitated. He had been ordered to not beat the horse, but his captain had given orders that the party was to be ready to travel. Anything that might spook his captain might be worth running from.

That made his decision easy. He brought out his whip and began beating Thistle about the head and snout. She again whinnied in pain and anger. Corporal Tapeni pulled at her bridle as he flogged her.

With his hands bound, Keven struggled to get up.

"No!" he shouted. "I'll tend to her. Don't hit her anymore."

Corporal Tapeni drew his short sword and tucked the whip back in his belt. He grabbed Thistle's hobble line, swung his sword and severed the line close to the tree. He then sheathed his sword, looked at Keven with contempt and turned to lead Thistle to the other horses. The other soldiers turned to packing what little supplies the small party had.

The warning shattered the silence: "Ginelli, behind you!" Kiel screamed as she ran into the small clearing. The alarm in her voice raced across the clearing an instant before the meaning of her words reached the men.

Two sounds then competed for registry in Keven's mind. The first was a piercing scream of pain and horror from Corporal Ginelli. The other was the familiar whine of an arrow as it cut the air in search of its target. Keven turned his head as fast as he could.

He was sorry he had; it was a nightmare come to life. Corporal Ginelli lay face down with what Keven could only describe as a man-sized mantis looming next to him. The giant insect dug his teeth into Corporal Ginelli's left shoulder. From the amount of blood he could see and from the way the beast was yanking the corporal backwards, Keven could only imagine the agony and fear the other man felt.

Kiel's first shot was sticking out from the monster's left side. The arrows did not stop the monster from yanking the fallen man into the woods.

Keven was frozen in horror as he watched the thing drag Corporal Ginelli kicking and screaming as easily as a full-grown man would drag a child. Movement caught his eye. He quickly turned to see three other giant mantises emerge from the brush. Kiel's arrows whizzed by his head, each finding its mark. Corporal Marsali swung his sword at one of the two other bugs.

That left Keven defenseless in front of a giant bug whose strangely mammalian jaw opened and slammed shut menacingly. It moved quicker than Keven could imagine, closing upon him in a flash to sink its fangs into the sturdy fabric of his left pant leg. It had a good hold of him. With strength he would not have thought possible, the thing yanked him hard enough that he landed on his bottom, and it jerked him towards the bush.

He quickly looked around to see that Captain Kiel, Corporal Marsali, and Corporal Tapeni were all engaged in a fight for their own lives. He kicked at the thing with his right leg. The hard shell made him feel like he was kicking stone. Panic set in as Keven twisted his body wildly.

As he was thrashing about, another form entered his vision, a gray blur. In a thunder of stomping hooves, Thistle was there, pounding the thing's hard outer layer. She delivered a flurry of heavy blows with her forelegs, and Keven heard loud cracks he could only hope came from the thing's shell.

Thistle changed tactics; she turned and kicked the monster with her hind legs. Keven could feel the impact of those blows. More importantly he heard sharp cracks come from the points of impact. The beast opened its jaws and retreated. Using that same speed with which it pounced on Keven, it withdrew into the brush.

Keven scrambled up. He could see a still twitching bug at Kiel's feet, its neck a pin cushion of long arrows. Corporal Tapeni was laboriously swinging his sword at the bug that faced him, landing each of his blows. Like a flash, Captain Kiel ran into the woods. "Watch him," she shouted to Corporal Marsali as she passed Keven at a dead run. She drew her sword as she leapt over a low hanging branch. Her grace and agility made her vanish in only a few steps into the trees, heading in the direction in which the bug had dragged Corporal Ginelli.

The two men exchanged inscrutable looks, then wiped their blades and waited for their Captain.

After a period of time none of the men could measure, Captain Kiel returned, her sword sheathed and her expression grim.

"Corporal Ginelli is dead."

"Did the bug kill him?" Corporal Tapeni asked.

"No. I did." The manner in which Captain Kiel said it let all three men know it had been a grim task. "He was past saving. The poison had done its work. When I reached him, he was no longer screaming."

"What were those things?" Keven was surprised to hear the question come out of his own mouth.

"They are called direbugs. I have read of them. You saw the size of them. Yet, they creep as silently as any bug. My kind fears them. Our senses are keen, but these bugs can fool even us."

After seeing her move into the woods and after hearing her words, Keven was acutely aware that she was not simply a beautiful woman. She was a true elven ranger. She fit the image of all of the stories he'd ever heard.

"I can offer you only what I have been told. Their jaws contain a sinister poison. It keeps their prey alive. The evil of it is, the prey is aware and can feel pain, but can not move. Corporal Ginelli was going to live for a long time as the bugs took pieces of him. In every way that counts, he was already dead. I just spared him days of agony." She said the last in a hollow tone. "It was a shame a devoted follower of the Dream had to perish."

Keven wondered if she felt the loss of Corporal Ginelli. Her face showed the barest hint of sadness. Any compassion she felt, however, did not change the fact he was a bound prisoner or that she seemed to enjoy violence. Surprisingly, she ordered Corporal Marsali to cut Keven's bonds.

"Keven, did it puncture your leg?"

He was a bit startled by her direct question. Thoughts of the poison and the monster's jaws on his leg assailed him. In a flash, he realized how close he had come to sharing Corporal Ginelli's fate. Would she have come for him, he wondered.

"No. It only had my clothing." It was all he could say.

"You are indeed fortunate. You seem to have a way with that horse. Hence forth, you will ride it."

* * *

The indignation of it burned him to his soul. He was the king, yet he was trailing behind a woman several years younger as if he were no more than one of her admirers. At first, he feared her mocking him in public. He was almost prepared for that, but discovered her casual acceptance of the situation to be much worse than any cutting words in public.

Walking behind her in the hallways as he did afforded him a chance to smell her perfumed hair. It was seductive, he had to admit. Worse, she had an ability to wear dresses that hugged her hips in a way that drew men's gazes. Violently, he ripped his gaze away from that part of her. He was king! He was not one to ogle those beneath him.

Her fast pace and the number of people walking with her gave Donius plenty to worry over. Though he did not know the assassins' guild well, he did know they changed their methods frequently. The variations in their methods were only matched by their ingenuity.

Walking several paces behind her was humiliating, but it gave him a good view of any possible dangers she might walk into. Additionally, he realized any assassin would not expect him to interfere.

One servant in the new livery approached her with a tray of delicate glasses. Donius was instantly on guard, though he did not show it. To approach the ruler of Atani with drinks while she walked was strange.

Ruler of Atani! Is that what he thought of Lilandra? Had he so quickly ceded that position to her? He had to guard his thoughts as much as he guarded her.

He marveled at how she allowed all to approach and speak with her. The servant with the drinks, like a puppy, simply could not wait to please her. Donius watched him approach. He walked gracefully, like an athlete. Only someone with extensive training could move like that.

Donius erupted in a series of fluid moves. Despite his age, he showed why he was still worthy of the title of Blademaster. He pushed one of Lilandra's admirers hard. The surprised supplicant slammed into the suspicious-looking servant. The tray of drinks flew out of his hands. Red wine was cast into the air. Donius could only imagine the poison those cups might have held.

The servant quickly scrambled to his feet, begging apologies. He did his best to slink away down the hall from which he had come, but Donius would not let him. In the time it took most to blink, the Blademaster drew his sword. "Surrender!" he ordered.

The man looked at Donius and paused, considering his options. In time even assassins would give up the secrets of their guild at the hands of a torturer. The faux servant made his decision; he drew a knife from the rear of his belt and attacked Donius.

His attacks were furious but clumsy. Donius did not realize the suicidal strategy. He simply saw a man with a knife trying to kill him or the Regent Lilandra. With little more than a flick of his wrist, he slashed the would-be assassin's throat.

Slowly, others of the castle staff appeared. Soon they would have to remove the body and clean the blood. The castle would be on alert for more assassins.

Lilandra, like the others in the hallway, pressed herself against the far wall. She was no coward, but she realized she could do little. Slowly, impressed with Donius' sword work, she peeled herself off the wall. That was not the reason for her sly smile, however. The smile came from the fact that Donius had passed his first test

Had Donius Lilandra's knowledge of people, he would have known that people grow to fit the roles in which they find themselves. Any servant would act like a noble if he were permitted the trappings. The same was true of even the highest nobles. Given a serving tray, an order, and an ultimatum, they will serve. Once a person agreed to one level of debasement, the next level was so much easier to fall into. Few could put themselves at risk without finding a reason. By putting himself at risk, Donius cemented his role as her protector. People would feel a greater need to protect her. In the end, this attempt and the other gave people a reason to worry about her. People only worried about things that were dear to them. He was hers and so was his kingdom.

* * *

Though his captors no longer tied his hands for the ride or mistreated him, he knew he was a prisoner. Each day they rode further east, further from everything he knew including where he thought Erin might be.

The nights were worse. After each evening meal, Captain Kiel would bind his hands and then tie his hands to a tree or a heavy log. He almost preferred either Tapeni or Marsali to do it since they were at least quick about it. They were also larger and intimidating.

The elf, Kiel was actually gentle when she bound his wrists. That did not mean she left slack; despite being graceful with her ministrations, she was thorough.

Each evening as she hobbled him, she tried to make conversation with Keven. Often it was about the glories of working for the common good. Keven found it difficult to keep his resentment at his position quiet as he stared at her crouching in her tight doe-skin riding breeches.

Though he was not bound in the day, they did take precautions. There were no supplies strapped to Thistle's saddle. Of course, Thistle was happy about that. But it meant that if Keven did manage to get away, he would have nothing to eat, spend, or keep himself warm.

Caelv and Corporal Ginelli's mount ended up being the packhorses. When Keven first met the squad, they were not carrying all of their supplies. They had buried some of their equipment and hung some of their food at various places along a trail. In general, the days on the road with Captain Kiel and her two soldiers were not pleasant for Keven. This day, however, was the worst so far. The sky had opened up and fat raindrops were beating him into the ground. The pitiful pieces of leather that he called his shoes would soon shrink, adding to his misery.

For no reason Keven could see, Kiel pulled her horse to a stop. It was a clearing, but they still had daylight left. Keven wondered how she could follow any trail with the rain as thick as fog. Shortly after they stopped, Corporal Tapeni and Marsali entered the clearing. It took Keven a moment to realize there was a heavy sack hanging at head height from a stout branch.

Corporal Tapeni drew his knife from his belt and cut the rope near its anchor point causing the bag to come crashing down, spilling open on impact. Oats. Keven had fed enough horses in his life to instantly recognize what they were.

"Corporal Tapeni, why did you not simply untie the knot?" Her tone was hard. The rain had pressed her hair to her forehead.

"This way was quicker." He knew he was caught. His expression said he was thinking quickly.

"And how much time do you think it will take you to pick up every oat that has spilled?" It was not a question. It was a blunt statement that contained an order and pointed out his error.

"You see, corporal, you must think of each moment as connected to the future. Do you wish you could relive the moment when you cut the rope and prevent the regret you now feel?"

"Yes." His hunched shoulders spoke volumes about his respect for her.

"Now, this present moment can be spent in different ways. If you diligently spend it picking up every spilled oat, you will prevent regret in your future moments. If you carelessly miss some, you will feel even more regret in your future moments. The choice is yours."

The heavy rain did not permit a fire and the lack of such hit Keven in two ways. The first was simple: a fire would keep him warm and maybe help dry a part of him. The second was much more poignant: the lack of fire reminded him of feeling the power of *Sublevato.* Now, captured, bound, and sitting in a downpour made him realize how little his will mattered.

Kiel did not eat with them. In fact, Keven rarely saw her eat. When he did, it was usually something she had foraged from the trail. After the men had eaten and after they had done their nightly business behind a tree, Kiel approached him with the now familiar bonds.

Despite her pleasantness, Keven could not wipe away the image of Gareloch with an arrow sticking out of his chest. She left him securely tied to a mid-sized tree. It was the corporals' custom to divide the watch. After the direbug attack, they all had trouble closing their eyes.

Corporal Marsali took the first watch. Tapeni lay down on one blanket and covered himself with another. Kiel simply lay down and folded her hands on her stomach.

For the hundredth time, Keven wished he could talk to Gareloch. The old man could tell him whether he should take the chance on his own or if he should safely go to Atani. Keven smiled to himself as he thought of the old man's answer. It would be a question. *Well lad, what is it you need?*

A new thought struck Keven. Gareloch did not instantly fall off Thistle because of the arrow. Instead, he disappeared by what could only be magic. If he could perform such magic with an arrow in his chest he must be powerful. If he was powerful, could Gareloch find him? Could he simply appear here and now? If he had power enough to disappear, the elf and her soldiers would be no match for him. The thought of revenge pleased him. He imagined taking the tether that held him to the tree and wrapping it around each of his captors' necks. Would their deaths meet his need?

With his hands bound as they were, he could not dig into his pocket and reach his flint. His hands were joined together in a useless stump.

It dawned on Keven that Gareloch never said the flint had to be in his hand. Keven concentrated on the flint. It was difficult; he was cold, wet and the rain was dripping off his hair into his eyes.

He began breathing like Gareloch showed him and the familiar pressure of the flint on his thigh was comforting. By clearing his mind, the image of the surface of the flint appeared on the back of his eyelids. Only when he made himself ignore the words, did they come.

The words were glorious. He both heard them and saw them, though he mouthed them noiselessly. The script was flowing onto his mind's page. The flint silently echoed the words: the spell was building. Keven directed the spell onto the knot of his wrist strap. He hoped he wouldn't burn himself, but didn't care as he needed it too badly.

The knot began to smoke, despite the rain. It was working! He reined in his excitement for fear it would disturb his fragile spell. Keven could smell the charring leather as he saw it turn black. The heat reached the skin of his wrists, but he pressed on. It was a balancing act, the breathing, the flint, and the words. The knot puffed into a small flame, but the rain quickly put it out. He hoped Corporal Ginelli would not notice the small flicker of light. Keven held the spell for a few seconds more.

He felt the pressure on his wrists release and let the spell evaporate. With a shake of his hands, the bonds fell to the ground. As quietly as he could, he got to his feet and did his best to imitate how Kiel moved. As he skulked to Thistle, he realized saddling her and scrounging supplies was impossible. He would have to ride her bareback. Somehow, he knew she would understand.

He guided her away from the sleeping forms. When he had tip-toed a fair distance and thought he was safe, he grabbed a handful of mane and hoped Thistle would not protest too loudly. As he was about to jump and swing his right foot over, he heard the disturbing whine of an arrow. An instant later, he heard it sink into a tree near his head. He realized with a certain coldness that the thought of that arrow or another one finding his head, did not scare him.

She appeared out of the rain like a silent ghost. Her elven grace made her as silent as night itself. "So you know the game of the opossum. You play it well. I'm curious human, perhaps you also play the fox?"

She was obviously looking for an answer. Keven felt no need to give her one.

"Human, you fight so hard against something you do not know. That is foolish, to hate something before you have met it. It is like fighting the coming of a new day. Why do you assume it will be bad for you?"

Her tone had nothing but curiosity. Again, Keven ignored her.

"You have not chosen your moments well. That will cause regret. You will need to be even further restrained. I assure you, I find more regret in that fact than you do."

"Captain Kiel, look here at his bonds." Corporal Tapeni was holding the ruins of what had held Keven.

Keven didn't know what information they could glean from the soaking bonds. She glided over to inspect them. She even sniffed them. Keven could see several thoughts flash across her almond shaped eyes.

"You do have magic. I was debating your worth against your cost. It seems both have increased dramatically. I'm sure Regent Lilandra will be interested in meeting you."

Keven hid his feelings at being thwarted well; he had had a lot of practice. Long ago, he had learned from Constance that if you let someone know what bothers you, they can use it against you.

"Human, I know a little of magic. You cannot be too skilled. You must have something aiding you. Corporal Tapeni, search him."

Keven stood passively as the bigger man dug the flint out of Keven's pocket. Keven bore the indignation silently. He continued to keep his face expressionless as his flint, his only link to freedom, was handed over the beautiful elf.

"Clever. Yes, you will be a good addition to the Dream. Regent Lilandra will definitely want to meet you."

* * *

"I tell ye, I know the way of it. This lad is special."

"Gareloch, that is easy for you to say. But, he never made it here. He has not been tested. Every youth who finds the palace seems promising. The question is whether he could make it through the trials to be a wizard." With that, the fat man took a drink from a mug that suddenly appeared in his meaty hand.

After a gluttonous swallow, he continued. "We have boys of all types making their way to us. We do not know how they know to come. We do not know if young women feel a different call. Are the rumors of St. Tabitha's true? Have they brought magic into the world by spreading magical artifacts across the known lands? Do the nuns hide a coven of witches under the nose of Sanctiloci? For all of the power of the oaths, we know almost nothing. How then could you know this boy is so special?"

"Why do ye think I've been out there? I'm learning about power and people. I'm planting seeds in the minds of the people."

"Only you could twist the One Oath so." A wisp of sorrow entered the bigger man's tone as he said this last.

"I fear fer ye, old friend. How can ye truly no believe there is knowledge outside of yer books?" He said it with true sadness. Both men knew the trap of the Wizards' Palace.

"I found the boy in a stable. I traveled with him fer weeks. I learned from him. There is no wizard in this whole palace who can no learn something from the meanest peasant. Tis the truth of it."

It was an argument they had had for years. As much as the bigger man wanted to believe it, he just could not make himself. He was a Wizard of Magic and had lived for many years. There just wasn't anything useful he could learn outside of the Wizards' Palace.

"This lad, Keven, had a way with animals. Most who are now Wizards of Magic first showed signs with animals. He had more talent with animals than I ever did."

"Yes, Gareloch, I know. And Wizards of Alchemy had talents for healing. Those who took to the path of technology were almost always millers, smiths, or even sailors. What does that prove about the boy?"

"Have ye used the orb ta scry him?" Gareloch said with exasperation.

"Yes, Gareloch. And I found nothing."

"Tis the way of it then," the skinny wizard concluded. "Ye did no see a grave. Wherever he is, and we know tis in Atani, he has magic surrounding him. Or maybe he has the way of need."

"Oh please, not more talk of the power of need." Though both men thought that need was possibly the most potent of the forms of power, the bigger man, like so many other wizards had given up on it. No one could master their need. "Next you're going to quote the prophesies. *'Forgiveness is the only weapon against evil* or some other ridiculous triviality."

"Ta discount the prophesies is the way of fools. Why do we make the adepts memorize them if we do no believe them? Aye, as ta need, how dare we deny the possibility of the unknown?"

"You, of all people, should give up on being a Need Master. No wizard can control his need; the One Oath prevents it. Need is what makes us human." Lucius believed his argument to be irrefutable. Only The Creator could fill all need. If a human had no unmet need, he would be The Creator.

As iron clad as that argument was, Gareloch refused to accept it. Gareloch had the sharpest mind in the Wizards' Palace. Simply refusing to agree with a certain truth was why Gareloch could walk out of the palace without breaking his oath.

"How can ye be bound by the One Oath and not seek out what could be the most powerful of all of the paths?"

"Because, Gareloch, I do not believe it can be achieved. No one except you does. Do you really think that sleeping on a hard bed with no mattress shows you have conquered your need? Does this bare room let you think you don't need anything? It is a fool's chase, Gareloch."

The arguing men had formed a deep friendship over many long years. The bigger man worried that Gareloch, who had the power and potential of three men, was wasting it on foolish ideas. "This man you have found is unfortunately just like any other young man who seeks us out. You cannot waste your efforts on him when there are so many other things we should do."

"Lucius, I saw a hawk land on him! We were under a tree. The hawk could have landed on the tree, but it chose the lad."

"Gareloch, I have to say, so what? Hawks land every day. That one chose to land on a human does not prove that human is destined to be a great wizard."

"There was something else. The lad had the way of trust with the Lady Thistle."

At the last statement, Lucius snorted his contempt. "Gareloch, my friend, you are the picture of a crazy old wizard. You have perfected *Situtum Domus* as well as other near impossible spells. You have gold beyond most men's dreams. Why do you insist on riding that irascible nag? And don't tell me it has something to do with *need.*"

"I am a Wizard of Magic," Gareloch said the simple fact to set up an argument. "Despite that, despite all of the horses I have had and that have loved me, I could do nothing with her."

"And?" Lucius challenged, though his tone suggested Gareloch might have a point.

"If ye must know, I'll tell ye. I can do nothing else as I lay in this sick bed." Lucius ignored his friend's attitude towards healing his recent wound.

"Years ago in a village in the Westlands, I came upon an inn. Twas like any other. I walked my horse ta the stable. At the time, I had a good gelding which served me well. As I came close, I heard boys having fun." His voice had a quality that only came about when he was speaking of his costly wizard price.

"Through cracks in the wall, I could see the way of their game. They had a pretty gray foal hobbled to the wall by her bridle. They also had one of her rear legs tied so that she could no put it down. She was standing on three legs and more helpless than the day she was born. It was thus that they were tormenting her. Nothing was so bad as ta cause injury. They would pull out some hairs, show her what each type of spur felt like or even make her flinch by slapping her nose. I watched a while. I did no do anything. Secrets are the way of the oaths." He spat the last words with contempt.

"The foal, she did squirm and resist, for a while. After a short time, she did no flinch at their blows. Her eyes had changed. With a simple spell of *Accipio,* I saw the foal's mind as she gave up and decided their torment was the way of her life. She had lost her hope."

Lucius remained silent. Gareloch had an iron will and could tolerate much more pain and torment than what the little horse had endured. It was not simply the pain the young horse had suffered that affected the Wizard Master; it was that the horse had lost hope. That was too close to Gareloch's Wizard's Price for him to ignore. Lucius knew in a flash of insight why his old friend insisted on traveling the lands instead of studying in the palace. He was looking for that which the Wizard's Price stole from him, hope.

"When I realized what the boys had done, I convinced them of the error of their ways. What fun is being a wizard if I can no scare some people inta acting right? Secrets be damned. As the boys ran from the stable, I was left with a foal who had been broken in the worst way.

"I was thinking kindness would cure the damage done by those boys. But, she had no the way of forgiveness or trust. Fer a long time after that, she would bite me or anyone else who got close. It took years fer her ta allow me ta ride her. Even then, she did no like me.

"The lad is the only one I have ever seen Thistle no try ta bite. When I found him, he was treated much the same as the horse. I had ta take him with me. He was on the verge of losing hope."

"Perhaps it is good that he has been captured. If the prophesies are true or will be true, the boy must suffer. I forget what book it is but the quote is burned into my mind, '*the one who will temper the needs of many is to suffer greatly.*'

"Aye, he knew the way of humiliation in his town tis true. But was it suffering enough to fulfill the prophecies? Surely there are others who have suffered more. What about the wizards in this palace or slavers? I can no reconcile the prophecy and my wish fer the lad's safety. If any of this was known, if we had a sign that he was the one, perhaps we could have hope."

Lucius had never heard Gareloch talk so openly of his Wizard's Price. To be the most powerful wizard in all of the known lands yet have no hope was a price no one should have to pay.

* * *

"You may go now. You have earned some rest. I am safe here." Lilandra said it affectionately, and it was true. In her own rooms that had already been checked, she was safe from assassins. Donius had watched over her faithfully. She had no desire to further humiliate him; there was no point in it. He was making the best of the situation in which he found himself and to rub his nose in it would only slow his acceptance.

It troubled her that she could not read his feelings. Was he waiting and planning? She believed she knew his needs, but a man so strong as he and with so defined a role should not have broken so easily. Did she misread his strength or was he playing at being the obedient dog?

His daughter was the key, though. Lilandra encouraged her to spend more time with him now that he had seen the light. Since he was always on hand, it was easy for Helena to join him in conversation. Lilandra was surprised how often a simple truth continued to surface: if you gave people what they wanted, they could not fight you.

Once people fell into a habit of obeying, it was next to impossible to change. In changing, they had to admit they were wrong. Most would go to any lengths, even ridiculous lengths, to avoid admitting they were wrong. That was why, despite working to have all of Atani believe in the Dream, she could find little dissent among the people. Those few who acted according to their role and resisted would be small enough in number to easily fit into the secret prison.

It was the same with Donius. The longer he served her, the more he would become his actions. Soon he would not be a king playing a bodyguard, but rather a bodyguard who used to be a king.

She lounged on her royal furniture and relaxed. She enjoyed meeting the needs of so many, but being cordial to the lowest citizens was exhausting. To constantly assure them that it was not their fault that they had ended up in their situation was quite an undertaking.

The idea of a luxurious bath pulled at her. Being near the lower classes for so long was a definite way to acquire the stink of them.

For a change, Nessy was not around. While Lilandra waited, she closed her eyes and rested on a velvet lounge. She let her mind wander. A wandering mind often found the best treasures.

In time, Nessy, her maid did appear. When Lilandra asked if it would be a great bother to have a bath drawn, Nessy told her to not think a minute on it.

Lilandra absently watched Nessy direct a crew of porters to carry buckets of steaming water into her bath room. It was clear that some men felt uncomfortable being in a room where the Regent would soon be naked, but Nessy ordered them around in a way that left no time for them to show their nervousness.

As she slowly immersed herself into the porcelain tub, Lilandra thought about her progress. She had to smile. The first part was almost done. She was the recognized ruler of a powerful nation. The nation was getting stronger and more unified by the day. In time, it would be the most powerful nation in all of the lands. She was nearly ready for the next part. With that, she was sure she would move ahead of Sogoth in preparation for their coming confrontation.

She had a firm grasp on the citizens' hearts. Still more was required; they were not ready. The road ahead was hard, and she needed to know that their minds were one with hers.

With all of the important decisions she had made, she had neglected to choose a symbol for the Dream. The lion crest of Donius' family needed to be replaced. It did not represent the people. It was seen as fierce and unforgiving; Donius and his ancestors were the the lions and the subjects were the prey. Lilandra needed something that allowed the citizens to think they could rise as high as their dreams. A bird. It had to be. All humans dreamed of flying. It would be perfect.

It was a little known truth that people's minds follow their behavior. Get them to do something and they will come up with their own reasons for why they did it. Those reasons would almost always be positive. She had reached a point where the citizens had given her much. They loved her as much as their deeds gave them reason to. The soldiers trained and readied themselves without pay. The farmers worked harder to compensate for their sons and daughters who answered the call and joined the army. No one sacrificed for something they do not believe in.

If asked, each citizen who gave would come up with his own reason for giving. They would not, of course, understand that adoring their

Regent demanded a price. In order to pay that price, they had to love her dearly. Lilandra knew that sacrificing both was a cause and an effect of love. She needed to increase their love for her. That meant a greater sacrifice.

Material goods, taxes, and work had assured her that they adored her. Yet, those prices did not show the depth of their love for her. She needed to bind them with a sacrifice that they would have to justify to themselves as worthwhile. She rested her head on the tub and let her mind go. As she absently soaped her breasts, she wondered how many mothers felt regret at having children ravage their bodies and destroy their dreams.

With a splash, she sat up. Hot water had done it again. Children. Every citizen had given much, but only in material things. If she could convince them to give their children, their most cherished possessions, to the cause, they would be bound to her forever.

Her mind whirled with the possible details. Any child under seven years would be suitable. The people of Atani would share in the joy and responsibility of raising the children. They would be given the benefit of a nation's knowledge and love. In time, those children would grow and would give back to Atani. Each one would be the perfect, selfless citizen.

Those parents would come up with their own reasons why giving away their child was a noble act. Even with those reasons, Lilandra thought that an extra incentive would be helpful. It wouldn't have to be much. Persuasion had three secrets, and she knew them all. The first was that the source of the message must have status. Parents rarely listened to children, but Atanians revered her. The second secret was knowledge of the audience. Lilandra knew what the people needed more than they did. The third secret was that the message must join the source and the audience, and that she had mastered with the citizens' assemblies.

All people had dreams of glory, if not for themselves, then certainly for their children. If one of the children who was given up and raised by the citizens was chosen to be the next ruler, the nation would see that as something beyond noble. It would be perfect.

No longer would the rulers be born into the privilege. They would come from the citizens and be raised by the citizens. No future ruler would know who his parents were, thus they would have no ties except those to the nation that nurtured and raised them.

The idea was so perfect, Lilandra hurried her bath. She wanted to begin to make plans. She leapt from the tub, splashing water everywhere. Like the clothes she had left strewn about, the water on the floor was beneath her notice. She could barely wait for the next citizens' assembly in the coliseum.

Lilandra

Małgorzata Ćwiek

Chapter 14

Tonay Denisio could hardly contain her excitement. She woke and almost sprang out of bed. She was in Atani City! In the dark of the night, too late to be officially signed into a company, she had been brought to the recruits' dormitory. There were several buildings just like the one she was told to enter. It was glorious: People from all over Atani, ignoring their own need for the good of the nation.

She had had to sleep in her clothes. She had to since there were young men in the dormitory as well. She'd have to get used to that. Being a soldier left little time for modesty, she reasoned. Her clothes were tattered. Weeks on the road with Lieutenant Deccia had her training hard and living rough, but she did not mind. Any hardship she felt was confirmation that she was indeed sacrificing for her nation.

When the call to muster in the courtyard in front of the dormitory was heard, Tonay hurried. She followed the flood of other recruits. She wanted to be noticed. As she pushed herself out the door, she was once again amazed at the number of recruits. They were her brothers and sisters.

The training officers quickly had the recruits in lines. Standing in the front row, Tonay did her best to look grave and capable. With her face set in a mask of seriousness, she waited to be given a practice sword so she could show what she could do.

People of every shape and size were in the yard. It gladdened her heart to see so many who cared so much. With so many people volunteering, she reasoned, how could the Dream fail?

The low, squat dormitories blended into the walls that surrounded the large training compound. The walls were high, almost half again her height and their tops bristled with wooden spikes. They obviously symbolized the strength of Atani.

The order came that once the recruits were divided into companies, they would get breakfast. With that announcement, Tonay realized she was very hungry. She wished the others would settle down so she could begin the day.

After what seemed like an impossibly long time watching officers shuffle papers and discuss orders, Tonay was told she was now a part of the seventh company. Her name was being written down. It was official; she was now part of the Atanian army. She was no longer a recruit: she was a Private! If only her father could see her; surely he would realize he had been wrong.

Under the direction of several shouting training officers, the mass of recently promoted privates began moving to the mess area, a large yard with a few tents and a lot of benches in neat rows. The tents covered only the cooks who tended large cauldrons of boiling food. Tonay followed her company-mates and got in line.

She shared bits of conversation with those who were around her. Like her, each of them was interested in serving Atani. Together they commiserated that their parents, among others, could not understand such noble ideas.

When she reached the food tents, she was handed a rough-hewn wooden trencher. The trencher looked like it had held many meals since it had last been gouged. Though the thought of eating off the rotten wood sickened her, she knew that sacrifice was necessary to bring the Dream to all people.

The food did not look nor smell good. Whatever it was, it had been boiled for so long, it had lost all texture. She did not care. She was doing what she had set out to do.

Almost as soon as she sat down to eat, the training officers began barking more orders. She wolfed down the mush quickly. In so doing, she burned the roof of her mouth. That, she thought, was better than being slow in following orders.

The long line exited the mess yard and entered the supply yard. Instead of food, the soldiers under the tents issued each private a training sword, boots, and a tunic. The boots were certainly more appropriate than what she had brought from home.

Each new soldier quickly donned his or her tunic. Once that was done, the disparate groups of former recruits began to look like an army. Without wasting any time, the training officers marched the members of the Seventh Company off to yet a third yard. After some more instructions, the new soldiers were to begin a long day of drills with their practice swords.

After hours of sweaty practice, the Seventh Company was allowed to take a water break. Tonay's head was on a swivel; she wanted to see everything at once. As the other soldiers of Seventh Company collapsed in whatever shade they could find, Tonay remained standing. She was exhausted, but she wanted to show her training officers that she was different.

In the brief few minutes of rest, Tonay asked about the bright orange arm bands that some of the soldiers were wearing.

"Didn't you hear?" came the friendly reply.

"Hear what?"

"This was the color of the Regent's last gown. It is said she notices people who notice the Dream. By wearing the color, you can show her you are with her."

Tonay almost fainted when she heard the news. She would hate to be ignored or passed over simply because she did not have the right color.

After too short a rest, the orders came again. "Seventh company! Stand and form two lines facing each other. Pick a partner." The lieutenant had a voice that cut the air and grabbed attention. The privates slowly regained their feet.

"Faster! I want you standing straighter than a dwarven line." As he continued his harangue, his corporals joined in. If a soldier was not moving quickly enough, they were given words that were seldom spoken in Ducca's Vineyard.

"Now, we'll see if any of you worthless dogs have anything worth giving the Honored Regent Lilandra. On my command, begin sparring. Hold and begin again if you best your opponent. Otherwise, wait for my command."

The only thing that entered her mind was the image of herself as a fighter, quick and sure. The bigger man across from her nodded in a friendly manner. If he was trying to say he was not going to try to hurt her, she did not see it. Her attention was focused on nothing and everything. She could feel each part of her body. As the lieutenant shouted to begin, only one thought crept into Tonay's mind. She desperately hoped the Regent Lilandra would see this.

* * *

Even wizards such as Sogoth needed sleep. He fought against it every time he felt the tendrils of exhaustion invade his mind. The cool silk of the black sheets caressed his naked body as if to speed his transition to the dream world. Dreams, however, were not always pleasant. It was one of the few places Oaths and his Wizard's Price had no power. His powerful imagination often constructed liquid dreams where his victims were not so powerless and alone in their anguish. Worse still were the vivid scenes of what The Book of the Word decreed would be his punishment at the end of his days.

As a defensive reflex, his mind called forth memories of a happier time. That it was a time when he did not exist meant nothing to someone who did not have a clear idea of what were his thoughts and what were not

The spring wedding ceremony was comforting in its peasant simplicity. The drab brown of homespun tunics and dust covered huts gave way to gay ribbons and flower garland. That three sisters of St. Tabitha's were eager to officiate the exchange of vows made eloping seem like the silly dreams of poor youth. Both sets of the betrotheds' parents beamed with pride. Families from far away farms contributed to the feast that was to follow the ceremony.

Sogoth's father wore simple but handsome clothes. His mother, however, wore a white gown that was shared by the women of the village for weddings. In one of the increasingly embarrassing gestures of gratitude, one of the sisters had altered the gown for Sogoth's mother and interwoven real gold thread.

The betrothed stood together under the white, arched lattice that was painted white and adorned with flowers as the senior nun read from The Book of the Word. After the repetition of ancient prayers, the young lovers exchanged the rings that the sisters had given them days before the ceremony.

The sublime subtlety of the white gold rings made Sogoth's parents initially refuse the gift. The gold and jewels of the rings, the sisters had insisted, were not the real gift. The gift, they said cryptically, was what the rings would bring. In words that the betrothed did not understand, the sisters explained that the rings would strengthen the wearers in the ways only The Creator could see.

Despite the heavy exhaustion that lay upon him like a thick blanket, the magic of the rings he had not seen in uncounted years pulled cool sweat from his warm pores. Even in his castle countless years away, the tingle of the magic the rings held made his exhaustion temporarily retreat.

At the height of the ceremony as the rings passed the second knuckle, Sogoth knew that the pleasure of his parents' marital bed would never match the taste of magic they felt. While not knowing the exact nature of the magic, he knew his parents' blooming marriage was doomed.

Sogoth fought his eyelids as he worked on a problem that had vexed him for so long. The rings clearly held magic and were from the nuns of St. Tabitha's. The nuns who passed the rings to his parents were bound only by their love of The Creator. Why then, did his parents' love falter? Why was he raised by his mother and Lilandra raised by his father?

The black master of sorcery and magic imitated the common behavior of the meanest peasant; he fought with his bed to find a comfortable position. He resented the need to shift to accommodate his weak body. Why could he not simply lie down, endure the necessary interruption to his work and be done with it? Always there was the undignified tossing, the nuzzling of a pillow, and fighting of thoughts that were better left ignored.

This time, his own memories intruded. Time and again, he saw instances of his warm father rebuff him as if he were tainted. Yet, his father made sure Lilandra was never far from his side. As much as the townfolk loved his father, they adored little Lilandra more. Always, there were sweetcakes and a kind smile for her.

For Sogoth, the townsfolk offered politeness, even fear, which was an echo of what was offered to his mother. Just as Lilandra never left her father's side, Sogoth was dragged to every injury, birth, and death of the town with his mother. He learned to see people's frailties and to hear what was said in the moments when people were weakest. In time, he outshone his mother's healing powers and her ability to use people's secrets against them.

As sleep crept into the mind of Sogoth the Soulless, a nightmare born of a true memory reared in his head. In their worst, the nightmares and memories were one.

The mob was terrifying in its alieness though he knew all of its members. He and his mother had comforted the fevered faces of those who shouted the worst of the hate. That they were simple farmers made their torches no less bright and their pitchforks no less sharp. The group tantrum hurled the darkest of all peasant accusations, *witch*. Encircling his mother's stoutly built house took the horde a surprisingly long time. The amorphous gang had precious little leadership. Hate was a poor substitute for courage. Making itself into a thin cordon allowed each member to be seen as dangerously close to an individual.

With a timid beginning, the mob made its desire known. Ignorant folk who had begged her to save their babies demanded she present herself for a trial. Everyone whose ears were rasped by the hate knew that the trial would only end one way.

"Come out now and your boy will live to leave this town." The statement hung in the cool night like a fog of evil. Sogoth remembered that was the first time he had ever known panic. The creak of the crude hinges was like a trumpet announcing her.

With regal pride, she had stood among them in her thin night clothes. Shadows flickered across her face as the torches of the ignorant foreshadowed her sentence.

Sogoth remembered his mother neither denying nor fighting. With a shame that heated the cool sheets around his naked body, he remembered himself walking away from his mother as the mob took her away.

The only thing that burned hotter than his shame was the rage that came with the memory of his sister standing among the crowd. As the mob turned its evil body to escort his mother to a tree for hanging, Lilandra stood still. Etched in Sogoth's brain was the smile in the young Lilandra's eyes. It was a smile that few peasants ever could smile; it was the smile of accomplishment.

* * *

The days had passed much like they had before Keven tried to escape. In truth, he had stopped counting how many there had been. His life in Village Donnell seemed so far away. His mother seemed to be a character out of a story. He convinced himself he missed her, but he could not make himself feel it.

The few oats that were left were for the horses, leaving them to eat rough fare, gathered from the surroundings by Corporals Tapeni and Marsali. Each evening, they would emerge from the woods with the products of their foraging, eager to show Kiel what they had found. Keven noticed their need to impress her dispassionately.

He cared little for the food they offered him. At first, he resisted eating, but he became hungry. He had no real reason not to eat, and he had suffered enough indignation. Having food forced down his throat by a beautiful woman while he was bound was not something he wanted to risk. He knew she was quite capable of it.

As they traveled, Keven noticed the landscape change to rolling hills of low foliage. From her previous attempts to make Atani sound inviting, Kiel had described in detail the plants of Atani. Even without the elf's lecture on the plant life of Atani, Keven knew he was in the far eastern land. He wondered if he would ever leave.

Thoughts of Gareloch carried with them a hard to define emotion. To Keven, Gareloch was hope. He had shown Keven how rich life could be. Indeed, Keven had begun to see the way of things. Keven inwardly smiled at the thought of Gareloch's words. Still, thoughts of Gareloch were mixed. He still did not know if the old man had been killed or was alive and not coming for him.

The only thoughts that seemed to bring much pleasure were those of Erin. Almost constantly, he reviewed memories of them in the woods near Village Donnell. Her sense of humor and her gentle way with him had made him feel safe from the world after his many torments.

Keven had almost grown accustomed to being a prisoner. They had not mistreated him; from their point of view it was only smart to keep a prisoner bound. He knew he had already half surrendered himself to their whims. Still, the latest development made submitting to Kiel's will much more debasing.

It was a roughly created device to further restrict Keven, little more than a collar and stick. The collar was a simple leather thong tied around his neck. Due to his hands being bound with the cloth, he could not untie even a simple knot. The attached stick hung down Keven's torso from the front of his collar where the others of his party could easily reach it. They used it to move him in the direction and manner they chose like a leash.

When he was on horseback, Kiel would tie the stick to Thistle's saddle horn. Thistle, surprisingly, rode smoother than she ever had. Keven didn't know if it was magic, luck, or something else. Whatever the reason, Keven was grateful. With his neck attached to the saddle by a rigid stick, he would have been very sore had it not been for Thistle's gentle gait.

"Human, your humor is foul. We are close to Atani City. Your past moments with us will become clear. I regret the need for such a brace, but it was your decisions that forced these moments."

Keven did not know why she continuously approached him. He knew she wanted something from him, but he just did not know what it was. As a result, he maintained his silence.

"You are a puzzle. It is true I have seen little of your race, but I have read much. You do not fit other humans. From your present moments, I can guess neither your past nor your future."

Keven listened, but he gave no outward sign of it. Even if he did hear something useful, there was little he could do.

"Your companion, he was one of great power and clearly an enemy of the Dream."

Keven knew enough not to argue with her. Her actions showed that there was nothing that would persuade her. Indeed, by attempting to do so, he might give her a reason to use her weapons.

"He obviously taught you some. You know of magic."

Keven was rendered totally helpless, far from any possible aid, and she was asking about what magic he might possibly know. He couldn't tell if she was asking or telling, and his thoughts flowed thickly. He decided to say nothing.

She broke the silence. "I, too, rode to Atani, unsure of my future moments. In a short time, I was welcomed and honored. It shall be so for you as well."

Keven broke his silence. "Were you forced?"

"In a manner of speaking. I was forced from my home. No one can control all of their future moments."

Keven heard her words, but dismissed them as meaningless. He retreated back to silence.

"I can not now control the past moments that led me to leave Elvenwood. Nor can you control the moments that brought you here. Were I to unbind you this moment, you might well resist in a future moment. I would not want that regret with me. Regent Lilandra values all who would help in the Dream of Atani. It seems you might have the ability to help a great deal. There human: behold!"

Keven followed her outstretched arm. What he saw made him feel smaller than he had ever felt before in his life. Sitting atop Thistle on a recently crested hill gave him a view of Atani city.

The city itself was huge. Keven could easily see the imposing stone wall surrounding the city. At regular intervals, towers rose up from the square walls. Outside of those walls was another city.

It was a city of wagons, carts, and tents. All of the people of Village Donnell could easily fit into the many makeshift shelters many times over. There seemed to be no logic as to how the tents and wagons were placed.

* * *

It had been a long and unpleasant journey. Though they did not deny him food, Tapio was far from the willing volunteer they said he was. The only thing that tempered his rage at being forced to Atani City was that he believed Tonay to be there as well.

The city looked much bigger than it had in his youth. King Donius always had an eye on the defense of his nation. He would have never allowed peasants to concentrate in settlements outside of the city walls. For those who could not make it into the city in times of siege, he had required them to spread out in the countryside where they would be harder to massacre. The city walls were obscured by tents and hastily built merchants' booths. It had to be this new Regent's doing. From the poles that held up the tents, Tapio could see bits of cloth that made it look like a festival.

It was so crowded that they had to slow their horses to a walk lest they trample a darting child. Many parts of the road were blocked by venders hawking their wares. Each person greeted Tapio and his guards with a smile or a wave.

As the party reached one of the city gates, their members wearily lumbered to a guard station. Horses were hobbled to a rope strung between two posts. Lieutenant Spudolli and his men dismounted and told Tapio to follow, handing the reins of their mounts to the guards. When one of the guards came for Tapio's old horse, Tapio did not protest. Doing so would gain him nothing.

He tried to unstrap his saddle and take his belongings with him. An extra pair of clothes and a few coins were all that kept him from being a beggar. Lieutenant Spudolli, his soldiers, and the eight guards of two other squads explained to Tapio he would not need such things. They seemed to be honest in their reassurance as his belongings were recorded. They told him repeatedly it would be redistributed to other citizens of Atani.

"From those who have to those who need," he was told several times. Tapio could not truly believe so many soldiers would not take for themselves.

In all of his descriptions to Tonay of how crowded Atani City was, he had thought he was accurately describing it to her. If anything, he had exaggerated his memories to dissuade her from wishing to visit. His exaggerated memories did not match what his eyes told him as he walked the city streets with his armed escorts. They had to push themselves through the crowds. Vendors had set up booths in the middle of the street. Some of the travelers set up their wagons as portable houses.

Despite how packed the people seemed to be, Tapio did not notice the hostility that usually accompanied such tight quarters. The people seemed to actually enjoy the closeness. As often as he was jostled or bumped, he heard a sincere word of pardon.

The crowd shifted and gave him a view of a slave standing against the side of a large shop. Of course, the slave was officially a former slave; the Regent had said so. Her false proclamation did nothing to fill the empty stare of the poor creature who leaned against the wall looking for direction.

As if The Creator wanted to emphasize the subtle sickness that surrounded him, a group of boys smaller than Tonay began taunting the slave. He put up no defense as the boys' words turned to pokes then slaps. Tapio, who had seen more blood than most did not know what what was more disturbing. The boys kicking the defenseless man who curled in a fetal position or the fact that no one made a move to stop it.

Tapio looked around and was sure he was the only one who noticed it. The crowd slamming into his back ripped him out of his disgust for the public brutality. He staggered and had to work to keep his feet. Others were knocked to the ground and that allowed him an opportunity to see the cause of the surge in bodies. Dwarves. There were a half dozen of them making their way through the crowd. Unlike Tapio and the other humans, they did not attempt to slide between people.

As they pushed the crowd away from them, not a word of apology or pardon was offered. Their passage took only moments. It took several more, however, for the crowd to regain its previous robustness.

The thought crossed his mind to use the crowd to his advantage. He might be able to separate from Lieutenant Spudolli and his men. His heart raced at the prospect of being free of them. He began to plot his course through the crowd.

As he was about to make his move, he thought better of it. He might be able to distance himself from them by a few yards but he would not be able to move very well through the thick throng. They still had crossbows. Tapio did not think they would fire in such crowded streets, but he was not completely sure. He would never forgive himself if he made it to Atani City only to be shot in what could be no more than a league or two from Tonay. He discarded his escape idea though it burned to do so.

He dutifully followed Lieutenant Spudolli through the crowd with the other soldiers fanned out behind him. As he noticed more of the city, he could not help but marvel at the amount and variety of people he saw. There were cobblers and barbers who were hawking their trades from rickety carts. Some of the merchants' wagons staked out quite a bit of street surrounding their opulent homes on wheels.

The sights and sounds swirled around him. They came too fast for him to focus on one. The smells, however, were anything but fast. They hung in the air in a nauseating cloud. Even the occasional aroma of roasting meat with spices was not enough to overcome the stench of so many unwashed bodies. The roasting meat reminded him of his hunger. That, of course, made him even more resentful of his position. He was in a unforgiving city with no coin, no horse, and no way to find his daughter except to follow his escorts. He was helpless.

He felt non-existent. He'd had no time to tell anyone in Ducca's Vineyard of his trip to Atani City, so no one knew where he was. Tonay obviously didn't know. If he were to get a crossbow bolt in his back, no one would know or mourn him.

At least he had his name and his daughter's love. Nothing could take that away. The very thought of losing Tonay caused the forge of his rage to heat up again.

The walk from the city gates took most of the day. He was hungry, tired, and angry. That was no combination to accompany the realization that he had just arrived at a set of barracks.

As they approached, Tapio could see the spikes on the wall that surrounded what he knew to be a training camp. It was not the same one he had been trained in as a young man. As lost as he was in the city, he was not sure if he could find that site again even if it still existed.

There was no let up in pace as his escort marched towards the opening in that wall. A squad of soldiers, some standing, some seated around a table, guarded the opening. There was a booth nearby that they obviously used for administrative purposes. The soldiers stood around in the bored, arrogant stance that only men who had not seen true battle could manage. They were young and filled with the false confidence that was given to them by others.

Each of the men loitering around the entrance, while older than Tonay, had few lines on their faces. Their uniforms were crisp and clean. Their swords, he could see, were fresh from the forge. Tapio prayed to The Creator that they would stay unused.

When they had reached the bunch of soldiers, Lieutenant Spudolli proudly said, "We have brought a recruit to help Atani reach her glory. Keep an eye on this one; he has experience. A report will be filed regarding him. The circumstances of finding him justified ending the expedition early."

There were genuine good feelings as the squad on duty congratulated him. Tapio was shocked. Was everyone crazy? Did they truly not know he was dragged here against his will? Would they care if he told them? He could not be the only recruit who was forceably brought here.

The officer in charge approached Tapio. "Name?" he said in an officious tone.

"I am Tapio Denisio. I am a farmer from the south, an area called Ducca's Vineyard." He said it confidently.

"It is good that you have come, farmer. The Regent calls us all. We all give what we can. You are a farmer no more. Despite your experience, you are a private in the Atanian Army," a round-faced soldier said with some triumph.

"It is an honor to serve. With all citizens working for Atani, our nation will know no limits." That seemed to pacify the officer. He nodded and then passed Tapio to two of the soldiers. Both were thin and had not gained the full weight of manhood. They, however, had swords.

As he was escorted into the training ground, he heard the officer in charge call to him. "Private Denisio, you are assigned to the Eighth Company."

That meant nothing to Tapio, but his two escorts nodded and steered him to the left. Once he got a clear view of the area inside the great fence, his heart sank. There were thousands upon thousands of people enclosed in the large series of yards and buildings. There were far more soldiers in this place than he ever recalled seeing before. As big as the complex was, he knew it was only one possible complex in which Tonay might be.

Because it was afternoon, he could see several large groups of soldiers marching, practicing, and doing their best to please the men who were yelling at them. He was led in the direction of a group of soldiers who were lying about in the shade. The officer in charge noticed Tapio and the two escorts approach.

"Identify yourself, Private," the officer ordered in a surprisingly friendly manner.

"I am Tapio Denisio. I am a farmer." He risked upsetting the officer by not using his new rank of private, but he simply did not want to be called by anything other than his name.

"I am Captain Amito. I'm sure you have traveled far. We train hard, but it will bring out the best in each soldier. Once you have reached your best, you can better serve the Dream." The tone was welcoming.

"*Private* Denisio, this is the Eighth Company of the fifth regiment. From this company will come the men and women who will make up your squad. This will be the best company." He said the last loudly. As the resting soldiers heard it, they perked up and enthusiastically offered cheers.

Captain Amito ignored the cheers. "You're a bit older than our normal recruit. It is no matter. We have thousands of people who seek out service in the army."

"You mean all of these people are volunteers?"

The officer gave him a questioning look. "Yes, even those from other nations are welcome. That lieutenant over there was rescued from slavers by Atanian soldiers. She came some time ago. Her father was a blacksmith, so she knew her way around the forge. She worked her way up from a private. Not easy for a woman so small. Now she is the weapons officer for some of the companies. She was a foreigner from the west but she gives everything she has for the Dream. The rumor is, she is going to be a captain soon. That is how the Regent wants it. Anyone can achieve everything.

"In a short time, you will join us in drills. You will get the hang of it. Your fellow soldiers will take it easy on you at first. After drills, we will get you situated in the barracks. Now do you have any questions?"

"I have a daughter who was ahead of me in coming to serve. I had to stay to close my small farm. After that was done, I came after her, but she was so eager, I could not match her pace. Would it be possible to find her?" His heart hung in his chest. Weeks of travel, worry, and despair hung on that one question. Tapio prayed to The Creator that this would help him find Tonay.

"I will do some checking for you. If she is here or in another camp, we will have record of it. But for now rest time is over. Please join your company in drills."

Tapio controlled his emotion as the officer stirred his men. He would join them and feign enthusiasm. He would do whatever it took. Tonay might only be a few hours away.

Tapio was handed a practice sword that had metal weights attached to the end of it. He was partnered with a young looking soldier who was holding a large sack of sand that must have weighed four stone. After watching the other soldiers begin, Tapio quickly realized he was to strike that bag as hard as he could. His partner's hands and arms surrounded the bag. Part of the drill was to learn control with a heavy practice sword. Fortunately, the young man wore padded mitts as one errant swing would easily break a hand.

It did not take long for the men, young and old, to become saturated in sweat. There were paint marks on the sack of sand to denote where the vital areas on an opponent's body would be. Despite himself, Tapio could not help but smile at the accuracy of his blows. Even while concentrating on his accuracy, he was hitting hard enough to force his young partner to take an occasional step.

After some time, the two partners switched. Tapio donned the padded mitts and hefted the heavy sack. It did not take him long to learn that his young partner was nowhere near as skilled as he was. Despite the padding, his arms, wrists, and hands started to ache.

The drill lasted for hours. After each round, Tapio and others in his line were ordered to move right to face new partners. He quickly made eye contact with each of his new partners. None of the members of the Eighth Company wished to hit their partners. Still accidents did happen, and there was always a sympathetic wince from the other men.

Tapio's exhaustion prevented him from noticing how the sun had fallen. He was surprised when Captain Amito ordered a halt to the drill.

"Not bad, Eighth Company. I am told I am not supposed to encourage competition between the companies, but I have seen you train and I have seen the other companies train. I'll deny this if I hear it repeated, but the Eighth Company is the toughest company in the army!" They all cheered as they clapped each other on the back.

"Now, you have three candle marks to clean up, assemble in front of your barracks, and ready yourselves for evening meal. Fall out."

Once inside his barracks, Tapio followed the soldiers to the far wall where he saw several open kegs of water. The first keg was simply for dunking heads and cooling off. The soldiers dipped their heads in and let the water drip down their sweaty shirts.

After they had done that, they removed their shirts. Even the women did so. They stood in line with the men in nothing but their underclothes. Tapio could barely control himself at the thought of Tonay standing about with her shirt off. It was not right. She knew better, but he knew there was little resisting when a group insisted on a certain behavior.

The next barrels had soap, wash water, rinse water, and one even had dry shirts for the soldiers. The women were given clean underclothes and a screen to change behind. The men paid them little attention. After some time, the whole company was clean, dressed, and ready for dinner.

As a group, they filed out of the building and assembled into lines. Tapio was guided by his new company-mates, who urged him to be quick and silent.

When Captain Amito arrived, he surveyed the company for a few moments. Each soldier pretended not to notice. They fixed their gaze on the unclimbable wall that surrounded the whole of the training grounds.

"Very good, Eighth Company. If you keep progressing, you will be ready soon," the Captain said matter-of-factly. If it was to be a compliment, he hid it well. Still, Tapio noticed many of his fellows struggle to hide smiles.

"Eighth Company, fall out for dinner!" They cheered as they began to walk briskly to the mess area. Tapio followed the crowd but was stopped.

"Private Denisio, as I said, I did some checking. There is a Private Denisio in the Seventh Company. She is a young woman. From that, I would say she is your daughter."

Tapio Denisio struggled mightily to keep his face blank. Tonay was here! He had to assume she was well.

"There will be ample time to meet her. *But,* I must stress you do not have permission to seek her on your own. She is a private in the Atanian Army, as are you. She is not your little girl anymore. You are not her father. You are a fellow soldier. Now, the other soldiers like me because I help them. I am an easy captain when things go as I wish. Do not think, though that I will permit disobedience." Captain Amito whispered the last and Tapio believed the man was deadly serious. There was a reason only the officers had real swords.

"Thank you, sir!" Tapio winced as the words came from his mouth. Old habits die hard and he was now acting just like any other soldier.

"One more thing, Private. You should be proud. There is a rumor that Seventh Company has impressed the Regent enough to be sent off. They are to take the Dream to those outside of Atani."

What was only moments ago a feeling of elation turned to leaden despair. He had seen battle. He had to reach her before she left with her company.

* * *

The expedition had to be counted a success. It was a shame that Corporal Ginelli was lost. He had the makings of a good soldier despite his abuse of the horse, a creature of nature. Perhaps *Agris* chose the manner of Ginelli's death as a consequence of his past moments with animals. Ginelli's death aside, it was important to know how far north direbugs had traveled. Direbugs and goblins were not something to be taken lightly, but they were fun to kill. Because of the Dream, she was able to use her skills to put an arrow into a wizard and kill direbugs.

Kiel's worries about goblins were soothed at the thought of the Regent meeting this man. If anyone could draw someone out of his seedpod, it was the Regent Lilandra. She could see the flower hidden in even the ugliest bulb.

The road was fairly crowded as they rode the last two miles. She stole a quick glance at the human, Keven. He wore no expression. It was as if the sprawling city did not affect him. He seemed to feel less and less with the passage of each day.

As the city loomed near, Kiel examined the buildings just outside the city walls. It could only be described as a small village made of metal. Stone and wood were bad enough. Who under nature's sky would ever choose to surround themselves with straight metal lines? It didn't take her keen elven eyes to find the answer. Dwarves. She had read about them of course. Elven books, she was learning, had not always accurately portrayed what was in the lands beyond Elvenwood.

Had she been in Elvenwood, she would have counseled herself to ride to another entrance into the city. She knew little about dwarves and their customs. In general, the stories painted an unflattering picture.

The wizard's apprentice seemed not to notice. Seeds that stayed dormant longest often grew into the tallest trees; she heard her instructors' voice echo a favorite lecture topic. She rode on, trying to keep him at her side. As they neared the city, she had to hold his horse's reins to keep the party moving. Corporals Marsali and Tapeni were only a few paces behind with the spare horses in tow.

She could see a dozen dwarves on top of different roofs of their village. Each one was alert and holding one of their legendary crossbows.

Right as that thought passed through her mind, she saw one of the dwarven sentries point their way. As he did, the others swung their bearded heads in her direction. To get to the gates, she would have to pass in range of their crossbows.

She did not take her bow from her back. Her skill with a bow would not prevent them from approaching. None of the humans who were sharing the road with her seemed particularly fearful of the dwarves. She should act as the road-side humans did. Trusting others, however, often led to regret.

Kiel gripped the reins of her horse and of Keven's more tightly as a group of stout dwarves ambled towards her. Their rough laughter did not instill ease in her. She hoped her two soldiers behind her would not do anything to cause regret. They were three while the dwarves coming towards her numbered six. Though they might be able to outrun the bandy-legged dwarves, they could never out run the crossbows on the steel roofs.

"Hey now, what's this? Three on one?" Each of the six dwarves approaching her carried a mug of what had to be ale in one of their meaty hands. With only one hand occupied with a flagon, the other hand of each dwarf was close to the heavy hammer or axe hanging from wide leather belts.

Kiel took down her hood. She had learned enough to know that her visage was striking enough to win concessions from some. She hoped it was so with the dwarves.

"Look, Maul, an elf. An elven archer and two soldiers for one skinny man. He must be fearsome to be tied so." Their laughter did not hide the rage in their eyes, as they formed a semi circle in the road. Kiel could ride around, but that might escalate the confrontation.

"I am Captain Kielasanthra Tylansthra of the Atanian army. I am on my way to see the Regent Lilandra. She will be displeased if I am delayed."

Kiel knew of dwarven hatred for her kind. Whenever she asked for an explanation of the hatred, the elders had always quickly reminded her that it was not her position to question them.

One of dwarves, who might have been the drunkest, said, "There's no sport in three-on-one." He offered in a mocking tone. As he staggered to her horse, it pranced a bit uncertainly about the strange figure. Dropping the guise of inebriation, he snatched the reins of her horse near its bit. Then with an arm span that could not possibly fit on such a compact form, he sacrificed his mug to grab the hilt of her sword. In a blink, he had her neutralized. He knew she would not be able to free her sword from his iron-like grip. Still, she remained calm lest Tapeni or Marsali act rashly.

The dwarves were merely bored. Kiel also reasoned that had they been intent on harm, the Regent would not have allowed them to stay. This waste of moments was insignificant. She could be patient.

Another dwarf ambled to Keven's horse. Thistle, with no warning, bit the dwarf. Keven did not react except to watch. Tied as he was, there was little he could do. The dwarf ignored what had to be a painful bite.

"Listen now, boy, we'll fight to free you, three against one shows no one's strength, but only if you prove your worth to me after. I have to know why they keep you like an animal."

Kiel broke in. "He is being brought to the Regent. He is no concern of yours."

"I did not ask you, elf. To keep anyone so bound, three against one does not ring true."

Kiel realized that the dwarves could take Keven to their steel village. Getting him away from the dwarves if that happened would be next to impossible. Her heart sank as she thought about Lilandra being disappointed.

"You, boy, what say you? To have your strength stolen like this or to contest with honor?"

To Keven, it was all happening too fast. First, it was magic and goblins. Then it was an elf and being held as a prisoner. Now, he was facing the prospect of freedom with dwarves. Would that be any better than what Kiel had told him awaited him?

"If I take your offer, I will then owe you. Your price may be higher than the one I am already being forced to pay." After he said it, he simply looked down at the dwarf with a blank expression on his face. The dwarf returned his stare from beneath bushy eyebrows.

"Hah! Did you hear this one? He does not need our strength. Truly, there is a reason he is held so. He has his own strength and resists an easy bargain." The dwarf punctuated his laugh with a big swig from his mug.

"Leave this one be. He does not need our help. He needs nothing. A true dwarf among humans. Boy, you can drink with us anytime." With that, they turned their back as a group on the riders and headed back to their small, steel fortress.

What Keven did not know was that the dwarf leader and Kiel shared similar thoughts. For the elegant elf, the thought was a little unsettling. For the gruff dwarf, the thought was something to be admired. Keven did not seem to need much at all.

Kiel

D. Cameron Calkins

Chapter 15

Keven noticed that it was Corporal Tapeni who was actually leading his Captain through the crowded city. It made sense to Keven that he would know the city better than she. Still, it seemed odd to have the intimidating, confident elf listen to another.

The confusion of the city and the teeming pace of the streets were a more effective prison than any ropes or knots could ever be. He did not wonder if the many people he passed would give him aid if he asked; he had learned the answer to that question in his own village. People did not worry themselves with the need of others.

Keven could sense Thistle's unease. She did not like much in the best of circumstances; being in a crowded city made her even more edgy. Even from his saddle, Keven knew her eyes were wide with fear and alarm.

Atani City did not match what he had imagined. The dress of the people and the look of the buildings were different from that of the Westlands. He was far from home and with each step, he felt the possibility of ever seeing the Wizards' Palace slip away.

As soon as he saw the intimidating wall, he knew that was his destination. There was an opening about which men in uniform were milling about. As they got close, a man stepped from the crowd.

"I am Lieutenant Burtoni. Are you lost, Corporal?" He sneered at Corporal Tapeni's bedraggled image.

"Perhaps I can tell you where my soldier needs to be, *Lieutenant*. I am *Captain* Kielasanthra Tylansthra. We wish to entrust a recruit to you. I trust you will show him that we all serve the same Dream, especially those who have been bravely scouting the lands while others have been polishing their boots and playing soldier."

The arrogant officer's eyes went wide in surprise. He realized the rumors of an elf in the army were true. Embarrassment and fear washed across his face as he mumbled unintelligible words.

After the chagrined lieutenant mumbled his compliance, all eyes turned to Keven. There were at least six men on the ground, all wore blank expressions. One of them barked orders for Keven to dismount. As

Keven was being yelled at, another man in uniformed strode forward to untie his bonds. Numbly and with more than a little regret, Keven swung down from Thistle's saddle.

Captain Kiel, Corporal Tapeni, and Corporal Marsali had fed him and to some extent, protected him. In Keven's mind, they represented life outside of this huge city. If they left him, he would be separated from any link to his previous life.

"Step lively, Recruit. Front and center," Lieutenant Burtoni said.

Keven did not have the energy to move quickly, nor did he have the need to rebel or fight this new authority. If he fought, he would not be any closer to freedom.

"What is your name?" As the lieutenant spoke, one of his men appeared with a tablet.

"It is Keven." He automatically spoke in a flat tone.

"It is Keven, Sir!" the lieutenant corrected him. "What is your father's name, recruit?"

For years Keven's lineage had been the tenderest of sore spots. The village of his youth knew that and used it to endlessly torment him. Years earlier, he had even prayed to The Creator for a father. He was ignored.

"I don't know," he said.

"Are you playing dumb with me? Most people strive to get here. It is an honor to serve Atani." The lieutenant's shout came from a distance of less than a thumb's width from Keven. "I'll say again. This time you had better think before you answer! What is your father's name?"

"I don't know."

With speed that would've made Gunter jealous, the back of Lieutenant Burtoni's hand impacted Keven's cheek. Keven was staggered, but resisted the need to feel his cheek.

"I'm a bastard. I have never known my father. My mother does not know his last name." He said it without shame.

"In the new Atanian army, everyone must be equal. You have to have a last name. You will now be known as Private Keven Whoreson." With that, the corporal next to Lieutenant Burtoni wrote on the tablet. "You are now part of the Ninth Company."

From seemingly nowhere, an arrow flew past the eyes of all present. It took the hat from Lieutenant Bertoni and stuck it to a post supporting the guardhouse.

"Lieutenant," the elf said with menacing calm. "I will be happy to give you lessons on the Dream. It seems you are in need of more education. Is this how fellow citizens are to be treated?"

"No, Captain."

"This man is to be treated like every other recruit. He cannot be expected to experience the Dream if he does not have proper examples. I will report this to your commander. If I hear of any other abuse, you will face me."

After that proclamation, Keven was escorted through the gate. Captain Kiel and her men turned their horses and rode off. When she realized what was happening, Thistle went wild. Two of the unsuspecting soldiers were knocked to the ground.

After a few moments of mayhem, one of the solders produced a cane about the thickness of his thumb. The air whistled as he swung it. Thistle screamed as it hit her again and again. Keven caught the look of defeat in her eyes as they led her away.

As he walked through the gate, he saw a courtyard filled with countless other young men and women practicing swordsmanship while others marched. A few seemed to be doing little but standing in straight lines. It was that group to which Keven was led by two of the corporals.

The lines of soldiers watched Keven approach. Though their heads did not move, he knew that their eyes were studying him intently. He paid little attention to the exchange between the corporals who escorted him and the one who was ensuring the lines were straight. He merely heard snippets of their conversation.

"Another one, huh? Well, I'll take him, but no more after that."

"You'll have your hands full with this one. He doesn't see the need to show respect to his superiors."

Keven knew from his experience with Banolf that to try and refute that claim would only make matters worse. He kept his mouth shut and tried to put his mind anywhere but where he was. He was roughly shoved towards the soldiers standing in line.

"Your place is here." The corporal in charge guided Keven to a spot in the rear line. "Keep the dung out of your ears, and we'll have no problems."

The next hours were spent marching in unison. Keven had spent his life doing hard work. Though he was not a strong man, he was not overly frail. He was therefore surprised when he realized how exhausting marching was. Physically, he reasoned, he had endured much worse, but marching was mind numbingly boring. As boring as it was, he could not let his mind drift. At any time, the corporal in charge would bark a command that would have the whole formation change their direction.

As long as the day of marching was, the end of it came suddenly.

"Ninth company! Dismissed. Three candle marks until evening mess." The well-formed group of soldiers disintegrated and moved as one to one of the low squat buildings. Keven, not knowing any different, followed the crowd.

They filed into one of the buildings that looked remarkably like all of the others. The coolness of the large building was a welcome relief from the hot afternoon sun. There were rows of low-slung cots on the dirt floor. Keven followed and watched as the others fell into their cots. He found an empty one and imitated them.

He watched with interest as one of the soldiers produced a candle. Another soldier went to the mid-sized hearth set into one of the walls. As hot as it was in the daytime, Keven knew from his time with Captain Kiel that Atani nights could become cool. The soldier returned from the hearth with a fist-sized chunk of flint. After a few quick strikes, the candle was lit.

Once that was done, the soldiers began to talk with each other. There was little serious conversation. The way they carried themselves was not like a group of people forced to train. He wondered if they all could be wrong in their choice to volunteer. Seeing them tease each other and make outlandish claims made him realize he had never had such friends. He was the only one in the large room who was unhappy.

It gave him a lot to think about. He lay quietly on his bunk with his thoughts racing. Keven followed the gaze of his fellow soldiers. Periodically, they would look at the table that supported the candle. It had only a short time to burn before they could report for evening mess. But as their eyes occasionally looked at the candle, Keven's stared at something next to it: the large chunk of flint.

* * *

Lucius was working to imbue a shirt with *Aestifer*, a delicate piece of magic that needed a touch of sorcery. The spell itself was not difficult and the energy and matter involved were comparatively small. Still, even a small amount of energy and a small amount of matter greatly resisted occupying the same space. By using sorcery, Gareloch could hold the shirtness, the essence of the shirt still, when Lucius pressed the magic into it. That was possible only if the Wizard of Sorcery was paying attention.

"Gareloch, are you still thinking of that stable hand? You have lived how many centuries? You have seen how many young men enter the palace? Forget this one. He may be fine. If he is as special as you say, he is probably handling himself just fine."

"Lucius, ye do no believe that anymore than I do. The madness in Atani might leave any number of peasants untouched. But, ye know such madness will land on the lad as surely as the hawk did. He is small boat in a roaring ocean holding onto a wee candle of hope and dreams. The madness will engulf him and his light, his hope will be gone."

Lucius was quiet at Gareloch's sad ruminations. There was no consoling a wizard who was intent on dwelling on the painful cost of his Wizard's Price. Lucius knew that no matter how many times Gareloch told him not to fret over his grotesque body, he could not help it.

"Lucius, ye do no see? After all the lad had been through, he was still willing ta take a chance with me. Most people outside of this palace look at the past no differently than they do the future. In only days on the road with me, he was imagining his future."

"You have convinced me, Gareloch. The man was special. What of it? Are you going to track him like a ranger? You're an old man with no horse. Are you going to spout fire from your hands and toss people about until you find him? Test your skills against a city? What would that do for the people of the lands, to have them know there are wizards among them?"

Gareloch sat in one of the rickety, wooden chairs that did little to add comfort to his bare chambers. Lucius took a chair that was across from an ancient table that looked as though it could barely hold the platter of sausages that had recently been emptied.

Lucius had seen his old friend confront his limitations many times. All people were limited; Gareloch knew that fact. He just raged against it more than most. Though he was old and spindly, Lucius knew Gareloch's clenched fists were anything but weak.

"Do I let him go? Give up like the rest of the wizards in this stone prison?" He said the last in anger. Lucius was one of those wizards; it was unfair for Gareloch to blame him for not finding a way out of the Wizards' Palace. Rather than apologize, he told his large friend the rest of the story.

"Lucius, there is more. I have told ye the lad had hope fer himself. Do ye know how rare that is, hope in a peasant? Hope, like despair, has the way of disease. Tis contagious."

"I know how your curse torments you, but aren't you reading too much into this one man?"

"But *I* felt *hope* for him. Don't you see what that means? A glimmer I have not felt in centuries of searching. *Hope* was magically taken from me. If he can show me the way of hope, could he no do the same fer peasant farmers? If he can ease my Wizard's Price, can he no do it fer other wizards? Fer you?"

Lucius, Gareloch knew, was undergoing his own mental struggle. Gareloch waited and watched his friend. The fat man's body might be soft, but his mind was as quick and sharp as any in the Wizards' Palace.

Gareloch continued. His excitement was that of a novice succeeding at his first spell. "Remember the prophecy. Tis true. He is the one."

Lucius ignored his friend's ravings. He, like all humans, would think of his own need first. He would imagine himself free of a body that was big enough for four men. He would then think of what the future might hold for poor laborers if they had real hope of their future. Lucius would need to know more and *that* was when the real explosion of possibility would happen in his mind. It had already happened to Gareloch. If

Keven, a nameless laborer, could possibly free a wizard of his Wizard's Price, then all wizards would seek him.

If they believed such important knowledge lay outside the palace, they would be free from the palace and possibly free of their One Oath. That belief, though, was near impossible to adopt. A whole palace of learned wizards was convinced they were trapped. Almost as rare as the power of need was the ability to separate from a group that is convinced it is correct. Gareloch knew his friend well enough to see the important thoughts cascade across the big man's face. The sought after honest belief that escape was possible bloomed in the man's eyes. Strangely though, Lucius' series of expressions ended in sorrow.

"If what you say is true, then you must hear the rest. While you were out these last years and while you have been recovering these last few weeks, news has come to us. Though wizards cannot leave the palace, hopeful students do find us. Some have come from Atani. It does not bode well for Keven." It was the first time Lucius had used the former stable hand's name.

"Reports are sketchy. This cursed palace confuses the messenger birds. It's a wonder we get any news from the outside. It appears that King Donius is no longer in control of Atani. It is the first time one of his line has not held power in Atani in generations. Atani is now ruled by a Regent. Someone named Lilandra. There is very little information simply because most people are moving into Atani and into Atani City itself. No one seems to be leaving."

Lucius paused to take a bite from a steaming bowl of stew that arrived on the table from nowhere. Driven by his Wizard's Price, Lucius hardly counted the extra effort it took to transport matter that contained energy like heat.

"But, from what we've been told, people are going into the city with clothes, food and coin. They are not fleeing as refugees. It is most unnatural. They seem to be going to Atani to *give* those things to others. There is more. I will tell you what I have heard, and you can piece it together. It is said that the young princess has turned against her father and given herself to this Lilandra. The reports say it is more than her support she has given. It is as if she willingly obeys every word from the new Regent."

Gareloch remained still as he absorbed the information. He did not like what he heard. Though he'd often been correct in ideas that others considered impossible, he never enjoyed being right when his conclusions brought bad news. His mind worked furiously even as he gave enough attention to what Lucius was saying.

"It is said that young and old flock to the city to volunteer for an army. It is not known how many have joined, but at this point it must be bigger than anything the Westlands have. Gareloch, each new student from Atani has confirmed that the people of Atani love the Regent. They would do anything for her. It was only the pull of the Wizards' Palace that kept them from joining her cause. The worst part is that no one can tell where she came from. This Regent Lilandra has done all of this in only a few short years."

Both men fell into silence while slowly working out the only explanation that fit. As their thoughts drew closer to the answer, each man's face showed fearful disbelief.

"Gareloch, do you think it is possible. Really, truly possible?" His dejected tone showed that Lucius believed it was not only possible, it was true.

"Aye, I wish...."

Neither man moved for a time, their thoughts racing.

Gareloch's worry caused him to speak first. "Lucius, if she is a Mistress of Need, Keven will not have a dwarf's chance in a tree."

"Could it be that he was simply taken by slavers?" It was an odd turn of events to hope someone was taken by slavers. So much in the lands was changing so quickly. It was as if the coming storm was preparing itself.

"No, I've told ye. I saw them, from a distance mind ye, but I know the way of Atanian riders."

"If he is held by her or by her people tis truly worse than slavery." Lucius said gravely. "Slavery only destroys hope. She can twist it. She will have him and everyone believing she cares for their need. In time, he will simply change who he is in order to meet her need. They all will. That will be the way of it."

"Damn." That simple word, however often repeated, did not seem to relieve any of the Wizard Master's rage. A moment after he swore, his spartan bed burst into flame. The table that separated the two men instantly shattered to fragments of its former shape. His one concession to comfort, The Magic Stick was left suspended in air.

As reckless as Gareloch's rage seemed, his cool words showed exactly how much control he had over his mind.

"I have been remiss in my duties as Wizard Master. Tis time I change that. I will request that all of the schools, magic, sorcery, alchemy, and technology work together on a project. I'll give enough hints ta let them think that if they take part, they will gain much knowledge. With that seed in their heads, the One Oath will drive them ta assist. I'm going ta Atani. I will have the full power of the Wizards' Palace behind me, whether they know it or no."

The normally reserved Lucius offered no objections. He too saw the importance of such an endeavor. In fact he offered his ideas. "Can I suggest starting with *Situtum Domus*? It can be modified to take a body anywhere." He was almost talking to himself. The scholar in him took over. "We'll need an exact measure of the distance. The Wizards of Technology have their tools. You'll, of course, need help from the Alchemists to let your body survive such a concentration of power."

As Lucius dreamily began to imagine the framework of such a large spell, Gareloch focused on darker matters. Wizards had to gain knowledge. They would in time find the reason for such a large concentration of power. They would sense the possibility of leaving the Wizards' Palace and of ending the horrible toll of the Wizard's Price.

Not all Wizards were bound by The Trinity, to actively seek to aid others. If those who were bound to only the Duality or even worse, to only the One Oath, left the palace, all of the known lands could suffer beyond anyone's nightmares. One wizard with no bindings was too dangerous. Atani was proof of that. If the palace emptied itself, only The Creator could stop what could be the end of all of the Known Lands.

Gareloch's thoughts were interrupted by Lucius' musings. "Anything we could create would have to have immense power. It wouldn't do to have you suddenly appear and then be trapped inside a tree or a wall."

It wasn't that Gareloch wasn't interested in the mechanics of the spell; he very much was. It was that his thoughts took a more serious turn. He knew it would only be a matter of time before the Mistress of Need found Keven. After all, he had. Keven was destined for great things.

He wondered how long Keven could resist. In the deep part of his mind, Gareloch nervously wondered if *he* could resist someone who could manipulate his needs.

They would have to act with all possible speed. It might already be too late. Keven might have already changed. He might have forgotten his mother and the village of his birth. A Mistress of Need could easily convince a young man that he had no need to pursue anything. It was a shame Keven had no faith in The Creator. Gareloch would have liked to have given him that, but it would have sounded hollow coming from a man with no hope.

Gareloch's particular affliction made thinking of Keven very painful. He could not hope things would turn out well. Keven would be so bound by Lilandra's need he might even forget his own beloved Erin. Lilandra could easily take that away from Keven, and he would not even know it was missing.

* * *

Like her brother, Lilandra had knowledge accumulated from years she had not lived. From that knowledge, Lilandra reminded herself that the regard of people was like a fine plate of delicacies. It provided momentary pleasure, but offered little in the way of real benefit. With that thought she maintained a tight control on her response to well-wishers.

As she rode with her escort through Atani City, she had to reign in her desire to interact with the crowds. Indulging in their adoration for her was something she must avoid. Despite near perfect execution of her plans, there were those who resisted her. The number of her escorts constantly grew so that her admirers could only glimpse her through the gaps of the guards' formation.

She had to admit, she missed being so close to the crowds. Adulation was better than any pleasure of the flesh. Still, like slaver's juice, temperance was the key. Public acclaim was too often a siren's song leading to distraction. Still, she rode on, giving a choreographed smile to the crowds that watched her pass.

Lilandra's horse and those of her party were the only ones on the road. By Helena's royal decree, the citizens were requested to donate horses to the Dream. The army and the laborers needed all that they could get. From the number of horses the purser's ledgers showed were donated, Lilandra could get a measurement of the dedication of the citizens. The measurement pleased her, but it did not eliminate the need for her guards or the purpose of the excursion, though she had giving Donius a supposed day of rest to hide her destination from him.

The ratio of those who were loyal and those who wished her ill approached a thousand to one. Still, it was a constant ratio and as the number of loyalists rose, so too did the number of enemies.

Of course, she had convinced the citizens that her enemies were their enemies. With such group think, Lilandra could assign only small numbers of her chosen ones to finding dissenters. Common citizens proved quite adept at assigning themselves the role of enforcers. That they quoted and enforced laws was delicious irony for the ones they had turned in. The ones who were turned in were often the older and more resistant judges and official peace keepers.

Despite the loyal guards surrounding her and the love of her onlookers, Lilandra knew she could not reassign roles to all inhabitants of Atani. Though she did not know when she learned it, it was a truth that humans became their occupations. Even the meanest of citizens identified with the tasks they did most often.

There was little she could to do to change the minds of those who had enjoyed a lifetime of judging and enforcing public values. Even with most of those spirited to the prison, any one of the faces peering from the open windows could hold the secret to a coven of dissenters. It was good that all loyal citizens were expected to donate all private crossbows and bows to the Dream.

The prison was constructed in much the same manner as the barracks, as it saved the carpenters' time. It certainly was not a permanent solution. Once Atani was fully engaged in a war with the west, then the final solution of terminating any dissenters who would not adopt a new role could be applied.

Upon her party's arrival, the guards at the gates swung the heavy doors open. With genuine nods to many of the guards, Lilandra spurred her horse ahead of her guard detail. With a bit of confused hesitation they followed her into the common yard.

The prison guards did not see themselves as body guards and her personal guards did not see themselves as prison wardens. Neither group of men was comfortable with the mass of naked bodies near the Regent Lilandra. Her guards were competent, intelligent men who had seen combat, yet the sight of nude prisoners stymied them. Clothing often dictated roles. Without it, the prisoners had one less thing to remind them of their life before the Dream.

Regent Lilandra had no such problems with seeing a horde of naked enemies of the Dream. In fact, she felt some satisfaction at seeing haughty judges and ministers meekly attempt to cover their genitals as they stopped their appointed chores. Few of the prisoners were women. Indeed under Donius' regime, rare was the instance of a woman rising to a social role of power.

That never meant that women were any less dangerous than men. That the women had more difficulty covering themselves than the men was inconsequential. What Lilandra wanted to know was whether the prisoners worried about their nudity when she was not facing them. If not, it meant they were accepting their new role and that would spare the expense and time of burying their bodies. More than that, if prisoners were returned to society eager to serve, other citizens would see that the Dream was too large to be resisted. That would further the Dream more than simply working them to death.

"Lieutenant Barillo, please instruct the prisoners to return to their work."

"With pleasure, Honored Regent." He flashed a smile that she was sure had never been seen inside the prison before. She had called him by name.

"One more thing, if I may?"

"Of course, Honored Regent."

"I gave instructions that only special soldiers would be assigned here. From what I see, many of these men are young, without special training"

Lieutenant Barillo visibly paled before he found his voice. "With respect, using such followers of the Dream as you ordered was seen to be a waste. Treating prisoners as they deserve takes no special training. In fact, nearly two thirds of any group of guards that have been assigned here will kill or punish any prisoner simply because they are ordered to. I assure you, Honored Regent, no special training is needed to be a prison guard."

"Excellent, Lieutenant. I'm not surprised that loyal Atanians would be firm enough in their treatment of enemies of the Dream." She squared her shoulders with his so that he and everyone watching would know her attention was fully on him. "Such naysayers and doubters must be separated and reeducated. You have earned my permission to reform these prisoners into model citizens by any means necessary."

At his instructions, the guards moved in with quirts and canes. The prisoners scurried to rejoin their tasks and to avoid being seen as too slow.

Shaping recently felled branches into arrows was a repetitive task that few would undertake willingly. And some might question giving prisoners access to long branches and rudimentary tools. But even before the prison was constructed, Lilandra knew who the prisoners would be.

Young people rarely had a social role long enough to resist a new one being thrust upon them. As a result, Lilandra knew there would be no youthful enemies of the Dream. Her prediction proved correct, the prison held only those with more than three decades of life.

With eager assistance from one of her guards, she dismounted her fine white mare. Though she could have agilely swung herself down from her saddle, it was important for the prisoners to see that courtesy and elegance did exist outside of their walls.

She inspected a barrel full of unfletched arrow shafts. She saw what she expected: they were perfectly shaped and would find a good chance of ending up in the body of anyone who opposed the Dream or stood with her brother. That the craftsmanship was of such high level did not surprise her despite lack of training of the prison workers.

From a memory that was not her own, she knew that no one could do a task for long and hate it. The mind would not let such a war exist in it. Since the prisoners could not stop making arrows, human nature dictated they would identify with the task they performed most often.

By looking down the shaft of the arrow, she knew that it must have been created with care. There was pride invested in the smooth wood of the shaft. Was it created by a former judge, a banker who had protested too loudly at agents of the Dream redistributing wealth?

On her way out of the prison, Lilandra made her rounds, dutifully exchanging pleasantries with as much of the prison staff as time allowed. She was careful to ignore the naked workers. Her parting words included instructions for the prison workers. Contests and a prisoner hierarchy should be introduced.

The makers of the best arrows would be rewarded with perhaps an extra blanket or some clothing. They would eagerly comply, though the physical reward would lose its value. The important part was that they would identify more strongly with their task, compliance led to conformity. The judge and banker would die as a new citizen would be born.

* * *

Denying herself the temptation to simply ride her steed to Regent Lilandra was torturous. She relied on her elven training of patience, knowing that if she approached the Regent in her tight leathers, she would feel regret. Every moment with Regent Lilandra was to be treasured: past, present, and future.

It was the need to impress Regent Lilandra that drove Kielasanthra Tylansthra to her rooms in the Atanian Castle. It was a measure of how important Kiel was that the servants were aware of her return. They had prepared a bath, and they pointed out several gowns that she might find suitable for a meeting with the Regent.

Kiel remarked to herself how silly she had been to reject human customs. Of course, the odors of nature were good and to be respected, but the warm, scented bath was just as Lilandra described it. The Regent's simple encouragement to prepare for the Citizens' Assembly had more wisdom in it than all of the lectures by her Elders combined. Truly, following Lilandra would prevent regret.

In this present moment in a tub of warm water being ministered to by a human, Kiel realized it was good to change. Elves, like the mighty trees, were too rooted in place. They needed to be like the leaves of the smallest flower, always turning toward the sun. Humans seemed to do that instinctually; they were born to adapt. They knew their needs and turned toward them.

Donning the elaborate gown was complicated, and Kiel was grateful for the help. There were so many layers of garments, each with its own sets of clasps and buttons.

In her past moments, she did not appreciate the beauty of human garments. After having been told that The Regent herself wore this style of gown, Kiel could see the beauty in it.

Walking through the long court room was an exercise in poise. Of course, word of her return and some of the harrowing, albeit exaggerated, details had reached the eager ears of the nobles at court. They had all but abandoned the pretense of not staring at her as she walked by. Her elven eyes let her know that many of the admirers looked at how the dress both revealed and concealed her body.

As she came within twenty paces of the crowd surrounding the Regent, something unexpected happened: Regent Lilandra rose from the throne and rushed to embrace Kiel.

242

"My elven friend, it is good to have you here. Though we value your skill, we value your company even more." Every face in the large and ornately decorated room was fixed on the two visions of beauty.

The ruler of Atani whispered discreetly in Kiel's delicately pointed ear. "Please do me the favor of mingling with my guests for a time. Then, you and I will discuss matters in private." Just that simple separation from the other guests put Kiel at ease. She would, of course, be happy to do any favor for Regent Lilandra.

The time spent socializing was hard to measure. There were many awkward moments where both human males and females simply stared at her. She was the most important person in a room full of important people.

She lost count of how many times she retold of her battle with the direbugs. Many of the guests politely begged for details of what would have happened to Corporal Ginelli had she not taken such a direct hand. Many of the nobles, especially the men who liked to talk of their exploits with a sword, had trouble understanding how someone so beautiful could do what she did. Her gruesome tales dramatically conflicted with her elegant appearance.

Regent Lilandra saved her. With a slight squeeze of Kiel's elbow, she let the elf know it was time to move away from the sycophants. Most were sorry to see her go, but all tried to conceal envy and admiration for her as she went to spend time with Regent Lilandra.

Despite the array of sights and sounds that came with visiting the nobles at court, Kiel had still not lost her well-honed skills. She became aware of another person who was making his way through the crowd. His path was parallel to the one that Regent Lilandra was making for herself and Kiel.

With a sigh of relief, she realized she did not have to worry. The person who was following them was greeted by Lilandra. They spoke quickly and glanced at Kiel as she made her way through the conversations of admirers. Once Kiel caught up to the pair, they began walking again. The man walked a few paces ahead, then behind and finally kept pace with them.

Kiel noticed two other things about the man. He had a sword strapped to his belt. Though the pommel was ornate and finely crafted, the scabbard was well worn indicating it had released the sword many times. The second thing she noticed was that the man walked with grace. He reminded her of some of the elven males with whom she trained.

The deeper she walked into the castle with Regent Lilandra and her strange escort, the more torches she saw. The dim, flickering light did not overly bother her. Her eyesight was keen enough; it was the thick smoke that bothered her. Trapping it inside a stone building was not natural.

As they approached the door, Lilandra attempted to dismiss the man. "You have been on your feet since before dawn. Please rest now. You have earned it. Who could harm me in my own chambers?"

"It is always good to be sure," he replied. He pushed past the two women and entered The Regent's chambers.

The candelabra and various sconces were already lit. It was a tremendous waste of candles to keep a room lit while unoccupied. Perhaps Lilandra's guard insisted on it. He quickly walked through her apartment, even into her sleeping room. With a nod, he began to exit the room.

Lilandra turned to him. "Once again Donius, thank you. I doubt there is anyone who could protect me so ably."

When he had left, Kiel could not help remarking on the man. "He seems to be a good one to have on your side. He is no stranger to fighting."

"You are perceptive. He is a true Blademaster. He has now found a new way to give to his nation."

Kiel did not ask anymore about the bodyguard. Once they were seated in Lilandra's personal apartments high in the castle, the conversation began in earnest.

"Thank you for spending your valuable time with my guests. Sometimes the nobles misunderstand their role in relation to the rest of Atani."

"It was a good way for me to spend my moments, sharing with others," Kiel graciously said.

"I'm glad it was not too troublesome. I value your contribution to Atani and so do they. It would not be right for me to simply steal you away without them hearing of your exciting adventure. But, tell me, what of the lands outside of Atanian borders?"

"There is much to tell," she said. Despite having told it many times to several foppish nobles, she gladly retold it to the woman who had given her so much.

Kiel recounted everything. The gritty nature of her tale did not match the opulent surroundings in which she found herself. She told how she had instructed her men in the elven art of woods lore. When she told of the direbugs, she made sure to emphasize the importance of goblin tracks. With Regent Lilandra, she did not leave out one awkward detail.

"There was a man we brought back. It seems he has some skills that might prove useful to the Dream." Kiel did not know how much Regent Lilandra or any human knew of magic.

"Please continue, Kielasanthra."

That Lilandra used Kiel's full name touched the elf deeply. Kiel was not sure how Lilandra learned to pronounce it, but she did know it was not easy for any human. That small act showed Kiel how valued she was.

"The man himself is young and has demonstrated some small ability with magic. In a hard rain, he managed to burn through leather straps." Kiel paused to read the reaction of the Regent. There was none, so she continued.

"The man, who is now in one of our training areas, may or may not cause us regret. He was traveling with an older man. The older man, I believe was a man who quite possibly knew much magic."

"Did you kill this man?" The genteel and elegant Regent could be, when necessary, a pragmatic and cold calculator.

"I don't know. I shot him. My aim was true, the arrow hit its mark in his chest. Then he…simply vanished. He left his horse and the young man who may be his student. He might come looking for the young man."

"That is interesting. He vanished you say, with an arrow in his chest." Lilandra was not asking, just confirming.

"Regent, I know only a little of magic. It is required learning for all elves. I know that being able to vanish like he did requires great power. If such a man came looking for his student, he could do great harm to this city."

"Yes, we must think of the citizens. Everyone must feel safe. Captain Kiel, I can not begin to express my gratitude towards your heroics. In fact, I feel I must ask you for one more favor. More information is needed. You have shown that you can meet the need of your new nation. The goblins, among other things, trouble me. We need to show the people of the neighboring lands we can protect them. Those outside of our nation need to believe in the Dream."

Time had no meaning for those who studied the flow of moments. Some moments could pass in the blink of an eye. Others could only be measured in the rings of a fallen tree. For Kiel, this moment stretched into an eternity. What did Lilandra need of her?

"Atani should send at least a division of companies west. We need to project strength and gather more information. I think you are the best choice to command that force. Will you accept such an offer? You will not answer to anyone but me, if you accept."

Damn regret, Kiel said to herself. "I would be honored to serve, Regent Lilandra," In ninety years with the elves, she had changed little. In a few short moments with the humans, she had grown more than she had in the past few decades with the elves.

Her instructors had it wrong. It was among the humans that she had found everything she needed.

Lilandra, ever polite, made very subtle gestures and remarks that let Kiel know her time with the Regent was over. Though they were made gently, Kiel reacted to the hints with the utmost haste.

"You are truly an example to the citizens. You continue to give for the good of all. I shall ensure you have everything you need for this expedition. Please rest, now, and enjoy your time in the castle. You have earned it." Lilandra watched the smiling elf go. As they frequently did, thoughts tinged with satisfaction rushed into Lilandra's head.

* * *

Lilandra had had no doubt that Kiel would accept the position of Commander. Kiel would change to fit the role. Roles and positions formed humans and elves as cups form even the finest of wines. She was amazed that more people did not know that or act on that knowledge. King Donius, the vigilant bodyguard was proof of it.

Lilandra reclined on her padded lounge, upholstered according to her latest fancy. With Kiel's news, Lilandra determined the known lands were in quite a stew. According to Kiel's report, there seemed to be a wizard making himself known outside of the palace. That certainly added quite a bit of spice to the stew.

Kiel had mentioned the wizard had a young companion.She had to get to him first. If she could find out what he needed, it might reduce him as a threat. Perhaps she should have the peasant Westlander moved to the prison for questioning. No, she caught herself; the prison was too clumsy of a solution. He was special and needed her personal attention.

Keeping him with those who were loyal to the Dream was fine for now. Prolonged exposure to other citizens was like marinade for the young man who she thought of as a tough piece in the stew. If he did have a connection to magic, he could be quite valuable. Such a potential asset or threat could not be blindly trusted to standard military training. She would have to see firsthand how or if such training was making a favorable impact.

The goblins and direbugs were bones hidden in the stew that could choke her. They were definitely Sogoth's work. Who knew what else he was doing? Waiting to see what spoonful would turn up the bones was a fool's way to eat. She was no fool and could not wait. She had to stir the pot to see what lurked in the bottom of it.

Goblins and direbugs did not scare her; it was the circumstances that drove them from Darkwood. Sogoth was on the move, and she doubted even The Creator knew what dark things he was conjuring.

Atani was strong, possibly the strongest nation in all of the known lands, but Atani alone might not be strong enough to stand against Sogoth and his army of Darkwood Denizens. She required more people and resources. It was time to start to move on the Westlands. Together, they could stand against Sogoth.

The citizens of Atani would be joyous at hearing their beloved sons and daughters were going to spread the Dream. Only days after Commander Kiel's force would depart, the whole nation would be starving for news and rumor of the progress. Of course, such news would only come from her. Their need for her would be driven to a new level.

Regent Lilandra, the cold pragmatist, knew it did not really matter if Commander Kiel's force was successful. The companies she would command were quite expendable. After news of the glories of the campaign was spread among the citizens, each dead soldier would be easily replaced by ever more eager peasants.

The parts of the plan fell together like a puzzle. To that end, Lilandra fully realized the propaganda value in Kiel's adventures. People love strange and exotic things. Both nobles and peasants would believe any tale if they thought it was true enough to distract them from their daily lives. With Lilandra's ministrations, Kielasanthra Tylansthra would be the source of countless more tales of glory and mystique.

Lilandra closed her eyes and allowed herself to sink deeper into the cushions. Her quarters were far removed from the din of the nobles' idle chatter. She could relax knowing that Atani was hers and the Westlands would soon follow.

* * *

Princess Helena sat in one of her rooms. She, being the princess, had almost a whole wing of the castle. It was more space than any one person needed, but she was the princess and that is how it had always been. In one of the many richly appointed parlors, she had the soft furniture removed. To replace it, she had brought in furniture that more fitted a meeting room.

The new furniture went with the new role she saw herself in. Of course, Regent Lilandra had encouraged her. It was not a good use of her talents, the Regent said, to simply be concerned with being pretty. She was the heir to the throne of Atani, and she needed to act like it.

So, upon the tables and desks in Princess Helena's new office sat piles of paper. Some of the sheets were maps, others were the stewards' records, but most important were the pursers' ledgers. Knowing who controlled the coin in the city was the key to directing the city residents.

For too long, she had been kept in the background. Her father had promised that she would one day rule, but as far as Helena could see, he had made no effort to teach her the important things. That was why she would be eternally thankful for Lilandra; she had shown Helena so much.

There was a light tap at the door. It gave her a slight shiver of power to be sitting behind a desk to receive people. In the past, whenever anyone had called upon her in her quarters she was usually lounging or experimenting with her hair.

"Enter," she called out evenly. She did not want to sound like a pretty young princess.

Helena was surprised to see her father peek his head around the corner. She did not know whether she should be on guard or happy to see him. It had been so long since she enjoyed his company. It was just that he did not understand so many things.

"Good afternoon, Father," she replied formally. It was best to be a little cautious. If he got the impression that she was simply his little girl, it would not help anything.

"Good afternoon, Helena." His voice had nothing but warmth in it, warmth and perhaps a bit of tiredness.

She wanted to let her guard down, but she still was wary. "I have been going over many of the reports. Lilandra gave them to me herself. Most of the major indicators report substantial growth. The City's coffers have never been so full. The newcomers pay their taxes happily. With the revenue, Lilandra has given much needed help to our most needy citizens."

"That is good. I'm sure they appreciate the help," he said as he continued to walk towards her. He plopped himself down in one of the chairs that faced her desk. It was odd to see him in front of a desk and not behind it.

"And there is more," she added. "So many recent recruits have come to the city that we have had to form many new companies. We've had to reorganize. The Fifth, Sixth, and Seventh Companies will form the Fourth Division. The Eighth, Ninth and Tenth companies will make the Fifth division. Fortunately Regent Lilandra had planned ahead. There are plenty of supplies in the city's storehouses."

"That is encouraging." He did not seem to be looking for a fight. "Tell me, how have you been? I know you have been working hard, and there was that scare on the tower."

"Oh Father, it was nothing. I work so hard because it is good for Atani. Everyone needs to work for the good of each other. That is the Dream. As for the incident on the tower, I have already put it out of my mind. We have good citizens who are joining the army to risk their lives. I can't be worried over what might have happened to me."

"Your courage is impressive. I know men who have melted at even the mere thought of death. When I heard, I was scared." He raised a hand to forestall her coming objection. "I know you can take care of yourself, but it is a father's prerogative to worry about his daughter." In a voice that so rarely showed emotion, he added, "I can't imagine losing you."

"I can't concern myself with that. One day, I might lead a division of companies to the Westlands. Will you worry about me then? I am a grown woman."

"Let us talk of topics with more cheer. I understand there have been some fine young men at court. Have you taken a fancy to any of them?"

It was a familiar game. He would tease her. She would squeal and protest in embarrassment. Secretly though, she had always loved the attention. That was before Lilandra's arrival.

Without a trace of the attention-loving little girl, she said, "Father, this is hardly the time to talk of such childish things. I have work to do. Lilandra is going to present her grandest idea yet at the coliseum soon. It will join all of Atani into one family." She said the last with youthful hope.

"Yes," he said noncommittally. "She does rally the subjects to her. Have you any word as to what she might say?"

"None. Usually she tells me everything." There was a hint of pride in her voice. "This time, she has said it is a secret for all. She did say it would make us all a big family. Isn't that great!"

"That would be fine," he said hollowly. "Helena, I am concerned about the amount of soldiers we have. You know my military history. I love the army and what it can do for young people and for our nation. But, why do you think we need so many?"

"Father, Atani has been blessed. We are beginning a new way of life. It is good for everyone. It would be wrong of us to keep that knowledge. We have to spread it."

"Do you think using an army to spread ideas is a good thing?" He said it as evenly as he could.

Helena immediately sensed his meaning. She strengthened her guard. "Father, we will not send our army out to conquer. They will be ambassadors of the Dream."

"And how do you think King Festinger of the Westlands will see this?"

"He'll come to see it eventually."

"When you say eventually, what do you mean? Will you force it on them?"

"Not at first. But, like a child, sometimes people have to be firmly guided into what is right for them."

"I see. You know that will mean battles, maybe even a full war. How many lives do you think will be lost?"

He said it gently. Still, it was an attack, and she reacted to it as such. "You don't understand. Sometimes sacrifices are necessary."

"Honey, I know better than most the sacrifices of war. I have seen war. I have killed in war, and I have sent young men to their deaths in wars. I am your father. Trust me. This is not right."

"Lilandra understands what is right. People need to follow her. Only she understands the Dream! Only her need is important, everyone else's is simply a selfish attempt to please themselves!"

The young woman's face was red, her tantrum in full bloom. Donius knew there was nothing he could say. This too was another lost battle. He quietly got up from his seat and exited. He had lost battles, dear friends, and even a wife. Never had he felt so empty.

Joseph Swope

Tonay

Paul James Mather

Chapter 16

Life in the training camp was certainly not fun. As dedicated as she was, Tonay could admit it to herself, though she would never admit it to anyone else. She did not want anyone to think anything of her except that she was one with the Dream.

The morning water break allowed her the time to have such thoughts. The drills kept her mind too busy to actively think. The drills, however, let her mind wander to a special place where she let her imaginary fighters do the thinking for her.

Even some of the biggest men eventually came around to ask her for help on their technique. She was, of course, happy to show them what she could. It wasn't much. She knew the same basic movements as they did. It was just that she saw the fight as a coordinated whole. She saw her opponents' moves as she would do them. She did not know how she knew what she knew; to her, it was just common sense. There were certain movements a body could do and could not do. When she tried to explain how she knew, she simply ended up reteaching something the training officer had shown earlier.

Even so, she felt a little uncomfortable with the thought that there was no one left in her company who could touch her with their practice sword. It wasn't that she could not improve; it was that she could not improve with her company-mates as sparring partners.

They took it in good humor. As she would beat them, they would routinely say that the only way for them to improve was by fighting someone with more skill. In Ducca's Vineyard, she knew boys that would rather die than get beaten by a girl in any competition. It filled her heart with joy to know that the soldiers in the Atanian Army truly lived the Dream.

"Seventh Company!" At those words, the soldiers jumped to find their places.

From around the corner of one of the barracks rode an officer with a dazzling display of decorations on his chest and shoulders. He had to be a captain or higher.

The captain steered his mount toward the middle of the front line. Tonay wondered if she could ever give enough to reach that high in the Dream.

"Soldiers of the Seventh Company!" he called out. "I have been given a very special honor by the Regent herself."

He paused for effect, but Tonay was proud to notice that not a peep escaped the lips of any soldier of the Seventh Company. Truly they had to be the best company in the Atanian Army.

"The Most Honored Regent of Atani has specifically invited every member of the Seventh Company to attend the upcoming citizens' assembly in the coliseum. She feels it important that all citizens feel included."

The discipline of the soldiers held, but just barely. Tonay herself had trouble standing still when she heard the news. The Regent had specifically invited her. As the Seventh Company was absorbing that information, the captain rode off. Tonay did not hear his closing words. Whatever he could have said could not come close to matching the importance of his announcement.

As the training officer took over and began directing the Seventh Company towards their drills, Tonay's mind was thinking of other things. She thought about running from her father's farm. She thought about the scary journey when she sought the recruiting party. It seemed so long ago. She felt foolish for ever having been frightened.

A single thought caught her in an unexpected way. It had been so long since she had seen her father. She was surprised to feel a sense of loss. She did not wish him worry. She even felt regret at leaving him. Still, if she had not left, she would not have had this chance to see the Regent.

* * *

Keven's eyes opened well before the hated drum came to wake him. It and the sweaty drills that would follow would come soon enough. Everyday, members of the Ninth Company were woken by a beating on a large metal drum; the only thing that could roust the exhausted soldiers.

Keven, like every other soldier, had learned to cringe at the sound. It gave the new soldiers something to hate together and from that commonality, a bond began to form. The others included him in the conversations of the drum and of the countless other things that these new soldiers spoke of.

He knew he should hate lying in his cot. He should resent the fact that he had been brought to Atani against his will and that he was imprisoned in a training camp for an Army that threatened his homeland. That hatred, however, was difficult to maintain. His life in Village Donnell had been no better. Worse than that was the fact that Gareloch had not come for him.

A new reality was growing in him. The whole company of young men and women did not care that he was a bastard nor did they particularly care that he wasn't very good with the practice sword. Instead, between drills, some of his company-mates would show him why they could score on him. They encouraged him to use their knowledge to be better.

They teased him about his strange Westland accent. It was different from the teasing of Constance and the Goodfolk. His company-mates offered their jibes with friendly smiles.

Keven began to understand the Dream about which Captain Kiel had spoken. Everyone seemed to be equal. There were no Goodfolk who thought ill of him because of his mother's crime. He realized in a flash for there to be Goodfolk, people who were seen in high regard, there had to be people against whom they were compared.

The Dream was different. No one in Atani seemed to care or even notice that he was a bastard. People were to be judged on what they did, not on the sins of their parents.

Keven had no way of knowing the time as he lay on his cot. He knew the drums would come for him and his company-mates, but tried not to think of it. Lying on his bunk in the dark gave him a chance to be alone with his thoughts. It was peaceful.

The sound of the early morning insects reminded Keven of the many early mornings when he would be doing some chore for Banolf. He forced that thought aside as aimless wondering. He was as alone as he could be. Every other member of the large company was sleeping. The drum for reveille could come at any moment, and Keven did not want to waste his chance. The chunk of flint was on the mantel, but the mantel was several paces away from his cot. Though his eyes were adjusted to the dim light of the early morning, Keven feared what he knew to be a squeaky floor under a dormitory of sleeping soldiers. Did he actually have to touch the flint?

Quickly and easily his breath found that rhythm Gareloch had taught him so long ago. He imagined his thoughts as a tendril of his mind reaching across the air to feel the flint. It was similar to what Gareloch taught him about sorcery. He did not know exactly where the flint was. He could not feel it nor did he know if his thought was near it. He could not even be sure if he was not simply imagining his thought being outside of his mind.

Though he could not feel the flint, he began the next stage. He could not say the words aloud. Would the volume of the words make a difference? It was frustrating to know so little. Still, he pressed on. Despite his mental probing, he could not feel the flint. He redoubled his efforts to feel it across the room. The inability to feel it distracted him from the task of keeping his mind clear. That irritation distracted him from keeping the proper rhythm with the words.

With a sigh of regret, he abandoned his efforts. Keven continued to lie in his cot. It wasn't long after his failed attempt at magic that two of the corporals appeared with the metal drum making an obscenely loud noise. Some soldiers reacted with violent jerks and threw their blankets while others groaned their dismay.

Keven was one of the first ones standing. He was heartened when he realized the corporals noticed how quickly he came to his feet.

The breakfast that was served was the same food they had eaten the night before. The whitish mush had only the flavor that was added to it after cooking, for breakfast, chopped figs and dates for sweetness. For evening mess, salt and bits of dried meat made it into the porridge.

The morning drills were difficult. Still, the officers in charge constantly reminded the soldiers that they could always work harder; it was for the good of Atani, they were told. One day, their lives might depend on the skills they learned during training.

Whenever they felt they were being watched by a corporal or the officer in charge, they would swing a little harder and grunt a little louder. Keven worked harder too. He knew his fellow soldiers were improving. He did not want to earn any more welts from them than he currently had, so he pushed himself.

For hours upon hours, the corporals would bark commands that would send the Ninth Company marching in various directions. The steps of each soldier had to be precise. Failure of that was cause for punishment of the whole company.

Keven could see aspects of the Dream in almost every part of the training. Still, he did not enjoy marching and doubted he ever would. After a day's worth of training, he felt as if the corporals were trying to march the individuality out of every soldier.

Before they were dismissed for the short mid-morning break, they were held in formation. "Soldiers of the Ninth Company!" The officer in charge bellowed.

"There have been many rumors. Some concern this company being sent west to spread the Dream. Others concern King Donius. I do not know facts relating to that. I am an officer in the Atanian Army. You are soldiers in the Atanian Army. Our job is to follow orders. No good can come from trafficking in rumors."

Keven could almost see the sighs of disappointment escape his fellow soldiers. The Ninth Company worked hard and routinely showed spirit in its training. The officer's words had the ring of chastisement.

"Once again, you will hear no rumors from me!" He emphasized in a stern voice. "You will only hear facts. It is a fact that I have been handed official notice that the Regent herself would like to visit this company." He did his best to keep his tone harsh, but the wide smile that spread across his face betrayed his true feelings.

Keven did not know what to think. He knew he should have no love for the Regent. He was born in Village Donnell in the Westlands. In fact, he reminded himself, he had been brought to Atani as a captive. Still, he had to admit, he felt the excitement. That she wanted to see the Ninth Company meant that their hard work had been noticed. Despite himself, pride bubbled up.

"There is one formality; The Regent recognizes she has no right to disturb the hard work of the soldiers of this company or any other citizen. She therefore would like this company's permission to visit. I will ask you. You will respond with your voice. Does this company give its permission for the most honored Regent to visit with its soldiers?"

Instantly, every member of the Ninth Company shouted his or her assent. The celebration went on for several minutes. Even the corporals lent their voices to the cheering. The only one who was not shouting at the top of his lungs was Keven.

After the roar died down, the officer continued. "This company is finished with fighting drills for the day. Every soldier is dismissed to the barracks. That building and every soldier in it will be spotlessly clean. Dismissed!"

What had been a model of discipline and order instantly broke down into a mob of joyful young men and women. Despite his efforts to remain unaffected, Keven wished he had some of the colored cloth that his fellow soldiers said the Regent appreciated to pin to his uniform.

When the soldiers of the Ninth Company rushed into their barracks, they could only be compared to a swarm of arrowflies. They acted as one, never questioning their purpose. Never had soldiers worked so hard to clean themselves, their barracks, and their uniforms. Keven, too, buried himself in the mindless chores of readying himself and other things for the Regent's arrival.

It only took a few hours for the members of the Ninth Company to scrub every part of their large barracks. With diluted lye and stiff-bristled brushes, the Ninth Company cleansed the barracks of the stench of their own sweat. After they were done, they had nothing to do but wait. They realized that the call for evening mess would come relatively soon and that the time of the Regent's visit was not certain, but each soldier would gladly miss a meal to wait for her arrival.

After each soldier had bathed using the kegs of water, the exertions and excitement of the day became apparent. Slowly, each soldier found his or her cot and stretched out on it, including Keven. Keven, however, laid down with something no other soldier of the Ninth Company had, a piece of flint. The prospect of feeling the touch of magic was sweet anticipation.

With many of the other soldiers lying in their cots, Keven figured no one would notice. It didn't take him long to find the correct rhythm for breathing. Immediately, he felt himself relax. As he felt his muscles slacken, he gently ushered all thoughts from his head. It was a balancing act: if he tried too hard to keep his mind free, he would think about the effort to do so. If he allowed his mind to wander, stray thoughts would enter his mind against his conscious wishes.

With his mind and body prepared, he thought of the words. Though he did not know all of them, he knew enough to make the spell work. He had proven that to himself while trying to escape from Captain Kiel. As he formed the words in his mind, he could feel the flint. It was as if the words sought out the surface of the flint.

With the flint so close to him, he could feel the spell building. Each thought was a gossamer strand of surprising strength. Like any web, the spell would only work if all of the thoughts were connected.

The pleasure of having the building magic resonate in every part of his body was magnificent. Keven felt alive. Though he had never really known the full touch of a woman, he could not imagine anything that would give him more pleasure.

He realized with sudden consternation that he had nowhere to put the spell. The spell was at the point that had he directed it to the edge of paper or wood, it would have immediately ignited. He could not very well have a small blaze suddenly appear in the middle of the barracks.

Just as he was deciding what to do with the energy of the spell, he was shaken awake, and the spell dissipated as quickly as smoke in the wind. He opened his eyes to find several of his fellow soldiers standing around his cot. They stared at him with curious, amused expressions.

"What are you doing?" the soldiers snickered.

"Nothing," Keven stammered. "I was just sleeping."

"You were saying something. It was in a strange language. You just kept repeating it over and over."

Nothing drew a crowd better than a crowd. More and more soldiers surrounded Keven's bed.

"What are you trying to be, some kind of magician?"

Keven stared at the crowd of faces. The silence was awkward. He did not want to do anything that would make himself seem different than those looking down upon him. That long pause in which Keven struggled to find something to say was ended by the sweetest sound that had ever reached Keven's ears.

"Ooh, perhaps you are the one the elven Captain spoke of," the voice said. The sound was so melodious that Keven longed to clasp his hands to his ears to trap the sound in his head forever. Every pair of eyes that looked at Keven turned to find the source of the exquisite voice. At the same time, countless mouths hung wide open. Standing in the midst of the Ninth Company was the Regent Lilandra

After a few moments of astonished stares, soldiers turned their heads back to look at Keven. The meaning of her words was delayed by the shock and embarrassment of having the Regent suddenly and unceremoniously appear among them. She seemed to know of Keven. Were the rumors true, they all wondered? Was there an elf serving in the Atanian army? Was Keven connected to those rumors? In unison, everyone looked again at the Regent and then back again at Keven.

Fortunately for them, the Regent was gracious. She easily overlooked their stunned silence and walked towards another group of soldiers. They were standing near their cots, watching the events unfold around Keven. As she moved, many of the soldiers around Keven followed her. Soon, every soldier in the Ninth Company surrounded the Regent.

Her fondness and appreciation for them was recognized by all of the soldiers. In turn they drank in her attentions like kittens lapping up cream.

As she walked around the large building, the crowd shifted. It was amazing how she managed to have different words for each soldier.

As her tour of the building brought her closer to the main doorway, she stopped and stepped up on a cot to make herself visible to the whole company.

"Noble soldiers of the Ninth Company, often citizens of Atani assemble in the great coliseum to celebrate our collective efforts. Unfortunately, it is usually only wealthy citizens or high ranking officers who are able to get seats for the event. I would like to take this opportunity to personally invite each one of you to the next event. We will celebrate our successes as a nation. I would like you to be there."

Astonishment and joy spread over the soldiers of the Ninth Company like a wave.

"I am sorry I have to leave now." With that, she stepped down from the cot. Though she was a delicate woman, she stepped off the cot with confidence. She did not look for a hand like a fragile noblewoman might have.

After she had left, there was an almost palpable void. Many of the soldiers began recounting the events that had occurred only minutes before. Each soldier had to tell his fellows how the Regent enjoyed talking to him. It did not take them long to notice that talking about past glory was a poor substitute for being close to such glory. As they tired of each others' conversations, they turned to Keven. He seemed to be closer to the Regent than any of them.

Keven had barely become accustomed to being accepted as an equal part of the Ninth Company. To suddenly be faced with soldiers seeking his attention was exciting. Keven knew it was temporary and that he truly had not earned the attention, but it felt so good. With that realization came a certain amount of shame that had he not been captured and brought to Atani against his will, he would not be the center of attention of his new friends.

* * *

Tonay Denisio was bursting from anticipation. This was the day she had awaited for so long: she was actually going to see Regent Lilandra in a few hours. The issued uniform was rather drab and worn, but she fought with herself not to fret over how she looked, since that was not what mattered to the Regent.

Regent Lilandra, Tonay knew, was more concerned about the inside of a person. Indeed, this afternoon's speech at the coliseum was proof of that. Hearing that the Regent made sure there was space for poorer citizens and the lower ranking soldiers only confirmed what Tonay knew. Regent Lilandra was not simply a leader for the rich and noble.

Still, Tonay wondered if she should adorn her uniform with the bits of orange cloth she had accumulated. That was never an exact science. Rumors spread among soldiers faster than they did among bored noble women. Some said the Regent had been seen in green; others said it was blue; still others said those stories and others like them were false stories designed to mislead them. For that very reason, Tonay decided she would not add any colored cloth to her uniform.

It was deeds that mattered. In the end, each citizen had to give to the Dream. Wearing bits of cloth that might or might not please the Regent was not what the Dream was about. If she kept the Dream in her heart, the Regent would notice her one day.

It was a rare morning off from drills and the gift of free time was spent sleeping or talking.

Tonay did not participate in what she believed to be gossip. Not everyone shared her devoutness. Earlier, some young soldiers complained about certain things. While Tonay agreed with them that the food could certainly use more flavor and variety, she did not think it was appropriate to criticize it. The food they ate represented the efforts of someone else. All Atanians were called to give their best to their fellow citizens. If the food they ate was the best of her fellow citizens, it was wrong to criticize it.

It was really only a few members of her company who spoke out. She did not engage them in debate as some of her company-mates did, she simply led by example. When she would swat them with ease with her sword, she hoped they would understand that if they worked more and complained less, they would have fewer bruises.

260

Even the worst of the complainers had eventually calmed down. As Tonay propped herself up on one elbow on her bunk, she looked around. There was harmony in the barracks. The officers had chosen not to discipline the protestors. They had punished the whole company and left it to the group to deal with the few who complained.

During that period of relative newness, the Seventh Company had not resorted to mob violence, they simply tried to counsel the ones who did not understand and complained. Other times, they had simply refused to talk to those who complained. Over a short period, even the loudest dissenters had begun to understand. To Tonay, complaining was a waste of time and effort. She did not see why they had to think differently. If everyone thought the same, the Dream would be achieved more quickly.

She was glad the discord had been eliminated, because today was the day she and the rest of the Seventh Company were going to be in the coliseum with the Regent. She forced herself to remain calm on her bunk. If she stood up, she knew she would begin to pace again.

The order to roust came suddenly. This was it. She was going to see the Regent. She could almost feel the excitement in her company. Still, they maintained proper discipline. No one spoke and every back was straight. She strained to hear what the officers whispered among themselves.

With little warning, Tonay and the many soldiers standing in formation around her heard the order to march. It was the most thrilling moment of her life. The endless drills had paid off, and Tonay could not have been more proud. She was a part of something glorious.

Her excitement at beginning to march grew as she proudly followed her company through the city. The city was packed with all manner of citizens. As crowded as the street was, everyone moved aside when her company approached. It was hard to keep her gaze steady. From the corner of her eyes, Tonay could see the respect in their faces. She wanted to turn and absorb the wonder and awe of the children as they watched the magnificent parade.

As she marched through the part of the city which housed the nobles and wealthy, she could see large flags of orange. It disgusted her that people would try to buy the Regent's approval.

A different kind of disgust filled her when she saw the dead dog near the side of the street. From the stench that reached her and the flies that buzzed about it, she knew it must have been there for days. How could hundreds of citizens step over it instead of remove it. Tonay hoped the Regent would never see the citizens ignoring their duty and she did not let it diminish her joy.

There was nothing in Ducca's Vineyard to compare to being a part of the Dream. She could actually feel the love of the crowd as her company passed by. The afternoon sun was reflected by the countless flecks of crystal in the white granite edifice of the great Coliseum. The carnival-like atmosphere washed over her. The crowds, disheveled as they were, made way for the orderly and impressive progress of the Seventh Company.

The pride she felt threatened to burst from her chest. Though the coliseum was huge, the entrances to the field were basically narrow tunnels. The soldiers of the Seventh Company maneuvered themselves brilliantly. Without breaking rhythm or cadence, they effortlessly formed themselves into one long column.

As they marched out on the field, it was only Tonay's ability to focus on her imaginary fighters that kept her from smiling like a fool. The ovation from the citizens lifted her soul.

The Seventh Company took its place on the field. That was a change from how she understood Citizen Assemblies were organized. She knew the King and even Lilandra used to address the citizens from a balcony high above the crowd. Tonay took the dais in the middle of the field as another indication of Lilandra's wish to be connected with the people.

The dais was huge. That so much stone was hauled to the coliseum to build the dais told Tonay there was nothing those who believed in the Dream could not accomplish. It was some thirty paces long, twenty paces deep, and had to have required a lot of dedicated citizens. Its height, maybe that of the average soldier, was such that all citizens in the field had a good view of it.

Near it was a large wooden building. Like all attentive citizens, she wondered what could be in it. Of course, the rumors about it were plentiful. Each person swore that what they had heard was the truth.

Her long wait was replaced by the glory of the Dream. With trumpets, drums, and a deafening roar, Regent Lilandra's escort made its way to the dais. Heading the long line of people who preceded the Regent was a banner of the Atanian Lion.

The seemingly endless speeches and introductions from people who Tonay did not know pushed her eagerness to a frenzy. Though she knew nothing about them, she envied them because they were sitting on the dais with the Regent. She could only imagine how selfless they must be to be given such an honor.

Tonay tried to listen to every word of each speaker. They were honored citizens who had been chosen by the Regent to give their wisdom to other citizens. Still, forcing herself to listen to every word was torture. She wanted to see and hear the Regent so badly, she almost felt the need physically.

After a speaker who had merely repeated everything the previous speakers had said was finished, trumpets blared, drums rolled, and banners waved. The crowd became a living thing, a huge beast that roared its triumph at seeing its prize. Tonay Denisio realized that this moment was what she was born for. She felt complete. The Atanian Coliseum was alive with love for the Dream.

Regent Lilandra was resplendent in her deep blue gown with a white sash wrapped about her shoulders. Her hair was swept up in a way that called attention to her elegance. Tonay knew she would never achieve the grace and beauty of the Regent, but at that moment, she was content just to be near her. As regal as the Regent appeared, her gestures were touching in their plainness. She motioned to the crowd to quiet their wild adulation. Lilandra had said many times she was only one citizen, no more important than anyone else.

* * *

When the crowd had quieted, the Regent prepared to speak. As she stepped forward, the crowd of countless thousands was unified in their silence. Not a boot scrapping the ground nor an errant cough could be heard.

"My fellow citizens," she called to the large crowd. "We have much to celebrate. The efforts of all of our citizens have yielded results that prove the Dream is alive and growing. Even as the chains that bind the slaves have been broken, so have the bonds that tie us to the past." The crowd roared its appreciation. Lilandra knew that a crowd had far from an accurate memory. It believed what was most easy to believe.

"There are countless children in Atani who are hungry and cold. We have a duty to them. They, too, are citizens." Lilandra paused. The grief for the children was evident on her face. "As of this moment… the nation of Atani will care for all of its children." She ended the statement in a crescendo. The crowd cheered as if to give her their very soul.

"All citizens who know of a child who does not get enough to eat or who is not being raised according to the Dream, please give that name to an official. We must secure the Dream for all generations of Atanians." Again, there was a wild cheer.

"Additionally, all parents are now encouraged to give their children to the nation. As you know, the whole of Atani can do more for a child than only two parents. From these children who are given to the state by true believers will be chosen the next Regent of Atani. In the future, only one who has been raised by the nation will rule the nation."

Upon hearing her words, the crowd erupted into a deafening roar. The citizens gathered at this particular assembly were poor and had little to give their children. Too often, they were denied things that would make their lives less painful. They had simply stopped hoping.

"There is change blowing through Atani," her voice sang. "Atani must ride those winds. The old must be put away, and the new welcomed with open arms." With those words, the pole holding the Atanian Lion fell and hit the ground in a heap of dust. Then, a new pole was raised. It had a blue background with a brown hawk soaring majestically.

"Accept this noble bird as the new symbol of Atani. Unlike the male lion of our past, which thinks only of taking for himself, a hawk returns from the highest heavens to fill the mouths of its young. So, then must we always deny ourselves our pleasure if it will ensure others are fed. It is the children of Atani to whom we must always return."

Lilandra's announcement stirred something deep in them. Her words gave them a reason to have hope for their children. To Tonay, nothing could have been more beautiful. She fought back tears as the wave of love and adulation rolled through the crowd. Lilandra was sharing what she had with all, even the poorest citizens of Atani. The crowd knew that and gave its gratitude in a wild ovation that seemed to shake the heavens.

After what seemed like hours of cheering and celebrating, Lilandra motioned to the crowd for their attention. It was a testament to her control that the riotous crowd again became silent almost immediately. "And now my fellow citizens, watch our hawk as it flies high, only to return to us, its people. That is what we all must do: reach for the heavens so we can share it with our neighbor."

The beautiful young ruler took the large bird from its handler who unobtrusively appeared next to her. The hawk was perched on his arm and had a small hood, which kept its eyes covered. Regent Lilandra donned a heavy leather mitt. It was only after the handler placed the taloned feet on the mitt and made sure his beloved ruler had the tethers in her hand that he removed the hood. Upon doing so, the bird came alive, flapping its wings and screaming its piercing cry. Regent Lilandra held it high for a few moments. She wanted the citizens to feel connected to the moment.

With a flourish, she threw her arm up and released the bird. Tonay Denisio thought she had known happiness before. She thought she knew what being a part of the Dream was about, and the sight of the majestic hawk made her soul soar. Thousands upon thousands of eyes joined Tonay's in watching the hawk leave the elegant wrist of the Regent.

Instead of flying high and free, the hawk flew in low, erratic circles. The crowd wanted to see it soar. It represented the new hope of Atani. The sighs of wonder turned to gasps of muted shock when the large bird landed in the middle of the crowd. Many people in the upper part of the coliseum could not see where the bird landed. It seemed to disappear in the crowd of soldiers standing on the field.

Tonay had trouble seeing at first. Despite her skill with the sword, she was shorter than the average soldier. It wasn't until her fellow soldiers shifted that she could see the bird. It was on the arm of an Atanian soldier. She did not know him because he was not in her company. From his position on the field, he must have been part of the Ninth Company.

He was not much to look at. Though he was a man, he did not appear much bigger than her. Had the bird landed on her right arm, Tonay knew she would have felt both surprise and fear. The private who was standing not more than thirty paces from her had a look of contentment on his face. Tonay did not know how, but he seemed to ignore the fact that a large part of Atani City was staring at him as he ruined the Regent's ceremony.

* * *

The morning came too soon for him. He had barely had any sleep. The wine the officers saw fit to pass out to the Ninth Company flowed too easily for those who had morning drills.

Despite his throbbing head, dry mouth, and exhaustion, it was the best morning of Keven's life. The night before had been nothing but cheering and celebrating, and it had all been for him. From the moment he'd been carried out of the coliseum on the shoulders of his jubilant company-mates, Keven did not spend one minute of the previous night without someone hugging him, screaming for joy, or filling his goblet.

At first, Keven was not sure if the crowd that surged towards the Ninth Company would tear him apart. The assembly did not seem to know if the hawk landing on him was a good omen or a bad one. Keven thought it was his company-mates' immediate reaction that influenced the crowd that it was right and good that the hawk landed on a private.

He had been brought to Atani against his will fully expecting to have to fight his way out of slave-like conditions once he arrived. Instead, he had found people who had accepted him. Now, he was beloved. Even officers had rushed to get him wine last night.

He dunked his head into a keg of water to help cool his face and wash the ache from his temples. He enjoyed the calm of being the only one awake. When the others awoke, he would be peppered by their attention. Even through his drunken haze last night, he realized he was now important to them. That feeling was new, and it was welcome.

He slid down so he was seated on the floor with his back against the water keg. Too many thoughts dashed around his mind. He wanted to remain honest to the idea that Atanian soldiers had shot Gareloch and dragged him off against his will. But, that thought was hard to hold onto. He was valued here. He fit here. How long could he wait for Gareloch to come for him, if he was even alive?

He just needed time alone to think; time without his new friends talking with him, time without officers telling him how well he was doing. Time to think, however, was not a luxury he had. The peace of the early morning evaporated as the groans from dehydrated soldiers filled the air. The hated clanging of the wake up call drove Keven and his company-mates into the training yard.

After several hours of swinging his practice sword, the officer in charge called for a water break. Discipline held and each soldier carefully placed his practice sword on the sword rack. Though he knew it was little more than a stick, Keven did the same.

To do otherwise would seem wrong. He had worked with it; his fellows in the Ninth Company seemed to value taking care of the weapons. Keven did not want to show disrespect for them.

When the line was halfway through the wait for water, he saw her. His heart froze and for a minute he feared it was yet another cruel trick he had to endure. She was taller and her hair had changed, but there was no doubt. Erin strode across the training yard.

It took him a moment to break free of his shock. His newfound respect for the customs of his company warred with his desire to call out for her. It was a short war.

"Erin!" he called in a voice that overflowed with wonder and hope.

She froze in astonishment. It had been years since she had been called by her first name. She had worked hard to earn the rank of lieutenant. For someone to yell her name across the training ground as if she were no more than a private infuriated her. She almost dropped the square board on which she had tacked the weapons inventory.

Keven knew that his outburst had attracted every eye. Still, he did his best to maintain his dignity and control the urge to run and sweep her up in his arms. He approached her reverently, still not entirely trusting that she was truly in front of him.

She had grown much in the years since she had moved away from Village Donnell. Keven noticed her uniform and officious gait. The formality of her bearing slowed Keven's desire to simply grab her.

"It's me, Keven." A torrent of thoughts was expressed in those three words. He felt the joy of their shared youth, the pain of their separation, and the untamed hope of what might still be possible.

Her eyes went wide. Astonishment washed over her face, though she quickly regained control. "I'll be beaten and forged! It is you. It is good to see you have come to be a part of the Dream. I did not know that the recruiting parties had gone so far west." Her tone did not match Keven's.

"Erin, how did you get here?" He could feel a protective rage building at the thought of her being hurt. Had she been bound and dragged halfway across the lands?

"It is a long story." She looked around as if noticing the eyes of many low-ranking privates staring. "My father is still in the Westlands." Something in her voice made Keven want to embrace her as she talked about her father. With the next thought her voice was filled with cheer. "But, I found the Dream."

There was more to that story, Keven was sure. What had been left out was obviously not pleasant. "Erin, I still can't believe you're here. I've thought about seeing you again for so long."

"Yes." She surveyed his company-mates taking their break. "This is the Ninth Company, so that would put you in the fifth division. You're still a private, so you probably have not been assigned a squad yet, but I'm sure you'll do fine."

Keven heard her words, but he didn't understand. Why was she talking about his company? He wanted to simply grab her and run off, but she held a board full of papers like a pikeman anticipating a charge. He awkwardly aborted his thought of an attempted embrace.

"Uh, this place sure is a lot different than Village Donnell." What else could he say?

"Aren't the training officers great? They really help new soldiers become part of it all. How is the sparring going?"

The pride he had felt just a few moments earlier at his progress was like bitter ashes in his mouth. Why was she acting this way? The ache that was developing in his stomach was far worse than any pain a sword, real or practice, could deliver.

When he didn't answer, she continued. "Well, you should be proud of me. The Regent herself gave me the duty of caring for all weapons of the fourth division. I have made lieutenant rank. So from now on you must address me as Lieutenant Dunn. But, don't worry. If I can make officer, you can do it too. Then we can talk properly."

Keven was a small bird caught in a windstorm. Each time he thought he could land, his perch was taken from him. He became very aware of his company-mates. It was all going in the wrong direction. Why didn't she remember? Why didn't she care?

"Remember, don't just follow orders. Live the Dream. It is only because of Lilandra's vision that I am not scrubbing pots like some scullery maid. She gives everyone a chance, even foreigners from the Westlands."

Keven sensed the conversation was ending. Despair threatened to engulf him. She had not told him how to find her again. Would she walk by again? Did their past not matter to her anymore?

"I must go now. I have a lot of soldiers and citizens depending on me. Remember, Keven, see to the need of Atani first. That is the best way to live the Dream."

With that she walked off, in crisp, military strides. Her uniform was perfect. As she walked farther away, Keven could feel his pleasant memories fade. His travels with Gareloch and Captain Kiel had helped him forget most of Village Donnell. With Erin's departure, there was very little left of the stable hand Gareloch had found so long ago.

Thankfully, the officer in charge ordered the Ninth Company to assemble and prepare for drills. For Keven, the afternoon drills were fierce. He put everything he had into every swing. He fought hard, but he also fought recklessly. Even with his elementary knowledge of sword play, he knew that he was giving his opponents plenty of openings. He did not care. Each meaty smack that landed on his body brought with it pain and the pain of each blow covered the real reason he hurt.

"Ninth Company! Attention!" Keven was the first to stand in formation. His body was rigid. He was a model of a soldier at attention. Following those orders kept him from feeling.

"Private Whoreson, front and center." As crisply as he could, Keven marched to the officer in charge. His movements were the very picture of proper military action.

"Private Whoreson," the officer read from a scroll. "Your presence has been requested by the Most Honored Regent of Atani. An escort will be sent for you this evening." The officer in charge let the scroll snap back to its coiled state.

Keven was the only soldier to maintain discipline. There were plenty of gasps and intakes of breath. The excitement was palpable. Keven felt it. But, formation was not the place to show such emotion.

* * *

Donius did not stay in one place. To do that was to become complacent. He needed to be aware, ever vigilant. He alternately walked through the crowd of nobles or perched himself on a balcony overlooking the celebration. During his passes through the crowd, he did his best to greet as many of the nobles as he could. None asked why it was not he sitting on the thrown.

The ball was extravagant, as they always were. It was attended by foppish people who overestimated their importance. The spoiled nobles always seemed to drink too much while forcing themselves to laugh at comments they found boring. Donius rarely enjoyed them. As king, he had felt they consumed too much of his time and the castle's resources. In his new role, he found he hated them even more.

There was a predictable pattern and tempo to the movements of the partygoers. The people below would move in slow, nonchalant movements across the polished courtroom floor. It would not do to be seen as moving anywhere in a hurry. Even the few who were brave enough to part from the crowd and approach the tables of figs, dates, and other delicacies did so with forced casualness.

For the fifth time that evening, he stood on the balcony. The view gave him an opportunity to see all of the revelers, the minstrels, and the servants. It was the same. Nobles came from their city houses or their nearby estates in their finest and traded opinions and esteem with each other in an attempt to get closer to the Regent.

A good warrior, he knew, never let his mind wander from the battlefield. Keeping Lilandra safe was all that was important. It was that focused thought that allowed him to notice a small rustle in the normal flow of the celebration. At the far end of the hall, Donius could see a young soldier being escorted by a castle servant. The servant he knew; which provided him with some measure of reassurance. A private appearing in a grand ball, however, was unusual. As a bodyguard, he knew that anything unusual was to be examined.

His men saw it as well. Clandestinely, two of his men approached the young soldier. Donius could see them act in accordance with their training. One of his men stood unseen approximately eight paces away. The other indirectly approached the young soldier's position. He did so in slowly tightening concentric circles. If the young soldier was an assassin, he would probably recognize the maneuver. If he was not, he would not know he was being examined.

While those two were examining the young soldier, Donius took his eyes from them. He knew well the technique of distraction, and he had to guard against it. He had to trust in the training of his men. After a few moments of scanning the crowd, he let his gaze fall back on the target of his men's investigation. His men were moving away from the soldier. Apparently, they determined he was not a threat.

He was escorted by a castle steward. That, Donius hoped, would mean that the soldier was invited. Lilandra frequently did that as a reward for some minor service they might have performed. She made Donius's job much more difficult when she invited commoners and nobles alike to speak with her.

As the young man made his way through the crowd, he gathered people's attention. It was not simply that he was dressed as a mere private in the army. He was something of interest to the assembled guests. In a flash, Donius recognized him. He was the soldier on whom the hawk had landed.

Earlier Donius might have enjoyed seeing the Regent's plans be so publicly and suddenly changed. However, she was not his enemy now. Donius had to believe that with all of his mind, or he might miss a possible threat to her. As far as threats, he knew his men were right. The young soldier below was no threat to the Regent. He seemed to be a lamb being led to the sheerer.

* * *

Keven had rarely felt more uncomfortable in his life. The hundreds of disapproving glares that accompanied him through the crowd of nobles were unnerving. His escort, dressed in the finest castle livery, seemed to want to be rid of him.

The castle servant led him directly to the throne. Keven's mind was awash in several powerful emotions. He stood on the perimeter of a circle of onlookers feeling excited and scared at the same time. Sitting on the throne, the Regent looked nothing like the casual friend who had dropped by the barracks. Her gown was a shade of green he had never seen. Beautiful red curls were swept up to expose her elegant neck. He was unnoticed at first. But, then, an admirer of the Regent across from Keven launched into a verbal attack.

"After you caught the new symbol of Atani, you released it. You're lucky embarrassment does not touch her. You coaxed the bird to your hand. How could you not bathe in the honor of sharing affection for the noble bird as it flew?" Though it was phrased as a question, Keven knew it to be an accusation filled with disbelief and venom.

He noticed many others nodding their agreement to the condemnation that was heaped upon him. It was nothing new to him; he had been the focus of an angry and disgusted crowd before.

Keven responded the only way he knew how, with simple honesty. "She was scared. The crowd bothered her. She was confused between her training and her instincts. A bird like that should not be kept." With boldness that none of the courtiers had seen in the face of Lilandra's charm, Keven continued. "Nothing should be bound and forced to serve others." As soon as he said it, he recognized how similar that was to his own history.

Again, thoughts in his mind pulled at each other. The resentment he felt at being treated no better than the bird welled up. It was matched by what the Dream could mean for him. The two thoughts battled equally until a melodic voice tipped the scales.

"Such nobility for one so young," the crowd became silent as Lilandra crooned the words.

She gracefully rose from her throne and glided down the steps. Her gown was like no other Keven had seen. He was sure that an emerald had been sacrificed just for the material. The green gossamer gave teasing hints but kept her best secrets dear. Her hair was as radiant as a new sun on a spring day. As she approached, his nervousness was only matched by his desire for her to reassure him. He wanted to talk to her. As she drew ever nearer, he became more certain that she would not do him harm.

"Please be calm, the first time at court is often overwhelming. You are a member of the Ninth Company. Were you not recently brought to our fair city?"

Keven almost swooned. All thoughts of resentment at being dragged to Atani evaporated. She remembered him! Someone as beautiful and admired as her, knew him.

"Yes, my lady." Keven tried to say clearly and loudly. His voice broke with excitement at responding to her direct question.

"Aw, poor dear. I know it can be nerve wracking, but you'll get used to it. I think you might fit in well here." She traced a fingernail gently down his cheek to his neck. It came to rest on his shoulder. The physical contact of one so beautiful gave him gooseflesh.

Keven's mind was reeling. 'Get used to it' echoed in his head. She wanted to see him after this! He was acutely aware of the others who were watching the Regent's attention on him. He was uncomfortable with the stares, but he was enjoying the reason for their jealousy.

He wished his company-mates were watching. He wished the whole coliseum and his old village were watching. She then put her arm in his and guided him across the floor. The crowds parted in automatic respect for her space.

"You're Keven, from the Westlands. Right?" The question was asked with a mix of seduction and compassion.

"Uh, yes," he stammered. He did not say his new last name. Though he had all but lost his need for pride, something prevented him.

"And how do you like our city?

He couldn't believe it. She was interested in his opinion. He said a silent prayer that somehow Constance would hear of this. Maybe even Erin would hear how valued he was and would want him again.

"Um, it is wonderous. It is grand." Wonderous? Grand? He had never used those words before in his life. Where were they coming from?

"Tell me, Keven, what did you do before you came to our fair land? Were you seeking the Dream?"

"No," he said reluctantly, "I was a stable hand."

"A stable hand," she said with enthusiasm. "You must be such a kind man to work with poor beasts."

Keven had never before been called a man by a beautiful woman. She said it effortlessly, as if there could be no doubt to the fact.

"Yes, I really do have a way with them. They seem to take to me." He said the last honestly and unabashedly. Keven felt that was what she wanted to hear.

"Keven" she whispered so only he could hear, "The Dream is growing. The good people of Atani are making it come true. But, success brings with it more opportunities to serve. I need good people to fill those opportunities. I can tell that you are a person of quality. You come from the Westlands and might have some valuable thoughts. Would you be interested in a position in the castle, working with me, for the Dream?"

His heart leapt. He was constantly aware of how her arm was touching his. Aside from what he and Erin had shared, this was the most contact he had ever had with a woman. He was afraid of moving because he feared it would cause her to move her arm and end the moment.

Thoughts reeled in his head. It was hard to pick one out of the swarm. Then, one found him. It was simple, 'think before ye speak, lad.'

That thought seemed to freeze the flurry of the other thoughts. Few of the thoughts that now hung suspended in his mind seemed right. Keven did not know if he was an Atanian. He had never really considered himself a Westlander. The familiar conflict between new and old loyalties re-ignited. Could the Dream offer more than the Wizards' Palace? Would accepting her offer close the door on reaching the Wizards' Palace?

"I, um… don't think that would be good for me. I'm sorry, but I must refuse."

Keven was aware of a pause in the conversation, but little else. He was too enamored of Lilandra to see the hardness that crept into the subtle lines of her face.

"Well, my dear Keven. It is noble to uphold one's commitments. It is always an honor to meet soldiers who so selflessly give themselves in service of their nation. Forgive me. I must attend to other less pleasant duties." There was a dark tone to her voice, and with that, she glided off.

Very quickly and very smoothly a lady in waiting appeared at Keven's side. She guided him away from the ball room and through the hallways of the castle. Keven knew that he had to return to training. The thought was a sudden rain cloud that cooled and dampened a spring day.

Keven heard his guide's words but did not respond. He was involved in his own thoughts. He trusted her guidance through the corridors of the large castle. To Keven the wide corridors were magnificent. He had never been in a building that was not made from timbers. It made him feel small with wonder. Without her to guide him from the castle, he would have been lost.

The Regent had wanted him. It could hardly be conceived, yet it was true. He could still smell her sweet perfume. He felt like kicking himself for turning down her offer. What could be better than serving her?

Almost in response to that and from the deepest recesses of his mind, he heard a long missed voice. "Is that the way of it, lad? Do ye give up magic and the lass so quickly?" Keven did not know why that thought popped into his head. It was disturbing how easily thoughts of Erin, pain and joy had slipped from his mind.

Joseph Swope

Erin

Hadassa I. Molnar

Chapter 17

Erin Dunn left her office. She carried the board to which she often tacked sheets that listed the types and amounts of weapons for which she was responsible. Because of her small size and lack of skill, it was recognized early by both her and her training officers that she would never be a good fighter. They did, however, recognize her value when she told them of her background and her father's trade.

That was the beauty of the Dream. Each citizen gave in the way they could. She had given her all over the last few years. It was with a heavy heart that Erin realized she had a new way she could give to the Dream. Keven's disturbance in the citizens' assembly might be causing the Regent discomfort.

If the rumors were true, Keven had been taken to the castle. He had to be somewhat important to the Regent if he was escorted there. Maybe Keven was to be promoted? A mix of feelings stirred within her. Would that be the best thing for Keven? Of all the people she knew, he, for some reason, seemed least likely to join the Dream.

Maybe that was it. Maybe Keven really wasn't part of it. He hadn't seemed committed to it when they spoke in the training yard. Was he against it? Was he one of those who were rumored to be working against the Regent? Questions swirled within her.

Was he a saboteur? Keven? Even if he was against the Dream, what could he do to it? Probably not much, she reasoned. Still, she had seen what even a few malcontents could do to a company. And, there was the incident with the hawk.

Keven did not fit into the dream. Try as she might, she could never make her imagination picture Keven as a happy citizen of Atani Her role as an Atanian officer made her duty clear. She must tell the Regent everything she knew of Keven.

There was a pang of guilt from what felt like betrayal, but how could she not honor the Regent and the Dream?

Her gut said that not only didn't Keven fit into the Dream, he was a threat to it. Her mind couldn't quite make sense of the feeling, but

Keven seemed different than every other recruit. Erin's practical mind warred with deeply rooted emotions. How could Keven be a threat to anything? He was, in his own way, the most simple and honest person she had ever known. Maybe he simply didn't understand. Maybe she should make it her duty to help him see why he should give everything to the Dream.

That thought didn't fit either. She knew he could never be convinced of anything, he always found holes in anyone's logic. Arguing with him was always worse than arguing with her father. Even if her father punished her, Erin knew she was on the right side of an argument.

When she had a rare argument with Keven, she was almost always wrong. It wasn't because he cheated or even because he wanted to win, he simply saw thing better than she did. In time, she had learned to simply trust his judgement.

Thinking about those days brought an unexpected lump to her throat. As she walked through the city, she could not help but let the too brief conversation with Keven enter her mind again. Each time she did, it was as if a barely healed wound was again ripped open. It had taken her a long time to adjust to being alone in Atani. Leaving Village Donnell had been tough, but she'd had her father's love as a crutch.

After being forced to leave Village Donnell, they had settled into a decent life in the northern Westlands. Her father, of course, worked at a smithy for a minor lord who was a close vassal to King Festinger, and she was his apprentice. One day, the king's guards came for her father. The rumor was the lord who had used her father's sword had lost a duel because the sword had broken. The feeble-minded King Festinger had blamed her father for it.

They had beaten him bloody in the street while she looked on helplessly. She had done her best to defend him. She had even struck one of the guards with a half-forged sword. The only real damage it caused was to her when the soldiers reacted to her attempt. Both she and her father were dragged from the smithy section of the city as other members of the guild looked on.

He was taken to the castle for a fate she dared not imagine. When they had first arrived in Wielseat, they had been told of the King's justice by weary laborers. Residents of Wielseat had eagerly told them each story and rumor of the dungeon. It was better to die than to suffer the King's punishments. The punishments he gave out lasted lifetimes in the depths of his castle. She had grieved for her father everyday until she found the Dream. The Dream distracted her from the possibility that her father might still be suffering at the hands of the King of Wielseat's torturers.

Erin had been sentenced to a different fate. The guards had brought her to their commander with lustful leers in their eyes. He had not let them ravish her. For that, she would be eternally thankful to The Creator.

276

However, soon after that, she ended up wishing they had had their way with her and left her in the city penniless. Instead, he had ordered them to sell her to the nearest slaver and split the profits. She remembered the horror of hearing that decree. She had been powerless to stop it. To them, she was nothing more than a good to be traded.

She almost faltered as she walked to the castle. Despite the warm Atanian sun, Erin wanted to wrap her arms around herself in protection from those memories.

Two years ago, when the King of Wielseat's men had taken her to the slavers, she was allowed no rest. To speed exhaustion, she and the other slaves had been tethered to a large wooden wheel that hung horizontally five feet above the ground. The device had several wooden poles extending from it like skeletal arms. She was tied to one of those arms. A horse was tied to the longest arm and was prodded to move. As a result, she and the other slaves were forced to walk around the slowly spinning circle. It was a gristmill that ground away at her spirit.

She had been a young woman of no more than fifteen summers when the recruiting party freed her from the slavers. The slavers were traveling from Wielseat to a slavers' market when the raid came. She and the people in the caravan were herded along like the livestock they were. Little about it remained with her except for the deep shame she had felt. She had thought of herself as strong-willed. Indeed, she had resisted her intimidating father often, but that counted for nothing with the slavers. Within a short few nights at the hands of the slavers, she was letting herself slip away. She would have gladly begged them to stop their training, if her saviors had not come when they did.

When she had first been taken to the slavers' camp she had been beaten and stripped of her clothing in front of the crew of slavers and the other slaves. It had been awful, yet neither group reacted to her nudity. At that point, she truly felt like an animal in a pen. When she tried to reason with them, they beat her. When she continued, they stuffed a gag in her mouth. Still, it was not the gag, the nudity, or the beatings that was the worst of her torments. It was the accepted idea that her fate was sealed and she was of no consequence.

Around and around she and the others had walked. When they faltered and let themselves be dragged by the horse drawn pole, the slavers would attach them to the pole by their necks. At night, they had been bound in various positions. Erin was frequently positioned on her hands and knees, bound to stakes in the ground. The speed with which the slavers could attach her ankles, wrists, and knees to the stakes was a testament to the number of times they had done it before. Six vertical poles imbedded in the ground at her ribs, hips, and shoulders prevented her from moving her belly away from the point. Small pebbles had been strewn about the ground so that, in only moments, they dug into her flesh.

Despite being left in one position, she could not sleep. When positioning her, the slavers would force her to arch her back. They would then place a sharp blade under her midsection with its point just touching her belly. She could not relax her position without slowly impaling herself. As a result, sleep was denied to her. The muscles in her back would quickly scream and beg her to relax and end it. Part of her had already given up. She had desperately wanted to let go, but she could not. She could not willingly impale herself.

That she couldn't escape, even in death, was the thought that almost broke her. Night after night, she sobbed tears of despair. The slavers would walk by, ignoring her as though she were nothing more than a piece of meat that was curing for sale at a market.

When the caravan was on the move, she and the others would be dragged behind a wagon. On the days when the slavers wanted to rest the horses, she would be forced to walk the wheel. She knew she would break, she could not stop it. Day after day, her decline was observed and recorded. She could still hear the demonic scratching sounds of the stick filled with ash as it marked her descent on the foreman's rough tablet.

In retrospect, she realized she was fortunate. She had not been given slaver's juice. She did not know why. Had she been given enough slaver's juice, she knew she would have fought to stay with those who tormented her.

When the Atanians rescued her, she had already given away much of herself. The rescuers treated her well, but at the time of her rescue and for some time after, she was barely more than a hollow shell. She took her rescuers' comforts warily, unsure of whether she could trust them. After a while, she realized that what they offered might fill the hole that had been created by the slavers and the loss of Keven and her father. Quite literally, Atani and the Dream had saved her life.

Though she had seen the Atanian soldiers kill all the slavers in a nighttime raid, she still feared those slavers for quite some time after their death. That shamed her deeply. Her mind knew they could not get her, but she still trembled at the thought of them like a small child trembles at nighttime shadows.

The memories of losing her life with her father and her thankfully short time with the slavers were almost as painful as her recent thoughts about Keven. She had thought she had successfully put behind her all thoughts of her life outside of the Dream. Keven's sudden appearance had had the effect of waking her up from a very pleasant nap. She had worked hard to achieve a secure and respectable life in Atani. The possibility of being promoted to captain was tantalizingly close.

Usually walks through the city helped to clear her head. This time the many flags bearing the new symbol of Atani reminded her of Keven. The awareness of a choice between loyalty to Keven and her devotion to the Dream crashed upon her. Whatever she chose, it would cost her dearly.

* * *

Lilandra sat in her chambers and reviewed her plans. The throne room had its purposes, but for the peace she needed to plan, her chambers were the best. She had the throne and its authority firmly in her grasp and the people loved her. A whole division of companies would soon be moving towards the Westlands. The best part about it was few Atanians noticed. Ambition, she knew, was best kept hidden.

As she reviewed a few sheets of paper, several thoughts crashed in. As always, there was the damned dragon to worry about. Her elegant plans could be torn asunder if the dragon decided to wake and eat the city. Her best efforts could not even wake it much less move it, and she knew there was nothing she had that could affect it if it did wake. Like she had done so many times before, she pushed thoughts of the dragon out of her mind.

Another worry crossed her mind. It was small and probably insignificant, but unlike the dragon, Lilandra knew she could control this irritant. It was the Westlander she had recently met. He was a mere stable hand and a simple private in the army. Yet, he resisted her charms. A man such as he should have crumbled at her attentions. She could tell he had never been with a woman, but her touch was not enough to get him to acquiesce. She did not try harder because she did not want to be seen as attempting to convince someone. It was always best if they accepted easily.

The elf had mentioned him several times, not just because of his apparently magical companion. Kiel spent an interesting amount of time describing the man and his curious reaction to being recruited. From Kiel's description of him, it seemed as if he had something with which she was very familiar, control of need.

She paused from her thoughts as the cool morning air made her feel grateful for the blanket that covered her legs. Still in her sleeping gown, she knew that if she simply moved about she would not feel the chill. But, one of the small pleasures in life was to hold onto mornings and make them last.

Lilandra sipped the still warm cup of tea and thought about the stable hand. He probably did not know what problems he caused. Most people would not see it as a problem. He had not actually done anything.

He, she was almost sure, did not know what power he possessed. Still, Lilandra did not want to leave anything to chance.

He might soon realize his capability. Perhaps others would learn of it. Perhaps even his whole company would realize they did not need her. That had to be avoided at all costs. Almost instantly, her mind wove the beginnings of a plan. He needed to be separated from other citizens. As a member of a company, having him simply disappear might cause future problems.

Nessy knocked and immediately entered. Lilandra chose not to chastise Nessy for not waiting for a response to her knock. The man from the Westlands reminded Lilandra that care had to be taken with people. She needed them to need her. If Nessy saw her as a source of criticism, she might not be so eager to serve. That thought blossomed into the rest of her plan for the stable hand.

"Nessy, I have a favor to ask."

Lilandra watched the big woman's posture change at the thought of being needed. "Yes, my dear, what is it?" No one else would think of calling the Regent, 'my dear'. Nessie, though, did it with the utmost reverence and affection.

"Could you arrange to have one of the stewards come see me? Mr. Passi, I think would be best. But, do not have him come too soon. I would like to get dressed for the day." She said the last with just a hint of girlishness. Lilandra knew Nessy valued her femininity and beauty. In fact, as a reward Lilandra would ask Nessy for her advice on gowns and jewelry.

With a smile that was almost coy, the large woman nodded and left the chambers. It was the simple system of rewards that worked so well for Nessy that gave Lilandra the inspiration for the plan with the private from the Ninth Company. She had to retrain him. She had to make sure the only good in his life came directly from her. In that way, he would come to need her.

As she dressed, she fleshed out the details. She needed a task to assign him. As long as he and his company believed the task was for the benefit of the Dream, no questions would be asked. Of course, she did not care if the task was ever completed.

Lilandra believed all of her plans were brilliant, but this one was better than most. She wanted to combine her two biggest sources of worry, the Westlander and the dragon. He was good with beasts, and she needed some type of control over the beast. He would become its caretaker. If he failed to wake it, then she lost nothing. The dragon and he would remain in the building.

She returned to her lounge and waited for Mr. Passi. A brisk set of taps ended her wait. He was a thin man with dark hair and rat-like eyes. He wore fine clothing that did little to mask his deceitfulness. Nothing about what people wanted or what they would do to get what they wanted surprised Lilandra. She had realized long ago that people were ultimately self-serving, but Passi made even Lilandra feel uncomfortable. There was no deed he would not do to achieve his ends.

Their exchange was relatively quick. Of course, he wanted it to last as long as possible. It was not often he was summoned by the Regent to do her a personal favor. Her instructions were clear. What he heard more than her instructions was the fact that he could see her again when he successfully delivered the man to his next assignment.

With the ball rolling, she knew she should have felt a bit more relaxed, but there was still a residue of unease from her thoughts of the Westlander. She was thinking too much about him. In a flash of horror, the thought hit her like a hammer. She needed him to need her; otherwise her control was not absolute. Was she no better than even the most common citizen?

The wave of resentment and anger was enough to make her forsake her usual self-control. It had been a long time since she had felt the need for happiness or safety. It had been a long time since she had felt the need for anything. If she could not control what he wanted, she would destroy him.

Again, she wished for Sogoth's power. It was rare that she envied him his power because she was well aware of the price he and other wizards had to pay. Even so, being able to smash something with a simple thought would help quell her frustration. He was a simple stable hand, a peasant. How could she need him?

* * *

Tapio Denisio was a religious man, but living in Ducca's Vineyard had not given him much opportunity to visit any holy places. Still, he prayed frequently. His prayers were not formal declarations that were so popular among those who called themselves holy. Rather, his prayers were more like one-sided conversations with The Creator. Did The Creator get tired of the same prayers? Would The Creator ever let him see her again?

"Private Denisio, I need a word with you."

Tapio pulled himself away from the crowd of soldiers who were heading towards the wash vats. He was tired. The officer in charge waited for Tapio to approach. He would not speak until Tapio had assumed the correct position of attention. So, Tapio quickly stood as the other man wished.

"This company has finished its drills early this day. You have done well. Many of the other soldiers see you as a leader. Perhaps you should think of your future in the Army. But, for now, the Seventh Company is still in drills. If you leave now you should be able to see your daughter as they dismiss for the day. Dismissed, Private Denisio," the officer in charge said with condescension.

A thousand thoughts ran through Tapio's head as he walked away from the Eighth Company's portion of the training grounds. Chief among them was fear of missing her, and that sped his steps. He walked as fast as he could without appearing to run. He was a private. If he ran, he might attract the attention of any corporal or officer who might not be sympathetic to his need to see Tonay. As he rounded the corner of one of the squat identical buildings, he saw them in formation. They were being dismissed for the day. There were too many soldiers in uniform for him to see anyone that looked like Tonay.

As the tight lines of formation broke up, he ran towards them. "Tonay!" he shouted with unabashed hope. "Tonay!" he called again. He saw the crowd lurch as if someone moved against the flow of bodies.

She emerged from the crowd, and his spirit soared as he ran to her. He was heartened to see that her face showed joy at seeing him. After his journey and his constant state of emotional anguish, he did not think he could bear it if she rejected him.

"Papa, what are you doing here?" She flung herself at him like she had done as a small girl.

"Tonay, how could I not follow you? When you left like you did, I came after you."

Her eyes dropped to examine him, and she saw his sweat stained uniform. "Papa, you're in the army too! What company are you in? Have they formed you into squads yet? I'm doing so well! You should see me! I'm the best with the sword in the company!" There was need in her eyes. She desperately wanted his approval.

As he struggled to find words, he embraced her again. The day full of drills had left her face red and her hair sweaty, but he held her tight. He felt that if he let go, he would not hold her again. Still, she pushed away from him.

"I can't believe it. You've decided to join. Have you seen the Regent yet? Isn't she beautiful?" The glow of happiness in her eyes was dazzling.

Unaware of the soldiers milling about the hard packed dirt of the training area, Tapio's eyes fixed on his daughter's face, the same face that had giggled with glee upon hearing a silly story so many years ago. He had to force himself to speak. If he did not, their time together would be finished.

"I have not seen the Regent. There was not enough room at the last Citizen's Assembly for the Eighth Company. The rumor is that we will be invited to the next one. I can't wait." It was a lie. He did not care anything for the Regent. His only need was to protect his daughter from the madness that had infected everyone around him.

"Papa, you'll love her. In the coliseum, all citizens come together as one. It does not matter if they are noble or common."

"Perhaps we could attend together. The officers of my company seem to be pleased with me. They might allow me to visit you for such an occasion."

"Oh, but Papa, my company has been chosen to march west. We are to be part of a new expedition. We will spread the glory of the Dream. Isn't it magnificent? Don't worry, Papa. The expedition will go smoothly. And, my skills are really good. You should see me. No one in my company can touch me with their sword. Maybe the Eighth Company will be sent out soon. We could be together, spreading the Dream."

Desperate panic forced him to try what he knew would fall on deaf ears. "Tonay, my love, if I dragged you home and forced you to accept my ways, what would you think?"

"Papa, this is not the place for such talk. You're here, surely you see the light."

"Just listen, you would resent me, even hate me if I dragged you home. Being able to choose of your own mind is the best gift I could give you. There is nothing more important. How, then, do you think those whose homeland Lilandra plans to invade will think? This is wrong. Think Tonay!" His desperate plea was whispered with every bit of love in his soul.

Her only response was the silent tears that filled her eyes. She moved her mouth as if she wanted to say something, but no sound came out. She dropped her eyes and turned away from her father as her chin quivered in anguish.

Tapio was a parched man watching a spilled drop of water disappear into dry ground. He felt powerless to stop her from drifting further from him. While enduring long nights with Lieutenant Spudolli and endless hours of drills, he had simply refused to think she might not choose to return with him. In one instant, long delayed grief crashed upon him. It almost brought him to his knees.

A harsh voice called out to them. "Private Denisio, you are holding up your company. No one goes to evening meal unless everyone goes to evening meal."

She skipped into a run towards her dormitory.

Tapio watched her go. Tears did not come to his eyes. He was too empty for that. The pain he felt towered above what even the best slaver could inflict. It was a special pain reserved for parents who could not prevent harm from coming to their children. A thought crept into his mind like a dark serpent. His daughter, the person to whom he dedicated his life, was gone. She was dead to him.

Returning to the area of the Eighth Company, he walked as a dead man. His heart had been ripped from him. He could not blame his daughter. She was acting for what she thought was best. The only person he could blame was the one Tonay chose over him: the Regent Lilandra.

Tapio had no coin, no allies, and very little hope of exacting any type of revenge. Still, as he entered the barracks of the Eighth Company, he swore revenge on those who had stolen his daughter.

He would spend however long it took to find a way to hurt the Regent. He would train and dutifully obey his officers and would play the part of a loyal Atanian. All the while, though, he would keep his eyes open. He would find those who also hated her. For he knew the enemy of his enemy was his friend.

* * *

The man who arrogantly confronted the officer in charge was certainly not from the army. His clothing was too fine, but he passed on a piece of paper and the officer obeyed.

"Private Whoreson, front and center!"

Upon hearing that, Keven properly turned from his position in the ranks and trotted to the officer. He stopped as he had seen other soldiers do, with a respectful flare. His officer noticed and gave the briefest of nods that made Keven feel good.

Despite Keven standing no more than four paces from him, the officer continued in a voice that was more suited to barking orders to a whole company.

"Private Keven Whoreson, your service has been requested by Regent Lilandra herself. She requests that you honor your fellow citizens by changing your duty. You are to now serve her personally."

As the officer read the orders aloud, the normally well-disciplined Ninth Company let out a collective gasp. As envious as they were, they were genuinely happy for him. Friendship and the cheerful ribbing about the way he pronounced words were far different than the spiteful jeers of the Goodfolk in Village Donnell.

Keven was told to follow the man named Passi to his new place of duty. When he asked about his few possessions, he was told not to worry. Everything would be provided for him.

The excitement of getting to meet the Regent again almost washed away the apprehension he had about leaving the hunk of flint behind. That piece of flint, though common and cheaply replaced, was a connection to his brief lessons in magic. It was the only thing that really reminded him of his time before the Ninth Company.

With no more ceremony, Keven was led across the brown dirt of the training ground by his new escort. The man offered no words, which Keven found more than a little strange. The lack of conversation allowed Keven to hear the command to continue training.

Keven had to hurry to keep pace with his escort. Keven wasn't sure if the man was running to leave the training area or if he was running to return to the castle.

When they reached the exit of the walled training complex, his quiet escort offered a few words. "The city is large, and we should not keep the Regent waiting." With that, he led Keven to two horses. Keven swung into the saddle and dutifully followed the man through the city.

The mare he was riding stirred thoughts of Thistle. Keven knew enough about her past to know she had not been treated kindly. Now, she was somewhere, far from anyone who would understand or care for her.

His thoughts of the horse that had acted to protect him echoed his thoughts about himself. He felt like a single leaf that had fallen into a fast moving stream. He had no idea where he was going. He tried to empty his mind and think of the Regent. Once he was with her, he knew things would be fine.

As the two rode through the city, the crowds slowed them, thus Keven couldn't help but end up riding next to the other man. Surprisingly, the angry little man broke his silence with some vehement words.

"I don't know who you think you are, but the Regent's time is too valuable to be wasted on one such as you. She has people who need her. Yet, in her endless patience she has made time for you."

Keven didn't know what to say. He tried to stammer an apology, though he was more than a little confused as to why.

"Do not offer your words to me. Save them for the Regent. She is the one who is upset with you."

Those words hit Keven harder than any fist. The Regent was upset with him. Instantly, he tried to recall every moment of his time with her. Did he insult her at the castle? He didn't know. His stomach developed into a pit of fear. She of all people! She had shown him nothing but kindness. He had to apologize.

Keven noticed the amount of dark blue cloth that hung from every building. He instantly knew it had to be the same color as the dress the Regent had worn during her speech. With a sharp sting of regret, he wished he had thought to bring some of that with him. Perhaps it might show her how much he was devoted to her.

He was surprised to see that they were riding to the coliseum. Their steady progress towards it made it loom ever larger. After following his escort right to the huge arena, Keven noticed there was a squad of guards at the gates. They were not milling about as he had seen so many guards do. Their hard eyes watched Keven approach on the listless horse.

Keven's guide did not slow. As he approached, he simply nodded to the lieutenant. When the lieutenant nodded in return, the guards stepped aside. Keven kept his gaze at his mount's mane. He had thoughts more troubling than whether or not the guards found him acceptable.

When he had been fortunate enough to be present at the Citizens' Assembly, Keven had seen for the first time the glory of the Atanian Coliseum. The field alone could hold Village Donnell. When he had walked to the field with his company, he had been too overwhelmed by the sights and sounds to really study the huge wooden building.

Riding with the Regent's man, Passi, Keven gained a better idea of the building's magnitude. The tunnel he and Passi walked their horses through was a hundred paces long. It was high enough to allow them to sit atop their horses. Though he could see light at the other end, the tunnel was as dark as night.

With a steady gait that unnerved Keven, they both approached the wooden warehouse and dismounted. Passi undid the heavy cross bar and pulled the door open. The skinny man struggled with the weight of it.

Keven could see nothing as he entered the warehouse. The door immediately slammed shut behind him, and Keven heard Passi thrust the cross bar in place.

The moments it took for his eyes to adjust to the dim light of thin beams slipping through the planks of the wall and ceiling passed slowly. His gaze was immediately captured by something that could not be clearly seen at first. Keven had felt small and insignificant next to the coliseum, but what he saw before him dwarfed even the coliseum in magnificence. His quick mind instantly wondered if what he saw was a trick. As soon as he wondered it, he knew in his soul that no human could create something as exquisitely powerful as the dragon he saw before him.

"I see you have noticed my surprise for Atani."

The voice of the Regent in her sultry manner could not compare to seeing a dragon.

"Is it real?" He knew the question sounded foolish as soon as it left his lips. He almost looked around for an arrowfly.

"Of course; it is merely sleeping." Her voice held no trace of the softness he remembered and desperately hoped to hear again. She walked in front of Keven so his gaze would fall on her instead of the dragon. With her interrupting his line of sight, he had to pay attention to her.

"My dear," she cooed with an edge to her voice. "I hope you realize how special I consider you. It is not often the leader of a nation personally sees to the accommodations of a stable hand."

She flashed him a smile like he had seen on Constance, so long ago.

"From now on, you will stay here. Away from the hot work of army training. That really doesn't fit one as special as yourself. This nice quiet warehouse is more suited to you."

The dread he held in his stomach during the trip to the warehouse, the stress of meeting the Regent again, and the outright shock at seeing a dragon prevented him from really understanding her words.

"Given your skills with beasts, I would like to invite you to be my special guest. This, my backwards farm boy, is a dragon. It was a gift to me from an admirer. I will regive it to the citizens of Atani. This gift, however, does nothing but sleep. It does not stir. It does not even seem to breathe. I am told nothing can be done to wake it."

She seemed to pout with sadness at the tale of the dragon. As hurt as he was by her treatment, he still felt bad for her, and he needed to make her feel better.

"But what if it wakes, what does it eat?" He tried to keep the fear out of his voice remembering what Gareloch had said about dragons.

Lilandra noticed Keven's gaze. She had seen it countless times. It was easy to produce in anyone. The first step was to find what a person needed. The second step was to give it to them. The third step was to take it away. The fourth step was to simply watch them do anything to regain whatever filled their need.

"My dear Keven, you told me of your skill with beasts. I have even heard you have some ability at magic. Who else could disrupt the flight of the noble Atanian hawk? Surely, you can tame this beast for the benefit of the Dream." Her voice was a mix of a scolding mother and a teasing vixen.

With his gaze still upon her, she knew she had to dangle the prize a little further from him. "Don't worry, I'll come visit you. You can still think of me."

As her words crashed upon Keven, he noticed her bodyguard. He was large, but not overly so. His eyes were trained on Keven as if he was a cat and Keven was a mouse. The man wore a long sword, and his hand casually rested on the pommel.

Regent Lilandra turned and began to walk towards the door. Her bodyguard's hard stare froze Keven where he stood. Then, he too followed the Regent towards the door. After a few paces, she stopped and turned towards Keven.

"Keven, please understand all of Atani thanks you for this service. Oh, don't fret. Meals will be brought to you. The door, however, will have to remain locked. If you would like to leave, simply use your magic." She said the last in a tone that made Constance's best efforts seem warm.

Keven was too stunned to say anything. First, Erin had treated him like any other private in the army. Now, he was going to be locked in a prison with a dragon that could awake at any time. Keven's heart sank lower with each step toward the door the Regent took.

After she and her bodyguard summoned the outside guards to open the doors, Keven saw them disappear into the sunlight. To punctuate their exit, the great door closed, and the heavy wooden beam fell across the outside of it. He was plunged into darkness again as the light of the mid-day sun barely poked through. Feelings of abandonment crashed down on him. His new friends in the Ninth Company would not think of him. They believed him to be in the Regent's loving company.

Keven had visions of the dung shed. No matter how far he traveled, he was still a bastard to be locked away at others' whims.

His mother, the people of his village, and even Gareloch would never find him. Keven knew in his heart, of course, they would not even search. Most of all, it was Erin's words that made his entrapment feel worse than death. He was truly alone. Whether he lived or died would be known to only one and cared about by none.

* * *

The breakdown of their settlement was quick and efficient. Of course, they'd had practice from the long journey to Atani. Even if they had not, the dwarves would have acted with a smooth determination, that was the dwarven way

Though their current tasks were mundane, many of the dwarves wore bits of their armor. Every dwarf wore at least one hammer or axe. Those who wore armor were quick to say the extra weight of thick weapons and armor was nothing. Those who did not were quick to say they were strong enough without armor.

Haft Oreshale watched it all with his deep set brown eyes. His bushy eyebrows added to his scowl. There was not much to scowl over, but he managed to do it. The equipment was being tightly lashed down and the supplies were being neatly stowed. He walked the square of ground that was inside the temporary metal fort. Short, powerful legs made his strides lumbering. His thick, calloused fingers held many papers. His workers would assume the papers were ledgers and reports detailing the condition and location of each piece of equipment. As fighters, his employees feared nothing. Fear was almost always born of weakness, and no dwarf would admit to that. As employees, they worried that he would find a reason to pay them less of the bonus he had said they might receive.

With an eye towards the papers in Haft's hand, each dwarf worked diligently. To an outside observer, Haft Oreshale appeared to be anything but shrewd. To some he was the picture of a slow wit pressed into service as a jester. He had a bulbous nose that showed enough red veins to be a road map of the caves of his home. His wild hair sprang from underneath his horned helm. He frequently looked at the papers in his grubby hands as if he had forgotten what he had just read. But, those features hid the sharp wit that was betrayed only by his eyes.

It was not forgetfulness that made him look at the pages again and again. Haft simply enjoyed looking at them. The papers held the numbers which revealed the profits from the sale of their goods. The final number was half again bigger than what he had dared hoped at the outset of the expedition. All of his workers were going to receive a bonus. But, he would not tell them till all of the work was done.

Haft had never had a session of negotiations go so well. The Regent of Atani was willing to grant him everything he asked for. He was suspicious at first. She came with but one assistant and that was just a young princess. A physically weaker pair he could not imagine, two thin human females. After haggling with her for some time, he realized she understood and respected strength. Indeed, he felt gratified when she sympathized with the tremendous effort it took to get the weapons to Atani.

She, too, demonstrated her strength. That separated her from the humans he knew. The secret to strength, as all dwarves knew, was believing in strength. Humans were filled with doubt. He tried to point that out to the few humans he drank with.

Before meeting the Regent and after having many conversations with Atanians over weak human ale, Haft picked up on the idea that Atani was a nation in change. The changes had to be costing a fortune. Still, she met her obligations unflinchingly. In fact, she paid more than the asking price.

It was that strength that endeared her to him. He would return to Atani as soon as possible and would bring double the number of weapons and charge half the price. If she could sacrifice for him, he would show her his strength. He would sacrifice double for her. She had need, and he had the strength to fill her need. How could he not?

Haft knew he would drive the caravan hard. The wagons were in near perfect shape, and he did not have to fear ambush. Atani was a nation of friends now. The normal suspicion humans had of dwarves was waning. On his last jaunt into town, more than a few humans had actually smiled at him. Some of the children approached him only to run away giggling.

Many in his craggy homeland had sneered at his plan to trade with Atani. Word of his success and more importantly the several chests of gold he had in his personal wagon would show them how wrong they had been.

The chance to boldly wave his success in the faces of those who doubted him made him wish his workers would pack up even more quickly. He did not openly urge them; he simply assumed his routine scowl. He would tell no one of his need to prove himself right. That need spoke of weakness deep within him.

The other dwarves would grumble at the pace he would soon demand of them. They could complain safely without fear of being thought of as weak; they had worked hard and performed admirably. They would not see his need to rush. With the success of selling the weapons, they had urged Haft to buy several cows and lambs. They were in the mood to eat well and travel slowly. When they had butchered the last of the livestock, they would still have plenty of dried and salted meat and at least one whole wagon was filled with kegs of ale.

They would, however, meet his demand for speed. As much as they loved to sit with big flagons of ale and share roasted meat and stories, they loved coin more. The sooner the wagons returned, the sooner they could reload them for another trip to Atani.

Haft knew he would lose some workers. A few would take their pay, buy a few wagons, hire some employees, and make a trip on their own. He did not mind, that was the dwarven way. Competition bred strength. Even so, he knew there would be little competition. The prices for weapons would rise, war was coming. Atani would have an even greater need for dwarven weapons. Many dwarves would profit in the next few years.

Many humans would suffer, but that was their way. They could not seem to prevent their own suffering. That did not mean dwarves did not feel some compassion for the suffering of others. But, there was little Haft or any other dwarf could do. Humans were weak and suffering followed weakness.

It had only been hours since he gave the order to pack up the encampment. In that time, the work had almost been completed. They would travel through the night. Humans could not see well in the dark and would be sleeping in their soft beds, so the roads would be clear.

There was little he would miss about the human lands, except the profits. Only two humans showed enough strength to make them worthy of note. One was the Regent.

The other was the prisoner who had been brought to the city. Dwarves did not bind their criminals, because no dwarven criminal would ever dare escape. Fleeing was the ultimate weakness. Any dwarf who was guilty would take his punishment readily and be done with it.

The man did not seem ready to flee. He had true strength.

* * *

Keven sat, as he had for days that blended into an amalgam of loneliness. He did not think his time in the warehouse had stretched into weeks, yet. Keven did his best to pass the time by sleeping in a ball on the dusty floor. He tried every position he could think of, but he could find no comfort on the packed dirt.

When food and water came, it was always with blinding sunlight that stabbed at him as the doors were opened by the guards. One guard would keep him from getting too close with the point of a spear. The other would drop a skin of water and a wooden bowl of bland food. It was the same type of meat-laced porridge he and the other members of the Ninth

Company had eaten regularly. Of course the bowl, like the wooden trenchers, probably had not been washed.

He had no idea if the food and water came at regular intervals. He thought it did. His short time in the army had taught him that schedules are not changed lightly.

Try as he might, he had reached a point, where he could sleep no more. It just did not come to him. He worked through Gareloch's breathing exercises. He even held the idea of nothing for quite some time, but his mind wanted to be active.

The warehouse was truly a prison. It took him awhile to overcome his fear of the dragon and explore. It was only after realizing the dragon did not breathe that Keven began to entertain thoughts of moving near it.

During his first circuit of the inside of his wooden prison, Keven had kept close to the walls. He wanted to keep as much distance between himself and the monstrosity that could so easily cause his death. The dim light let his eyes confirm what his groping fingertips had told him. Each wall was solid. Keven reasoned that the building was probably built to cage the dragon, not him. If that were the case, he would have no chance of breaking out. Once again, he had no mechanism to achieve his will.

After some time, he became increasingly accustomed to his new fate. He used a pebble to scratch marks on one of the planks. With those marks and the shifting angle of the sun's rays, he had some measure of time.

He would challenge himself not to look at the progress of the stream of light. He would reward himself with allowing himself to dwell on pleasant memories. Sometimes his memories would take him to working with his friends in the Ninth Company. Most of the time, his memories were split between Erin and Gareloch. Those memories, however pleasant they began, always rotted with the pain of betrayal or isolation. He tried to keep the memories of Erin centered on the bright spots in his past. The thoughts of Gareloch brought him to the realization that a future of learning and power was not for him.

The dragon, being similar in form to a small lizard, lay in a curved position with its feet in a pile on top of themselves. Its delicate wings were folded against its sides. Keven first approached the dragon from the back. Even so, he was intimidated by the sheer size of the beast. Lying as it was, it was still as high as he was tall. Each time he looked at it, he was reminded of its magnificence.

On several occasions, he would take a few steps in its direction only to turn away in fear. To Keven, his approach to the dragon reminded him of the time he and Erin had dared each other to touch a wasps' nest. Even as children, they knew the pain of wasps' stings would ebb quickly. With a dragon, Keven knew he could be touching his death.

291

In a startling revelation, he wondered why that would be a bad thing. He had lived long enough to see that every living thing fought for and clung to life. He had remained as still as a rock when the goblins approached. Now, he was imprisoned in a warehouse and would not be missed by anyone. His dream of wedding Erin had been dashed by her need to serve Atani. The dream of being a wizard had vanished with Gareloch. There was nothing he needed outside of the warehouse. Why then would he care if he died in it?

It was that strangely emboldening thought that freed him to approach the dragon's head. No writer's stories or artist's painting could have created such a visage. Its reptilian brow and long scaled snout should have inspired revulsion. Instead, it made all human attempts at art look like a child's mud sculpture. The multihued scales made him think of the finest gossamer dancing in the sun.

On one attempt, he forced himself to touch the terrible visage. The dragon was everything he was not. It was strong and beautiful. It feared nothing and needed nothing. At that point, he wished it would wake. If it was so magnificent when it slept, Keven could only wonder at what the beast would look like standing or even flying.

After staring at the closed eyelids for some time, Keven reverently backed away. Instead of returning to his corner near the beast's back, he chose a position against a wall that allowed him to be in direct sight of the dragon's head.

He remembered Gareloch's words on will and mechanism. In the dung shed, Keven had a burning need to get out of the manure. Now, Keven also had no mechanism, and he lacked the will to escape.

If he could break out, he had no place to go. The officers of the Ninth Company surely would not let him simply rejoin if they thought he had been assigned elsewhere. He could not very well hide in the city; he had no coin. For that same reason, he could not attempt the long journey back to Village Donnell.

In truth, Keven did not really want to return to Village Donnell. His life there was over. He loved his mother, but he did not miss her. He missed Gareloch, but he was reasonably sure the old man was dead. No one could have survived long with an arrow in their chest. Keven had to believe Gareloch was dead. If Gareloch had survived and was a powerful wizard, surely he would have come for Keven. It was less painful for Keven to think the old man couldn't rather than he wouldn't.

It wasn't even that Keven wanted to leave Atani. While training with the Ninth Company, he had felt like he was getting close to happiness he had only sporadically known before.

He could not fathom why the Regent was so upset with him. If he could just figure out what he had done wrong and how to please her, he knew she would let him serve in the Ninth Company again.

He tried to be angry with the Regent. It was difficult to do. His thoughts returned constantly to the idea that somehow something he'd done had created his present predicament. She was the beautiful Regent of a powerful nation who had everything she needed. It simply did not make sense for her to torment a private in the army for no reason.

For the thousandth time, he reviewed his interactions with her. He could find only two possible reasons for her to be angry with him. The first was the hawk in the coliseum. She wasn't angry with him for that, he reasoned.

The second was his refusal of her offer. He understood little of the niceties of their exchange. Why had she offered the position to him? He was a private and a newcomer to Atani. She surely had a line of people who would jump to accept what she offered. Why would she care if he denied her request?

Gareloch

Mike Lafferty

Chapter 18

Gareloch entered the large, spherical chamber and did his best not to do so triumphantly. The curved walls and floor were made from a polished metal that could only be the result of some arcane art. The shiny surface reflected the light that had no apparent source and cast no shadows.

On Lucius' urging, Gareloch wore special white ceremonial robes that were tailored for him alone. Gareloch had even agreed to don a traditional conical wizard's hat for the occasion. He imagined Lucius had imbued his new garments with some type of *Sospitix* to prevent them from wrinkling or absorbing stains.

He cared little for appearances. But, as Lucius explained, if so many wizards were helping him, they needed to believe their efforts were going to something worthwhile.

The needed spell could not be cast without the knowledge of all of the paths of power. Many of the wizards looked up from their books, vials, or machines upon his entrance. Individually, they had all been chasing knowledge to prevent the punishment of breaking the One Oath.

By working on the spell that Gareloch and Lucius had designed, each wizard was learning more than he could do alone. Gareloch tucked away that fact in the back of his mind. It was related to other thoughts of Keven. That many wizards were working together gave him a glimmer of hope. If it were not for his need to reach Keven, all of the involved wizards would be sequestered in their own workshops.

He toured the chamber walking from one group of conversing wizards to the next. The Wizards of Technology brought the most equipment to the specially designed room. There were only three of them. Though he looked over their shoulders, he had little understanding of their conversation. Without their precise measurements of the distances involved as well as their understanding of the forces he would be subjected to, the spell and his body would simply disintegrate.

The Wizards of Sorcery were the quietest. Their task was simple to put into words, but difficult for any but them to truly understand. Each of the Masters of Sorcery was to construct an intricate thought, hold it until the spell required them to apply the thoughts to the spell. Their task could best be described as picturing every detail of two places at once.

Each sorcerer had spent many long hours quietly yet excruciatingly practicing for this spell. If any of the Wizards of Sorcery let a stray thought appear in his mind, the spell would fail and Gareloch would die. Because it was a spell of *Situtum Domus*, he did not know where he would die. It might be that he would die in this room or in the intended destination. It might simply be that his body would never be found in any of the lands.

Gareloch resisted the urge to share pleasantries with them. The concentration that would soon be required of them would be extreme. Any word he might say to them would be a potential interference that might distract them at the critical time.

The Wizards of Magic had practiced in their way. During many sleepless days and nights in the library, the wizards poured over countless old tomes.

They searched for any spell that contained elements of *Covinnus*. There were many theories, but precious few spells. In the end Lucius was correct; the platform would have to be *Situtum Domus*. The magicians would have to add to and subtract from that spell to create what Lucius and Gareloch specified.

There were eleven Wizards of Magic present. Some chose to wear robes that were adorned with magical symbols. Most of the symbols were powerless, merely for show. Few truly powerful Wizards of Magic would rely on runes and symbols.

Gareloch then walked to the four Wizards of Alchemy. Alchemists were rarely bound by the Trinity. They saw no reason to limit themselves for the sake of others. It was, after all, the discipline that created slaver's juice. After some questioning that came close to violating the Trinity, it was revealed that the Wizards of Alchemy created slaver's juice somewhat by accident. Fulfilling the One Oath often lead wizards' inquiries in unexpected directions.

It was what they did with it that was most disturbing. By using the juice on a powerful, albeit trusting Wizard of Magic, certain Wizards of Alchemy coerced the Wizard of Magic to transport a small amount and the recipe out of the Wizards' Palace.

Their motives, they claimed, were simply inspired by the One Oath. Once one of the involved Wizards of Alchemy wondered aloud if it would be possible, he and the others were then driven to discover if it was. Their explanation was given with a smirk that could only be removed from their faces by resorting to methods the Trinity forbade.

In investigating, Lucius and Gareloch found that the spell the Wizard of Magic used was a clever version of *Situtum Acus*. The Wizard's fondness for slaver's juice ensured his decayed mind would never again allow him to cast a spell. The only book in which that version of spell was written was hidden in Lucius' study and warded by several spells.

As a result, Lucius and Gareloch had but a few possible Wizards of Alchemy from whom they felt they could safely choose.

They huddled together like black robed skeletons. Their pale, gaunt faces revealed little of what they thought. They were poorly regarded by the other schools. They did little to combat that notion as they whispered to themselves about the proper amount and type of substances to administer to Gareloch.

Without their help, even Gareloch's legendary ability would not be enough. For a short time, Gareloch's mind and body would be a vessel into which immeasurable amounts of power was poured. Without augmentation of his mind and body from the potions and herbs, he would crumble under the onslaught.

What he was trying belonged in the exaggerated legends of old. In those tales, it had become accepted as fact that wizards were all-powerful beings able to teleport at will and to see the secrets that all men hid in their souls, but that was a legend.

The theory of the spell was sound. The twenty-three wizards who were working on the effort were very good practitioners of each of their disciplines. Each one of those wizards understood the spell and could see no reason why it would not work.

There were some variations that even the best calculations and plans could not account for. The energies and distances involved were huge. He had been over the plan many times. He was beginning to think it would work. That was when it hit him again, a fleeting feeling that he knew was linked to Keven. It was gone as soon as he noticed it, but it was there. Hope.

* * *

It was the sound of the great door being opened that woke Keven. He did not know how long he had been in the warehouse, nor did he know how long he had been asleep. His only measure was the increasingly long growth of hair that sprouted from his chin.

As per their unspoken routine, one of the nameless, silent guards dropped the wooden bowl on the dirt floor. The other kept his spear handy and a needlessly wary eye out for Keven. Keven, as always, stayed well away from them. In fact, he doubted if they could see him. He was crouched in the shadows while their eyes were accustomed to the bright sunlight.

As always, a portion of the mush slopped over the side of the bowl. With a resentful scowl, they picked up his partially empty bowl. Rarely could he finish the food that was brought to him.

Over his predictable meal, Keven thought about Lilandra. While her words still stung, he could think about them clearly. He knew from his often-painful time at Village Donnell that words can hurt. She, he reasoned, must know that too. Why then he wondered, did she purposely say things to hurt him?

Words hurt, but they could lose their edge if used too much on a tough hide. Once, he had cringed every time he heard the word bastard. Since leaving Village Donnell he had learned that the words of others had very little to do with his needs. His indifference to the name Whoreson was proof of that. The name bothered him no more than a butterfly flapping its wings.

It was true her words had hurt, but with his thinking, they hurt less and less. As the pain of Lilandra's words was reduced by Keven's insights, the wound left by Erin was revealed. It was the reoccurring thoughts of Erin's rejection that made his time in the warehouse the most painful. With nothing to distract him, his thoughts seemed to return to his memories of her. All of his pleasant memories of the two of them were burned away by the knowledge that now she valued him not at all.

Those thoughts made him almost wish the dragon would wake. He was not scared of that possibility anymore. His only regret at having that possible fate would be not learning more about the dragon before it ate him.

As he shoveled the last of his porridge into his mouth with the thick wooden spoon, he thought about will and mechanism. He had neither. As bored as he was, he could not think of anything he needed. There was nothing outside of the warehouse for him, and he was becoming quite content with his thoughts.

It occurred to him, that without mechanism, he had no control over death. He could not prevent his death at the will of the dragon or the guards, and he was helpless to cause his own death. He could of course antagonize the guards into running their spears into him, but that seemed like cheating. He needed to have the mechanism come from within. He did not have the will to die. It just struck him as strange that without mechanism, he was forced to live.

He wished Gareloch had taught him more about sorcery. Having ability at sorcery or even a whole spell would be a tool to reach Lilandra. He knew they shouldn't, but somehow his thoughts returned to her.

In many ways, that inability to impress people had been his largest problem. He had no tools to please other people. It was the same with Banolf and the other Goodfolk of Village Donnell. They, like all people, needed certain things in life. He had no tool to fill those needs.

With that crushing realization, he felt the pain of Erin's loss again. He had nothing she wanted or needed. He was, in the truest sense, worthless to her. With a renewed sense of sorrow, Keven wondered if he had ever had worth to anyone.

Gareloch had taken him from a life of drudgery. He had asked nothing in return. He had taught Keven more than he could remember. Without the distractions of the Army and the Dream, Keven could see it was the best chapter of his life.

With Gareloch, he had felt alive. The old man had the ability to whittle off all but the important part of the question. Why *did* he have to need things?

He looked at his empty wooden bowl and thought more about Gareloch's other teachings. For the thousandth time, he wished he had a piece of flint. He missed the feeling of magic coursing through his body and mind.

Despite his many thoughts, Keven had not tried *Sublevato*. He was almost certain it would not work and had refrained from trying. If he did not try and prove to himself it would not work, he could still have hope that it might. It was foolish, and he knew it. No question was ever answered by ignoring it.

In frustration, Keven kicked the half-empty wooden bowl away from him. It landed a few paces away. He did his best to recall every detail of practicing with Gareloch. He remembered the breathing and the feel of the magic. The monotony of the warehouse contained no distractions and allowed Keven to dredge up some of the words. If he had the words, he might not need flint.

He closed his eyes and slowed his breathing to the gentle rhythm he so enjoyed. His mind imagined the bowl begin to char and blacken. When he had his breathing right and his mind clear, he summoned the words. Though he did not know their meaning, he remembered their sounds. He poured all of his effort into making the spell work. Without the flint, he could feel his energy flowing away like water through a flask with a hole.

He knew it did not work. When he opened his eyes, he saw the wooden bowl sitting on the dirt unaffected.

His disappointment and defeat were short lived. His heart jumped in his throat as he saw something much more impressive than the hoped for tiny flames on a wooden bowl. The dragon had stirred.

With his heart in his throat, Keven's gaze moved slowly from the mundane porridge bowl to the magnificent dragon. His thoughts of not caring about being eaten disappeared like seeds in the wind as overwhelming feelings of fear and excitement crashed upon Keven. Despite his intense terror, the dragon had barely stirred. In truth, it had only opened its left eye.

The scaled face showed no expression.

Part of him felt fear, a primal fear that only those who are prey could know. Another part of him felt nothing. He wondered if elders on their deathbed felt the same way when their moment had come.

As silently and as unexpectedly as the dragon had lifted its eyelid, it closed it. Had his attempt at *Sublevato* done it? Should he try it again? Did he *really* want to wake a sleeping dragon?

The thoughts that flooded into him were like much needed rain falling on a farmer's dry fields. They changed everything. He did have a tool! His little bit of magic might be able to wake the dragon. He wished Regent Lilandra was here to see it.

As soon as the thought revealed itself, he realized he still craved her approval. But, why? That question had to be answered before any others were asked.

* * *

Sogoth did not need a throne. One could barely consider him a ruler. He rarely made laws or issued edicts. In fact, few of the people of the villages and hamlets surrounding Ebensburg had ever spoken to him. Still, he sat upon one. Even without his threatening presence on the carved seat, any would-be visitor would be awed by its forbidding countenance.

The chair was conceived and created by Sogoth. Though the unforgiving granite would steal the warmth from any body, it felt to Sogoth like a prize feather bed. *Commodum* was a spell Sogoth seldom used; he did not need much comfort in his life. But, like all knowledge the spell was to be horded. No one came to see him on the throne. But, they would when the battle between he and Lilandra was well and truly joined.

Goblins were pawns in the game he was playing. Pawns were expendable, but positioned just right, they could topple a king or a queen.

The peasants around his castle were good people. He had, on several occasions, dressed as a traveler and passed through the villages over which he was considered lord. They welcomed a strange traveler warmly. Since they believed he was a simple traveler, they spoke openly about their fears of their lord. It was gaining that little bit of knowledge that allowed him time away from his workshop.

He ended that thread of thought because it brought nothing useful. He could pine over the dark deeds he had done for years. It would not change the fact that he had done them nor would it change the fact he would do similar deeds in the future.

Perched upon his throne, he wished his orb of *scrying* would work on dragons. Its power fell short of that. Lilandra, too, was not visible in his orb. That was a testament to how far she had traveled down her path of power that she could block him. With extreme concentration, he scried near her and sometimes saw enough of her assistants to cobble together some idea of the happenings in her adopted nation.

The One Oath drove him to learn of her progress; it gave him need. He was not exactly sure how her mastery of need interfered with his need to spy on her. Still, he was satisfied with the knowledge that it must give her extreme bouts of frustration to know that she was powerless over the dragon. Putting it in the city had been a brilliant idea. Sogoth had no false modesty. He was brilliant, he knew it, and he enjoyed reminding himself of that fact.

The dragon's potential to cause devastation was enormous. Granted it was not yet in its prime, but still it was large and powerful. The size and strength of the thing alone would level any building.

Lilandra had nothing or no one who could combat it. Perhaps she had a few who called themselves wizards. He had made it out of the palace, and there were rumors of others. Frustratingly, any attempt to use the orb to find magic failed. If magic was present in the site he was scrying, it interfered with the orb's ability. As a result, Sogoth had very little ability to find information regarding St. Tabitha's, the Wizards' Palace or magical creatures.

The beast's power was such that Sogoth knew he was lucky to have been successful against it. The spells he had used had been ten years in the constructing, a composition of many spells. At most, he had been able to hold that amalgam for a fraction of an hour. Had he not flown when he did, he would be nothing more than yet another memory in the mind of the long-lived dragon.

His research into dragons showed that they did not have the same needs as humans. For their inactivity, Sogoth was grateful. If others knew enough, they too would pray to and thank their precious Creator.

It was unbridled arrogance that allowed him to do what no other man had done, face a dragon and not be eaten. Still, Sogoth had been careful to keep his talents hidden during his time at the Wizards' Palace. Keeping power concealed was truly the only freedom. Had he shown his brilliance, the other wizards would have expected things from him. He resented that. He was bound to seek knowledge, not to provide it for those who were too slow witted to gain it for themselves.

The ancient texts often conflicted, but in the palace and later in his library, Sogoth gleaned passages that many of the tomes foretold. *Two of unimagined power will clash. The greater will win and the weaker will lose. The greater shall bide time. The weaker will act in ignorance of the greater. Naught but true forgiveness can defeat the collected power of one who gains for himself.*

Sogoth knew he had a right to be content. The fools had no knowledge of his power, but that would not appease the One Oath.

As powerful as he was, Sogoth knew he had barely been a match for one dragon. Had one attacked him, ambushed him as he had it, it would have had an easy victory. If there had been more than one, his death would have been assured. For the thousandth time, he wished he knew more about them.

They had magic, but whether that magic was a part of them or whether they had to learn it was not in any tome. Sogoth ached for the knowledge. Was dragon magic similar to human magic? Was it more elven in nature? Did they speak their spells? Those questions as well as his need to beat Lilandra had driven him to attempt his risky endeavor.

Would the dragon be angry? He assumed so. He truly regretted harming and humiliating such a magnificent creature. But, it had had to be done. Knowledge was paramount. As a result, everything else had to be sacrificed.

As much as he felt regret, albeit delayed, for the harm he had caused the dragon, he felt no such thing for goblins or direbugs. As evil as they were, both had to be studied for their method of incapacitating their victims before killing them.

It was not that he enjoyed watching them take their prey in an agonizingly slow fashion. He simply could not help himself when the spark of curiosity was fanned into a flame. Like all wizards, he was bound to the search for the most intimate details of the last moments of the prey's life. Sogoth oversaw countless attacks of direbugs and goblins. There was much that interested him. But, in the end, neither of the two offered him the knowledge he was pushed to learn.

As a result, he had begun working with some of the people of the nearby hamlets. They were poor folk with naïve beliefs and quaint customs. At first, he did not feel anything at causing them the harm that was necessary for his research. Perhaps if he had, he would not have gone through with some of his more ghastly works

Direbugs and goblins took away the self of their victims. Direbugs were a bit more tidy and did not do so out of maliciousness. Sogoth had learned through several spells of *Attingo* that the victim of the direbug was quite conscious and aware of being dismembered. The poison which rendered them paralyzed did nothing to alleviate the pain.

His former teachers at the Wizards' Palace had shied away from such study while the One Oath drove him to it. Through other re-worked spells of *Attingo*, he could intimately know the pain of the victim of a direbug. After the initial bite, the first excruciating pain was felt in the eyes. The venom of the direbug prevented the eyes from blinking. As a result, each eye would be left to dry and shrivel. The only thing that extended the victim his sight was the tears which would only prolong the agony.

Sogoth did not know why the victims would not bleed to death as various pieces of them were removed by the hive members. That too was a piece of knowledge he was driven to find. He doubted whether The

Creator would ever forgive him for what he did in pursuit of that knowledge. He was glad that the poison he used to imitate the direbugs attack did not allow his subjects to beg.

The Goblin's method, while crude, also took away the self of their victim. The first part of their sport was maiming their prey. All goblins were skilled at maiming. It was a practice that was diligently taught to their young. The favorite method was to cause the terrified prey just enough of an injury so that it could not run or fight well. Then they would begin their sport in earnest. They would feign inattention and let the prey escape. The longer the chase lasted, the better, and the goblins would hunt it until exhaustion took over. That was what the goblins most enjoyed, watching their victim give in to terror and more pain when their bodies would no longer let them flee.

Sogoth needed to know more of that moment in the victim's life. When they gave up, what exactly was given up? In too many experiments to ever allow him back in the grace of The Creator, he had taken that indefinable thing from local peasants. He preferred to work with the young because they more easily gave it up and saved him time.

His experiments often left them with a choice: their cherished ideas of what was good or an end to suffering. Life long devotees of The Book of the Word would forswear it willingly and quickly. Pure maidens would repeatedly debase themselves if it meant the end to the agony or fear. Other times, he would simply have them choose between physical pain and the agony of a loved one.

The Wizards of Technology provided many of the machines that could methodically tire his subjects. His favorite was a machine that required a subject to hold a heavy stone. After some hours, the subject would tire and want to drop the stone. The closer the stone came to the ground, the more a loved one was stretched on a rack.

That was the easy part. The more delicate part was questioning both subjects. His questions had to be precise. It was only after he learned what was given up that he could learn what it was that made them who they were.

It did not matter who the subject was. Both men and women pleaded and promised to pay any price. In his earliest experiments, Sogoth was surprised at how quickly even the most dedicated parents would offer him their children if he would stop tormenting them. Some would even beg him to take their limbs. After a sufficient number of experiments, the only person who was surprised was the broken parent at how easily she would sacrifice her child.

After the tests were over, they were allowed to return to their homes. Sogoth had no interest in keeping them, and he had no interest in killing them. Physically they would be fine. Sogoth's methods and machines rarely left marks on a body. On the rare occasions a subject's body had to be damaged, a moderate level of *Curatitus* would restore them to the health they had had before they came to him.

Though they returned with a healthy body, they did not return whole. Something had been taken from them. Few people in all of the lands knew what it was that made them who they were. With each subject and after each test, Sogoth learned.

It was simple really: the first step was to measure the subject; the second was to inflict unbearable pain while taking away any mechanism they had to stop it. They would try everything and test each mechanism at their disposal.

The pattern was remarkably similar among all subjects. The first was always their body. They would squirm and test their bonds. Then, they would use their mind to try to reason their way out. Next, they would use whatever endurance they had to ignore the pain. That, of course, would not work. Predictably, they would then try to communicate with him. He found it best to simply not be seen by the subject. It reduced the time it took them to realize their will did not matter.

The time of the realization did not vary much between subjects. After an interval where their will did not matter, they became accustomed to being helpless. Once they had given up hope that they would ever own their needs again, they were finished. Even his crippled conscience recognized the evil of such a crime. Stealing a person's self, their very soul, was unforgivable.

Joseph Swope

Norbert Pustan

Chapter 19

Once more, he awoke, unable to sleep. The warehouse, as always, was unchanged. He had wondered what would happen if he could sleep continuously. How long could he sleep and ignore the occasional pain of hunger and thirst?

He did not have total control of his mind. No matter how often he slept, he would always wake. He knew his mind should rule his body, but it felt like it was his body that ruled. He could not ignore the bland mush that was brought to him for more than a day. He needed to eat. He could not hold his breath for more than a few moments. He needed to breathe.

Keven wondered about death. If he died in his sleep, would he notice? Were sleep and death so different? He did not seek death, but he certainly would not fight it. It meant little to him.

It became clear to him; he was not a just prisoner of the sturdy wooden building. He was a prisoner of his body and mind, but he was quickly gaining control of his mind. It was his body that still ruled his existence. Hunger, thirst, and pain, they were still his masters. Though they did not always issue orders, when they did, they could not be denied.

Keven felt like he was one step away from the answers. He tried to remember Gareloch's words. If he did not need to live, he did not need food. If he did not need to feel comfortable, he did not need to avoid pain. He needed to find that which he most needed. In examining his needs, he had to honestly ask himself, why he had to live?

He knew that people clung furiously to their lives. That was their greatest need. More and more, the answer he came up with was that he did not have to. No one knew he was alive, and no one would care if he were dead. He certainly did not fear death and had nothing to lose by it because he had no need to live.

The dragon was unchanged, yet Keven began talking to it. Of course, it did not talk back, but speaking his thoughts aloud helped Keven to work through them. He would sometimes pretend the dragon was Gareloch, guiding him through a conversation.

His time in the warehouse, talking to the dragon and answering for it, had taught Keven much. Though he thought of Lilandra and Erin often, he did not think of the two of them in the same way. They had both deeply hurt him. He had needed them, and they had rejected him. But, he could see a difference.

It was why he needed them that most concerned him. His questions and subsequent answers chased each other in a dizzying fashion. He needed Lilandra and Erin because they made him feel good. Then, he would ask himself why he needed to feel good. He could not find an answer that fit. The best he came up with was the supposition that feeling good meant that for a brief time, pain was kept at bay.

His thoughts were interrupted by the tell tale sound of the large door being opened. He looked up from his spot against the wall. The routine of the soldiers exchanging the empty bowl and water skin with full ones did not interest him much. He could immediately tell, however that this time, it was different. The door was swung wide open and the incandescent daylight seemed obscene to his dark-accustomed eyes.

Two figures entered the warehouse and strode across the large space. With the sunlight behind them, he struggled to identify them. Though he could not see details, he could see that one was a man and one was a woman. By the woman's confident, graceful gait, Keven knew it had to be Lilandra.

He did not know if he should stand to greet her or continue sitting. He could feel the lure of her approval pulling him. But, he had learned enough to know he had no mechanism to reach that. She kept it away from him. His mind knew he did not need her approval, yet he still felt drawn to her.

"Ah, Keven I have been thinking about you." Her tone held none of the hardness he remembered. She spoke with sincerity. She was glad to see him. "I was hoping you would have success in waking this beast. I knew if anyone could, it had to be you."

She continued to walk towards him with her bodyguard trailing her, his eyes always searching for threats. She was wearing a dress that was surprisingly simple. Despite the dress's intention, it could not conceal Lilandra's curves. It only made them seem more accessible to the eyes of a poor stable hand.

She looked around with wide innocent eyes. "You poor dear. I know it must have been tough being here for so long."

Her tone oozed sympathy. Keven dearly wanted to believe it was genuine. He was distracted from the Regent by a grunt and a thud. He looked over the Regent's shoulder as she turned towards the sounds. Her bodyguard had taken it upon himself to try to wake the dragon with his sword. There was no visible effect on the dragon, but the very act of it offended Keven.

"Hey! Why did you do that?" he challenged as he stormed passed Lilandra on his way to confront the man with the sword. He noticed her look of amazement at being ignored.

Keven did not feel even a twinge of fear as he walked towards the bigger man. Either the man would use the sword, or he wouldn't. Neither of those two possibilities particularly bothered Keven.

When Keven was standing in front of the bodyguard, he learned how paltry his training had been. His clumsy swings with sticks could never compare to the fluid arc of the man's sword. In a heartbeat, the steel edge went from pointing towards the floor to pressing against Keven's neck. From the sting, he knew the sword had made a shallow cut. He also knew that since the strike was so quick, so sure, that there was no doubt that the man was in total control of the blade. The gash that was on his neck was put there purposely.

To Keven, it was a minor irritation. With his breathing exercises, he could control that little bit of discomfort. He stared the man in the eyes, but had nothing to say. Either the man was going to swing again, or he wasn't.

King Donius had faced many opponents in his life. All had some weakness to exploit. Finding them was the ultimate skill of a Blademaster. Donius had never, however, faced a man who did not react. Not at the motion of the attack or at the sting of the small wound. He had heard of battles where one side was so mad with emotion, they would fight to the death. Even they, however, would react. An opponent needed to react; otherwise it was not a fight.

Donius knew why he had struck at the dragon. Having his kingdom and his daughter dangled right out of his reach grated on him. Having to submit to Lilandra's will while she took them further away made him quiver with anger and hurt.

Just as he knew why he struck the dragon, he knew he shouldn't have. Discipline and control of one's actions was the center of success. If he could not control himself, he was not fit to be king. Perhaps Lilandra was right.

Looking in the eyes of the poor wretch who Lilandra kept in this building told Donius one more thing. He would not strike the dragon again. The man's eyes contained no threat, just a simple statement of fact. To hit the dragon again, he would have to kill the gaunt man in tattered clothing. Donius was many things. He could be as hard as iron. He had killed on the battlefield and had sentenced people to die. However, he was not a murderer.

He lowered his sword and walked away. Donius had only backed away from two people in his life. Both were in this large wooden prison.

Lilandra had watched the exchange with intense interest. "So, Keven, tell me about this dragon. You must care a lot to want to protect it so."

"In truth, honored Regent, I know little about it. Probably no more than you," he said in a flat voice.

"Well, do tell what you have found. I knew you could find the secrets of this beast," she said encouragingly.

"I would be happy to tell you." That part was true. Despite all he had learned about himself, he still wanted to impress her. "But, it will have to wait until your next visit." He said the last with forced enthusiasm. He did not want to give in to her. It was with a tremendous effort that he tore his mind from what she needed.

His cheerful tone was the second to last thing she expected. The last thing she had expected was to be denied. He walked away from her. The last time she requested something of someone and was refused had been at the gala so many weeks before from the same person.

Before she had time to recover, he strode to the large door. Though closed, he knew it was not barred. His action was so sudden and so smooth, that Lilandra and her bodyguard were caught unaware.

She called to him in a voice that barely contained her agitation. "Keven, you are not finished with your work. I need you to do it. You are the only one who might be able to wake this dragon."

Keven kept walking toward the door. His back was to the Regent and her bodyguard. He could not see her frantically gesture towards her guard to go after Keven to make sure he would not make it to the door. Reluctantly, the bodyguard trotted after Keven.

* * *

The prisoner was not walking fast, and Donius knew he would catch him well before he reached the door. It was as if the prisoner did not actually care if he escaped or not. It amused Donius to see Lilandra flustered.

Donius looked over his shoulder as he jogged towards the door. He caught up with the man within ten paces. Instead of grabbing him, Donius jogged past him, reached the door and waited.

The man did not look at Donius as he walked towards him. His scraggly beard and unkempt hair added to his otherworldly bearing. Donius was more than a little nervous. He did not personally care if the man walked out of his prison, but Lilandra still controlled his daughter.

With part of him not wanting his daughter hurt and the other part of him not wanting to use his sword against the defenseless man, Donius was wracked with indecision. Thankfully, the prisoner stopped at the door and said nothing to Donius. In fact, he did not even look at him. He simply waited for Lilandra.

When Lilandra finally caught up with the two men, Donius knew the moment was awkward for the Regent as well. Donius certainly did not know what to say. From her silence, he guessed that Lilandra did not know either.

When the man made a move to push open the door, Donius once again swung his sword. He stopped it at the man's neck. This time, however, he did not mark him. It was simply a warning gesture. He felt shame from that and from the fact he had struck the only man he knew who had stood up to Lilandra.

The man did not move or even react to the blade that was kissing his neck. Instead, he continued to push the heavy door open. "Please, Honored Regent, hurry back. I will have more information for you then. You do not deserve to spend one more minute here."

Donius was amazed. This prisoner, a man who had nothing, was dismissing Lilandra. It was unheard of, but to Donius, who valued tradition and respect for authority, it was welcome.

With nothing left to say, Lilandra stepped out into the sunlight. Donius followed and barred the door. He had learned and seen much in his rich life. But, he had never before seen such a spectacle. He would look forward to Lilandra's next visit. He needed to see that man again.

* * *

Keven did not know why he had acted in such a way, but he did know that it felt good. That, however, only led him to examine himself again. Why did he need to act that way around Lilandra, why did he need to feel good?

He walked back to his familiar spot against the wall. In an epiphany that was becoming increasingly common, Keven realized that winning a victory did not count if he needed to win it.

From too much time spent against the wall he knew there were no splinters left on his spot. For weeks, he had experimented with many positions. None were very comfortable. Sitting with his hind end on the dirt and his back against the rough wall gave him the best view of the dragon.

After his excitement with the Regent, he wanted to wake it. To Keven, it seemed beyond concern. Nothing could bother it. He envied its peace and strength.

He stared at the empty porridge bowl. Through countless meals and many soldiers, its wood had become very dry. His encounter with the Regent and the recent thoughts his mind produced encouraged him. He cast the bowl a few paces from where he sat. It rolled to a stop in the dirt.

He began the ritual that he hoped would result in at least a blackening of the wood. Without the flint though, he had grave doubts.

With his rhythmic breathing reflecting the void in his mind, he began to speak the words. Though he remembered only part of them, he could feel them deep within himself. The magic felt just beyond his reach as though he were trying to catch handfuls of air. After a period of time, he gave up.

He opened his eyes to see an unchanged wooden porridge bowl. But, again, something was different. A tremor rippled through him. While holding his gaze on the bowl, he felt himself being watched. There was no other set of eyes in the prison except those of the dragon.

When Keven forced himself to look at the dragon, he swallowed in fear. He had indeed woken the beast! Both eyes were open, and it had raised its scaled head. The yellow eyes with the hourglass shaped pupils peered at Keven. Though he could tell nothing from the blank reptilian expression, he was frozen in fear. He tried to tell himself he shouldn't be. But, the dragon's eyes were far worse than the point of a sword.

How long their eyes met, Keven could not tell. It was the dragon who broke the contact first. The huge yellow orbs flickered downward. Keven followed the line of the dragon's sight. It was focused on the wooden bowl. With no warning, the bowl burst into flame. As it did, Keven could feel the familiar pulse of magic deep in his core. The simple porridge bowl was reduced to a pile of ash in mere moments.

The dragon was not finished with its awesome display of power. Without turning his head or otherwise indicating his intention, it threw fire against a wall. The flame lasted barely a moment, but it left a black soot mark several feet in diameter.

Keven understood true power as he looked at what used to be thick planks of wood. He had no doubt he could push through the charred wall. Keven wondered if it was noticeable from the outside but could not stir to examine it. He did not want to call the dragon's attention to him.

The magnificent, alien dragon then did something that was too mundane to be believed. It stretched. First, it opened its mouth wide, revealing rows of dagger-like teeth. After that, it flexed its great claws digging substantial gouges in the hard packed earth.

It gracefully lowered its head to the ground. During the descent, Keven was the direct focus of its powerful gaze. Despite knowing nothing of dragons and little more of magic, Keven was certain the gaze was filled with curiosity.

To Keven, the length of the exchange between the dragon and himself could not be measured. While the fearsome eyes held his with casual interest, Keven felt as a rabbit must when eyed by a wolf. Then for no reason Keven could see, the dragon closed its eyes and resumed its slumber.

Keven's mind was thrown into disarray. He wished others were with him to validate what he had seen, or even better, he wished he had kept his wits and asked the dragon a question. He wanted to speak to the dragon, to learn from it. He knew he could wake it, but he did not know that it wouldn't simply kill him.

That was not the reason he was hesitant. The real reason was that it was too magnificent to be woken simply to alleviate his boredom. As if he felt Gareloch's teachings, Keven knew he did not have the right questions for it.

He had questions, more than he could count. It was just that he did not know which were the most important. His mind was fighting itself. As soon as he settled on a thought that was worth exploring, a competitor would vie for his attention.

Keven wanted to prepare himself for another encounter with the dragon when thoughts of the Regent's bodyguard popped into his mind. Keven could see the man's hatred of the Regent. Why then, Keven wondered, did he protect her? As soon as his mind asked it, the answer sprang to his mind. She had something he needed.

The lightning flash of thought hit again. She wasn't who she pretended to be. Lilandra was truly evil. Goblins sought out and fed on weakness in others while Regent Lilandra *created* weakness in others. She created need so she could fill it.

The elf, Kiel, his company-mates, Erin, all of them worshipped Lilandra. They were not evil. She convinced them she had something they needed. Countless numbers of people loved her. He, however, did not love her. She had personally put him in this prison.

Why? That was the question that overrode all other thoughts. She had everything. Her every whim was catered to, her every possible need was met. What more could she want, Keven wondered.

In the same mysterious manner in which all thoughts come, Keven knew that having all needs met and not having needs were two entirely different things. Lilandra sought one while Keven had the other. She needed his adoration, while Keven realized she had nothing he needed. Keven finally understood Gareloch's lesson. Keven felt free. He did not need to be free of the warehouse. He did not need anything.

* * *

The stench was not overpowering, but she could smell it even as she approached. Too many bodies in any one spot would always produce a certain unwashed aroma. It didn't matter that the bodies were small. Children could stink just as badly as and often worse than adults could. Still, it wasn't too difficult to maintain her smile as she approached the set of three squat, wooden dormitories.

They were hastily built warehouses that had little in the way of comfort except being low-roofed like other buildings in Atani. Even with the pleasant Atanian weather, buildings trapped heat. The children's housing was similar to the barracks in which the growing Atanian army was housed. The three warehouses of the Children's Corps, as it was named, did not have cots. There had been no time to obtain such amenities. The children slept on thin sheets on dirt as only one in three of the warehouses had a wooden floor.

The children seemed ambivalent about their new homes. They did not particularly want to be in the Children's Corps, but the conditions from which they came were much worse. The oldest child the Corps would accept could have no more than seven summers.

There were currently hundreds of children that now resided in the three warehouses. More were arriving everyday. It was anticipated that the ranks would swell to several thousand. Most were children of parents who simply could not afford to feed them. It was the eternal curse of the peasants; fornication became recreation. The poor could not afford the herbs and treatments to prevent too many children.

The group of children Lilandra was most interested in were the ones who were forcibly taken from their parents. When people had needs they could not fill, they would turn against neighbors. As part of her plan, she had many Agents of the Dream conspicuously tour the neighborhoods in Atani city. It would only take one report from neighbors to have a special squad of soldiers take a child away from the accused parents.

Lilandra studiously counted the number of instances of children who were forced to come to the Children's Corps. That number, like the amount of colored cloth displayed, was a measure of the citizens' commitment. She instructed the Agents of the Dream to make such seizures public and noticed. It was important for all citizens to see that the Dream was alive and active.

Lilandra readied herself for the act she knew the children would need to see. The white gravel path that led to the first of the squat dormitories was freshly laid. When she came near, several of the guards nodded to her. The guards had traded their usual soldiers' uniforms for a different garb. Their bright yellow, baggy pants and multi-hued tunics were comical. It was a testament to their commitment that they did not balk at wearing the jester's hat.

Despite their reassuring presence to the children, they were not men to be trifled with. Though their choice of weapons was very discreet, their hidden blades could easily dissuade any parents who had ideas of reclaiming their child.

She took time to speak with the guards. They, too, needed to know they were important. After a quick exchange of pleasantries, they opened the door for her.

The stink was much more intense. Many of the youngest children were still learning to control their bowels. There were several young women who had the title of The Children Corps' leaders. They did their best; still, children were messy. Through the stench, she could smell the newly cut timber that made up the walls of the building.

The children were arranged in groups in one corner of the rectangular building. Though there were no internal walls, the leaders of the Children's Corps had done their best to divide the interior with colored sheets hung from ropes.

The play corner of the large building had no adornments. Each child was occupied with a toy that had been donated by citizens who were happy to give to fill others' need. The idle chatter and noises they pretended came from the carved toys meant little to her.

She knew the training activity well because she had helped the leaders develop it. Each child would be allowed to choose a toy or an activity. Some chose carved animals while others dug in the dirt floor with tiny shovels. After some time, they were told to stop what they were doing and begin playing the games of the other children.

The boys, of course, did not want to play princess games. The girls did not want to play with the pretend swords. But, it was important for them to learn that no roles were bad. Equality for all was part of the Dream. By learning that they owned nothing and could never own anything, they learned that all things belonged to all citizens.

The leaders of the Children's Corps noticed her entrance. They tried to be nonchalant. Of course, they wanted to talk to and be noticed by the Regent. They couldn't simply act like sycophants or let themselves run up to her like the children in their care.

This part of her plan was going well. People did not give much thought to events that were going well. Soon, the citizens would forget about the multitudes of young children that had been given to the state.

Children were presumably more valuable than anything. By giving them to the nation, many citizens had placed their utmost faith in the Dream. Such a sacrifice would have to be supported by thoughts of dedication. Lilandra wanted more.

She wanted to permanently and irrevocably bond the citizens to her. If she could prod them to give a little more, then the upcoming sacrifices of war she would soon ask of them would not be so onerous. Giving poor children to the nation to raise was a big step, but it was a relief to many. That relief reduced the price of sacrifice.

Lilandra knew that few things brought people together like grief. War brought grief, death, and sacrifice. The citizens needed to see loss as a whole. It would cement them as one and prepare them for the future sacrifices the coming war would demand.

Only the loss of a child could do that. Having grown children sent to fight and then be lost in battle was painful. But, the parents of such children were, at some level, prepared for the possibility of loss. That preparation allowed them to cope and carry on with their lives. That preparation was a defense that allowed them to remain whole. For her plans to work, the citizens needed to be torn down and rebuilt together.

Watching the death of a young child or, better yet, an infant would test even the most dedicated citizen. They would be conflicted. They would question whether the Dream was worth such a terrible price. One or two citizens might step from the crowd to voice a lone opinion of dissension. It was a gamble, she knew. But, the odds were in her favor, the bigger the crowd, the less of a chance of dissension.

She was confident that a coliseum of citizens would idly watch a child be sacrificed for the Dream. It would happen quickly.

After that, they would have to change. No person who believed himself to be good could live with the thought that they had passively watched a child needlessly suffer. They would have to believe the suffering was not needless. They would have to believe the suffering was an important part of something that would benefit all citizens.

They were ready. Their need for her now, she believed, was greater than their own fundamental needs.

Lilandra strolled to the huddled Children's Corps leaders. Meeting the need of a nation could be done en masse at an assembly. It could also be done by letting each person know they were receiving undivided attention. She talked with them and shared jokes about the foibles of young children. The women were eager to tell her of the children's progress. They were proud of their work and wanted the Regent to know that all of the children had learned that their individual needs did not matter. Only the group's needs mattered.

The young women were eager to demonstrate how the young citizens responded. They stepped away from the Regent and approached each group of playing children. There were few protests as the children regretfully ended the activity they had been enjoying and engaged in the new games to which they were directed. Lilandra was impressed. Children were usually consumed by their own needs. This group of young women had impressed on the children the need to please. From that small step, the children would fulfill their potential to be perfect citizens. She had seen enough. She said her goodbyes and made her way out of the dormitory.

As she walked from the Children's Corps dormitories towards the castle, she found herself thinking of Keven Whoreson. More and more her thoughts sought him. She did not know whether he had magic. She wondered if magic allowed him to protect his need. Even the resistance of one private could spread to others. She needed to reach him. She needed to find why he could resist her.

Mario-Elisa
Vaisanene

Chapter 20

His daily meal continued to arrive. As always, it was bland and the water was stale. He had made marks in the dirt for every time it did come. Eventually, he stopped counting. It did not matter to him. All that mattered were his thoughts and questions.

The sunlight, as always, moved itself across the walls of the warehouse. It changed nothing, though. Occasionally, he would walk the inside perimeter of his prison. He examined the scorch mark the dragon had left on the wall. It was more than a simple mark of soot and carbon. What was left were brittle timbers.

The dragon sat unmoving. Keven toyed with finding a name for the great beast. He could come up with none that did not demean the dragon. Such magnificence could not be labeled. He would in time attempt to wake it again with *Sublevato*. He waited because he wanted to be certain he was ready for that moment.

At first, he wasn't sure he heard the noise. Eventually, it repeated itself, became louder, and was a mix of many sounds. After a few moments, Keven could make out horses, the creak of wagons, and men's voices. He could not resist the urge to abandon his important thoughts for a chance to hear what was being said.

The sound was coming from outside of the wall with the burn mark. Keven walked to it and put his ear to the damaged part of the wall. He was certain those on the outside could not see the dragon's work.

The noise was getting louder and more diverse. From that, Keven realized, the men outside were readying the coliseum for another Citizens' Assembly.

The dais on which the Regent stood to address the citizens was directly in front of the burned wall through which Keven spied. From his position, he could only see the side of the dais.

It didn't take long for him to lose interest in the workers' activities. His thoughts were what mattered. He sat back down in his customary place across from the dragon's head.

His mind easily recaptured the delicate thoughts that so occupied him. Ideas of will and need swirled in his mind. The two were connected

319

sides of the same coin. Keven had precious little of either. In that, he was like the dragon. It lay motionless, neither eating nor breathing. It did not seek life nor did it run from death.

Keven was close to that. Absently, he wondered about pain. If the guards who brought his food ran him through with a spear, what would his need be? He answered that with another question. Did he need to live?

That he felt was his best question yet. The answer to it would be the key to unlock so much more. If he was dead, would he know what he had lost? Would it matter?

Despite his concentration, the peacefulness of his mind was again disturbed by the increasing noise from outside the warehouse. The coliseum was filling up with citizens eager to hear the Regent's words. At an earlier time, Keven would have desperately wished to be one of them. His time in the warehouse had allowed him to know the untruth of her words.

Though he cared little for the Regent or her opinions, he was surprised to feel pity for the masses of citizens who looked to her to fill their need. He would have to examine that pity. He had never been overly concerned with the need of others. Rather, he had always been concerned with his own need to avoid a beating.

He had learned much in the warehouse. Not having need was very different from not feeling. He had sought the elimination of his need to protect himself. In doing so, he had insulated himself from feeling. So much of human need was imbedded in emotion. To eliminate one meant risking the loss of another.

The noise grew as more and more citizens poured into the coliseum. Keven wished he could talk with them. Perhaps if he shared with them what he had learned, they would realize the truth. He imagined himself talking to them as Gareloch had talked to him.

Keven sat for some time pondering his future. Sitting in the warehouse was an existence, but not much more. He wanted a life that contained joy. At the same time, he could not let himself need it.

The blaring of trumpets brought him out of his reverie. Keven knew the ceremony had begun in earnest. The cheering of the crowd had reached a crescendo. He heard the words of the first speaker, the same he had heard from too many other citizens. They all believed her illusion. It had seduced him as well. He, too, had come to see the Dream as something good.

The words of the multiple speakers droned on. Keven could have ignored them with ease, but he listened to them. Each word stirred feelings of anger in him. They reminded him of the many times when his will was denied, where he was helpless. The citizens of Atani were helpless before the Regent. They, however, did not know it.

The current speaker's mad devotion to the Dream was evident. Keven heard the insanity that laced the speaker's words, but, of course, the crowd could not. He knew how seductive it was to feel a part of something. Some of his happiest moments had been sharing stories and jokes with the Ninth Company. It took great pain and isolation to break the illusion.

Lilandra was bending them to her will. Keven did not want to feel the inevitable need they would feel after their betrayal. Somehow, he felt their need more than he felt his own.

He stood up and walked purposefully to the scorch mark on the wall. As he had suspected, the blackened timbers gave way under the slightest pushing. He squeezed through the opening he made while smearing his tattered clothes with soot. It mattered little. His time in the warehouse had reduced his appearance to that of a beggar or slave. Both his head and chin sprouted unkempt hair that reeked of sweat. His clothes were a match for his dirty body. They were caked with the dirt and dust in which he had slept for countless weeks.

The crowd was such that only those nearest his exit hole noticed him. Their faces betrayed their alarm at being confronted with something that should not be. Still, they quickly turned their attention from him. Regent Lilandra had walked to the front of the dais, and they feared missing a word.

As he moved through the crowd, few noticed him. Keven was an island of calm in a sea of hysteria. Their loud cries of exuberance were so powerful he could feel the roar of the crowd resonate through his body.

Their craving for her and the feelings she gave them were palpable. Keven watched her beckon the crowd for silence. Thousands upon thousands of people were instantly silent, so they could bathe in her words. Keven closed his ears to her words. Instead, he watched her interaction with the people.

She was a conductor and the citizens were her symphony. Her hands moved to emphasize the importance of her words. By ignoring her voice, he could watch her body. She swayed and moved across the stage in a hypnotic dance. The people seated behind her were every bit as entranced as those standing on the stage and the crowd on the field. The few guards that were positioned around the dais were turned inward toward her. They, too, did not want to miss a word.

There were a few others who were not hanging on her every word. They were climbing stone steps on the far side of the dais. One of those who climbed the steps separated from her fellows. In her arms, she had a bundle wrapped in bright blue cloth. Keven immediately knew it was a baby.

He began to listen to her words. As he became aware of them, his horror mounted. The Regent took the infant and continued addressing the citizens. She passionately explained the need for them to be bound together by tragedy. It would strengthen them for the upcoming travails as they spread the Dream. The crowd's reaction only increased Keven's horror.

Lilandra cradled the baby gently, lovingly. In a perverse action, the Regent subtly pulled a silken cord from somewhere in her gown. She continued to speak. She was giving the crowd time to become accustomed to the evil they were about to witness.

The crowd seemed ready to watch the atrocity in the name of sacrificing for the Dream. By sacrificing so much, they would be chaining themselves to Lilandra's will. Keven had to prevent that. She would use such a bond with less mercy than any slaver. He worked his way through the unseeing crowd towards the nearest set of steps.

No one made a move to stop him, even the guards were transfixed. The crowd's attention was so attached to Lilandra and to the now crying infant that they did not even react to Keven's sudden arrival on the stage. One set of eyes did register Keven's presence on the stage. Those eyes belonged to the Regent's ever-present bodyguard.

Keven watched impassively as the intimidating man's hand drifted to the pommel of his sword. Though he was not afraid, Keven felt disappointment. If the bodyguard drew his weapon, Keven would have no mechanism to combat the man. The man's will to stop Keven would prevail over Keven's will to stop Lilandra.

The man stared intently at Keven and while keeping his hand on the pommel, he almost imperceptibly nodded.

Keven wasted no time. He sprinted undeterred to the Regent and snatched the screaming baby from her arms. The sound of thousands of gasps of surprise was loud in Keven's ears. He did not fear his future fate. But, as he held the baby who clung to him, he knew he could not let any harm come to it. For a single instant that seemed to stretch into a year, time stood still. The shock on the Regent's face was something no one in the coliseum could ever have imagined.

As Keven backed away towards one of the front corners of the stage, the Regent Lilandra quickly recovered her composure. A moment or two after that, the citizens acted as one. The crowd reacted like an angry beast deprived of its meal. It surged forward as if to grab the man and rend him to pieces.

Surprisingly, Lilandra made her voice heard over the tumultuous cries of rage. Her call for the guards calmed the crowd and the sudden silence in the large coliseum was unsettling.

The guards snapped out of their stunned trance and advanced on Keven. Three approached him with swords drawn. With nothing but his tattered clothes and a baby in his arms, his only need was to protect the child. He had no mechanism to support his will and backed towards the edge of the stage. If he fell into the crowd, he would be helpless to stop them from having the baby. If he stayed on the stage, the three swordsmen would take the scared baby from him.

From the corner of his eye, Keven saw a flash of movement. The Regent's bodyguard ran towards Keven, covering the distance in a few strides. He then drew his sword and glared at Keven. Though they shared no words, much passed between them, and Keven knew the man understood the depths of Lilandra's evil.

Suddenly, the man turned his back on Keven and faced the three soldiers. He did not lower his sword. Though each of them was bigger than he, they stopped. Their expressions changed from confidence to confusion. The impasse lasted for a time that could not be measured.

"Donius, you surprise me," came Lilandra's smooth voice too soft for the crowd to hear. "How very noble of you to act to protect this peasant spawn. What about your own child? Do you care nothing for her?"

A realization broke upon Keven. The man who was now defending him was the feared King of Atani.

With confident contempt, Regent Lilandra turned her back on Keven and the king.

"Princess Helena, please attend me." The crowd was silent in its stupefied inactivity. Keven watched, fascinated, as the princess walked across the stage to the Regent.

One voice screamed in protest from the front of the crowd. Bodies were pushed aside as the owner of the voice pushed forward. Keven jumped, startled as something approached him from behind. He was so captivated by the drama on the stage that he had failed to watch his backside. What he feared would be a strong grip tearing the baby from him was a gentle touch of reassurance. He did not know how, but Erin was beside him. That she removed herself from the crowd and stood with him against the Regent was all he needed to know.

When he turned his attention back to the Regent, he saw that the princess stood with her. With surprising stealth and grace, Lilandra pulled a slim dagger from the folds of her gown. She slowly and deliberately moved the edge of it until it pressed against the pale skin of the princess' neck.

To Keven, that shock of betrayal only proved his opinion of the Regent to be correct. What bothered him was the reaction of the princess. Instead of pulling away and resisting, she stood passively offering her veins to the Regent.

"Tell me now, Donius, where do you stand? Sheath your blade and I will sheath mine." Her glib satisfaction of outplaying him was evident.

"She has made her choice; I have made mine," was Donius' only response.

323

Anger flashed across the beautiful eyes of the Regent. She nodded to the soldiers nearest the king. They spread out to attack him from three sides. Erin put herself in front of Keven. Any pain she had caused him vanished in that gesture of love.

Keven had been beaten by many swordsmen in his time with the Ninth Company. As badly as he was often beaten, he had never seen true speed and grace with the sword until he saw King Donius dance between the three men. The three men worked together. Their attacks were concerted and vicious in their speed and power, yet, they moved like clumsy children in comparison to the Blademaster. He cut down two of the three with fluid ease. His strikes were of such smoothness that the soldiers did not know they were dying until they felt the wetness of their own blood.

The third guard was lucky enough to escape with a large gash on his sword-arm. His arm hung limp as his sword slipped from his bloody grasp.

Though Donius had easily won the contest, sorrow was all that could be seen on his face. He did not sheath his sword. He simply placed the point between his feet, closed his eyes and hung his head.

Lilandra broke the silence by addressing the crowd. Keven was amazed at her ability to look as though she had planned every occurrence. "Your princess who has been born with everything and was to be the next ruler of Atani chooses to give all that is hers by birthright to the citizens. This is a true citizen, an example to us all. The princess herself has chosen Atani over her own life. Not content to live out her life as a former princess, she wishes to demonstrate her dedication to the Dream."

Lilandra tightened her grip on the princess and pressed the knife under her ear. King Donius of Atani, Blademaster and feared general kept his head low and wept silently. Lilandra brought her mouth close to the princess' ear and whispered words only they could hear. Many in the coliseum closed their eyes in defense of what they did not want to see. Keven was one of them.

With his eyes closed, he could not see what transpired between the Regent and the princess. He only heard Erin's scream as he felt hot agony rip through his arm. The impact staggered him to his knees. Erin was knocked off the stage by the collision. He opened his eyes to see the princess on top of him. She was bringing her arm back in preparation for another stab. Keven was defenseless and so was the babe in his arms. He turned his body to shield the infant from the impending attack. It never came.

Again, he saw a flash of movement. Again, the King of Atani moved with fluid grace. His sword was a blur as it arced through the air. The swing stopped at the body of the princess. Unlike the deliberately minor wound the King had left on Keven's neck, the impact with the princess' body grunted with a wet thud. The king did not hold back as his blade swung deep into the body of what he had once loved as his daughter.

The dying princess fell to the ground. She turned to the Regent and mouthed words of apology. Keven did not know if King Donius noticed that his daughter did not turn to him. Even in death, she was still captive to the Mistress of Need.

* * *

Lilandra was in a situation in which she had not found herself in quite some time. She, for the moment, was powerless. Thousands of eyes were observing her lose control of events on the dais.

She addressed the crowd. "Citizens of Atani," she called to them. "The former King of Atani still clutches at the evils of the past. He stands in the way of the Dream." She paused for effect. Keven could tell the words were sinking into the confused masses. "Citizens of Atani help me. Help yourselves to a future of possibilities."

The crowd roared its willingness to come to her. Thousands moved forward in a crushing wave of humanity. Keven clutched the child to him in preparation for what he knew would be his death at the hands of an unthinking mob. He feared that Erin would be trampled.

His thoughts from the warehouse echoed faintly in his mind. Whether he died or not did not overly concern him. He had no needs, but the child in his arms did. Keven had adopted the child's need to live.

In desperation, he reached for the words Gareloch had taught him. Pushing the fear of death away for a moment, Keven held the child tight and closed his eyes. He breathed as if he were coaxing a spark to grow to a flame, and said the only words of magic he knew.

It was a futile gesture, but it was the only mechanism he had to meet his will. Perhaps he could throw the spell at the Regent and delay the inevitable death of the orphan in his arms.

Suddenly, sounds of countless trees being snapped by a gale made themselves heard over the riotous mob. It was immediately followed by what could only be the dragon's roar. No one in the coliseum had heard a dragon's roar before. The babe in his arms shrieked in a fear that was shared by everyone.

The sound came from the junction of the roof and the nearest wall of the warehouse. The thick timbers that had once imprisoned Keven were broken outward. They looked to him like a wooden toy of his that Banolf had smashed many years before. Keven hugged the babe tightly to his chest.

As the crowd stared intently at the huge opening, an enormous gout of flame erupted into the sky, its brightness equaling that of the Atanian sun. Even those far below the inferno could feel the wave of heat. Like a practiced move, thousands of citizens threw arms over faces. With another gut-wrenching roar, a nightmare that could not be burst forth from the ruined wall of the warehouse.

The dragon's flight was short. It did not land with a heavy thud as Keven would have expected. Even though it landed close to him on the stage, he barely felt it.

The terrified minds of the crowd were slow to realize the true horror of its sudden appearance on the dais. The target of the scythe like claws and malevolent power was the Regent. She was violently knocked to the stone of the dais. Lamely, she flailed her limbs in an attempt to stand.

With a great-clawed hand, the dragon roughly grabbed the limp form of the once imperious Lilandra, her head and legs dangled from the scaled grip.

With the thoughtless speed of a mob, a large number of the citizens on the field again surged forward in anger. It was a testament to their love and loss that they would face such a monstrosity. The dragon was perched uncaringly on the dais. Its magnificent scales reflected the bright sun. Its beauty and form had too many facets to be comprehended at once. Its hourglass eyes flashed hatred to the hoard of humans menacing it.

As the crowd grew nearer, Keven heard the dragon hiss its defiance as it held their beloved in its grasp. He did not know whether to keep his eyes on them or the dragon. Could a beast as powerful as a dragon be overtaken by a horde of enraged humans? He thought the answer was yes, but he was heartened to notice how little fear he felt.

Erin. She had fallen off the stage. He feared for her. He feared for the baby in his arms. His eyes sought her as one more sound from hell assaulted the coliseum.

Like the screeching howl of a windstorm, the dragon let loose its breath. Sheets of flame streamed from the toothed maw of the great beast. Those on the field directly below the stage were the first to die. Keven was sickened as he saw the tongues of the flame reach the first line of the crowd. Many did not have time to scream.

The Book of the Word could not have described a more horrifying torment for sinners. As some crumpled and fell, others scrambled vainly to run, only to find the crowd behind them blocking their path to safety. Their panic and the pain of their burns leant them frenetic strength. The dragon once again raked the crowd with its fiery breath. This time, he aimed deeper into the crowd. Many fell in frantic attempts to run from their own burning clothes.

The dragon roared in triumph. With surprising swiftness, the wave of people receded from the dais. They fled to the tunnels, screaming their terror. Citizens ran over each other. They cared for nothing except flight. For those who participated in the selfish crush of bodies, all vestiges of the Dream had been burned away. The panic was palpable. Those who remained on the back of the stage clung to each other in fear. Keven held the child with all of his strength. He looked at the dragon and hoped the child would feel no pain when death came for it.

The dragon swung its beautiful head towards Keven. The sharp angular features looked to have been carved from a diamond. What Keven once saw as an expressionless face, was now a face that said much. Its awesome gaze held Keven's eyes.

As in the warehouse, there was a connection. Keven realized he had no reason to fear the dragon.

Before he could begin to understand, the dragon looked to the sky spread its great wings. Despite their thin appearance, Keven knew they contained power. With a mighty leap and a great flap of his sinuous wings, the dragon was aloft with the barely struggling Regent. Keven followed the rapidly disappearing dragon as far as his eyes would allow.

The magnificence of the dragon had distracted him from the horror and gore that littered the coliseum field. There were still some citizens fleeing the stadium. They did not seem to notice that the dragon had left. Their cries were becoming less as the crowd funneled itself into the exit tunnels. There were others left moaning on the field, and there were those tending their fallen comrades. Their efforts were in vain; the only way they would escape the pain of their burns was death.

There were some who hid to the side and to the rear of the stage. The dais still held a few honored citizens, but Keven knew they were no threat. He looked at the baby and with sudden fear realized it was still. Despite all he had seen, he was amazed when he realized the child was sleeping peacefully against his chest. Had the dragon done that?

Those on the stage and those around him began to stir. Keven walked to the side of the stage where he had last seen Erin. As he did so, he saw her sluggishly climb the steps. Her face bore plenty of marks from her struggle with the crowd. Keven ran towards her. She, too, hurried to meet him. She hugged him firmly, but mindful of the babe he still held in his arms.

As they struggled to find words, King Donius approached. "You have done this." It was a statement of fact. There was more in the tone than Keven could decipher. "The Regent Lilandra is gone."

Keven did not respond. He simply returned the King's gaze.

"I will be king again." There was no hint of triumph in the Blademaster's voice. It was eerily hollow. "Still," he said to himself. "There are many who loved her and will still love her." He looked around the coliseum as if to survey the damage. Erin and Keven followed his eyes. His sweeping gaze stopped for a moment at the crumpled body of his own daughter.

"The people will be angry. I will regain the castle, but they will not rest if they know you are alive inside of it. There can be no order if you live."

Once again, Keven did not know how to respond to the emotionless voice of the man who had just killed his own daughter.

The king spoke to himself, almost absently. "Perhaps it will be best if the subjects can rest with the knowledge that you are dead."

Keven exhaled a sigh of frustration as Erin clutched his arm.

Citizens were moving about the stage. Many had come up from below and the honored citizens had approached where the King Donius stood. They too were looking for answers. More and more of the survivors surrounded the trio. The growing crowd waited silently for direction from man they had obeyed for most of their lives.

"Uh, a thousand pardons, Your Majesty." An older soldier boldly stepped from the growing circle of onlookers. He approached with reverence, yet there was a hint of confidence.

He continued in a low voice. "Your Majesty, I can take this man to do your justice." He finished his statement with a quick look to make sure he was not overheard.

The King gave no reaction to the man's words as he easily wrestled the infant from Keven. He simply proclaimed loudly, for all to hear, "Private, take these two away!"

Keven was too surprised to think of a protest as the larger private grabbed Erin and him by the arm. He roughly pulled them through the crowd of onlookers who stepped aside for him.

Keven had never been strong, and his time in the warehouse had weakened him. Erin, small as she was, had no hope of resisting. As a result, the soldier easily dragged them towards one of the tunnels exiting the coliseum.

Finally Keven asked, "Where are you taking us?" There was some alarm in his voice. It was not for him because he was past fear. It was for Erin; he felt her need more than his own.

The man turned on him with a face full of emotion. "We are going to a place where no one will ever find you. We are going to a place where no one from the Dream will ever come. You will be safe in Ducca's Vineyard."

* * *

Gareloch was too angry to sneak. Instead, he strode through the Atanian Castle as if he were the rightful king. He clouded the mind of some who noticed him and used *Occaeco* to be unseen by others.

The whole damn city was crazy. Despite his efforts at scrying, eavesdropping, bribing, and befriending any who would talk to him,

Gareloch could make no sense of the hysteria that gripped the city. He stopped trying to piece it together from hearsay and peasants. The one consistent tidbit he could glean was that King Donius was definitely in the castle.

Walking through the castle was easy. Most doors were open and most guards were easily distracted.

The heavy door to Donius' chambers was closed. Two guards stood at attention in front of it.

Ordinarily, Gareloch preferred to use as little force as necessary. But, his impatience and frustration with the city pushed him. With little more than a moment of concentration, he sank his thoughts into the wood of the door. Once he felt the other side of the doors, he jerked them open.

The heavy doors exploded towards the burly guards. They were knocked off their feet and thrown several paces. With the noise, still echoing in the stone corridor, Gareloch strode through the ruined doorway.

To his credit, the man sitting behind the desk recovered quickly. Upon seeing the old wizard suddenly appear, he sprang to his feet and drew his sword. Gareloch was not concerned at that. The man, who had to be King Donius, was twenty paces away. A wizard who could not defend himself from a swordsman at twenty paces did not deserve to pass the wizard test.

"Guards! To me!" the king shouted.

Without turning his head, Gareloch again used his skill at sorcery. An unseen wall stopped the guards.

They desperately wanted to enter the room, but their only mechanism was muscle. Gareloch had no more will than they, but his mechanism was his thoughts turned loose in the world. It took minimal amounts of concentration to keep the room blocked. With the two guards prevented from entering the room, Gareloch turned his attention to the king.

"Yer Majesty, King Donius." It was a simple statement.

"I am. Who are you to come in to my chambers?"

Gareloch noticed two things about the man. The first was that he had not put his sword away. The second was that the man had not advanced on him. That was good. It would not start things well to have to humiliate a king with a sword. Words were always best. He took a deep breath and swallowed his anger.

"I am Gareloch. I am the Wizard Master. I do no come ta harm ye. In truth, I apologize for yer doors. I simply seek knowledge."

"I've read enough of the histories and stories of wizards. I did not know it was still true. But, I'll believe my eyes and your words. What information did you want, wizard?"

"Yer Majesty, I seek much. I ask fer yer time and honest telling. If ye would grant me such, I would have all that ye would tell me. If ye wish no ta say anything, well, tis a different matter."

"Is that a threat?" The king's eyes were flat. He was a warrior sizing up an opponent. There was no fear.

"No. In truth, Yer Majesty tis no the way of me. I'll no force ye anything. I simply ask. I suspect ye too have questions. Perhaps sharing be the way of it with us?"

Gareloch could see King Donius evaluate him. Gareloch knew from his readings that being a Blademaster meant knowing when to sheath it. King Donius did so with practiced grace. Gareloch was happy to see that wisdom in the king, though he knew the king really had no choice.

"Let us talk as friends." The king then gestured to two leather couches.

"In that case, I shall open yer doorway. Do tell yer guards the way of it now. Aye and perhaps ye could use a spell or two fer privacy." Not thinking of something was not a conscious thought, so it took no effort for Gareloch to let his thoughts dissolve. The doorway was open. Instantly, a group of large, well-armed men rushed in.

"Hold!" the king bellowed. "This man is our friend until I say different." The soldiers looked confused. Well trained, as they were, they obeyed quickly. They reluctantly backed out of the room. King Donius understood their hesitation. After what many had believed and still believed, it was difficult to determine who was in their right mind.

The conversation between the powerful monarch and the Wizard Master went on for hours. After some initial conversational sparring, they both realized they could trust each other.

Their talk wound its way around dragons, armies, wizards, and peasants. Each man gained a few pieces that made a large puzzle clearer. Neither knew exactly what to think of the dwarves. Both knew that if the dwarves believed there to be a profit in Atani, they would return. From Lilandra's evilness, Donius knew that whatever terms she made with the dwarves were to help carry out her plan. If he could find record of what the agreement was, would he fulfill it? Could he? Or would it be better just to send word that she was dead? With the Known Lands in such flux, the last thing Atani needed was an army of dwarves angry over a broken agreement.

Gareloch tried not to ask the king the same questions over and over. Perhaps it was the One Oath demanding clarity. Perhaps it was the fantastic nature of the dragon's involvement. The part that most intrigued the old wizard was Keven's time in the warehouse prison. As far as Gareloch knew, no man had ever encountered a dragon and lived.

Regarding Keven's location, the king did not know. He could only say that a soldier had taken Keven and a woman from the coliseum in the aftermath. Donius was left with the fragments of a kingdom and a people who would never be the same.

Gareloch doubted Keven was dead. That thought might simply reflect that Gareloch needed to believe Keven was alive. That need resembled something that had been taken from him a long time ago. It was a simple thing to many. To Gareloch, it meant everything. Hope. If Keven could restore that to Gareloch, he could do so much more for others. He must be found. Gareloch would use all of his power and that of the Wizards' Palace.

* * *

Kielasanthra Tylansthra sat atop her dusty, brown roan. The army that looked to her for guidance filled her with joy. The members of the army could not seem to wait for the next moment to greet them. Humans were so quick to act.

The army was young. Packing tents and stowing gear was still a slow process. But, with a few more morns of practice, they would get it right. She was pleased with herself. She had adapted well to the role of military leader.

The humans under her command did not know of her past moments of shame with her own kind. To them, she was an exotic tracker whose skill with a bow was legendary. That thought made some follow her. For others it was the idea that following her was the best way to live the Dream, to make all people equal.

Her elven eyes picked up a rider thundering towards the large camp. His horse appeared near death, and the rider looked as if he himself had run the distance. Normally, the sight of such a bedraggled soldier and an ungroomed steed would have offended her newfound military sensibilities. It was the look on his face that forestalled her from disciplining him as he rode past several of her officers. Wordlessly, he handed her a rolled up parchment.

Reading the hastily scrawled words, she wished she did not have the knowledge of human script.

> *The Regent is gone.*
> *The Princess is dead.*
> *The Dream is in chaos.*
> *King Donius has the city again.*
> *Please send instructions.*

It was not signed. Kiel knew as well as anyone that Regent Lilandra had many loyal followers. Anyone of a thousand citizens could have written the message. As many admirers as the Regent had had, she named no one as the heir to the Dream. It hit Kiel like a great oak falling that the other citizens believed her to be the heir.

Too many emotions to count flooded into the young elf. Grief and rage fought with admiration and pride. She was an elf, a newcomer, yet they valued her. The Dream was big enough for all to share. If her new countrymen could accept her as they did, then she would die before she would let her fellow citizens lose the Dream of Lilandra.

That was where her present moment seemed to rip at her soul. She was leagues away from Atani City with an untested army. If she turned back with her army, would she ever spread the Dream to other lands? If she continued to spread the Dream, would she be turning her back on the birthplace of the Dream?

Perhaps it was her human side or perhaps it was her grief and rage. Something, however, made her forget about choosing her moments carefully. Damn any regret that might come in her future moments. The Regent had been taken. Regent Lilandra had always worked for others' needs.

If she was to be the heir of the Dream, she had to ensure the Dream would spread. That was how Lilandra would have wanted it. Her small army was enough to begin the task. It would spread west teaching and absorbing those who wanted to be enlightened. In time, the army would grow, and the Dream would cover the known lands.

She, however, would find the guilty ones personally. It would not be difficult and it would not take much time. With the loyal citizens' eyes and ears and with her tracking skills, she would find whoever had taken the beloved Lilandra. That required her personal attention.

* * *

Sogoth watched it squirm with intense interest. The One Oath, of course, drove him to perform the experiment that brought the abomination to wriggle across the floor. The creature mewing pitifully before him was a non viable failure, but the experiment was a success in that it had eliminated one course that should not be repeated.

The lump of flesh was a cross between a mole and a hawk. Of course, being different species, they could not be joined in the traditional manner. Sogoth had used a version of *Commisceo*. From the books of magic he had aquired from countless years of searching, there had never been a successful merging of two members of differing phylum.

His goal was to develop a type of vision that had yet to exist in the Known Lands. The vein of research began with a simple question Sogoth had asked himself. Rather than keep *Sublevato* engaged nearly constantly, Sogoth wondered how he could proceed without light. Few wizards saw the benefit in the simple premise that it was easier to change oneself than to change one's environment.

The feathered larvae-like shape nudged the base of the brass brazier that stood next to his throne. Sogoth surmised that such action stemmed not from the beast's inability to see the brazier. Rather, the beast seemed to be unable to move its body in a coherent manner. With barely more than a snap of his finger, which oddly was part of the spell of *Caesum,* Sogoth could have ended the life of the malformed feathered rodent.

Instead, he walked from his throne to the orb of scrying. More than the One Oath made him wonder how long the thing could live. Its beak was on top of its skull and while it could open and close, it was not connected to its throat. In short, it could not eat.

Sogoth had seen countless examples of human cruelty. Always though, there was a limit. The suffering even the cruelest person caused lasted only for a short time. Even jailers and inquisitors had been known to be inexplicably lenient. They too must face The Creator in their prayers. They too must recognize that what they did was known to others. In their mind there was always the hope their deeds could be forgiven or justified.

Sogoth's new thought distracted him from his interest in his creation's suffering. If others could be convinced there would never be consequences for cruelty, how far would they go? Would they plan the torment of their victims carefully instead of acting from wanton violence?

A sly smile could be seen in the flickering light of the brazier. Such questions he knew would be answered. The answer might take a long time in coming, but the asking would be most enjoyable.

Once having his new area of curiosity placed correctly in his mental queue, Sogoth's attention turned to the fate of his sister. As usual, his sister's power made the orb nearly useless with regards to her. Of course, the dragon also blocked all attempts to scry it or the area around it. When Sogoth used the orb to scan the present, evidence of the dragon's wrath in Atani was plain to see.

King Donius and his immediate area were blocked to him. Sogoth was unaware the king had any magic. Indeed, in the time before what could only be a war in the coliseum, King Donius was easily scried. How had he gained magic?

Over and over Sogoth had used the orb to find news of his sister or what had happened in the coliseum. As had been the case in the past, there was nothing. No, he corrected himself, in the very recent past there were faint glimpses of her. Always though, the faint glimpses included Lilandra and an unremarkable young man. Sogoth had called forth the images countless times. The man had no sword or magical adornment. In fact, he looked like a slave.

The first image showed Lilandra and the man in a military barracks. The second image the orb showed was the man and Lilandra in what could only be the Atanian castle. The few others showed Lilandra visiting him in a dark prison. The last and most puzzling showed the man cradling a baby while Lilandra looked on enraged.

Lilandra's power of need had always blocked any attempt to scry her. When Sogoth attempted to scan the man, that effort was blocked. The man must have some type of power. Could it be that their two powers together negated each other? That could be the only explanation. If so, what type of power did he have?

That possibility of having such knowledge made Sogoth almost drool with anticipation. While her path had never been his, he nevertheless was well aware of its power. Whatever it was that the man had, Sogoth knew he must acquire it. That endeavor inserted itself at the front of his mental queue. There was nothing more important than finding that man and taking his power.

* * *

King Donius stood on a castle balcony that overlooked much of Atani City. He held the babe in his arms. The weight of it, while small for a man with arms hewn from years of training, was comforting. King Donius, Blademaster and ruler of Atani needed that comfort. He had lost so much.

His kingdom was once again his. The riots had ended and many of the city's newcomers had returned to their homes. Most of the people of Atani, like himself, were left with many questions. Many of his subjects had again sworn fealty to him.

New thoughts crept into his once proud head. He had lost more than his kingdom. He had lost his daughter. He did not grieve for her death in the coliseum. He had lost her well before her blood was spilled. He did not know how long the pain would be with him. He considered himself a good man, tough but fair. He had made his mistakes but certainly no more than other men. Why, then, he asked himself, did he have to lose so much?

He knew that many of his advisors and the holy men would say he had been given a rare gift, a new beginning. The people wanted him to lead them again. The babe in his arms also represented a new beginning. To Donius, the boy was more than that. He was his son. It was right to adopt the babe that was so nearly lost to insanity. Donius had named him Keven. He and all of Atani owed that simple man more than they could count.

Many of the citizens did not know that. They still hated him and blamed him for Lilandra being taken away. Donius would work hard to change that. They needed to know the truth. He would build monuments to Keven and spread the true word of Lilandra. He had learned much. It was what a good king and more importantly, a good father had to do, listen to others' needs.

Appendix A: Spell List

Abeo subucula	Changing clothes
Accipio	Sensing
Adfirmo	Strength
Aestifer	Heating
Ambedolucer	Eating of Insects
Arcessito	Serving
Aspecties	Scrying
Attingo	Feeling
Caesum	Killing
Cavio	Guard
Commodum	Comfort
Conligatio	Binding
Contego	Shielding
Covinus	Traveling
Curatitus	Healing
Dedisco	Forgetting
Delenio	Soothing
Desidero	Finding
Diffugio	Dispersing
Dilucesco	Lightening
Effingo	Copying
Excipio	Spying
Morsus	Pain
Nascondersi	Hiding
Occaeco	Invisible
Perdomo	Subduing
Permisceo	Confuse
Restitum	Replacing
Situtum domus	Homing
Situtum Acus	Teleporting short distances.
Sospitix	Keeping
Sublevato	Lighting
Urishol	potion created by alchemist to deny sleep through pain

Stone = 14 pounds

Hand = 5 inches

Appendix B: Index of Social Psychology concepts

1. 'Zimbardo Vineyard' is in the southeast section of the map. The is a reference to Philip Zimbardo and the STANFORD PRISON EXPERIMENT

2. 'Village Asch' is in the southwest section of the map. This is a reference to Solomon Asch and his LINE CONFORMITY EXPERIMENT

3. pg 13 'King Festinger' This is a reference to the psychologist who came up with the idea of COGNITIVE DISSONANCE.

4. pg13 'The Goodfolk of Village Donnell did nothing to stop their neighbor and friend being taken away.' This is a reference to the BYSTANDER EFFECT.

5, pg 26 'There it was. Even he was not immune' This is a reference to classic gender roles. By complimenting and confirming his ability to fulfill a male role she reinforces his role and his worth.

6. pg 31 'Shared goal if they were recognized.' People need to be part of a group. According to social psychology, not being part of the group causes extreme discomfort and possibly illness.

7. pg 32 'A few confidential, woman-to-woman, talks had let the woman feel needed.' When a high status individual confers a role onto a lower status individual, the lower status individual perceived more self-worth.

8. pg 33 'By asking the opinion of commoners, she changed the role they saw themselves in.' To confirm roles is to convey value. This is seen in the power of nicknames, either positive ones or negative ones.

9. pg 38 'You think I am poor because of who I am. Would you be different if you lived in a barn and shoveled dung for a meal?' This is a reference to the FUNDAMENTAL ATTIBUTION ERROR. The fundamental attribution error suggests that people will blame others permanent attributions for failing. In contrast, they will blame a bad situation for their own failings. Conversely, people will assume it was good luck that caused others to find a positive outcome. They will credit a good outcome for themselves to their own work or personal attributions.

10. pg 57 'He was the King. His daughter was speaking to him as if he were one of her servants.' A change in roles or no roles makes people uncomfortable.

11. pg 74 'No one can be happy with two thoughts fighting in his head.' This is a direct reference to COGNITITIVE DISSONANCE.

12. pg 91 'Keven did not know what to think." People hate not knowing as a result they will almost always look for clues from others. This situation is often the beginning step of cults or why new people often conform quickly.

13. pg 109 'It was not malice, but simply the expectation that she would not be able to stand up to him.' This is an example of the FUNDAMENTAL ATTRIBUTION ERROR it is assumed woman are not good fighters because they are woman not because of the social situation into which girls and then woman are placed.

14. pg 111 'From this moment on, you will be Second Recruit Tonay Denisio' Roles are supported and strengthened by ritual, adornment, and titles. By making it as formal as he can given the situation, Lt. Deccia conveys much worth to Tonay. Indoctrination into a cult or religion often comes with such ritual.

15. pg 122 'Though he disliked having to do it, he made himself find positives in it.' COGNITIVE DISSONANCE is the unpleasant state of having two conflicting thoughts at the same time. As a result, it is difficult to do something for a long period of time and hate it. Since Lucius cannot stop doing his task, reduces the dissonance by reducing his dislike of the task

16. pg 126 'Aye, there is more. Once ye learn something, can no be unlearned. If I gave ye a reason to doubt yerself, could ye ever forget it?'This is a reference to the harm caused by the MILGRAM and the STANFORD PRISON EXPERIMENTS. Once the subjects were shown how they would act under social pressure, they can not easily forget that information.

17. pg 130 'But M'lady! Surely you do not think to visit those savages' This is blatant RACISM. It is thought racism stems from the fundament attribution errors where a group of people are blamed because of their physical attributes rather than their social situation.

18. pg 150 'Maybe my father was right. Maybe that is how poor people are. "This is blatant CLASSISM. According to the FUNDAMENTAL ATTRIBUTION ERROR, many people assume people are poor because of a personal and permanent shortcoming rather than being in a difficult social situation.

19. pg 150 'Few people could resist the lure of a crowd when that crowd decided to feel a certain emotion." Perhaps the most extreme example of social psychology is a RIOT. In a riot, concert, or sporting even, there is SOCIAL DIFFUSION where individual roles disappear and peoples' behavior, thoughts, and emotions echoe that of the crowd.

20. pg 165 'To be beaten so by a woman was humbling' King Donius having the role of protector of conservative values is very susceptible to the FUNDAMENTAL ATTRIBUTION ERROR. He believes women are weaker, less able or less competitive because of their fundamental attributes, not because of the social situations women often find themselves in.

21. pg 167 'Kiel was a demanding taskmistress.' This is a reference Kiel's changing role. Contrast this with the nervousness she had felt when

she was in the subordinate role of her instructors. Consider an employee who gets scolded at work proceeds to act contrite and then goes home to be the authority figure at home.

22. pg 184 'Most of the time, women, and especially men, acted awkwardly around her.' The citizens of Atani did not know what role to assign Kiel. While she often played the role of haughty regent, she would change her role and mingle with common citizens. That produces discomfort, people prefer to have a system of secure social roles.

23. pg 194 'The men were given authority to hold the door. Challenging that authority would only strengthen their resolve. She paused, forcing the man to think.' Once someone does something, they will resist thinking that behavior was wrong thereby bringing up cognitive dissonance. By asking the a question, she changed their role from automaton to that of a thinking person. Also, she drew them away from their role as a guard to that of a male.

24. pg 195 'Donius,' she used his first name to drive home the importance of her words. By using his first name, she is threatening his role as king.

25. pg 203 'It was a blunt statement that contained an order and pointed out his error.' This is a reference to Kiel's changing social role from meek student in Elvenwood to tough instructor.

26. pg 209 'Once people fell into a habit of obeying, it was next to impossible to change. In changing, they had to admit they were wrong.' Cognitive dissonance occurs when there is a difference between thoughts and actions. Because past actions cannot be changed present thoughts must be reformed to reduce dissonance.

27. pg 210 'Get them to do something and they will come up with their own reasons why they did it.' A person can be forced to do something. That leads to compliance. Because doing something a person hates for a long time, creates cognitive dissonance, they will create reasons why they acted a certain way. Once a person believes those reasons, conformity happens.

28. pg 210 'It was a little known truth that people's minds follow their behavior. Get them to do something and they will come up with their own reasons why they did it.' This is a refernce to COGNITIVE DISSONANCE. Once a person does a behavior, especially a bad one, dissonance shows guilt. To reduce the guilt or dissonance, that person will convince himself that the original behavior was valuable.

29. pg 210 'To constantly assure them that it was not their fault that they ended up in their situation was quite an undertaking.' This refers to the correct understanding of the FUNDAMETAL ATTRIBUTION ERROR.

30. pg 211 'Persuasion had three secrets and she knew them all.' Persuasion is a large part of social psychology because at the heart of

persuasion, there is a social interaction between people. As mentioned in the story, the three parts are souce of the message, nature of the message and target of the message.

31. pg 211 'The boys who kicked the defenseless man who curled in a fetal position or the fact that no one made a move to stop it.' This is a reference to the KITTY GENOVESE tragedy. She was murdered over several hours in front of an apartment building full of witnesses. Despite her numerous cries for help, no one acted or called the police

32. pg 223 'Private Denisio, you are assigned to the Eighth Company' Titles accompany roles and roles require titles. By emphasizing his rank, his role is confirmed.

33. pg 225 'She knew better, but he knew there was little resisting when a group insisted on a behavior.' This is the extreme danger of conformity and group power.

34. pg 226 'Thank you sir!' Tapio winced as the words came from his mouth.' Tapio was forced to comply with military discipline. Because it is difficult to do something for long and still hate it, Tapio conformed. Examples of this can be found in any boot camp or indoctrination effort.

35. pg 226 'Old habits die hard and he was now acting just like any other soldier.' This is a reference to conformity based on roles, titles, ranks and insignia.

36. pg 233 'Keven, not knowing any different, followed the crowd.' This is the very essence of conformity. People conform when they do not have a role or knowledge of their own to guide them.

37. pg 239 'Once Atani was fully engaged in a war with the west, then the final solution of terminating any dissenters who would not adopt a new role could be applied.' This is a reference to the Nazi Halocaust.

38. pg 240 'In fact, nearly two thirds of any group of guards that have been assigned here will kill or punish any prisoner simply because they are ordered to.' This is a reference to STANLEY MILGRAM'S OBEDIENCE EXPERIMENT

39. pg 241 'Young people rarely had a social role long enough to resist a new one being thrust upon them.' This is a reference to the evidence that young people are particularly more susceptible to CULTS than older people.

40. pg 243 'Please do me the favor of mingling with my guests for a time. Just that simple assignment put Kiel at ease.' By asking this, Lilandra is separating Kiel's role from those of the other guests. This confers status and importance upon Kiel.

41. pg 243 'Her gruesome tales dramatically conflicted with her elegant appearance.' This is a reference to the FUNDAMENTAL ATTRIBUTION ERROR. People at the social event were measuring her by her permanent physical attributes such as being female and beautiful

42. pg 246 'Roles and position formed humans and elves as cups form even the finest of wines.' This is a reference in the story to the idea that a person's self is completely flexible.

43. pg 247 'The new furniture went with the new role she saw herself in.' This is a reference to the idea that roles often need trappings to support them.

44. pg 248 'She wanted to let her guard down, but was still wary.' Helena is experiencing cognitive dissonance between role of daughter and role of burgeoning leader.

45. pg 254 'It gave the new soldiers something to hate together and from that commonality, a bond began to form' - GROUP BOND look it up in a book military boot camp

46. pg 254 'He should resent the fact that he had been brought to Atani against his will and that he was imprisoned in a training camp for an Army that threatened his homeland.". Keven is feeling discomfort of guilt due to being trapped between two thoughts. This is an example of COGNTIVE DISSONANCE.

47. pg 257 'They acted as one, never questioning their purpose.' This is a reference to GROUP THINK. Group think was thought to be a factor in President Johnson's advisors pushing the escalation of the Viet Nam conflict.

48. pg 261 'How could hundreds of citizens step over it instead of remove it?' This is an example of the BYSTANDER EFFECT.

49. pg 309 'The Prisoner, a man who had nothing, was dismissing Lilandra.' This references an unexpected change in role. Keven should have by the subordinate one, yet he behaves as if his role was the superior. Gestures such as salutes and bows support roles.

50. pg 314 'No person who believed himself to be good could live with the thought that hey had passively watched a child needlessly suffer.' – This is a reference that even in a large group, of people will do almost anything to avoid the COGNITIVE DISSONANCE of knowing killing a baby is wrong while doing nothing to stop it. Since they do not have the ability to stop it, they will change their idea that killing a baby is wrong.

51. pg 319 'She was a conductor and the citizens were her symphony. Her hands moved to emphasize the importance of her words.' This is a reference to Adolf Hitler's public speaking ability.

52. pg 323 'Thousands moved forward in a crushing wave of humanity.' This climactic sceen at the end of the story is a reference to the most extreme form of conformity, participating in a RIOT.

Before writing *Need for Magic*, Joseph Swope earned a modest living as a costumed adventurer. Sadly, that career was ended in a barrage of circumstances that is still being untangled. In writing *Need for Magic*, Mr. Swope worked to make magic real. In between writing the second and third novel of the Need Trilogy, Mr. Swope is working on a religion that brings people with odd and even birthdays together. Due to the lenient agricultural laws in Maryland, he lives west of the Chesapeake Bay with his family. www.knowyourneed.com